IT'S TECHNICALLY LOVE

KAT VINSON

1

———

Theresa Alberts stared at her desk at work, her chest tight, while Mrs. Winters listed suggestions and named specialists on the phone. Theresa's seven-year-old son's struggle with reading had reared its ugly head again. She'd talked a little about it with Mrs. Winters at the last parent-teacher conference, but things had gotten worse instead of better since then. She glanced at the montage of photos of Liam hanging on her white fabric cubicle wall, and her heart twisted with a mixture of apprehension and pride. Then her gaze landed on his drawing of a zebra they'd seen at the zoo. He had an uncanny ability to draw anything—pictures even most adults couldn't manage.

"Okay, thank you," Theresa said after Mrs. Winters finished. She took a deep breath to calm herself. "Could you give me the last one's last name again?"

She wrote it down this time, her hand shaking.

Liam's reading difficulties were putting him at serious risk of being held back a year, as well as simply being heartbreaking to watch. They went to the library regularly, and he always fought her when she tried to get him to read, because it was so hard for him. His long pauses between words, entirely wrong words or sounds... everything. Somehow, she had to get him beyond this. Being held back would destroy his self-esteem. He was too sensitive.

Plus, what would Michael say? Her ex blamed her for everything that went wrong with Liam. And her mom—she usually echoed Michael.

Theresa headed over to Casey's office. Casey was one of her best friends in Portland as well as her boss. The white door stood open, and Theresa leaned against Casey's doorway. The tall woman sat behind her two giant computer screens with a frown, her dark blonde hair messy like she'd run her hand through it.

After saying hi, Casey asked, "Find anyone for your mother-in-law?"

Theresa had an ad for the finished basement unit under her house hanging in the company's kitchen. "Nope, not yet."

"Maybe some studmuffin will want to rent it."

"Ha. No men for me. You know I don't want a repeat of Michael." Out with the girls one night, she'd made the mistake of saying it would be nice to have a man around to help at home. They wouldn't let her live it down. But she hadn't meant it.

Casey nodded. "Yeah, I get it. You can't trust them not to become cavemen."

Theresa cocked her head in agreement and leaned against the door. It was complicated, but that was the crux of it. Michael had made her feel like the worst wife and mother in the world. He'd basically taken any confidence she'd salvaged after growing up with her disapproving mother and thrown it out the window.

Casey added. "But even I don't think they're all like that."

Theresa shrugged. That might be true in theory, but the problem was that you could never tell until it was too late. So, she'd sworn off all men since her divorce. Michael had turned out how he was despite having been a stellar boyfriend. She wasn't at all sad that he'd stayed in Seattle when she'd moved to Portland. She stretched the elastic cuff of her red shirt, and let it pop back to her wrist.

"You okay?" Casey asked.

Theresa shook her head. "I have to take Liam to a specialist to get him tested for a learning disability."

2

"Oh, man, it's not getting better?"

"Nope." She told Casey about the conversation with the teacher.

Casey raised her eyebrows. "The school won't test him?"

"It will just take too long. I want to get started."

"Well, maybe they'll find something you can work with. They know a lot more about that kind of thing now."

"Yeah, you're right." Theresa sighed. What would she do if he really had a learning disability? She'd have to manage by herself. It would be so hard. Thinking about it had her heart speeding up again.

But Casey could be right. "No, it's true. Maybe it won't be so bad."

Casey lined up a programming book with the corner of her desk. "Maybe you can help me out and take your mind off this."

"What is it?"

"We've got an interview loop going on, and Guru can't make the two o'clock slot—can you fill in?"

"For a software dev position?" She could do it, but who truly enjoyed doing interviews? Awkward people, time away from real work. The last guy she'd interviewed had worn a sweater vest inside out, and she couldn't stop staring at the seams.

"Yeah. Nobody on their team can fill in, so they asked me to find someone." Casey led the data engineers and data scientists, but they all had expertise in software development, too.

"Tag, I'm it?"

Casey laughed. "Something like that. Are you able to do it?"

"Yeah, of course. Which interview is it?"

"Team suitability."

Theresa's least favorite part of the interview loop. Technical interviews were easier because they were black and white. This one was fairly subjective. Would the candidate be a good fit for the company?

Casey smiled sheepishly and reached for some papers on the other side of her desk before handing them to Theresa.

She read the top of the resume.

"Conall O'Donnell?" Theresa giggled. "Seriously?"

"Rhyming names aren't your thing?"

"No. But seriously, who could look at a tiny baby and write that on the birth certificate?" She glanced further down. "M.S. from Stanford. Nice."

"He definitely looks good on paper."

Theresa rolled up the resume, and they made plans for lunch before Theresa got back to work.

Conall leaned forward in the white task chair—everything in this office was stark white and modern—and rested his left arm on the edge of the meeting room's table. He studied his red and blue argyle socks. A bit too bright? A tiny leaf stuck out from the side of his shoe. He pulled the it off and let it sink to the floor under the table.

No, the socks were fine. Everyone he'd seen in the office so far was dressed very casually. Most in jeans and sneakers, and he'd seen several ThinkGeek t-shirts. But he'd followed the advice he'd read online about software job-hunting on the west coast: dress a little better than everyone else at the company.

His HR contact had said business casual. His khakis weren't overly casual, and he'd worn a simple pale blue button-down shirt. He was good.

So far he'd had two of the four interviews planned for today. He was waiting on the next interviewer, who was running late. This was the behavioral interview.

He thought the others had gone well. It was standard computer science fare—data structures and algorithms. How do you reverse a string? How do you avoid deadlock in a transactional database? Et cetera.

He heard a rustling sound and raised his head to see a woman wearing a long denim skirt and a red shirt standing in the doorway scanning papers in her hand. She had shoulder-length ash blonde hair pushed back behind her ears, which were strangely enticing. Delicate.

"Conall, I'm so sorry I'm running late. I—" She looked up, and their gazes locked.

It was still her turn to speak, which was good because he couldn't think of anything except how pretty she was. She might be average height, yet the rest of her was anything but.

Her eyes were velvet brown, and they had widened ever-so-slightly as they gazed into his.

"I—" she continued, still staring at him. She looked away, blushed, and confidently said, "I'm Theresa. It's nice to meet you."

She extended her hand, and he finally remembered his manners, so he stood and shook it, catching a whiff of mint mixed with citrus. Her grip was respectably firm, and touching her was a treat that he felt all the way past his belt.

"Nice to meet you, Theresa." He focused on being calm and not gripping her hand too firmly.

Theresa. A classy name. He imagined whispering it into her ear.

Nope. Focus. This was a job interview, not a night club.

They both sat down. She glanced back at him and blushed slightly before her gaze settled on some point over his shoulder.

"So," she began while setting his resume on the table. "This part won't be too technical. I'm just going to ask you some questions so I can get to know you a little."

"Sure." He gave her a smile, thinking it might be nice to get to know her, as well.

She asked about his experience at Stanford and then had him talk about the job he'd held for a while in Hawaii before moving to the mainland for his Master's. He watched her mouth as she talked, noting that her lips were full and red. She kept tapping on her chin with her matching fingernails.

"Can you tell me about a time you had to deal with a difficult coworker?" Theresa's eyes flitted to his for a second before returning to the spot over his shoulder.

"Fortunately, I haven't had a lot of that. But during my first month on the job, I worked with a woman who grew frustrated with me because I had trouble explaining to her the way the system would to work. And she said, 'You're not very good with people, are you?' That was a little awkward."

Theresa laughed and glanced at him again. "What did you say to her?"

5

He noticed a blush creeping up her cheeks. Cute.

He put the thought out of his mind. "I think I stuttered and then continued explaining, and she finally got it. I mentioned it to my boss because I was worried she might be right. He told me she had a reputation for being difficult to work with. Still, I worked on getting better at translating technical speak to customer speak."

Theresa nodded, and her shiny hair moved gently over her shoulders. "That's always difficult. In this role, you won't be interfacing with the end customer, and everyone here is very technical, all the way up to the CEO, but it's still good to have those skills."

They went over a few more behavioral questions, and then Theresa rose and said, "It was nice meeting you, Conall."

He stood and stuck his hand out, wondering if touching her would again bring on that internal fire. "You, too."

As soon as her palm touched his, there it was. He watched her watch him with her mouth hanging slightly open.

She turned, and rushed out the door.

Her fingers and head appeared inside the door frame. "Sorry, I forgot. Your last interviewer will be in here shortly. Then the hiring manager will be in to have a quick chat with you."

"Great."

Theresa's gaze fell on the papers she'd left on the table. She rushed in to snag them and disappeared again.

Wow. If he worked here, he'd get to see her all the time. Every day. In the break room. At the holiday party. Everywhere.

Conall wasn't sure if that would be a good thing or not. Besides the distraction, it could never lead anywhere. He sensed that she was the type to marry and have kids, if she hadn't already. If they dated, she'd eventually dump him—just like Clarissa had.

His ex-wife was the reason he'd left Honolulu to attend grad school in California. After the divorce, he couldn't go anywhere on the island that didn't remind him of her. He wouldn't go through that again. But his mind threatened to go down the old rabbit hole.

He needed to get his shit together. He was in the middle of an interview loop, for fuck's sake.

2

After leaving the interview, Theresa raced straight to Casey's office because she had to get this off her chest. She poked her head in. "Hey, boss."

Casey rolled her eyes and laughed. "Shut up, I hate that."

Theresa stepped in, closing the door behind her.

Casey took her hands off the keyboard and rested them on her stomach. "What's up?"

"You didn't tell me he was hot." She couldn't keep the accusatory tone out of her voice.

"Who?"

"Conall O'Donnell!" Theresa stepped in and plopped down in one of Casey's extra chairs.

"He's hot?" Casey raised her eyebrows.

"Oh, my God. My mouth fell open, and I stared at him for forever. Then I stuttered to introduce myself. Humiliating." She held her face in her hands.

"Ouch."

"He's lean and tall. He's just... lovely." Theresa sighed, remembering that sleek black hair and those gorgeous blue eyes and how she'd felt lost in them, like she was bobbing in the sea somewhere off the coast of Cancun.

Casey picked up a pen and tapped it on her knuckles. "It's been a long time since you've been interested in somebody."

"I'm not *interested*," she scoffed. "I don't have time to be interested." Or the inclination. Five years since the divorce, and she was fine. Too busy with work and being a mother. She didn't miss having a man in her life.

"Maybe we'll hire this guy, and you can spend your time lusting after him," Casey teased.

No. But he *was* undeniably appealing. "Speaking objectively, he looks like a male model. Except not, you know, effeminate at all."

"A male model? What, was he wearing underwear stuffed with toilet paper?" Casey mimed a basketball over her crotch.

Theresa cackled. "Very funny. Did I mention his striking light blue eyes? Soft black hair. It's hard not to notice. And oh, my God. His voice." She shivered just thinking about it. "Deep and masculine."

Casey laughed again. "You're lucky we don't have a proper HR department to hear you go on. So I take it you're voting yes?"

"Actually, he was really good. I'd vote to hire him even if he was butt-ugly."

"That's great." She moved her mouse. "Because we need more developers. We've got all these projects coming up. Three new clients just this past month, and they're in talks with two more right now."

Theresa nodded. "All good news for the stock." InfoQuest gave stock options as incentives. Theresa's options had only recently begun vesting, but she got several hundred dollars' worth each month because it was doing so well, and her option exercise price was so low.

"So are you okay, really?" Casey asked. "Wanting a man is so unlike you."

Theresa tapped her fingernails on her knees. "I know."

"Do you think you're changing you mind about the other half?"

"No, this was pure lust." She closed her eyes and pictured Conall's solid shoulders.

"Well, you know what they say about a woman's sexual peak, after all. It's only natural."

Theresa's eyes popped open, and she laughed.

The corners of Casey's mouth perked up. "It's true."

"I know, but I try not to think about it. Besides, the same holds true for you."

"I think I'm past mine," Casey said, looking away.

She was a little sensitive about men. And although they were close, Theresa still didn't have the full story.

"Oh, yeah—Theresa? Don't forget you owe me a configured server."

"I'll get it to you by lunch tomorrow." Crap. Now she'd have to focus on work again. But first she had to make Liam's appointment.

She returned to her desk to get the notes she'd taken while on the phone. And frowned at them. Poor Liam. At least tomorrow night was a little pre-Halloween trick-or-treating at the mall. He'd enjoy that.

She'd perused the testing center's website earlier and needed the phone number, so she moved the mouse to wake her computer. The movement made her think of shaking Conall's hand and the zap that had charged up her arm. If she wasn't so committed to a life without a man, she'd find it a challenge to have him around the office.

Enough of those errant thoughts. She truly didn't want a man in her life.

She headed over to an empty meeting room and called. The earliest appointment she could get was over two weeks out, but at least it was set. Progress.

As CONALL HEADED into the parking garage after the interview, he reflected on it. It had gone well. But the hiring manager told him he'd hear about the job by early next week. It was only Thursday. Many days of not knowing.

He climbed to the third floor of the parking garage, recounting the interview. From his research, InfoQuest seemed like a good company. Not very big—maybe 1000 employees in two offices now. He'd found it when he looked into the Portland tech market. When it had gone public, many of the employees had become multimillionaires overnight, and most of them still worked there. If they gave him an offer, they'd likely provide stock options, something he'd been hoping for.

His favorite cousin had just started at M.I.T. on partial scholarship but his tiny college fund would only last a year. Mark was too smart to waste away at a lesser college. Stock options typically started vesting after a year, so the timing would work as long as the value kept going up. He had another cousin who would also help. The plan was for the two of them to stick as much money aside as possible to get Mark through. Later Conall might wish he'd held onto some of the stock, but this was family. And family just mattered.

He opened his teal Camry's door and slipped inside. The rest of his money would go toward his own student loan debt, which wasn't bad because of his teaching assistantships at Stanford. And he'd had a full ride at the University of Hawaii for his undergrad. He'd double up on payments and be all paid off in five years.

He should also get a new car. This one was on its last leg—wheel? It was the car his parents had given him when he went to college, eight years earlier. The car had come over on a ship from Hawaii along with the rest of his life. He hadn't been back in the two and a half years since he'd left. He dreaded running into Clarissa.

He took a deep breath and pushed away all thoughts of his ex-wife.

Conall turned the key. The engine came to life, and his mind flitted to Theresa. She'd practically turned him on by just standing in front of him. He rested his head on the steering wheel. She had the prettiest little nose. And her cute ears. Also, though her skirt and loose shirt hid it, his instincts told him she had a fit body under all that fabric. She moved like she was all feminine muscle.

She'd be nice to look at, but that was all he'd do. No reason to risk the heartache of another failed relationship.

He pulled out of the garage and drove to the hotel, stopping for a burger on the way. He hoped he got the job, even though he'd have to figure out a place to live. That was true wherever he landed.

He was sitting at the computer desk in his room, the to-go bag wadded up on the corner, when his phone rang. He recognized the number as the same one HR at InfoQuest had called from to schedule the interview.

His heart sank. It was too soon to be a yes.

~

"MOM, stop walking in front of the TV." Liam lounged on the cream-colored couch in his pajamas, intent on a Saturday morning rerun of "The Dog Whisperer."

Theresa decided not to dignify what he'd said with an answer. She leaned over the side of the couch and dusted the windowsill. She wanted to get all this done so they could leave for the zoo and then the library. She'd already gotten up early enough to get her workout in, but there was never enough time for everything.

"Scoot over, Liam."

He made a little grunt of irritation but moved over after picking up Mr. Bark—his stuffed husky—and hugging him. She climbed on the couch to dust the middle of the windowsill.

"Stop complaining. You know we're going to the zoo." She was bribing him to get him to the library afterward. She had to keep trying until he was tested. After that, she'd know better what to do.

The windowsill done, she crossed in front of the TV again and tackled the kitchen windowsills. Just being in her bright kitchen made her smile. She'd make something hearty for dinner tonight, though she hadn't decided what yet. Maybe a beef stew? Root vegetables sounded nice.

Once the dusting was done, she stood with her hands on her hips watching Liam. He looked happy enough, relaxed on the couch under a blanket. His slightly wavy blond hair rested on his ears, like his father's did.

Don't think about Michael.

The TV rested on a black stand with an Xbox underneath and a coffee table filled much of the space between the TV and the couch. She regretted getting a light couch because there was already a water stain on it. She should have gotten a slipcover, too. Still should.

She still needed to vacuum upstairs and downstairs. She headed up with the laundry basket first.

It was at moments like these that she wanted a man. Not for sex, but for someone to help with all the household chores. Not that all men were willing to do housework, but in this fantasy, she'd found one who both wanted a clean house and didn't mind doing the actual work.

Today her fantasy man looked like Conall O'Donnell. Which was ticking her off.

Theresa pictured him standing at the kitchen sink filling a mop bucket in his khakis. Without a shirt. Because who would mop in a dress shirt?

She grimaced and shook her head to clear the image, then gathered all the dirty clothes. Conall did look good in that button-down he'd worn to his interview. She had to talk herself down. He probably hated puppies or something.

Once she had the laundry in the utility room, she grabbed her Dyson to take it upstairs. A knock on the door sounded before she was halfway up. She left the vacuum and headed back down.

Theresa's older neighbor stood on the porch in her ratty old sweater and Birkenstocks. "Hi, honey, how are you?"

"Good, Pat. How about you? Did you get all your plants brought inside?" It was getting cold enough that the morning frost would damage them.

The white-haired woman nodded. "Listen, honey, Lucy got herself stuck again."

"Uh-oh." Lucy was Pat's tortoiseshell cat, who had a penchant for climbing up and a fear of climbing down. "Where this time?"

"The roof."

Pat peered in and spotted Liam. She regularly babysat for him on Theresa's Friday nights out. "Hi, Liam. Enjoying your weekend so far?"

"Hi," he said absently. He was laser-focused on his show.

"You get the cat food. I'll get the ladder," Theresa said. Pat was well into her seventies and shouldn't be climbing ladders.

Pat headed back toward her house.

"Liam, I have to go over to Pat's for a little bit. Don't move from the couch unless the house is on fire."

"'Kay." He didn't look at her.

Theresa stood outside the garage waiting for Pat to open it. Soon, she heard the groan of the opener, and the brown door rose.

Pat stood just inside the garage. "Thanks again, Theresa—you're a lifesaver."

Theresa smiled and stepped in to retrieve the ladder. "Where is she?"

"In the back."

Now that she'd said it, Theresa noticed a faint persistent meowing emanating from the backyard. She dragged the ladder around, and set it against the roof.

At the top of the ladder, she eyed the mostly-black tortie crouched against the side of the chimney. She held the dish of cat food out, and slowly Lucy loosened her claws on the shingles and began inching her way toward the ladder where Theresa was perched, mewling pitifully the whole time.

"Is she coming?" Pat asked.

"Yep." Theresa reached out to expertly scruff the cat, who meowed sharply in protest but then relaxed as she held the bowl of food up to the cat's nose. Lucy sniffed it and took a mouthful.

"Sorry, Lucy," Theresa said as she dropped the dish onto the grass.

Lucy meowed again but Theresa began worming her way down the ladder. She deposited the cat into Pat's waiting hands and stepped down.

"Thank you so much, honey," Pat said as she hugged the cat tight.

"No problem. I never thank you enough for all the help you give me with Liam." Once Theresa had the ladder safely stowed, she headed back inside.

"Mom, some guy called," Liam announced.

That was odd. She picked up her cell phone from the coffee table and looked at the last number, which wasn't in her address book. An area code she didn't recognize. She dialed.

"Hello?" Something about the voice struck Theresa. Warm. And familiar.

"Someone from this number called me."

"I was calling about the mother-in-law unit you've got for rent."

"Oh!" Awesome. Though she'd been imagining a college girl, not a man. She told him about the features, and he was interested in seeing it today.

Every time he spoke, Theresa's sense of familiarity kept flaring. "Okay, so five it is. What's your name?"

"Conall O'Donnell. What's yours?"

Theresa's heart nearly stopped. No wonder he sounded familiar. "Theresa Alberts," she stammered.

He laughed, a sound she couldn't help but love. "I *thought* that was you. You have a memorable voice."

"You do too."

"So, you wouldn't mind renting to a coworker?" His smile was clear from his voice.

"You got the job?" she asked stupidly.

He laughed again. "I did."

Of course he had. She needed to stop being an idiot and get herself together. "No, I don't mind renting to a coworker. Let me give you the address."

Now she was going to have to see this sexy man in her house. Or at least at the front door. Maybe she wouldn't let him in and would just show him around the back. Yeah, that would be better.

She dropped the phone back on the coffee table and sat next to Liam, who asked, "Is Dad calling tonight?"

"He is, honey."

Liam sighed.

She knew he didn't enjoy the calls. They were a chore. Michael would bore him with sports talk and barely listen when Liam tried to tell him what he was up to.

Maybe Michael would forget to call. That would piss her off, even though she'd also secretly be a little relieved to not have to talk to him. Every two weeks wasn't enough for a boy to know his father. Still, it was the best she could manage with him living three hours away in Seattle.

"And we're going to the library, aren't we?" he asked.

She nodded, and he sighed again. "You'll enjoy the zoo. Maybe we can find some books about goats."

His eyes brightened. "They eat anything."

"That's what I've heard." She ruffled his hair, and he leaned into her.

She hoped Liam didn't have a learning disability. If he did, it would be hard to manage on her own. Michael would be no help, as she knew he'd blame her. Even thinking about that scenario made her stomach twist. She'd do almost anything to avoid telling him, even though she knew she would have to. As much as she despised him now, he was Liam's father.

3

Conall smiled again at the thought of seeing Theresa—in just a few minutes. He pulled off I-205 and headed into Milwaukie, a city a few miles south of Portland. The commute wouldn't be terrible, and he could take the train if he felt like it.

Google Maps guided him to a cute red bungalow with white trim. It looked like it was in good shape. He hoped the MIL was as tidy.

Before he'd even gotten to the door, Theresa was on the porch, waving. She wore jeans and a sweater that was too loose for his liking. He couldn't help himself—he wanted to see more of this woman.

He waved back and headed up the walk. "Hi there."

"I was so surprised you called. I didn't expect to hear from someone I'd actually met." Was that flush on her cheeks from the cold?

"I know, I had no idea whose listing it was. Guess I'm just lucky it was you." He'd seen the flyer in the kitchen while waiting for the office admin to get him a water, and it seemed perfect. The price was right so he'd snagged a tab off the bottom of the sheet. He hadn't even met Theresa so certainly hadn't had any ulterior motive. At least not at that point.

Her flush deepened. "This way." She pointed to a gate next to the garage. Conall glanced over at the front window to see a young blond boy staring out at him from the back of a couch.

So she had a kid. Was she married? He hadn't spotted a ring, and there was just one car in the driveway. Not that he planned to attempt to date her.

She opened the gate in the full-sized wood fence, and he followed her through. A few concrete steps led down to a white door she unlocked and pushed open.

He followed her in. The apartment smelled fresh, like she'd cleaned recently. Linoleum floors. A decent living room, two rooms off the back. He looked to the right and saw the kitchen. Bigger than he would have expected, which was nice since he liked to cook.

"The bathroom's back here," she said, pointing at the door on the left and giving him a sideways glance before looking away. Was she avoiding looking at him because he made her uncomfortable? He didn't see how he could. She wouldn't be reading his mind.

He smiled at her and said, "I'll just take a look."

The bathroom was a three-quarter, but that would be fine.

He turned around to see her standing back and looking toward the next room, which he followed her into. He was getting a definitely different vibe off her then he had in the interview. This despite the strong pull he felt toward her. They were just a few feet from each other.

"I know it's small. You might be uncomfortable with these low ceilings, being as tall as you are." This time she looked at him and he saw her eyes were green and bright. She had a dusting of freckles across her nose that he found so appealing.

"I can deal with the ceilings," he finally said, his voice low. He watched her, trying to read her face and active eyes, but she simply nodded and stepped around him, close enough that he caught her citrus scent.

She was right, it was a tiny bedroom, but a double bed would fit in here fine. A queen, maybe not. Not that he needed either. However, a twin was just too short.

Once they were back in the living room, whatever thing they'd shared in the bedroom had passed, and she was all business. He wished he could read her mind, because she seemed to have more going on than this rental. Did he remind her of someone she didn't like?

She showed him around the kitchen, which had small but new appliances. The washer and dryer were on the wall opposite the kitchen.

As they wrapped things up and stood near the front door again, Conall asked, "How do you feel about dogs?"

"Oh." Her eyes widened, and she tapped her red fingernails on her chin as she looked at him. "I hadn't really thought about pets. Do you have one?"

"No, but I'm hoping to get one. A larger one, but just one. And he'll be trained and crated when I'm not home. He will be very well-behaved." He put on a winning smile.

"I think I'd be okay with that. But you can't let him run free in the backyard unmonitored. My son plays out there, and I don't want piles of poop around."

"Understood. I'll pick it up each time. Maybe we can also designate an area for him to go. So, have you rented this place before?"

She shook her head, looking at him with that unreadable expression again. "No, I just finished it up a month ago. You'd be my first tenant."

"It looks perfect for me. Does the price include utilities?"

"I expect to split the electric and water bills thirty-seventy. The electric is much higher in the winter because we have baseboard heating. You'd have to get your own cable, though."

They talked more about the rent and bills.

"Come on upstairs, and you can fill out the application," she said as she stepped back outside. She stood to the side to let him pass. "I'll have to do a background check and everything.

"Of course."

As they went through the gate, Theresa said, "My son's inside. He's curious about you, but he's shy."

"I saw a boy watching out the window. How old is he?" he turned around as she shut the gate.

He loved the way she looked up at him again. "Seven."

"That's a great age."

She nodded and smiled fondly before leading him inside. The kid was still on the sofa.

"Liam, this is Conall. He's may be renting the apartment downstairs."

"Hey, buddy, nice to meet you," Conall said, extending his hand. Liam smiled and looked down, but he took Conall's hand, and they shook.

Conall looked back at Theresa and saw her smiling at them. He wondered what she was thinking again.

"Come on into the kitchen," she said and Conall followed her past the dining room table and into a small kitchen. More linoleum. She pulled some papers out of a drawer and set them in front of him on the counter.

Conall filled out the application and headed back to his hotel, imagining all sorts of scenarios with Theresa, even if she seemed uninterested. Still, he'd need to be careful. She was a coworker, and he didn't need to make things awkward.

"I'LL BE BACK after I let Conall into the apartment," Theresa told Liam, who was lounging on the couch watching TV. She'd called his references and heard on the background check, and everything checked out.

She pulled open the front door to the sight of Conall standing sideways, looking off toward the driveway, a navy backpack in his hand.

Even his profile was appealing.

He turned and smiled at her. "Hi there."

And his smile was breathtaking. How was she going to work with this man, much less live above him? She managed a friendly response, put on a brave face, and followed him toward the apartment's door.

Her gaze fell to his butt, which appeared quite firm.

Lord, what was she doing? She had made a terrible mistake letting him take the MIL. She had to get over this thing.

He opened the gate, and they stepped through. "You mind if I park in the driveway while I'm unloading a few things?"

"Sure, that's fine." She fumbled with the key, nearly dropping it, before sliding it in the lock. She handed the key to him and stood to the side to let him in.

Was that a smirk he gave her as he passed by? Had he noticed her checking him out? Mortifying.

Then she spotted Liam peeking around the corner of the house.

"I'll leave you to it," she called to Conall, only to turn and see him watching her from the doorway. She hopped up the steps quickly.

"I'll just walk with you," Conall said.

Liam waved at him.

"Hey, buddy," Conall called as Liam slipped through the gate, out of sight.

"He's still shy," Theresa said.

"I can see that. A lot of kids are."

The way he said it surprised her. "Do you have kids?"

"No, just lots of younger cousins."

That made sense. He was definitely old enough to have kids, but for some reason she hadn't expected it.

"Do you have a lot of things?" Theresa asked when they reached the driveway.

He laughed. It was infectious, though she forced her smile to a minimum.

"I have some suitcases but the rest of my stuff is in trash bags. I feel like a hobo. I lived pretty simply in California."

"What are you doing about furniture?" Theresa asked.

"I'm going to hit up the stores today and see how soon they can deliver."

Before she could stop herself, Theresa said, "If you can't get it by today, you're welcome to sleep on my couch."

Did his eyes widen slightly?

"I might take you up on that. But I'll head out as soon as I get my car unloaded."

"Great." Theresa forced a friendly smile. No need for him to see how horrified she was by her offer. What did he think? That she was coming onto him? "Well, welcome to Portland. I'll leave you to it."

"See you around, Theresa." The way he said her name melted her heart. Like she was special.

Yes, she had made a mistake.

CONALL LAY on Theresa's couch later that night, all the lights out, the house quiet. The boy had already been in bed when he'd arrived, but obviously Theresa hadn't.

Christ, that woman. She was gorgeous. It would to be a challenge to live under her house and not come up with all sorts of excuses to come up to see her.

He'd just have to focus on work to keep himself busy and sane.

Work. He really hoped this would be a good thing. Working for the state in Hawaii had been pretty great in terms of benefits, but it wasn't that inspiring as far as the actual work went. InfoQuest seemed much more exciting.

There was a shuffle across the room, and Conall looked toward the stairs and could barely make out the outline of a small person.

"Hi, buddy," he said.

The boy stood there silently, one hand on the wall of the stairwell.

"Did you need something?"

Liam answered after a few breaths. "Some OJ."

Conall moved out from under the sheets and blanket. He headed into the kitchen with Liam following him.

There was enough light coming in from above the kitchen curtains that he could see the cabinets. "Which one has cups?"

Liam pointed. "How come you don't have a shirt on?"

Conall laughed as he pulled two plastic cups down. "This is how I sleep. In just shorts."

"Oh. Don't you get cold?"

"Nope." He got the orange juice out of the fridge and poured some into each cup.

Liam took the cup Conall offered him and took a sip. He watched Conall over the top of the cup.

Conall smiled at him. He wasn't sure what was going on here, but he thought Liam was probably just curious. He didn't seem to have a dad around, so maybe he didn't get a lot of exposure to men. Conall figured he'd probably be seeing a lot of the kid. "Did you get enough?"

Liam nodded and set the cup on the counter. Then, without saying anything, he turned and ran up the stairs.

Conall chuckled and rinsed the cups out before heading back to the couch. Eight more hours and he'd be heading to his first day at InfoQuest.

4

M onday morning, Theresa sank into her desk chair, dropping her bag on the floor and pushing it to the back of the pod wall. She loved her job, but Mondays were such a drag after the relative luxury of the weekend. Though Conall would be starting his job today. Seeing him might mitigate the Monday-ness to some degree.

No, it wouldn't. There was nothing about a man that would make any aspect of her life better. And certainly not her work life. Anyway, today she needed to get back into the swing of things quickly. She had to code two different programs, which would require all her focus.

She heard the software manager's booming voice and looked up. There was Conall right behind him, wearing a green and blue plaid shirt. He caught her eye, and the corner of his mouth quirked up as he and the manager passed by her pod. Her heart started a ridiculous pitter-patter, picking right up where it had left off the last time she'd seen him, this morning.

She tried to ignore it, but her gaze followed him long past the point where she could see him. Even the back of his head tangled her insides. After all, she could picture what was on the other side. He was getting set up in her friend Sujata's pod, which would mean that every time Theresa went to talk to her, she'd see him. Hmm.

God, she was being ridiculous. She would *not* lust after a man. She'd sworn off them. Michael had wanted her to give up working after Liam was born. As if. He claimed he'd "tolerated" her working before that, but afterward all they did was have horrible, hateful fights terrifying in their intensity. His go-to label for her became "whore." Turns out he had definite views on the roles of women and men, which she hadn't learned about while they were dating. She still didn't know how—or why—he'd kept it so secret.

She should have read him better. She felt like such a fool. Her cheeks flushed at her naiveté.

She shook her head and focused on getting back to work, but her thoughts went to last night. Conall had come in with a small duffel, and she'd found herself looking at him too long again, mind in the gutter. He'd totally busted her too, grinning as he dropped his bag on the couch.

Liam had already been in bed, and a crazy thought had crossed her mind. She could kiss Conall, and no one else would have to know.

Fortunately, she had not done that. Instead she offered him a glass of wine but he declined so she showed him where the bathroom was and headed upstairs. Lying in bed that night, she hadn't felt so alone in a long time.

She shook her head again and made herself focus on work. She first had to set up another server to handle the large amounts of data that would need to be analyzed soon. This part of her day wasn't very exciting, and her mind kept wandering to the goings-on a few pods over.

After a little while, she caught something out of the corner of her eye and saw Conall come to a stop in front of her cube wall. He looked around a bit and then settled on her, his blue eyes shining.

She swallowed as her heart began its rhythmic march.

He greeted her and shot her a gorgeous smile.

"How's your first day going so far?" She asked.

"Oh, you know how it is at a new job. I'm working on getting all my account access and installing everything on my computer."

She nodded and gave him a knowing smile. Before she could think of anything intelligent to say, he asked, "Could you point me to the men's restroom? Someone told me it was around here."

"Yeah, just continue on that way, and it's on the right." She tore her gaze away from him to look the direction she was pointing.

"Thanks."

As he passed her again on his way back from the restroom, he smiled and raised his eyebrows.

Theresa turned to her computer screen, pulse faster than normal. Stupid. Why get all worked up? He was just a guy—no big deal. She worked with loads of them. She'd started on the programming, and now he'd distracted her. She had to focus.

She was able to get the first program written by three, and her phone rang soon afterward. She checked the display. Her mom.

"Hi, Mom." She got up to step into an empty conference room, dreading a call that was almost guaranteed to make her feel terrible.

"Hi, Theresa. How are you, dear?"

"Things are going well. How are you? How's Dad?"

"He's been doing really well."

"Great." So far, so good.

"And I am well, too. We have a potluck at the church this weekend, and I have my retreat coming up. Your sister and I are looking forward to it."

Of course, her mom would mention Sarah. "That's nice. Look, Mom, I'm at work. I should go."

"So tell me again about the church you've been going to."

Theresa sighed and fell into one of the chairs. "Oh, it's small. Everyone's really nice." She wasn't going to church, but she didn't have the nerve to tell her mom. "What are you taking to the potluck?"

"My ham casserole."

Theresa knew it well. It had spaghetti, chunks of ham, and lots of cheddar cheese. She'd never make the thing, given how unhealthy it was.

"Have you met any nice men there?" her mom asked.

She groaned internally and rested her forehead on the table. Not this again. "Mom, I don't have time for that. You know I'm busy with work."

"That was your problem the first time around. You need to rethink your priorities. Liam should be at the top."

"He *is* at the top." She closed her eyes in frustration.

"He needs a father figure. And I know you can't be home with him now, but if you hadn't run Michael off, you wouldn't be in this situation."

Her mom sure knew to aim for the gut. "It wasn't like that. Stop blaming me."

"I just wish you took after your sister more."

Twist the knife. Perfect Sarah, who wasn't perfect at all, but she *was* a stay-at-home mom and married to a lawyer.

"I'm just glad you never went to finishing school," her mom continued, using her term for grad school.

Theresa sighed again. Her mom thought advanced degrees effectively ruined a woman. "I didn't need to get a Master's. I got a good job without it."

"That's the problem. You love that job more than your son."

"Mom, I have to go. Talk to you later." She waited an appropriate length of time before saying, "Bye."

She sat with her forehead still on the table and regrouped. Her mom had such a way of making her feel like crap.

ON THE DRIVE TO pick Liam up from the after-school center that evening, Theresa planned out the rest of the day and thought about Conall only once. Progress.

After parking and heading inside the center, she found Liam sitting at a table drawing a semi-truck. He was leaning over so his blond hair hung down over his eyes—she needed to get it cut. She stopped to inspect the drawing, which showed an eighteen-wheeler at an angle from the front. Her heart swelled with pride at the fact that he'd already mastered perspective without any training. Would he really be this talented if he had a learning disability?

Michael blamed her for it. "If you'd stayed home with him," he'd

26

told her with a sneer last year when they'd been dealing with Liam's reading challenges the first time, "he'd never have these problems."

Even though Michael was a jerk, she worried he was right, despite her reading to Liam every night. She had to fix this.

"Liam," she finally said to draw his attention away from the paper. She rested her hand on his shoulder.

He looked up, his brown eyes focusing on her as a smile broke across his face. "Oh, time to leave."

"Yep." She leaned down to give him a hug and ruffled his hair once she'd stood back up. "Get your stuff, honey."

He picked up the sheet of paper and ran over to the wooden pegs where the backpacks hung to snag his blue one. His pack swung in his hand as they walked toward the car.

"What did you do today?" Theresa asked as they stepped into the parking lot.

He was quiet. "I don't remember."

"Did you do math?"

Liam nodded, and she opened the back door of her Nissan Rogue, watching his stuffed dog fall out and flop against the back tire.

"Mr. Bark!" He cried as he dropped his bag and reached down to pick the toy up.

Theresa tossed the bag to the other side of the car, and Liam set the dog down next to his car seat and climbed up, still clutching his drawing. She reached in to buckle him in, and he pushed her hands back. "No, me."

"Okay." He was growing up so fast. She watched him click the buckle shut. "So, what math did you do?"

"Subtraction."

"How'd you do?"

"Good."

"I'm so glad." She squeezed his shoulder before shutting the door and getting in the driver's seat. "You still like math, don't you?"

"It's okay. Did you see my truck, Mom?" He held the picture out, and she took it.

"It's really good, little man. Looks like a real truck. You hold onto it, okay? You can finish it when we get home."

He took it back and held on tight.

Theresa pulled out onto the main road so they could hurry up and wait in the evening's traffic. "What else did you do today? Did you read?"

"We had story time."

"That's nice. What did you hear about?"

"Bunnies."

"Ah." So he wasn't very talkative today. He was a quiet kid so she decided to leave him be.

Which wasn't necessarily a good thing, since it let her thoughts wander to a certain man with fair skin she wanted to lick. And soft-looking black hair that would be perfect for running her hand through.

"What's for dinner, Mom?"

She shook her head to clear it. "What would you like?"

"Vienna sausages?"

"Sure. What else?"

"Spinach." He said this with finality. He adored the canned stuff. He was under the impression it would give him muscles like Popeye, and she saw no need to correct this belief.

"Sounds good. After dinner we're going to practice your reading, okay?"

"Do we have to?"

"Yes, we have to. I promise you'll thank me later." She knew in her heart it was true.

5

Monday afternoon, Conall stared at the green installation status bar slowly stretching longer in the middle of his screen. He yawned. He was downloading yet another piece of software to make his computer useful for real work. He hadn't yet gotten the right permissions on the knowledge base to be able to start reading about InfoQuest's products or even look at the code documentation.

So he was bored. He really needed access to everything to start being productive.

He turned toward Sujata, the woman who sat in the corner cube opposite him. She wore a white blouse over jeans, and when she twisted to look at him, he saw a clear gem stud on the left side of her nose. He smiled.

"Still getting all set up?" she asked.

"Yeah. How long does it usually take to get access to the code?"

She cocked her head. "If I remember correctly, not long. Should happen today or tomorrow."

"Great." At least here they gave him administrator privileges on the computer so he could install software himself. Some companies had everything locked down so tight that IT would have do all the installations.

Sujata was half-smiling at him. "Bored?" she asked.

"You guessed it. So, if I can ask, what's there to do for lunch around here?" He'd brought a peanut butter and honey sandwich, but he'd soon get sick of that, and he hadn't gotten set up with good kitchen implements yet. He would have to invest in some serious cookware if he wanted to avoid starving.

"I usually bring my own lunch. So does Guru." She nodded at the other guy in the pod. "There's a Safeway nearby that people go to. But you should ask the guys—or, guys and gal, I should say—in the pod by the men's restroom. They go at least twice a week." She smiled at him, and he sensed just the slightest edge of mischievousness in her eyes.

He glanced toward the pod in question. "Theresa is the 'gal?'"

She nodded, still smiling.

"Well," he said, "great. Thanks. I'll check with them." What luck— now he had a legitimate reason to talk to her. Sujata hadn't planned that, had she?

She spun her chair back so she faced her computer screen.

The status bar on his computer hadn't hit a hundred percent yet. He stretched and headed toward the kitchen for coffee. As he passed Theresa's pod, he looked in her direction and caught her glance up at him, but she quickly averted her eyes.

Some jerk had put a completely empty pot back on the burner so Conall dumped the filter and put a fresh liner and grounds in. He filled up the water basin and leaned against the tacky orange counter, listening to the machine's spraying sound before the stream of coffee emerged. It did not look appetizing at all, but it would do the trick of waking him up.

He glanced over at the counter on the other side of the microwaves and noticed a cake. Pineapple upside-down cake. He got a paper plate out of the cabinet and cut a piece before returning to his spot leaning against the counter.

He turned his head when he heard fabric swishing and saw Theresa walk in. She had on a long skirt, this one colorful patchwork, and a short-sleeved blouse that showed off her arms.

"Oh, hi," she said and glanced at the coffee machine. "No coffee?"

"Not yet." He smiled and set the plate down. "Soon."

She nodded. "But I see there's cake."

"Yeah, and it's really good."

"One of our project managers is training for a second career as a baker."

"Really?"

She laughed as she leaned against the counter a few feet away from him. "No. Not really." She grinned. "Is your furniture getting delivered tonight?"

"The important stuff is. The rest is coming this weekend."

"Good."

His gaze fell to what she held. "Is that a Final Fantasy mug? Are you a gamer?" Maybe they could hook up on one of the gaming networks.

"Yes it is, and not anymore. But I've had it a long time."

It was a bad idea, anyway. He shifted against the counter and smiled at her. "So, what is it you work on? What's your job title? I noticed you're not in my department."

"I'm a data engineer." She swung the mug in her hand. "I basically serve as support for the data scientists and data analysts, managing databases and doing data extractions to make sure they have good data available to them."

"So I guess you work with data, then?" He leaned over to see if the coffee stream had stopped completely. "Looks like it's ready. Go ahead."

"No, you were here first."

He laughed. "No, I insist."

She smiled and stepped forward. "A gentleman, I see."

He gave an exaggerated shrug and arched his eyebrows.

Theresa filled her mug and Conall watched her, glancing down at her bright skirt. How nice her curves would look without the fabric hiding it. Bring on the leggings. She came back to the counter and poured a bunch of powdered creamer in. His gaze fell to her chest for a second while she focused on stirring the dissolving powder. He was enjoying the view—they were a good size—but then she looked up.

"Aren't you getting some?" she asked.

Given where his mind already was, he had to stifle a laugh and failed to suppress a grin. If only.

Her eyes widened, and she blushed and looked away, but Conall could see the corners of her mouth quirk up. Fortunately, it looked like she wasn't offended. He'd need to be careful, though. He didn't want to get a reputation as a work perv.

After he'd filled his cup, they headed back. She took a sip. "Good luck getting all your access soon. In the old days, you had to have somebody call in favors to get all hooked up, but it's better now."

"Would you have called in a favor for me?" he teased.

She glanced over at him, her expression unreadable. "Oh, sure."

They'd reached her pod, and he nodded at her before continuing to his, unable to stop thinking about getting some. With her.

He logged into the computer, saw the status bar still chugging along, and sighed.

Now nothing would keep him from thinking all about Theresa and how she looked like she was firm all over.

THERESA SAT with her feet propped up on the coffee table Monday evening while Liam played his video game. She was chatting with Casey on the phone.

"They shouldn't have killed him off yet," Casey said. "Now they're going to have to clean up the Rupert storyline a different way."

Every Sunday night Casey and sometimes Sujata came over to watch an edgy fantasy show. But Casey had missed last night's because she was in Oklahoma visiting her family. Once a month she took a long weekend and flew down there.

Theresa ran her finger along the end of the couch arm. "I agree, but it was kind of inevitable that it happened. They'd kind of worked themselves into a corner."

"True."

Theresa could imagine Casey nodding. She glanced over at the clock. 7:30. "Hold on a second, Case."

She wrapped her arm around Liam and pulled him in for a hug.

"Mom! You're messing me up."

"It's time to get ready for bed."

"Aw, can't I finish this one?"

Theresa glanced at the screen. He was playing a vet game and was currently performing surgery on a dog.

"Nope. Go ahead and pause it, and you can finish it tomorrow. Or if you get up early enough tomorrow morning, then."

He paused the game and scowled before heading upstairs.

"Okay, I'm back," Theresa said to Casey.

"How's your new tenant?" Casey asked. "He started at work today, right?"

Even the mention of him warmed her. She had it bad. "Oh, he's good. He moved in yesterday. He slept on my couch last night because he didn't have any furniture."

Casey teased her about having a hot guy in her house and doing nothing about it. Theresa didn't admit the thought she'd had about kissing him.

At 7:45, Theresa headed upstairs. She found Liam brushing his teeth. "Why don't you have a shirt on, buddy?"

She thought he said, "I want to sleep like this," around his toothbrush.

How odd. "Why?"

He looked over at her. It sounded like he said, "It's how Conall sleeps."

Dear Lord. Conall had been shirtless in her house? Her insides were aflutter. What did he look like? She imagined very good.

"Okay, little man. Finish up so we can read a book."

She sat on the side of his bed to wait for him, all her thoughts on Conall.

FRIDAY AFTERNOON, Conall checked his calendar for the meeting room, locked his screen and pushed back from his desk. This would be his first meeting at InfoQuest. He obviously didn't love meetings—what programmer did? But at least he was on a real project, so things were getting started now. He'd been reading the documentation so he knew the basics. This meeting should get him deeper into the work, so he'd be able to start progressing.

As he neared Theresa's desk, he realized he had no idea where the meeting room was, so he stopped when he reached her. She looked up at him, her gorgeous velvet brown eyes glowing under her long lashes, but she kept her fingers on the keyboard.

"Hi, Theresa. How are you?"

She tapped her chin and studied him. "Good. Busy."

"Is that a good thing or a bad thing?"

"It's good, I suppose. Keeps me focused." She blushed after saying it.

The color in her cheeks was a little distracting, but he managed to say, "I was wondering if you could tell me where room 603 is."

"The Athena meeting? I'm going, too. You can follow me."

"Great." He was unable to stop a smile. Not that he needed to. Nothing wrong with being friendly.

She finished typing and got up.

Today she wore a long navy skirt and a loose white shirt. Her hair was pulled back in a short ponytail so he could see her delicate ears. Simple silver hoops swung from them as she moved.

She rounded the corner, notebook in hand, and led the way. "The conference room numbers start on the south side of the building at the elevators and increase counter-clockwise."

"Oh, that's helpful. Thanks." He caught her citrusy aroma. Her shampoo? "How long's this project been going on?"

She filled him in until they reached the room and then she took a seat near the center of the long, oblong table. Conall sat next to her because many of the other chairs were already full. He wanted to see if he could catch another whiff of her shampoo.

"Who's the project manager for this?" he asked Theresa.

"Iryna," she said. Just then, a woman wearing more pink than he'd ever seen on a single human walked in. She had on pale pink jeans, a hot pink vest over a white t-shirt and fringed pink suede boots. A woman-shaped bottle of Pepto Bismol. And she smelled like a bouquet of fancy flowers.

Theresa looked at him and must have detected his surprise because she smirked and raised her eyebrows before turning away.

Otherwise, she was all business today. That was good. He shouldn't pursue her, however much he wanted to. He should avoid the old workplace romance thing. Don't fish off the company pier and all that.

But he did want to pursue her. Badly. It was almost too bad there wasn't a policy against it. He'd actually checked the employee manual, which was a short, stapled handout. But unless it was a superior-report situation, it was fine.

Conall watched the pink woman's long, pale pink fingernails clack on the keyboard.

The pink woman looked up and her eyes widened. "Oh, hi. You must be Conall. I'm Iryna." She stood up and sashayed over, hand extended.

They shook, and Iryna reached for the projector in front of her. She turned it on but it was very blurry. She adjusted it but then the screen turned into a trapezoid shape. "Oh," she said, clearly frustrated. "Could one of you men...?"

When none of the guys in the room immediately moved, Theresa got up and adjusted the controls until the screen was shaped right and the letters were crisp.

"Okay, everyone, let's get started," Iryna said while Theresa sat back down.

Iryna logged into the computer being projected onto the large screen. "Since we have a new developer, let's all introduce ourselves quickly. Also mention your role on the project. Conall why don't you start?"

"Sure. I'm Conall. I'm a new developer here, new both to Info-Quest and Portland. I moved here from California, though I'm originally from Hawaii."

He heard a few murmurs of approval, a reaction he was used to whenever he mentioned his home state. They went around the rest of the room and Conall tried to memorize everyone's names and what they did.

Then Iryna began the meeting. "Let's start by going over RTCs."

He glanced over at Theresa, who whispered, "Issue tracker." Ah, the software they used to log bugs and program enhancement requests.

"Number 64156. Who's the DM for the new DW objects?" Iryna said. This he knew. Data modeler and data warehouse.

Theresa spoke up and he studied the outline of her arm in her loose shirt, wishing she was wearing something sleeveless.

"64211," Iryna said. "Update?"

He wrote down more nonsense—HSA, SRAS, DMD. He'd have to spend more time reading the project documentation, and googling abbreviations.

"We're not on track for W28," Iryna said.

Theresa caught his eye. "We're in week 25 right now," she whispered.

He nodded. The meeting continued. He wrote down more abbreviations and terms, trying not to let all the uncertainty get to him.

6

Theresa watched herself in the mirror as she pressed her lips together to even out the lipstick. It was Friday night and Liam was in Pat's safe hands so Theresa could play a little. She had on a pair of nice jeans with a shimmery top and was ready. She, Casey, and Sujata frequented Clement's, their favorite bar in downtown Portland, to celebrate the beginning of the weekend. And she really needed a night of release tonight.

She trekked down the block to catch the bus to the MAX train station that would take her from Milwaukie into downtown. After a few stops, the wheels screeched as the train pulled into Sujata's station. There she was in a cute knee-length black dress waiting to get on. They always met up because it wasn't exactly a good idea to walk alone from the station to the bar.

Sujata spotted her and waved before boarding. She gave Theresa a little hug before sitting next to her. "So, I've been meaning to ask. Isn't Liam's testing coming up?"

"It is." Theresa gave her the lowdown.

"I hope they don't want to just medicate him," Sujata said. "Adderall is so over-prescribed now."

"Yeah." She didn't know what else to say. "I'm still nervous about it."

"Well, I think it's going to be okay. I have a feeling." Sujata put her arm across Theresa's back and hugged her again.

"Thanks." Theresa hoped she was right.

The train pulled into their stop, and Theresa held onto the yellow handrail waiting for the doors to whisper open.

"So, tell me about Conall, you," Sujata said.

"There's nothing to tell."

"Wait. Not yet. Not until we're at the bar."

Theresa shook her head at a mental image of Conall today, his shoulders straining his blue shirt ever-so-slightly. She would *not* think about what it would feel like to have those arms around her.

When Sujata pushed open the bar door, the heat of the room pushed against them. The unrecognizable pop music competed with the background hum of voices. There were a handful of booths, but the rest of the tables were bar-height. She headed over to the red bar while Sujata went to the restroom.

After waiting for a couple other women in front of her, she caught the attention of the blond bartender with a neatly-trimmed beard. "House Chardonnay, please."

Theresa slid a twenty across the bar and put her change back in her purse. She turned around and took a sip.

Ah. Nice and crisp.

She spotted Casey in their regular booth in the back corner. As she headed over, her friend looked wistful.

Theresa raised her glass in hello. "Hey, Case. You look like you have something on your mind."

Casey looked off behind Theresa. "Just thinking about a guy from college."

"Which one?" Theresa asked. Casey didn't normally talk about men. It was a sensitive topic with her.

"Like there was more than one," she scoffed.

Theresa raised her eyebrows as she sat. "You've never mentioned anyone you dated." She ran her hand across the smooth lacquered surface of the wooden table.

Casey sighed. "We didn't date. He was married when we met."

"What, *you* had an affair?" That was totally out of character for the Casey she knew.

"No." Casey shook her head. "Nothing ever happened. It's just, if I believed in soulmates, he'd be the one. But I don't want to talk about it."

"Okay, if you're sure." Theresa was quiet and took another sip when Casey said nothing. Theresa closed her eyes and let the flavor wrap itself around her tongue. So nice.

Sujata slid into the booth next to Theresa. "Hey, yous."

Before Casey could even get a hello out, Sujata bumped Theresa's shoulder and said, "So what is it you and Conall talk about?"

Theresa rolled her eyes. "Nothing."

Casey said, "He is good-looking, for sure. He's sexy in his jeans."

"You think so, too?" Theresa asked.

"Ha! You do like him," Sujata said. "He's a little skinny and pale for my taste, but he looks built on top."

Theresa took a sip of her wine to hide a smile.

Sujata chuckled. "And he's on the Athena project with you now. Not to mention living in your house."

"It's not *in* my house," Theresa said. "It's a totally separate unit. And it doesn't matter, anyway. You know I'm not interested in dating."

"And why is that, exactly?" Sujata asked. She hadn't been hanging out with them for that long so she hadn't heard Theresa's story.

Casey took a sip of her wine and didn't say anything. She already knew.

"They can just be so controlling. And judgmental."

"Surely not all of them," Sujata said.

"The problem is, you never know. Michael wasn't like that until after we were married. I don't know if he changed, or always expected me to become a housewife after we had a child, but that's how it was."

Sujata shrugged. "That's not all of them."

Theresa didn't see the point in rehashing this. She nudged Sujata's elbow. "So, you, how's *your* boyfriend?"

Theresa and Casey laughed, since Vivek definitely wasn't her

39

boyfriend, and Sujata groaned, crossed her arms on the table, and rested her head in them.

They loved to tease her. He had a huge crush on her, and she wasn't interested. He was really shy and a few years younger than their friend.

Sujata lifted her head and said, "I didn't tell you what happened yesterday."

"What?" Theresa said and she and Casey both leaned forward.

"So I was in the break room heating up my lunch and he came in. His head sort of jerked back when he saw me and his face turned red."

"So, par for the course," Theresa said.

"Up to then, yeah. He was holding his lunch and he just stopped and stared at me."

"Okay…" Casey said. "Then what?"

"He said, 'Sujata, would you do me the honor of coming to dinner with me tomorrow night?'"

Theresa barked a laugh. "He finally asked you out!"

Sujata groaned again. "Yes."

Casey also laughed. "'Do me the honor?' He can be so formal. It cracks me up."

"What did you say?" Theresa asked.

"I told him I already had plans for tonight. That seemed to knock the wind out of his sails, and he muttered something and left the kitchen. He was still carrying his lunch, and later I saw him having to go back in there to heat it up."

"Poor guy," Casey said. "You crushed him."

"I wonder if you should give him a chance," Theresa said.

Sujata shook her head. "He's not my type."

"You don't really know him, though," Casey said. "Maybe he's great in the sack. For example."

They laughed. It really didn't seem likely, given how inexperienced he probably was. She had trouble imagining him taking charge in bed. Theresa wondered if it was shyness or if it was a self-esteem problem.

They were quiet and each drank a little from their glasses.

Sujata grinned wickedly. "I want to tease you about Conall some more. The ice queen comes alive."

Casey snorted.

"Ice queen? I am not. I've just… I learned my lesson about men."

"Why not just go for it?" Sujata asked. "See what he's like?"

Casey took a sip and watched Theresa, probably curious about what she'd say.

"Honestly? He's attractive, and if I was going to try with any man, maybe it would be him. But dating isn't practical as a single mom. Not to mention the whole romance at work thing can be awkward."

Sujata smirked. "That's no different with Vivek."

"Not true," Casey said. "It's *already* awkward with him."

They laughed.

"Oh," Casey abruptly said, eyes wide.

"What?" Theresa and Sujata both said.

"You know, I never really thought about it before. I wonder if we have a policy against employees dating each other."

"Huh," Sujata said. "I can check with Gwen." She was friendly with the office manager.

Theresa shook her head. "Don't worry about it."

"No, I'm checking for *me*. Could get Vivek off my back."

Casey raised her glass. "Good point."

Sujata squeezed Theresa's shoulders. "You know, Conall asked me where to get lunch. I told him to talk to you and the guys since you go out a lot more than I do."

Theresa's eyes widened, and Casey said, "So you should prepare yourself."

Sujata smiled. "Depends what her intentions are, I guess."

"Ha." Theresa said. "I'm not going to do anything. I'm just going to try to not make a fool of myself. You know, try to not publicly drool and so on."

"I have faith in you," Sujata said. "You can do it, you."

Friday night Conall lay on his new couch reading a sci-fi book he'd picked up at the library. He was trying to concentrate on it, but lying there on the couch made his mind wander to other things that could be done horizontally. Which of course led to Theresa.

After the meeting, he'd walked back with her, and she'd helped him with some of the abbreviations. And before she'd walked away, she'd reached out and touched his forearm.

Which had felt nice.

Her mouth had fallen open like she was surprised at herself, and she'd blushed again.

He smiled thinking of it. She was beyond cute.

But he needed to divert his thoughts because he was not going to try to start something with his coworker and landlord. Instead, he sat up, set the book down, and looked around. What could he do to this apartment if it were his own? It had been a while since he'd been able to do any home improvements. Conall's dad had been a builder and taught him how to do almost anything around the house. Theresa hadn't done a bad job with this place, though he was partial to tile flooring.

But man, that touch. Theresa's fingers were on him for a mere millisecond, but he'd felt it everywhere. He shook his head.

His new dog, Maddy, stirred in her spot next to the couch, raising her head and looking at him. She probably needed a walk.

"You ready to go, girl?" He leaned over to rub the top of her head. In a flash she was fifty-five pounds of happy yellow lab, bounding around. He got her leash off the hook by the door. She forced him back as she jumped up on him and barked, her tail swishing energetically enough to power a small city.

"Calm down, girl." He crouched down and rubbed her behind the ears, and she licked his face, which made him smile even as he stood and wiped the wet spot dry.

He pocketed a couple plastic baggies, and out they went.

She pulled on the leash, dragging him a good ten feet before he caught his balance again. He laughed. "Maddy, chill out." He'd only gotten her Wednesday and still needed to sign up for obedience classes.

He missed Chelsea, the dog Clarissa had kept when they'd divorced. She was a big black lab and unusually calm. Conall had been hoping to find another one just like her when he'd spotted Maddy at the shelter. She was his the moment he set his eyes on her. She'd jumped against the cage wall and given one quick yelp. Her eyes had said, "Please take me home."

As they made their way down the sidewalk, his mind flitted back to Theresa. No woman had distracted him so much in years. He wasn't sure what it was, but every time he noticed something about her, he liked it. She must know she had delicious ears because she always wore interesting earrings to bring attention to them.

He shook his head. He'd never really been an ear guy. Maybe if she showed more skin elsewhere, he'd fixate on something else.

Maddy stopped tugging and began sniffing around on the grass.

He could pursue Theresa.

No. He shouldn't set himself up for the inevitable rejection. Probably, he just needed to get laid. It had been too long. He should hit up a bar.

He'd had a sort-of girlfriend in California, but it had never been serious for either of them. The sex had been good enough, but they hadn't been exclusive. She'd relished that freedom.

After Maddy finished her business, they rounded the block and soon he was walking up Theresa's driveway. Once Maddy was inside and off leash, he went into the kitchen for a late dinner. He should head over to Williams-Sonoma this weekend and pick up whatever kitchen stuff he saw and needed. He slathered some pesto mayo he'd made the night before onto a couple slices of bread and added turkey and Havarti cheese. After he pulled the melt out of the toaster oven, he sat down to eat and read his book.

Hopefully this would keep his mind off the beautiful woman who haunted his thoughts from the house above him.

7

Saturday morning, Theresa and Liam sat on the navy bedspread of his twin bed reading a library book. "Can you read that word?" she asked him. She wanted to get through at least this one before they headed over to the hardware store for paint and supplies.

He squinted and started, "Pen—" He paused before finishing, "—cil. Pencil."

"Good, honey." She rubbed his back and turned the page to the scene of a classroom full of kids doing all sorts of activities.

They continued through the book with Theresa reading most of it but asking him to read a word here and there.

She smiled and closed it. "Now we need to go to the store to get the paint so I can start fixing up the living room. You ready?"

"What color are you painting it?"

"I don't know exactly, but let's go find out. Come on."

She leaned across the bed to put the book on top of the boxy white nightstand. Liam's bulbous blue nightlight—with eyes and ears—stared her down. Why didn't that thing freak him out as much as it did her? He raced down the stairs and was outside before she even had the keys in her hand. She didn't know what had caused his good mood, but she hoped it stuck around.

Once at the hardware store, Theresa extracted one of the orange carts by the entrance, and the doors slid open for them.

"Look, Mom!" Liam said, pointing to a line of carts under a sign that said Dog Carts. Each one had a placard on the front. He pointed. "It's Snoopy!" At first she thought he'd read it, but there was a picture of the dog next to his name. The next cart said Puppy Patrol.

Liam gripped the side of the cart and skipped as they rolled past the plumbing section, one of the cart's wheels spinning and squeaking. An end cap displayed fancy bathroom and kitchen faucets. The next one was full of paint brushes. She pushed the cart around the corner. A bear of a man in paint-covered jeans leaned on the paint counter. She passed him and stopped the cart in front of the paint sample display. The rainbow effect created by the cards was strangely appealing. She moved to the browns while Liam studied the brighter colors.

Theresa found several light beige cards that she thought would be sufficiently inoffensive. She didn't plan to sell her house any time soon —or any time at all, really—but you never knew what might happen.

"Liam, what do you think of this one?"

He looked up. "Boring." He held out a bright red card. "This is better."

Theresa smiled. "We can't do anything that exciting, honey. We have to stick with neutral colors." Part of her wanted to do something bolder, but it wasn't practical.

Liam sighed. "What about electric blue?"

"Not neutral enough."

"Theresa?" a deep voice said.

She spun around and faced Conall, his eyes wide in surprise. She must have a similar expression, but hers was partially because she'd been struck again by how attractive he was—and the jolt of lust that had run through her body. He looked casual in faded jeans and a Stanford sweatshirt.

"Hi," she managed.

Conall grinned at her and said, "How's it going?" He looked down at Liam, who had plastered himself to her side, and his smile widened.

She put her hand on Liam's back. "What are you doing here?"

"Just came to pick up some shelving and storage." He was still smiling.

She tried to keep the surprise out of her voice. "Small world."

"Hi, buddy," Conall said to Liam.

"Hi." Then Liam looked up at Theresa. "Mom, what about cerulean?"

"Cerulean?" Conall asked. "The color?"

Theresa cracked up and ruffled Liam's hair. "How do you know that word? I don't even know what it means!"

Liam grinned at her. "It's a crayon."

"A good color," Conall said.

Liam grinned at him.

"How'd you know how to say it?" Theresa asked.

"Mrs. Abrahms told me."

His art teacher. "Ah. Well, what does it look like?"

"It's like blue with some green in it," Liam said.

Conall watched this exchange, apparently amused.

Theresa pulled out her phone and googled the color. "Same problem, sweetie. It would look funny if we had a bunch of bold colors in there." She touched Liam's cheek.

He nodded, frowning.

She hoped this was temporary, and his mood hadn't turned.

"I don't like neutral colors," he said grumpily.

"I know, but this is for the downstairs, not your room. When it comes time to paint your room again, you can pick the color."

She wondered if she would come to regret that. Even so, it prevented him from spiraling into a bad mood right now. Liam returned to the reds.

"I'd better let him choose before puberty, or it'll be black," she said to Conall.

He laughed, and they stared at each other for a few powerful heartbeats, until Conall said, "I guess I'll let you get back to it. I've just got to pick up a few things."

She nodded. "Nice seeing you." Too nice. She watched his butt as he walked away, enjoying herself more than she wanted to admit. Down, girl. She shook her head and called Liam.

46

"So, which one?" She held out the three cards she'd been holding.

"That one," he said, pointing to the one in the middle. "The others are too yellow. Ugly."

She looked at them and could see what he meant, though she'd never have noticed it if he hadn't mentioned it. "Wow, Liam—how do you know so much about colors?"

He shrugged but smiled.

She carried the card to the counter, where the assistant was helping another customer. She needed paint for the trim, as well. "Hey, Liam?"

He was studying the reds but turned.

"Would you pick a white out that will go with this beige? For the trim?" He probably could do that better than she.

"I don't want to." He was pouting now.

"Honey, don't be difficult."

"No." He moved over to the blues again.

"Liam."

He ignored her.

She went over to the white samples and held several up to the beige sample card. But she had no idea what to look for, as all the combinations appeared okay. She picked one and put the other cards back before heading to the counter.

Liam stood next to her.

"That one looks stupid, Mom. It's too yellow."

"Fine." She couldn't keep the irritation out of her voice. "Pick a good one."

He frowned, but she watched his face as cogwheels turned in his mind. He liked being needed.

After a moment, he came back with two sample cards and held one out. "I like this the most. It's still boring."

She took the card and didn't see anything wrong with it. She held it up to the beige, and the colors did look right together. "Looks good, honey. Thank you."

He returned the other card to its slot, and by the time he got back to the counter, the assistant was going over the paint options with her.

"What color are your walls?" he asked. His orange vest clashed with his red hair.

"Sort of a dusty pink," she said.

"It's mauve," Liam whispered.

The man looked at Liam and smiled. "You know your colors, huh? Want a job?"

Liam blushed. "I'm not old enough."

Theresa and the assistant both laughed. Then he said, "With these and walls that dark, you'll need to prime first." He proceeded to mix her paint and pointed her to the primer she needed. She filled her cart with gallons of primer and paint and she and Liam went to pick up tape, brushes, several plastic dropcloths and an extendable roller handle to get the ceiling. She tried to visualize the completed rooms because this would be such a chore, but the end result had to be worth it.

AFTER RUNNING a few more errands once he left the hardware store, Conall wanted to lounge around on the couch, but Maddy panted and ran to the door and back. She needed a walk.

"Hey, girl."

Maddy stopped in front of him and stretched her front legs out in a play-bow before giving a high-pitched bark. Her mouth hung open, and her ears flopped as she barked again.

"Wanna go for a walk?"

There went that tail. He stood up, and she followed him to the door.

Once she was leashed up, they headed down the block. Fortunately, it was just misty at the moment, even though there was a chill in the air. Maddy sniffed everything and even marked a few bushes, which was a little out of character. Conall trailed behind her, again reminding himself to call and sign her up for obedience class.

Thoughts of Theresa floated into his mind. He'd caught her watching him yesterday while she talked to Sujata, and it had stirred him. She definitely found him attractive, based on the way she looked at him. And then today. She'd been checking him out at the hardware store, too.

But he'd never be good enough for her. She had to be about his age —early thirties at the most—and surely wanted more kids.

He and Maddy rounded a corner and were soon heading back to the house. When he was a few houses down, Theresa's maroon SUV pulled in. From the back, Liam stared at him. Or maybe at Maddy.

As soon as the car had stopped, Liam jumped down and came tearing down the sidewalk toward them.

Theresa ran after him. "Liam! Slow down!"

Liam stopped a few feet in front of them. Conall pulled on Maddy's leash to get her to stop.

Theresa's eyes were on the kid. "Liam, don't run toward animals you don't know."

"But Mom, he's friendly. I can tell."

"Actually, she's a she," Conall said with a smile. "But she is friend-ly." Maddy barked once, as if to support what he'd said.

Theresa had reached Liam and put her hands on his shoulders.

"Hi again," Conall said, his smile widening. He felt Maddy's tail slamming into his leg over and over.

Liam turned his head back toward his mom and asked, "Can I pet her?"

She glanced down at Liam. "If it's okay with Conall, yes."

"Go ahead. But watch out—she'll want to lick your face."

Maddy pulled on the leash as Liam approached. He reached out for her head and soon got a face full of tongue.

Conall pulled back on the leash as Liam jerked back. "Ack! Gross!"

Theresa laughed. "He warned you."

Liam started spitting on the ground and wiping his face on his sleeve.

Conall glanced at her to apologize but she was studying Liam with a big smile on her face. She had no makeup on today, and he could see the dusting of freckles across her cute nose he'd noticed before.

"You're fine, Liam," she said.

Conall looked back at Liam, who'd finally calmed down. "Now that she's greeted you, you can probably pet her without being assaulted."

Liam approached her again, and Maddy let him pet her head. He very tentatively touched her between the ears and rubbed timidly. "You can scratch her a little further back. She likes that."

Maddy flopped over on her side.

"Go ahead and rub her belly," Conall said, and Liam dropped to his knees and started scratching her.

"He's desperate to get a dog." Theresa's eyes met Conall's again. And held.

"Oh, yeah? A lot of boys want a dog. I wanted one all through grad school, but my apartment wouldn't allow it."

"I'm the one putting my foot down here. Liam's not responsible enough yet. He's only seven."

"I understand." He'd been wrong about the makeup—she wore something a little shiny on her lips. "Dogs do take some effort."

Liam was still petting Maddy, and Theresa stepped forward to put her hands on his shoulders again. She looked down at him and said, "Let's go, sweetie. We still have some things to do today."

Conall's eyes took the opportunity to glance a little lower on her body. She looked lean in her jeans—she definitely worked out—and her breasts pushing against her green t-shirt seemed like a bonus on her slim body. This was the first time he'd seen her not in a skirt. He felt a distinct pressure below his belt.

"But, Mom."

"Come on. We have to get all the paint and stuff out of the car." She glanced up at Conall as she got Liam away from Maddy. "Tell Conall thanks for letting you pet his dog."

"Thank you." He said with a pout.

Conall smiled down at the boy, who hadn't let go of her, so it was clear he wasn't done with Maddy. "You're welcome." He looked up at Theresa. "Are you just getting home?"

"Yeah, we stopped at the library."

"Let me help you get all your paint inside." He couldn't let her go just yet, even though he should. He glanced down to see Liam petting Maddy again.

"But your dog…"

"Liam can take her to the back yard and run her tired, right,

Liam?" Conall looked at Theresa again to make sure she was okay with that.

The boy reached for the leash Conall held out and took it with a big grin.

"Just make sure to hold on tight," Theresa said.

"Okay!" Liam said and took off.

Conall smiled at her as she watched Liam running across the yard, concern belying a small smile of affection.

She turned back to him like she was again surprised he was there.

"Let's get the supplies."

"Sure, yeah. In the car." She turned away, which gave him the opportunity to check out her perfect butt, nice and round. He didn't bother to stop the thought that came next—of his hands squeezing it and how firm it would feel.

She leaned over and picked up a stuffed dog the kid had dropped behind the car and opened the back, where several gallons of paint sat. She picked up a can and the plastic bags and smiled at him as she maneuvered past him toward the front door.

Conall managed three cans and followed her inside. There was a subtle floral smell but he didn't spot any flowers. To his immediate right was a cream couch with a black coffee table and black TV stand on the opposite wall. To the left was the dining room.

He set the cans down next to hers just to the left of the door.

She turned around and gazed at him for a moment, the beauty of her brown eyes pulling at his insides. Her mouth parted ever-so-slightly.

Christ, it was tempting. Then he remembered what they were supposed to be doing and headed back outside. Liam was around. They couldn't do anything, even if they both wanted to.

They got the rest of the painting supplies inside. Theresa seemed to avoid looking at him.

From just inside the doorway, he said, "Are you painting now? You want some help moving this furniture away from the wall?"

She waved her hand dismissively. "No, I think I can get it myself."

So, she valued her independence. He could respect that.

He chuckled. "I'm sure you can, but it's easier with a second person."

"You're right. Let me get Liam in the backyard." She looked up at him and their gazes locked.

Conall felt that tug again. He moved further inside and tried to distract himself. "Are you going to be painting the ceiling?"

She stepped past him to tell Liam to take Maddy to the backyard.

"Yes, the same color."

"You may want to pull the light fixture away from the ceiling."

Theresa looked up at the cheesy chandelier that hung over the dining room table. "That thing needs to go."

Conall laughed. "It's not contemporary, that's for sure."

"When I bought the house, the listing claimed that, 'The original vintage features shine through.'"

"That's hilarious." He looked up at it and didn't see any visible screws, but he knew what they usually had. "Do you want me to help you with it?"

She tapped her chin before saying, "Sure."

"Got a step stool? And a Philips screwdriver?"

"Let me grab them."

She headed into the kitchen, and he looked around a bit more. There was a great room with the kitchen off to the left. The walls were an ugly dark pink straight out of the 80s. It was good that she was painting. A cherry table with six chairs filled the dining room area. The fireplace and hearth were nice—stone, but the area to either side begged for some shelves.

Theresa returned and soon he had the base plate of the fixture detached and hanging. Theresa had been watching him the whole time, and he felt like he'd made a good showing. He wondered if she'd been checking him out.

"The furniture now?" he asked.

"Sure, that would be great." She turned back toward the living room and nodded.

He studied the curve of her hips as he stepped down and folded the step stool.

"You grab that end of the coffee table," he said. She lifted her end, and they moved all the furniture away from the walls. He caught her eye as they hefted the last piece, and she smiled again, almost like she couldn't help it.

"When are you going to start painting?" Conall asked as they edged the TV console away from the wall.

"Sujata and Casey are coming over to help me this evening. We'll do the primer and maybe one coat." She was breathing a little heavily from all the furniture moving, and it was so hot he had to mentally talk himself down.

She stepped back, crossed her arms, and surveyed the room. "Then I can do the paint tomorrow."

"That's cool."

"I've also got to pull the trim off because I'm replacing it. I bought a little tool they recommended."

"Pry bar?"

"Yeah."

He was quiet for a moment because he didn't want to seem over-involved. "Actually, do you want help doing it? It's easier with a second person."

She squinted at him with a half-smile. "Are you a DIY guy even though you're not a homeowner?"

He laughed. "Yeah—my dad was a general contractor, and I grew up helping him around the house."

"That's nice. I want to know how to do more stuff around the house myself."

"But you know what a big job this is, don't you? You can't do it all in a day by yourself." Despite the futility of it, he wanted to spend time with this woman. He wanted to help her out.

"You don't think?" Theresa narrowed her eyes in thought.

He shook his head. "No chance."

"So I'm happy to help you paint tomorrow if you want a second person."

She shook her head. "Conall, I couldn't ask you to do that."

"It's no big. I actually miss doing all this stuff. It's fun and reminds me of my dad. He passed a few years ago."

"Oh, I'm so sorry."

"Thanks. The offer stands."

Her eyes were still narrowed, and he felt her studying him. "If you truly mean it, I wouldn't mind the help. But only if you don't have anything else you need to do."

"I really don't. Let's pull the trim off."

8

—————

Theresa stood in the dining room, between the living room and kitchen, with her hands on her hips. Liam was upstairs drawing. After Conall had left, she'd spent some time reading with her son. His stubbornness was impressive, like he didn't want to try because he already knew he couldn't do it. She prayed she could get him past this.

But Conall. Wow. She had to remind herself that men could not be trusted, because he was unbelievably appealing. And seemed so genuinely nice.

Sujata and Casey should be over any minute. Theresa looked to see what other home improvements she might want to make. She focused on visualizing the painted room and found it a little hard. She didn't have the eye.

She'd fallen in love with the house the second she'd seen the listing online. The exterior was fire engine red with white trim, and it was adorable. The inside was a nightmare in terms of decoration—gauzy drapes littered the windows, lace slipcovers concealed the age of all the furniture, and there were little knick-knacks on every surface—but she'd instantly felt the potential, despite the "vintage" look. Fortunately, the old couple she'd bought it from had taken all their kitsch with them when they'd left. But they hadn't taken the thirty-year-old carpet or flowery bathroom wallpaper. Or the pink toilet.

She thought she might go with stained concrete floor. She'd pondered tile, but liked the idea of smooth concrete. Super easy maintenance. She was already saving up for that. Picking something she could do herself, like painting the walls, made sense.

She glanced back into the kitchen. She knew she also wanted to completely redo that room, starting with some cabinets that looked like they belonged in this century. She wasn't even saving for that yet. It would be a while. She would start cashing in her stock options soon enough, and that's when she'd be able to begin the more expensive home improvement jobs in earnest. Like the pink bathroom.

A knock sounded on the door, and she opened it to find Sujata.

"Hey, you. Your doorbell doesn't work."

"It doesn't?" Theresa poked her head out and pressed the button. Just a subtle buzzing outside. "Huh."

They went inside toward the kitchen.

"You want some wine before we get started on the fun task?" Theresa asked.

"Sure."

Theresa uncorked a bottle she'd opened the night before and poured two glasses.

Sujata swirled her wine and inhaled its scent. "So what's the plan?"

"We've got to tape everything off first, then put the drop cloths down. Conall helped me take the trim off, so it should make things easier."

"Wait, what? Conall?"

Theresa smiled sheepishly. "Yeah. He was walking his dog when we got home."

"And so, what—you just batted your eyes and said, 'Hey, will you come in and help me take the trim off my walls?'"

Theresa snorted. "No. He just offered to help me carry the paint in and things went from there."

"It's like fate!" Sujata said.

No, it couldn't be. "After we had the paint in the house, we got to talking, and he volunteered. Apparently, his dad was a general contractor so he grew up doing this stuff and knows all about it."

Sujata gave Theresa a light punch in the shoulder. "So you've found your perfect man, then."

Theresa looked to the side. "Let's get started."

"Change the subject much?" Sujata teased.

Theresa responded by cutting open the pack of painter's tape and handing Sujata a roll.

Sujata took it and said, "Okay, then. Let's get to it. When's Casey getting here?"

"Soon."

They started working, chatting about the office.

As they finished taping plastic sheeting to the hearth, Liam came racing down the stairs.

"Mom!"

"What, honey? Be careful of the plastic."

"I drew a bear!"

Theresa stepped carefully across the room to where he stood on the bottom step.

"Hi, Liam," Sujata said.

He smiled shyly.

Theresa took the picture from him and inspected it. "This is wonderful, sweetie." She could tell it was a grizzly rather than a brown or black bear.

There was a knock at the door.

"Let me see," Sujata said.

Theresa handed it to her friend before opening the door for Casey.

"Wow," Sujata said. "His eyes make him look so scary."

"He's a mad bear," Liam explained.

Theresa and Sujata laughed.

"Who's mad?" Casey asked.

"Liam's bear." Sujata handed it to Casey, who nodded appreciatively before handing it back to Liam.

"Why's he mad?" Theresa asked.

"A camper stole his honey."

The women smiled at each other.

"Of course he did," Theresa said with a laugh.

"Why do you have all this plastic?" he asked.

Theresa ruffled his hair. "It's to protect the floor and furniture when we paint the ceiling."

"Can I help?"

She rested her hand on his shoulder. "Not today."

"Tomorrow?"

"We'll see. Why don't you sit in the kitchen and draw something new. Then you can show us."

The idea of drawing seemed to placate him. His feet pounded the stairs on his way to his bedroom.

Just after they got Casey set up to help, Theresa's phone rang. She looked at the screen and grimaced.

"Michael?" Casey asked.

"No. I have to take this." She accepted the call. "Hi, Mom."

"Hello, dear."

"Isn't your potluck tomorrow?"

Sujata crouched down to pry open a can of paint.

"That's sweet of you to remember." Her mom sounded so saccharine sometimes. "I've got it in the oven now. What's the name of your church? I want to have your dad find their website so I can see pictures."

Theresa sat down on the stairs, watching as Sujata lifted the lid off. "Oh, they don't have a website."

"Maybe he can find it on a map."

Casey handed Sujata a paint tray and she poured some of the primer in and wiped off the excess with her finger, which she dragged along the edge of the tray several times to get most of it off.

She covered the phone and sighed. "It's called Grace Unitarian Church."

"*Unitarian?*"

"There aren't a lot of local Baptist churches up here, Mom." At least, there weren't any in Milwaukie she knew of.

Her mom clucked, obviously still trying to absorb the fact that her daughter was taking her grandson to a Unitarian church. She was spoiled for choice in Baptist churches in Texas.

Theresa closed her eyes because lying didn't come naturally. The smell of the primer had wafted over to her spot on the stairs now. She pulled the hem of her shirt down where it had ridden up in the back.

"Watch out, Mom," Liam said as he squeezed past her with an armful of supplies.

"Are you going on any retreats?" her mom asked. "They are so wonderful for your soul. Does your church even have them?"

She hated this but didn't know what else to do at this point. "No, it's very small. Nothing like that."

"You know they're often offered by larger churches and anyone is welcome. Surely you could find a weekend one for mothers and their children."

Not right now. That sounded draining. "I'll look into it."

"What else is going on?" her mom asked.

"Not a lot. Liam's having a little trouble in school. His reading." She said it quietly and reopened her eyes to see Sujata looking at her in concern as she put the lid back on the can.

"You know if you spent more time with him it wouldn't be like that."

"Mom, would you just leave it? I know you think I'm a failure, but this is how it is. I have to work." Another lie. She was getting enough from Michael that she could quit. Instead, all that money went straight to Liam's college fund. She couldn't imagine not working.

"Yes, I know." Her mom sighed. "I guess I will just have to accept it."

If only.

"I just wish you'd move back to Texas so I could see Liam. They have computer jobs here, too."

Theresa needed the distance between her and her mom. "Listen, I have friends over, and they're helping me paint. Do you want to talk to Liam?"

"Of course!"

"Okay, one sec. Let me get him. I'll talk to you later. I love you." She pulled the phone away from her ear before she could hear her mom say it back.

She glanced back at Sujata and Casey, who were extracting rollers

59

from their plastic wrap, and shrugged before heading into the kitchen, where she found Liam spreading out watercolor supplies.

"I thought you were going to draw?"

"I changed my mind."

"Okay. Let me prepare the table for you. Grammy's on the phone."

He smiled and took the phone from her. "Hi, Grammy!"

Theresa sighed again and cleared the placemats off the table. Liam was telling her mom about goats. She got out a trash bag and spread it out on the table to protect it. Now he was all set up and she went back to the living room to Sujata.

"Sorry about that."

"Fun call?" Sujata said as she handed her a roller.

"Yeah." As fun as surgery.

"She sounds as critical of you as your ex."

"Let's get started." She really didn't like to talk about it because people thought she let her mom walk all over her.

Sujata looked like she might want to inquire further. Instead she said, "So when's Conall coming over, then?"

"Ten." She pictured him standing there with Maddy earlier, his jacket's collar tucked under on one side. She'd resisted the urge to reach over and fix it.

As intense as her weakness for Conall was, the fact that Liam would be here tomorrow was a good thing. Nothing would happen with Conall with her son in the house.

Not that she was tempted. No. Not at all.

9

"Liam, Conall's here!" Theresa called as soon as she heard the knock on the door. Might as well get him down here from the start.

She opened the door to the sight of Conall in a thin white t-shirt and a pair of worn, faded jeans, which sat invitingly low on his narrow hips. He wore his royal blue North Face fleece unzipped.

Her gaze met his, but not before she saw him checking her out, too. He smiled a little sheepishly, and her heart warmed, against her better judgment. She should not be thinking this way about him. He was a nice guy helping her out, that was it.

But there was no harm in looking, was there? If he ever suggested they be anything more than casual friends, she'd just let him down gently and carry on with her life. Because a relationship was out of the question.

He'd shaved, which Theresa appreciated because she'd never liked the feel of stubble.

A stupid thought because she'd not be feeling his face, however much she'd like to.

"Looks like you need a new doorbell," Conall said after the long pause.

"Yeah, Sujata pointed that out to me yesterday."

"Maddy!" Liam called.

That's when she noticed the yellow dog next to Conall. She laughed out loud. She'd been so distracted by him she hadn't even seen a fifty-pound lab pressing against his leg.

Liam leaned up against Theresa's hip, and she rested her hand on his shoulder.

Conall said, "Hi, Liam. She's looking forward to playing with you."

"Really?" Liam asked.

"Sure. She might not know specifically, but she knows something good's about to happen. Check out her wild tail."

Theresa glanced down and saw that the tail in question wagged so fiercely that Maddy rocked side to side. "Let's take her to the backyard."

Liam ran off the porch ahead of them to open the gate to the back-yard. Once they had Liam and the dog safely back there, Conall followed Theresa back inside, and they stood between the living room and dining room.

"You know, doorbells are easy to install," he said. "You can get a wireless one nowadays too. I'm happy to show you."

"Oh, that would be great." He was too much—so nice it hurt. And he made her stomach flutter. Yet what was she doing getting nervous? This was not a first date.

"Can I get you something to drink?" She looked back toward the kitchen. "I have some flavored waters. Wine." Wine? What was she doing offering wine in the middle of the morning? Good lord.

"I'm good right now." He held his head up a little. "What's that I smell?"

"I'm making a pot roast. You'll stay for dinner, I hope? I figured it's the least I can do." She really wanted him to say yes.

"Oh, sure." He grinned. "What man would turn down a home-cooked meal?"

"Fair point." She returned his grin and then made a colossal effort to tamp down her emotions. She was getting carried away. "Should we get started?"

"Sure."

His easy smile relaxed her a little. He was just being friendly.

Conall crouched down next to the paint cans before looking up. "Did you get it shaken at the store?"

"Yeah." She stood right next to him.

He nodded, picked up the screwdriver, and opened the first can. "Stir stick?"

Theresa pointed, and he leaned over to snag it before stirring the paint.

"This is a good beige," he said. "Not too yellow."

"Thanks. Liam picked it. He said the others were wrong." She got down on her knees, the smell of the paint hitting her. She wasn't a fan. She handed him the pour spout the guy at the store had recommended and held the first tray for him so he could pour. Then she gave him the second tray, which he filled.

"Here's a trick," Conall said. "Got a nail and a hammer?"

"Sure," she said, curious.

"A small nail."

She went to the garage and came back with a few nails of different sizes, and he picked one out of her open palm after she crouched down, the heat from his fingers giving her an unexpected tingle.

He took the nail and tapped a hole in the rim. "The paint will drain back in."

"Clever," she said.

They stood up at the same time and each leaned over to grab a tray, bumping heads. "Oh, sorry," Theresa said as she backed up, rubbing her forehead. "I'm a total klutz." He probably thought she was coming onto him, which both thrilled her and made her feel like a fool.

"No, that was all me." Conall grabbed a tray and a roller. "Here you go."

"Thanks," Theresa said as she stepped back to put more distance between them.

Conall picked up his own roller.

They decided to start on either side of the hearth, since the stones on it reached the ceiling and weren't being painted. They'd paint away from each other and meet up again on the wall that backed up to the kitchen.

Just after she'd applied her first roll of color on the wall, Conall said, "So, tell me some gossip from work."

She spread more paint on the wall. "Hmm. There isn't a lot of juicy stuff there. Most people are boring. Lots of family men."

"Yeah, there really aren't too many women, are there? Aren't you, Sujata, and Iryna the only ones? Oh, and the woman who has an office. What's her name?" He crouched down to get the bottom of the wall.

"Casey. She's my boss. Also, my friend."

"Ah."

He was right about the lack of women, but he'd forgotten one. "Well, there's also Gwen, the office manager."

"Oh, of course. I was thinking of technical people."

"Yeah. But it's okay with just the four of us. I don't have a problem with men." She turned to look at him and laughed. "Especially when they come over to help me paint my house." Boy, did she not have a problem with him. Having him here was really nice.

She looked over her shoulder and caught a glimpse of his lower back as he reached up to paint near the ceiling. She could see the top of the elastic band of his black boxer briefs. She felt herself warm.

Just then, he turned around and gave her a grin that said he knew she'd been admiring him.

"So," Theresa blurted, "uh—how did you like California?" Decent save.

"It was good. I didn't partake of the culture all that much. I was focused on my degree."

"I was pretty serious myself as a student." She stared at the wall, trying not to visualize his butt filling out his jeans.

"Where were you?"

"Seattle. University of Washington."

"How'd you end up down here?"

"I moved down after I left my husband. Ex-husband." She rolled the beige paint across the white of the wall, the familiar frustration building as she thought about him. "I prefer to think of him as just 'Liam's father' or 'Michael,' rather than anything to me."

"Liam seems like a good kid."

She smiled. "He is. Though he's going through a morose phase right now. I am not sure what to do with him half the time. Being a parent's tough."

"What's he do?"

"He's just moody a lot. I never know what to expect." She rolled more paint on, her heart swelling a bit with love when she thought about Liam.

"One of my cousins was a little grumpy when he was a kid."

"Tell me he's a success now." She wanted to turn around and look at him, but resisted.

"Well, he's fifteen, wears black skinny jeans and a fair amount of dark makeup, and listens to incomprehensible music."

Theresa groaned. "You're not helping."

Conall chuckled. "But... he'll be fine."

"Who? Liam or your cousin?"

"Both of them."

She hoped that was true. "You know the worst thing right now?"

"What?"

"He's struggling to learn how to read. I just want to fix it for him, but I don't know how. I'm having him tested for learning disabilities this week."

"That's rough." He paused. "I might be able to help."

"Really? How?" She spun around to see that he had made it all the way to front door.

He must have felt her eyes on him because he turned and said, "It just so happens that I have experience working with kids facing reading difficulties. I already signed up for InfoQuest's tutoring program. I did a similar program at my last job."

"Really?" Theresa said again, eyebrows raised. What were the chances? This guy... seriously. Was he for real?

What were the chances their lives would keep intersecting? Maybe the universe was telling her something.

Yes, it was reminding her how to exercise self-control.

"I could work with him," Conall said. "Or just tell you the right books to get."

She thought about this. She'd already been thinking maybe Liam would respond better to a man than to her. Probably part of Liam's lack of confidence came from the way Michael treated him. She knew Michael had called him a pussy for liking art instead of sports. Remembering this started a slow simmer in her blood.

"You okay?" Conall asked with a furrowed brow.

"Oh, fine. Fine." Michael was a world-class jerk. She'd tried to get sole custody, but of course the courts don't care about unprovable "pussy"-calling-accusations. Emotional abuse didn't "count." He wasn't physically violent, after all. It was so frustrating.

She went back to painting and glanced at Conall, muscles flexing in his arm as he moved the roller down the wall.

"Hey," he said.

His voice was a little lower than normal, and something about it heated her core.

Plus, he was still looking at her, watching her.

They were mere steps from each other. She could close this distance in less than a second, and she was so tempted.

"Hey, yourself," she said.

He blinked slowly.

Sense returned. She shouldn't do this with him. They needed to just be work colleagues.

But it was hard.

They smiled at the same time, and Conall blinked again.

Rationality won out, and she looked down to dip her roller in the tray before pressing it to the wall, her heart feeling the loss of his gaze. She felt him look back at the wall and continued painting, breathing in the smell.

But when their rollers met up, they smiled at each other again and worked together until the wall was finished. The heat in her core hadn't gone away. And when she glanced at him again, his jaw clenched as he returned her gaze. They were a couple feet from each other, and his eyes flitted down to her mouth, warming her even more.

Conall set his roller down in his tray and took a half step forward.

He was definitely in her space now, and she liked it. She raised her head a little to meet his gaze as her heart sped up. He reached out to brush some of loose hair behind her ear, and his touch made her shiver. She instinctively leaned into his hand.

His eyes were intent on her mouth as he moved his hand to her shoulder and bent forward. He was absolutely going to kiss her, and it was the only thing she cared about at that moment.

"Mom!"

She jumped back at the same time Conall stepped back and dropped his hand. Thank goodness Liam was calling from the back door. She hadn't heard it open.

"Crap," she muttered and glanced back at Conall, who grinned at her before she set her roller down and headed toward the kitchen. "What?"

"Can you bring me some water?"

"What? You can't come get it yourself?" He was standing in the doorway.

"I'm busy," he said.

Conall snorted.

"Liam, I'm busy, too. I'm not your personal slave." He was testing some limits. "If you want some water, come in and get it."

He sighed and stepped inside.

She could hear Conall chuckling behind her and turned to give him an exasperated look. His smile made his eyes glow, and she was instantly back to the moment when he'd touched her. Her heart sped up. She turned back around as Liam walked into the dining room.

"Are you having fun with Maddy?" she asked Liam, knowing what he'd say.

"I love her! Can I get my own dog, Mom? Then they can play together!"

"Liam, we've talked about this. When you're a little older, we'll revisit a pet, but not now." Theresa stood with her arms folded and watched him. Wearing a frown, he got on the step stool to get a plastic cup down and filled it with water from the pitcher in the fridge.

He took a sip and Theresa leaned down to catch him in a quick hug as he passed before he could escape back outside. He giggled as his arm slipped around her waist to return the hug.

She turned back around to face Conall, who's eyes twinkled with amusement.

"Honestly," she said.

"It's worth a try. What boy doesn't want a mom slave?"

"Apparently."

"So," he said, motioning at the unpainted ceiling. "We aren't done."

She looked up. "Oh, yeah. I sort of forgot about that."

"Good thing I'm here."

Their eyes locked again.

"It is." That felt like a bold statement.

As they stared at each other, she gradually realized this was still a bad idea. Liam was just outside. She broke the gaze and went to get the roller extension off the dining room table.

"I've only got one of these."

Conall went all business. "I can follow you around and patch up the edges, if you do the ceiling perimeter first."

Theresa nodded. She screwed the extension onto the roller and started on the ceiling over the wall they'd just finished. She worked her way around the room with Conall following behind her, cleaning up the wall and ceiling where her roller didn't quite reach. He was tall enough to get to the junctures without a ladder.

They were quiet considering their earlier chatting and escapades. Yet she felt at ease in the comfortable silence, rather than awkward.

Conall finished his task, and she started working on the rest of the dining room ceiling.

"Hey, Theresa."

She turned to find him holding the paintbrush up and watching her. "Yeah?"

"I'm sure Maddy's ready for some food."

"You're not staying for dinner?" She was more disappointed than she should have been about this.

"I was thinking I could come back, if your pot roast offer still stands."

"It does."

"Great." He stepped closer and lightly touched her arm before moving past her and into the kitchen, where he proceeded to rinse out the brush.

She stood there feeling the burn where he'd touched her and eventually made herself start painting again.

She heard him approach and felt his hands on her shoulders.

"Are you sore yet?" he asked.

"No," she said, the heat returning to her core as she lowered the roller.

"You will be." He massaged her shoulders.

"Maybe not. I lift." Why didn't this feel weird? A man she barely knew touching her. It felt way too good.

"Really?" he sounded impressed.

She closed her eyes, enjoying the sensation of his strong hands. "Yes."

He dropped his hands and touched her waist as he moved around her. "I'd better go. I'll take Maddy down and feed her. You'll be done by the time I get back."

She watched him head out the front door.

Some time soon she needed to kiss him.

No, no, she did not.

10

When Conall knocked on Theresa's door after taking care of Maddy, Liam opened it wearing a big smile.

"Do you want to see my tiger?" he asked.

Conall laughed in surprise. "You have a tiger?"

"Noooo," Liam said. "It's a drawing!"

"I'd love to see it." Conall stepped inside and shut the door as Liam went tearing off upstairs, pounding back down seconds later.

"Here." Liam reached up to hand him the drawing.

The sketch was remarkable. It looked just like a tiger crouched in the grass, so realistic and a little scary to look at. This tiger was ready to eat him. Conall didn't know anyone who could draw this well, and this was a little kid. "Wow, Liam, this is great."

Liam's face lit up in a giant grin.

"What are you drawing next?" Conall asked.

"A goat."

Conall laughed. "Why a goat?"

"Because they eat anything!" He took back the picture Conall handed him.

Conall headed into the kitchen with Liam at his heels.

"Hey," Theresa said while scooping potatoes, carrots, and onions from the crock pot into a white dish that already held the pot roast. "You came back."

"As promised." They looked at each other for a moment, both smiling. She'd changed into a pair of nice-fitting jeans and a t-shirt that gave him a prime view of those arms.

"Conall." Liam poked Conall's hand.

"Hmm?" He turned toward the boy, who looked at him expectantly.

"Do you want to see my other drawings?"

"Sure, buddy. That'd be awesome." Conall did want to see them. He already liked being here. It was comfortable.

"Liam," Theresa said. "Why don't you go upstairs and grab them? You can show him down here."

He headed back up, and Theresa glanced at Conall again. "You have an odd effect on him. He's usually quite shy."

"Yeah?" He leaned against the counter and crossed his arms. He wanted to touch her again, but Liam would be back any second. "He's very talented."

"Yeah." She beamed. "I'm trying to find an art program for him. There's a local arts academy, but it doesn't start until high school." She got the last of the potatoes in the dish and placed the crock pot stoneware in the sink.

Conall loved the proud look on her face.

"I got them!" Liam called. He brought a stack of paper to the kitchen table.

Conall raised his eyebrows at Theresa and went to look. He sat down next to Liam and studied at each picture as the boy passed them over.

There were all sorts of animals, a house, cars. And they were all very realistic. Liam had drawn a recognizable Corvette and a robin plucking a worm out of the ground.

"These really are terrific." Conall collected all the drawings and stacked them up. He handed them back to the kid. "Will you draw me a picture of Maddy?"

Liam's mouth fell open like this was the best idea he'd ever heard. "Yeah!"

71

"Why don't you take these back upstairs to keep them safe? We don't want to get food on them."

"That's true," Liam said.

Conall pushed the chair back and watched Liam reach the stairs. Then he caught Theresa's eye and sidled up next to her, putting his arm around her waist and looking over her shoulder as she rinsed the stoneware out.

She leaned into him as he inhaled her scent. Christ, he wanted her.

But then she turned off the water and stepped away. "He'll be back down in a second."

"He sure will." Conall rested his hand on his thigh as he leaned back on the counter.

Theresa smiled at him as she pulled a bowl of spinach out of the microwave and poured it into another dish. "Sorry, Liam believes in the power of spinach."

Conall laughed. "Muscles?" He picked up the pot roast to put it on the table.

"Yep."

She breezed past him, her arm brushing his, and put her dish next to the roast.

Liam reappeared and sat in the chair in front of the window.

Theresa said to Conall, "Go ahead and sit down. What can I get you to drink? I don't have any beer, but I've got some Chardonnay if you'd like that."

Conall said, "A glass of water would be great." He sat down.

Theresa reached into the cabinet for three glasses.

"Conall," Liam said.

"Yeah, buddy?"

"That's my mom's seat."

Conall laughed. "Oops, my bad."

"Liam, it doesn't matter where we sit," Theresa chided. "It's not assigned."

But Conall got up anyway and moved to the only other chair. The table didn't have a chair on the side that faced the counters. Theresa gave him a wry look as she poured water out of a filter pitcher over ice into a couple glasses. She brought those over and then poured Liam a glass of milk.

"This looks amazing, Theresa," Conall said as they started eating.

"Thank you." She looked pleased.

Liam chattered about drawing and what he'd gotten to do with Maddy.

Listening to the kid ramble on made Conall miss his cousins, the first time he'd missed Hawaii in a long time. He loved kids and wished he could watch his youngest cousins grow up. He also loved seeing the way Theresa looked at Liam, like he was the only thing that mattered. She was a gorgeous woman, inside and out.

"Liam, I need you to eat something. Have some of the pot roast."

Liam frowned and pulled a little beef away from the roast. As he finished chewing, Conall asked, "So tell me about school. What's your favorite thing there?"

Liam's eyes widened a little. "Art. Duh."

Conall and Theresa both laughed, but then she said, "Liam, don't be rude."

"So what's your least favorite thing there?" Conall asked.

"That's easy," Liam answered. "Madison."

Conall laughed and Theresa said, "Who's Madison?"

"This girl," Liam said.

"What's your least favorite *subject*?" Conall clarified.

"Oh. Reading."

"Are you serious?" Conall said as he set his fork on his plate. "Reading is awesome."

"Nuh uh," he said. Yet doubt colored his voice.

"It's my favorite thing to do. Except play volleyball."

Theresa nodded. "See, honey, I'm not the only one who likes to read."

Liam frowned.

Theresa caught Conall's eye and smiled at him as she popped a small potato in her mouth. "Eat some carrots, Liam."

"How many do I have to eat?"

"Four."

There were six on his plate, so Conall thought the kid was getting off easy.

He scowled. "I don't want four."

"Liam, you love carrots. Why are you arguing this time?" She forked one off her plate and opened her beautiful mouth for it. There could be something so intimate about watching someone eat.

"How much meat do I have to have?"

Theresa finished chewing. "Four bites."

"If I have five bites of pot roast, can I have three carrots?"

"If you eat five bites of pot roast and finish all the spinach on your plate, you can have just three carrots." Theresa looked exasperated, and it made Conall chuckle. He remembered the dinner table negotiations at his own family dinners. His entire family got together every Sunday, and there was always at least one kid who wasn't eating.

After Liam had finished the spinach and started pushing a carrot around on his plate, Conall asked, "You don't like reading at all?"

"It's okay when Mom reads to me," Liam allowed.

"Well, that's something." Conall thought of a different approach. "I think it's a way into secret worlds. How else can you find out about talking robots or spaceships?"

Liam looked at him while Conall chewed. "TV."

Conall's mouth stretched wide in a grin, and he glanced at Theresa, who was also smiling.

"I'll give you that, buddy. TV's pretty cool. But I still say reading's better."

Liam smiled, too, obviously proud of himself. "Will you read a book to me?"

Theresa said, "Honey, Conall doesn't have time. I'll sit with you later."

"That sounds fun," Conall said. "I can read with you a little after dinner, if that's okay with your mom." He glanced over at Theresa, hoping he wasn't overstepping some boundaries. Her eyes were a little wide, but she didn't look annoyed.

She returned his smile. "Thanks, that's generous of you."

They talked a little more about Liam's art projects at school, and once he'd finished his last required carrot, Theresa suggested he go pick a book.

He slid off the chair.

"Don't forget your plate, Liam."

He deposited it in the sink and headed upstairs.

She looked over at Conall and said, "You didn't have to say yes, you know."

"I know. I like kids. He reminds me of my cousins."

"Do you have a lot of them?" Theresa stood up and took both their empty plates to the sink.

"Yeah." Conall grabbed the pot roast dish and spinach and set them on the counter next to Theresa. "Eleven. I'm the second oldest."

"Thanks. That's quite a crew." She rinsed the plates off and opened the dishwasher while Conall carried the glasses over.

Liam came down with a book in his hand. "Found one!"

"What'd you pick?" Conall asked.

"It's about a dog."

Conall laughed and glanced over at Theresa, who shrugged and said, "Fixated."

"What can I do to help?"

"What? Oh, just go on and read with him. I'll finish the dishes."

"Are you sure?"

She nodded, then whispered, "If you can get him to read to you, I'll... be very appreciative."

He laughed. "That could be nice for me."

"It could be." Her voice had gone a little smoky again but then she looked away.

He reached out and touched her wrist quickly. "I'll do my best."

She glanced down at her arm, and he turned to see Liam standing at the end of the counter, watching.

"Let's go, buddy," Conall said. He scooted a chair closer to Liam's at the kitchen table while Theresa continued at the sink, soap bubbles stuck to her forearms.

Liam opened the book and pushed it toward him.

"Aren't you going to read for me?" Conall asked.

"No, you." Liam pushed it even closer.

Conall chuckled a little and turned to the first page so they could both see. "Max was one hot dog," he began.

"Hot dog!" Liam said with a laugh.

Conall smiled over at him. "Not one you'd want to eat, huh?"

"No!"

"Max was one hot dog," he started again. This time Liam just smiled, and Conall continued on, making sure to do all the right voices. They read through the book twice, with Conall convincing Liam to read a few of the words.

Conall closed the book. "See, you *can* do it." He looked up again and Theresa, who gave him an admiring look. He grinned widely at her before asking, "Have you ever read about Carlos the dog?"

"Is he funny?" Liam looked up at him, and Conall's heart broke a little. Moments like this were fleeting. He'd never have this with a kid of his own.

Something about being in this house, with a child and a beautiful woman, reminded him so much of Clarissa and what might have been.

Thinking about that was still a punch to the gut and the familiar sense of something missing in his life descended.

"Is he?" Liam asked again.

Exorcise the thought. No point firing brain cells with thoughts of the kids they'd both desperately wanted but never had.

All because he couldn't.

But none of that was this kid's fault.

"Very." Conall's voice was tight.

Theresa reached the table. "Liam, I think it's time for Conall to go."

"Will you read to me again?" Liam asked.

"We'll have to see, buddy." He squeezed between Liam's chair and the windowsill, and Theresa walked him to the door. He grabbed his jacket off the arm of the couch as she opened the door. He was bummed to be leaving, even though this superficial taste of domestic life was all he could ever expect. Fucking low sperm count.

"Thank you again for all your help today. Especially with Liam." She was looking into his eyes like it mattered.

"No problem. I should be the one thanking you for the wonderful meal." He reached out to squeeze her arm. He couldn't help it. His body wanted it—and last he checked, his hand was attached to his body.

Her face revealed nothing and he wondered if he shouldn't have. He glanced over at Liam again, who was still looking through the book. "Bye, Liam."

"Bye," Liam called.

Conall stepped out, and Theresa said, "Bye, Conall." If he wasn't wrong, her voice was just a tad lower than normal.

"See you tomorrow." Against his better judgment, he was already anticipating it.

On the short walk home, he remembered the good times with Clarissa and how much they'd looked forward to their life. Even when they'd first started dating, they knew it was for the long haul. Until everything was ruined by his failing.

11

Wednesday afternoon, Conall was trying to get through a document on the Athena project when Theresa's voice floated across the air into his ears. He turned around. The short-sleeved polo shirt she wore allowed him to admire her arms, which were draped across the pod wall in front of Sujata.

"Conall, hi," she said. "How are you?"

"Good. Yourself?" Out of the corner of his eye, he could see Sujata giving Theresa a smirk.

"Oh, you know, fine." She glanced at Sujata and clarified, "Good."

When she smiled at him, he nodded and turned back to his computer.

"Uh," she said quietly to Sujata. "Anyway. Friday night?"

He shouldn't have turned around. He should just let this go. A work fling wouldn't be good for either of them, considering they worked so closely together. It's not like he was in IT, and she was in legal.

He got back to his reading. He was still getting acquainted with the background to the project. His role wasn't going to be too difficult. He'd built a data warehouse at his last job and knew all the ins and outs. He was just trying to get to know the specifics of the data they'd be warehousing.

Theresa and Sujata were still chatting when Martin, one of her pod mates, came over. "Hey, brah."

"What's up?" Conall asked.

"So, Conall," Martin started, "what do you say to bringing Aloha Friday to Portland? Bernard's on board."

Bernard was Theresa's other pod mate. They were both from Hawaii. Conall rubbed his chin. "I could do that."

"Great. This Friday?"

Conall nodded.

"How 'bout you, T.?" Martin turned to ask.

Theresa looked over. "I don't know what you're talking about."

"You should do it," Conall said. "Pod solidarity through fashion. Well, plus me."

He needed to clear up the confusion still on her face. "In Hawaii, people wear aloha shirts and khakis on Fridays. It's like casual Friday, Hawaiian-style."

"You mean a Hawaiian shirt?"

"Yeah," Martin said. "It's mostly men, but there's no reason you couldn't join us."

"Well, except I don't have a Hawaiian shirt. Also, you guys are casual every day. It would be more like dress-up Friday."

They all laughed.

Conall cocked his head to the side. "Still, you could buy a shirt."

Her gaze was still on him. "Maybe I will."

"Cool," Martin said, heading back to his desk.

Conall scrolled down in the document. InfoQuest's data warehousing situation was a little unusual because they didn't have that much data. The plan was to use their warehouse for reporting on everything—finance, human resources, and customer relationship management to start. InfoQuest was planning to do something unusual with their system—every time they ran code on a client's system, they'd track that as a transaction. He was quite curious to see how it would be implemented, and how it would actually work.

It would be interesting.

He heard Theresa say, "You know how Casey is with her family. Can't get enough of them."

He'd been so close to having a family of his own. He'd believed it was imminent. He clenched his teeth to try to forget.

But things had been so good with Clarissa in the beginning of their marriage. They'd really been in love. They'd started dating when he was seventeen and she was sixteen, and it had lasted almost nine years. Seven of those had been good. They'd gotten married when he was twenty. The last two years had been full of heartbreak. That's when he'd learned he was broken.

Fuck.

Theresa laughed, and he realized he loved the way she sounded, kind of throaty, almost smoky. Her regular voice didn't go too low, but her laugh was sexy.

This was the first time he'd been genuinely interested in a woman since Clarissa. He didn't count his grad school friend-with-benefits.

"Hi, Conall."

He turned back around to see Iryna. Today she'd toned things down—she had on jeans that weren't pink.

"Hello." He smiled at her.

"How are things going for you? Are you getting settled on the project and everything?"

"Oh, sure. Everything's great. Theresa's been helping me out some."

"That's wonderful. Nice to see the group functioning as a team."

Conall could see Theresa over Iryna's shoulder, watching as she continued to chat with Sujata.

"The main reason I came by was to let you know that I brought cookies."

"Oh, really? Sugar cookies, by chance? That's my favorite."

Theresa glared before saying, "Okay, I should get back to my desk."

Iryna continued. "Sorry, no sugar cookies—just chocolate chip and snickerdoodle."

"Later, you," Sujata said to Theresa, who headed back toward her desk.

"Snickerdoodle will do just fine." He pushed his chair back and stood. They headed to the kitchen.

"So where were you before here?" Iryna asked.

"I just finished my Master's. First job since then. Worked for the state before that." Conall saw Theresa pointedly not look at them as they passed her desk. "What about you? How long have you been here?"

"Just over a year. I came down from Microsoft."

They reached the table beside the break room, where Conall spied the platter of aforementioned cookies. Awesome.

"Nice." He lifted the plastic wrap and pulled out a snickerdoodle.

Iryna watched him as he took a bite, and he wondered if she was interested in him.

"Mmm."

"You like it?" she asked.

"I do," he said through a mouthful.

"Good," she said. "It makes me happy when people eat my baked goods."

She was just being nice. Which was good, since he'd just been being polite—plus, he loved cookies.

He grabbed a napkin. "I'm just going to grab another one of these and get back to work."

"Okay, sure. See you around."

Iryna's very pink lipstick reminded him of Theresa's naturally red lips, which he'd been just inches from a few days ago. That's what he thought about all the way back to his desk.

He grinned at Theresa as he passed, and she returned it. He caught a glimpse of her arms below the hem of her sleeves.

He fell into his chair. No, he wouldn't think about those arms. Looped around the back of his head, for instance. He wouldn't think about where his mouth would be and what it would be doing in that scenario, either. Or what she might taste like.

He'd never find out. She'd made that clear.

THE NEXT DAY, Theresa stood and grabbed her mug, inspecting the dried sludge that ringed the inside wall. She had to get out of there to pick Liam up from school and get him to his appointment. She heard the faucet running before rounding the corner into the kitchen.

There stood Conall, looking gorgeous despite the fact that he was stooped forward slightly to reach the sink. One of the disadvantages of being tall, she guessed.

Look at those fine arm muscles flexing as he rinsed his mug. She was glad his sleeves were rolled up.

Okay, she hadn't been expecting lust to hit her so hard.

"Hi," he said when he looked over, the corners of his mouth turning up.

"Hello." She forced her own into a smile and tried to get rid of the heat that had coursed through her. Where on earth had that come from?

He shook his hands and pushed the faucet lever down. He stepped back while drying his hands with a couple paper towels. "Your turn."

"Thanks." She turned the water on waited for it to heat up.

"You look out of sorts," he said. "Everything okay?"

"Oh, sure, fine." When she glanced at him, he was grinning rather than looking concerned, almost like he knew he was the cause of her flustered state.

She furrowed her brow filled the mug with steaming water and some soap before dunking the scrub brush and powering away at the sludge. Did he know how he affected her?

"You sure?"

"Yeah, you know. I've got Liam's visit to the psychiatrist today. It's his test for learning disabilities."

"D-day. Hopefully you can find out what's going on."

"Well, I'm hoping it's something we can work through rather than something he'll always have to deal with." She dug the brush into the bottom edge of the mug.

"I hope so, too."

He was standing behind her, a little to the side, and she couldn't see him.

She ran her finger along the bottom of the mug and could still feel the dried-on gunk, so she rubbed harder. Her stomach twisted at the thought of the test. She wouldn't even find out the results for a couple weeks, at least.

Conall moved to lean against the counter next to the sink. "So, I wondered if you wanted help putting the trim back up in your place? I'm free this weekend."

Her heart did a stupid little dance. "Oh."

Of course, she could use the help. And she was an adult. She could get this attraction—or whatever it was—under control.

"Sure," she said. "That would be great." She rinsed the mug clean and turned the water off.

"Good. What time?"

"Can we talk about it tomorrow? I need to get going." She pulled a couple paper towels off the rack and looked up at him, struck again by his remarkable blue eyes, lit up by his easy smile.

"Sure."

On her way out, she noticed a tray of—no, it couldn't be. Sugar cookies. That woman was not subtle. "Would you look at that. Sugar cookies. On a pink tray."

Conall grimaced and followed Theresa back to her cube.

"Good luck. I'm sure everything's going to be fine."

"Thanks." She reached under her desk for her purse, and he stepped out of the way so she could get back into the aisle. "See you tomorrow."

"Bye, Theresa."

Even the way he said her name revved her heart.

Oh, stop.

THERESA PICKED Liam up from school, and they got in the car to head to the testing center.

"Ready for this, honey?" She'd told him he'd be taking a test that morning.

"What is it about?" He eyed her in the rearview mirror.

"The test?"

"Yeah."

"They are going to figure out what kind of learner you are. They'll ask you lots of questions. Some things you will just say, but they might want you to work through some problems. I just want you to do your best. Don't worry, okay?"

"Okay." He was quiet for a moment. "What are they going to ask me?"

"I don't know exactly, but I think there will be puzzles." She'd done the research she could. "But I'll be there with you the whole time."

He was quiet the rest of the trip, and they went into a building that looked like a renovated house, gray siding and all. A classic waiting room full of chairs and bright plastic toys for little kids. A rack full of magazines sat in the corner, and a few had been abandoned on empty chairs.

"Have a seat, little man." She went to check in while Liam wandered over to the colorful bead maze and started pushing the wooden beads around.

Once they were checked in, she sat in the chair next to him.

"This is boring, Mom."

She smiled. "It's for little kids, honey. You're not a little kid anymore, are you?"

"No." He sounded offended. "Obviously."

She laughed and ruffled his hair. "It is obvious."

"Liam Smith?" a dark-haired man in a gray argyle sweater said from the door next to the check-in desk. Theresa thought he looked familiar. He had a short peppery beard but she couldn't place him.

"Come on, honey." Theresa stood, took his hand, and they headed back.

As they passed the man, he smiled at Liam and said, "Hi, there. I'm Dr. Schwartz."

Liam looked up and muttered, "Hi."

"Just this way," Dr. Schwartz said.

Theresa had insisted on being in the room while the test was going on. They followed him, turning a corner and going into the next office, which had a wooden desk in the corner and a short table set up near the entrance

84

with some red and white cubes and cardboard sheets on top. He headed to the desk and motioned for them to sit in two chairs opposite him. Liam was still holding on tightly to her hand, and she led him over there.

Dr. Schwartz took the paperwork Theresa had brought with her and went over how the tests would work. First there would be an IQ test, then some reading and language tests, with others possible based on the performance during the IQ test. The testing would take approximately two and a half hours.

"Liam, will you come with me? We're going to start. There will be several different activities that will be a little like games."

Liam looked at Theresa, eyes a little wide in fear.

She squeezed his hand and released it to rub his back. "It's okay, honey. I'm going to be right here. Just remember—do the best you can."

He got up and followed Dr. Schwartz to the table, and they sat across from each other. Theresa moved her chair so she could easily watch.

"I want you to be comfortable, Liam," he said. "Do you want to take your jacket off?"

Liam nodded and pushed it off his shoulders so it fell against the back of the chair. Theresa went over and took it from him, then scurried back. Dr. Schwartz's back was to her so she couldn't see everything that was happening.

"Okay, Liam, first we're going to play a little game with these blocks. Are you ready?"

Her son nodded and watched as Dr. Schwartz pushed items in front of him.

"Do you see this picture?"

"Yeah."

"You can make the picture out of the blocks." He shifted some of the items around in front of Liam, who was watching enraptured. "Do you understand how it works?"

Liam nodded. Theresa was tense in her chair, worried.

He shifted something else. "I want you to make this picture out of the blocks."

Liam reached up and started shifting them around. Soon, he looked up at Dr. Schwartz, who wrote something down.

"Now make this picture out of the blocks."

They went through several rounds of this, with Liam looking pretty relaxed, before Dr. Schwartz said, "I'm going to show you some pictures and then ask you some questions about them. Okay?"

"Okay."

"Look at this picture. Something important is missing. Can you tell what it is?" He listed off some body parts and Liam said, "Toe."

Theresa thought he answered pretty quickly, but she still found herself tapping her fingers on the arm of the chair.

They went through many of these picture questions. Then Dr. Schwartz asked Liam similarity questions before moving on to some number tests.

There were many more tests and finally they got to the ones clearly about language. Dr. Schwartz asked Liam to break words into syllables. Theresa's heart ached as she listened to him struggle with these. He also struggled with a test that involved reading a list of words and a spelling one. From the look on his face, he was getting tired, although he was still trying. She was impressed with his focus.

Eventually, after another test that involved Liam doing a lot of writing, Dr. Schwartz said, "Okay, Liam, that's it. We're all done."

Theresa could feel Liam relax from across the room, and the tension in her shoulders loosened.

"Why don't you sit here for a little bit while I go talk with your mom? You can play with the blocks if you want."

Theresa moved into another chair to face Dr. Schwartz as he sat at his desk behind her.

"How did he do?" she asked.

He glanced at his clipboard. "I need to look at the history you've provided me with and then compile the report before I can really say. Though he was fast with the block exercise."

Theresa smiled. "He's artistically gifted."

"I will give you a call once I have the report ready. However, it won't be until after Thanksgiving."

"Oh, that's a while." She'd go crazy.

He nodded. "Yes, it takes me some time to analyze and write up the results."

When Theresa got to the table, Liam had an intricate design with all the blocks. "That's really nice, sweetie. What is it?"

He shrugged.

"Ready to go?"

He took her hand as they left the room.

12

Saturday morning, Conall worked on a decent lunch and planned to spend the rest of the day avoiding work. He had a friend from grad school coming over to pick him up to shoot some hoops.

He chopped green onions, the sharp tangy smell filling his nose and reminding him of when his mom first taught him this recipe. He put them in a large glass mixing bowl along with soy sauce, sesame oil, sesame seeds, and chopped macadamia nuts.

Of course, it also reminded him of all the cooking he and Clarissa had done together. They loved to spend time in the kitchen, laughing and working. And she'd been willing to just give that perfection up. The pain was as raw as ever.

The limu was on the stove, blanching, so he drained that before chopping it nice and fine and sliding it off the board into the bowl. Next came the fresh tuna out of the fridge. He cubed it.

He was almost as skilled at chopping things as Clarissa was, but she was definitely faster. Did her new husband cook with her?

Stop remembering.

He was glad he'd gone to the store last weekend and picked up all the kitchen basics. The place was starting to feel more like a real home.

There was a knock at the door. Isaac was early.

"Hey, man," Isaac said as he came inside. He was tall and built up and had a little blond goatee. "Nice place. I expected something smaller."

Conall nodded. "Have a seat if you want."

He went back to the kitchen and dumped the two pounds of cubed tuna into the bowl and squeezed two lime quarters on top of the combination before mixing it up. One time he'd been doing this when Clarissa had come up behind him and wrapped her arms around his waist. They'd had great messy sex, and he'd had to finish it later.

Isaac stopped at the end of the counter and stared. "What's that?"

"Poke." He let the liquid drip off his hands into the bowl and bumped the kitchen faucet on with his wrist so he could scrub the oil —and the memory of Clarissa—off.

"Huh." Isaac stepped closer and peered into the bowl. "What'd you say it's called?"

"Po-kay. Marinated tuna. There's enough for you if you want some later."

"What's that green stuff?"

Conall laughed, knowing what he meant. "You mean the green onions?"

"No. The... other stuff."

"Limu."

"What's that?"

"Seaweed."

Isaac grimaced and shook his head. "No thanks."

"Suit yourself." Conall smiled. "But you're missing out."

"Fine by me."

He put on sweatpants and a green and yellow wicking shirt he pulled off the shelf of his barebones closet.

Conall followed Isaac out to his blue Subaru BRZ and they sped off to the park. It was close and Conall wondered if they could have just walked.

The park had a couple courts, both free. It was November, after all. They did several warm-up shots, which Conall felt in his calves. Still, it was great to get his body moving again, even if he did miss an embarrassing number of shots.

"Man, you suck," Isaac said. "What the hell happened?"

"Hell if I know. I guess I'm out of practice." He bent his knees for a shot, lined up his elbow and this time sank the ball.

Isaac retrieved the ball. "Better. I was worried you'd turned into a girl."

"Ha."

Isaac stepped back for a three-pointer. "So, any hotties at your new job?" He released the ball with nice form, his fingers on his ball hand pointing down.

Conall laughed and jogged after the rebound. Of course, an image of Theresa filled his mind. "You know how it is. Not a lot of women." He dribbled up to the three-point line and leaped with his shot.

"Too bad. You didn't date much at Stanford, either."

"No." He'd slept around a bit at first, but then had just the one regular casual hook-up. He'd had trouble getting close to anyone else. He figured he was still sort of mad at all women because of how Clarissa had treated him.

Isaac nodded. "So no one you've got your eye on?" He took another shot. "Doesn't every office have at least one? The receptionist, maybe?"

Conall ran up to the basket to get the bouncing ball and dribbled a distance before shooting again. He wondered what Theresa was up to. Probably doing something with her son.

He wasn't going to think about it.

"Why not break your dry spell?"

Conall tossed the ball back. "Who says I'm in a dry spell?"

"Aren't you?"

"There's one with the nicest upper arms I've ever seen."

Isaac snorted as he prepared his shot. "Upper arms? Who gives a shit about that? What about her other assets?"

"Not to worry, they're a perfect handful." Conall pictured her filled-out polo shirt yesterday and imagined what her breasts would feel like. "She's maybe five-eight and kind of wiry, but in a very good way."

"If you say so, bro." Isaac dribbled a couple times before dropping another basket.

He did say so. Conall jogged over to the ball. He wasn't going to say the rest. That she was smart and friendly and a wonderful mother.

They took several more shots.

Isaac's shoes squeaked against the concrete as he lined up another one, ball in the air. "You interested in joining a coed league volleyball team? We just had a guy leave the team so there's an open slot." He sank the ball.

Conall retrieved it and headed back. "Sure. When do you play?"

Isaac jogged over to where Conall had stopped and held his arms out to block his shot. "Games are Thursday nights. We usually practice on Tuesdays. Sometimes Sundays, too."

Conall turned his back toward Isaac and started dribbling to the side to try to get around him. He spun around and made the shot right between Isaac's outstretched arms. "Ha!"

Isaac jogged to get the ball and laughed. "You think it's over yet?"

Conall kept Isaac from shooting but then Isaac managed a crossover and did a quick layup. "How're your ankles, bro?"

"Sturdy and ready to support my foot as it kicks you in the ass."

Over the next hour, Isaac barely edged Conall out. But Conall's moves improved over the game, and by the end he didn't feel so incompetent.

He was also looking forward to a shower where he might, just might, ponder Theresa a little more. No harm in thinking about what he'd like to do to her, right?

13

Conall knocked on Theresa's door Sunday morning, nail gun in hand, to work on the trim.

Liam answered wearing a big grin. "Hi!"

"Hey, kiddo. How's tricks?"

"Huh?" Liam's brow furrowed, and he stood with his hand still on the doorknob.

"Liam, let the man inside," Theresa called from the kitchen.

He took a step back, and Conall walked on in.

"What did you say?" Liam asked.

"How's tricks? It just means 'How are you?'"

"Oh, okay. I'm good." The boy smiled up at him. "How's tricks?"

Conall chuckled. "Good."

Disappointment filled Liam's face after he looked past Conall. "You didn't bring Maddy?"

"Not this time, buddy."

Theresa came around the side of the counter into the dining room, and Conall took in the sight of her. Pony tail, yoga pants, and a fitted t-shirt. Finally, something that let him see the shape of her. She did not disappoint. She was very toned. He looked back up as she glanced at him and touched Liam on the back. A surge of longing went through him.

"I want to show you my gator!" Liam said.

"You can show Conall your drawings before he leaves."

"I'd love to look at them." Conall swung the door shut.

"For now, can you work on your Legos?" she asked.

Liam frowned. "But I want to help. You never let me help."

"Honey, we're going to be putting the trim back up so the house will look normal again. We're using a tool that's dangerous."

Conall stepped back toward the door. Theresa needed to deal with this alone.

She led Liam to the kitchen and talked to him quietly until he sat at the table.

Theresa returned and stood with her arms crossed. She seemed cautious while she looked at Conall.

He touched her shoulder. "Ready?"

She wrapped the fingers of her other hand around the spot he'd touched, which warmed his heart, and said, "Sure."

She led him through the kitchen where Liam sat in front of a jumble of Legos on the table and into the garage. They began bringing in the pieces through the kitchen, some of which were very long and awkward to get around the counter. Liam kept turning around to watch them, but to his credit, he kept quiet.

"Good thing we labeled them," Conall said. "It will make this much easier."

"Yeah." Theresa put her hands on her hips and looked around the room.

He took the opportunity to take a quick peek at her full chest.

"So how do we do this?" she asked.

"We can start with the door. Basically, you hold the piece in place, and I'll shoot the nails in. It'll be quick."

She nodded, looking at him again. This time she held his gaze, and he couldn't have looked away if he'd wanted to. The adorable freckles on her nose stood out but her eyes locked on him made it almost impossible to avoid going over there and kissing her. She wanted him too, that much was clear.

Then she looked away. "Should we get started? The pieces are all in the garage."

He nodded and followed her out there. He handed her a stack of trim. "I'll get the rest."

As she carried the load in, he had to adjust himself. That little look they'd shared had given him a semi, which was crazy, but that was what this woman did to him. He needed to get control of himself. There was a kid around.

He carried the rest of the pieces back inside and dropped them next to hers. "Ready?"

She nodded at him and looked at the bathroom doorway.

"Let's find the right pieces." He started rifling through the pile of trim they'd made and pulled out the doorway trim. He handed her the top one. "Okay, here we go."

She smiled and looked away from him. He wondered why. Maybe she was trying to be sensible.

"Hold it here." He pointed to the right spot.

She got it centered, and he put the first brad in on one end, catching a citrusy whiff off Theresa, which made him hope he hadn't started to stink yet. He did a quick sniff test and turned back to see her smirking at him, so he grinned at her.

He finished nailing the rest of the brads in, and she picked up the piece for the right side of the door and got it in position.

Being this close to her was not going to be easy. He needed to distract himself.

After glancing at the table and seeing Liam engrossed, he quietly said, "Liam's a friendly kid, isn't he?"

She held the trim piece and looked up at him. "It's funny. I'm still surprised at how he's so different around you."

"Huh. Does he have a lot of men in his life?" He got the top brad in and crouched to get the one in at the bottom.

"Not really. He doesn't see Michael often. And it's worse than that, because he's such a terrible father. He has a scheduled phone call every other week on Saturdays, but he cancelled yesterday's because Liam's going there this week for Thanksgiving. The calls themselves are painful—he's not really interested and Liam senses that."

Conall nodded.

"And that's it."

He stood back up and ran his fingers across the back of her hand. "You can let go now."

"Oh." She blushed slightly and stepped back, dropping her hand from the trim.

He put in a few more nails. "Maybe he's responding to me because I'm a guy. Boys are sometimes like that."

"Oh, right. The volunteering."

"Yeah. I did Big Brothers/Big Sisters as well." He finished the brads for that piece of trim.

"Wow, Conall." She laughed. "You're quite the guy. What else do you do? Rescue lost mountain climbers? Sick kittens?"

"Ha. Not a chance. I'm a dog person and scared of heights."

Theresa smiled and picked up the piece for the other side of the door, and they started working on that one. She looked over at him, and their eyes locked.

After a silent moment, she broke the look.

God, he wanted to touch her for real. "How did Liam's testing go by the way?"

"I don't have the results yet. Not until after the holiday." She looked tense when she said it. He wanted to rub her shoulders. She needed it.

"Mom," Liam called.

"Yeah, honey?"

"I made a dog."

"Hold on a sec," she said to Conall. She took the sculpture from Liam. "Look at that. You did."

"Let's see," Conall said. This was a good distraction from his thoughts.

She showed it to him. It was made of mixed colored bricks, but was clearly a dog-shaped thing.

"That's cool, buddy."

Liam beamed at him.

Theresa took it back and asked Liam, "What are you going to build now?"

"I want to draw again."

"Okay, sweetie. Please clean up the rest of the Legos and take them upstairs with you."

Liam started dumping the pieces into a clear plastic bin on the table, and Conall shot the rest of the brads in the piece of trim.

Liam stood at the base of the stairs and said, "You will look at my gator before you leave, right, Conall?"

"Sure thing."

Liam grinned and headed up.

Theresa returned to stand next to Conall. "What next?"

Conall looked over toward the fireplace. "You know, I'm thinking you need shelves in here."

"Yeah? I've thought about bookshelves over there." She pointed toward where he'd been looking.

"They'd look really good. And I can show you how to build them, if you're up for it." He smiled innocently and shifted the nail gun to his other hand.

"Really? That would be pretty nice. I could paint them to match the trim."

"They'd look great."

Then she seemed a little flustered and stared past him at the fireplace. "Uh, when were you thinking?"

"Whenever."

"Well. If you mean that, Liam's going to his dad's for Thanksgiving, so we could do it then." She looked at him again and smiled.

Thanksgiving was in just a few days. And it would be just the two of them. Not that anything would happen. She wasn't up for a fling, obviously. "That works."

"So, tell me—are there any tricks to that gun?" she asked.

"Not at all. Do you want try?"

She looked at him and nodded. "I'm trying to learn this stuff."

"Okay, sure." He handed her the nailer, pleased when their hands brushed again. However, much more of that, and he would have a problem. Then he returned to the pile of trim and found the piece that went behind the TV. He got on his knees to line it up. "Come here."

She knelt next to him and reached out to line the trim up against the door piece. In the process of shifting to angle the gun right, she

96

bumped his hip, which he didn't mind one bit, even though it made his crotch situation more uncomfortable.

"Just get the piece lifted up against the other, and I'll hold it for you. You'll want to put the brad in right here." He pointed at the right spot.

She got the first brad in, and Conall shifted to the other end to hold it in place, watching her as she moved along, adding brads, until she reached him. He didn't move. Instead, he looked at her.

She looked back, and the desire came washing back in. He finally couldn't resist. He reached out and brushed a strand of hair that had fallen loose from the pony tail behind her ear and looked at her lovely red lips, slightly parted. He leaned forward, inhaling.

But just before he reached her, she turned her head.

"Conall, I can't."

Surprised, he held his hands up. "Did I misread?" He didn't see how he could have.

"I just can't." She was staring off to the side. She also still looked like she wanted to be kissed.

"Okay. I'm sorry if I overstepped." He got up to retrieve the next bit of trim.

"You're fine." She nailed in the last brad.

Okay, did that just happen? Had he really misread her or was she lying? Or had he just tried to soon?

Fuck, he shouldn't have done anything. Now he'd screwed everything up.

They proceeded around the room, silent discomfort stretching between them, yet still working perfectly in sync.

After she put the final brad in the final piece, they stood up, and Conall brushed his jeans off.

She looked up at him again and smiled, though it looked forced. "You really are a great guy, Conall. Thank you so much for your help." She handed him the nail gun.

The fog of awkwardness was still hanging around, and he wanted to get out of there, but he couldn't leave just yet. "I promised Liam I would look at his drawings before I leave."

Her eyes widened. "Oh, yeah. He would have been upset if you'd left without giving him a chance to say bye, too. I'll go get him."

When they came down, Liam carried a handful of drawings to the kitchen table, each more impressive than the last.

"These are wonderful, Liam," Conall said after the last one, of a dinosaur eating grass.

Liam grinned, obviously proud of himself.

Theresa stood next to the kitchen counter with her arms crossed.

"Okay, buddy, it's time for me to get back to Maddy. Thank you for showing me your drawings. Some day you need to make one just for me."

"I will!"

Conall followed Theresa to the door and Liam trailed behind. She opened it for him, and he stopped on his way out.

"Let me know about the tutoring," he said. "The offer still stands. Same goes for the bookshelves."

She nodded and smiled up at him. "Thank you. I'll see you tomorrow."

He was still glad about that, as pointless as it was.

Sunday evening after dinner, Theresa loaded the dishwasher while Liam played his video game—fortunately the vet one was his favorite, and the objective was to heal pets, rather than to go around targeting people. She'd never allow him to play a first-person shooter, though some day he'd encounter them with friends. She didn't mind a little pretend violence—she'd played her share of fantasy video games and she and Liam often played laser tag. But first-person shooters took it a little far.

She just needed to get this stuff done, and then it would be time for him to get ready for bed. She had the last dish squeezed into the bottom rack when her phone rang.

Her mom again. She hadn't talked to her since last weekend.

"Theresa, we need to have a chat."

"Mom, how are you?" She opened the cabinet below the sink for the dishwasher soap pods and dropped one in.

"I'm fine. The retreat was very nice." She'd been at one with her church for the weekend. "But Liam told me you aren't going to church. I've been stressing about it all week."

Theresa closed her eyes, put her hand on the counter, and took a deep breath. "Fine. It's true."

"And why not?"

Theresa opened her eyes to push the dishwasher door shut. "Mom, I work long hours, and weekends are dedicated to Liam."

"Your brothers and sisters all manage to find time to go to church."

She knew that wasn't true for all of them. June still lived at home and Kevin lived in town, so they both went to the same church they'd all grown up going to, but Will worked on a cruise ship, and she doubted there was a church there. Rob was a lawyer in New York and could go to church but she knew he didn't.

"How can you expect Liam to become a godly man if you don't teach him right?"

Theresa leaned against the counter and looked at her bare feet. The red polish on her toenails was chipped and half-grown-out. "You know he's sensitive and sweet. I've taught him to never fight. He will become a fine man."

"You know what happens to children who grow up in unchristian homes. I can't believe you are neglecting him like this!"

"Mom—"

"Theresa, do you remember Hazel Winston?"

Hazel was Rob's ex-girlfriend, and her mom had never approved of her.

"Her son is in rehab for drugs! Rehab. He's fifteen! That's what happens."

She didn't say anything and instead went into the garage, the cold floor painful on her feet, and unloaded the dryer into the laundry basket. It was like getting reamed by Michael. She still couldn't believe she'd married someone who turned out to be as judgmental as her mom. They'd met at church, and he'd seemed like a good man. He'd done all the right things, but he'd changed after they'd married. The metamorphosis had been stunning. She still wondered why. His mother was a bit overbearing and got more so after Michael's dad died, right before the wedding. She thought it might have been somehow related to that. Or she had just been oblivious to who he really was the whole time.

"What do you have to say for yourself?"

"Did you call me just to yell at me?" The truth was that Theresa wouldn't mind going to church, but she hadn't been able to find a new one yet. Plus, the idea of trying to fit church into her weekend was exhausting. She rested the basket on her hip while shutting the door into the kitchen.

"No, you're right. I'm sorry. It's just, I love you and Liam so much it just hurts to see you making bad choices."

"How's Dad doing?" Theresa sat next to Liam on the couch with the basket between her feet.

"He's doing well. Still spends all his time watching Wheel of Fortune."

Theresa smiled. He'd always done that. "Do you want to talk to Liam? It's almost bedtime, but he can talk for a few minutes."

"Of course!"

"Liam."

He was intent on his game and didn't respond.

She looked at the screen and saw he was taking the temperature of a dog. She touched his arm. "Sweetie, Grammy's on the phone."

He paused the game and took the phone.

She pulled all the clothes out of the basket and piled them next to her hip.

Liam told her mom about his latest drawing.

She picked up one of Liam's shirts and studied it. He was getting so big. There was a time when his clothes were almost doll-sized. Now they were nearly as big as hers. He was probably going to be tall. Michael was, and she wasn't short.

"Mom had a friend over," Liam said.

Theresa thought of Casey because she'd been over for dinner last night, while she folded a pair of Liam's jeans.

"No, he has a dog."

She jerked her head in his direction. Conall. Crap, this would be bad.

Liam laughed. "No, Grammy." He continued, "Maddy is so fast!"

Theresa set his folded jeans in the basket and picked up another pair.

"A dog." A pause. "Conall." Then, "I don't know."

She put the other jeans in the basket.

"Mom, is Conall Irish?"

"I think so, honey."

Into the phone he said, "Yeah."

"Okay. Love you." He pulled the phone away from his ear. "Mom, Grammy wants to talk to you."

Great. "Why don't you go on up and get ready for bed? Don't forget to brush your teeth."

"I want to finish my game!"

She took the phone from him. "You can finish it tomorrow after school. We'll save where it is."

He frowned and pushed himself off the couch and squeezed between the basket and the black coffee table.

"Mom," Theresa said into the phone.

"You're dating a Catholic?"

"I'm not dating anyone." She put the phone on speaker and finished another shirt.

"What's he doing in your house then? Are you sleeping with him?"

Theresa flushed, because she had thought so much about it. Still, her mom had no sense of boundaries. "No, Mom."

"I should hope not. You don't want a repeat of what happened with Michael."

Theresa gritted her teeth. This again. "We were already engaged. It just happened a little sooner than we would have planned."

"I'm just glad no one here ever did the math." She paused while Theresa carefully folded underwear. "You can't marry a Catholic."

"Nobody's getting married, Mom. Come on."

"What's he doing in your house?"

"He's my new tenant, and he's offered to help me with some of the remodeling I'm doing." She wasn't going to mention him reading with

Liam. Her mom would imagine all sorts of malicious conversion attempts. Her minister growing up had always been very anti-Catholic.

Her mom sighed loudly. "He lives in your downstairs apartment?"

"Mm-hmm." She'd finished the last of the clothes. "Mom, I've got to go get Liam to bed."

"Theresa, you need to be careful with that man."

She almost said she was always careful with men, but then her mom would say Liam wouldn't be seven years old if that were true. So she settled on, "Okay. I love you."

"I love you, too."

She ended the call, tossed the phone across the couch, and leaned back with her eyes closed.

Conall was not going to be a problem.

She forced herself up, dragging the laundry basket up with her. She heard the water running in the bathroom as she put Liam's clothes in his dresser. The water went off, and Liam came in still wearing his superhero pajama pants and no shirt. He'd been doing that since Conall had stayed the night on the couch.

"Did you brush your teeth?"

"Yeah."

Something about the way he said it felt suspicious. "Let me smell."

She leaned down, and he opened his mouth and exhaled. Smelled like mint. He hadn't been lying after all. Her mom had just put her in a bad mood.

"Sweetie, remember you're going to your dad's on Wednesday for Thanksgiving, okay?"

He nodded and smiled. "Do you think he's excited I'm coming?"

"I'm sure he is. And you'll get to see your brother and sisters."

"Yeah." His expression darkened a little.

"I thought you liked them?"

He shrugged and climbed into his bed.

She had no idea what that was about. He'd always gotten along with them. He even liked being the older brother. Maybe something had happened over the summer when he'd last visited. She couldn't imagine what, since the oldest was only four.

"What do you want me to read to you?" She ran her hand along his forehead and pushed his hair back.

He pulled the bedspread up to his chin. "The one about the dog."

After she finished, she put the book in the nightstand and turned on the funky blue nightlight that freaked her out a little, with its permagrin.

She leaned over to kiss Liam goodnight, and he smiled a little more while hugging Mr. Bark tighter. She watched him until the smile faded, and he was breathing evenly. There was nothing like watching him sleep.

14

Conall got into work early on the Monday before Thanksgiving, and there was nobody in his area. He hung his jacket on his chair before grabbing a simple white mug he'd picked up at Williams-Sonoma when he bought the rest of the kitchen stuff.

Theresa's cube was empty as he passed it. Bummer. He'd been hoping to talk her into letting him help her with the bookshelves. He'd to flex his carpentry muscles and spend more time with her, even though nothing other than that would happen.

On his way back, he inhaled the coffee aroma wafting up from his mug as he approached Theresa's cube. She stood in front of her desk, getting settled. She looked fresh this morning, with light makeup and red lipstick.

She looked up, and their eyes met. She smiled at him, and he returned it.

"Morning," he said as he reached her cube.

"Morning."

The sleeve of her black cardigan got caught as she tugged off her jacket. She quickly pulled it back into place over her light blue tank top, but not before he'd seen a flash of her bare shoulder. His smile widened, and he rested his mug and elbows on her cube wall.

"Everybody must be taking the week off," he said.

"I know Martin's back in Hawaii because he can't go at Christmas, and Bernard's somewhere with his wife's family." She straightened the collar of her jacket after she hung it on the chair. "Sujata also went to her parents'."

"Nice. Where's she from?"

"St. Louis."

Conall nodded. "How's Liam?"

She raised her eyebrows. "Nothing dramatic has happened in the last eighteen hours since you saw him."

He smiled. "Well, that's a good thing, right?"

"It is." Her eyes were glowing as she held his gaze.

"So, are you ready to build bookshelves while he's at his father's?"

She frowned thoughtfully and looked away.

"We don't have to," Conall said. "I'm just offering."

"No, I want to. It's just, I don't know if it's a good idea." Her gaze seemed packed with meaning.

He chuckled. "Don't worry. I'll be the perfect gentleman." He followed that with a wink, which made her laugh.

"Okay, fine." She paused. "Let's do it. Liam's father will be there to pick him up about eleven on Wednesday. I'm available afterward."

"Why don't you call me when they're gone, and then I'll come over. We'll take some measurements and then head over to the hardware store for all the supplies."

Theresa nodded. "That sounds good."

"Great." He waggled his eyebrows at her and headed back to his cube, her pretty smile embedded in his brain to carry him through the day.

He set the mug down and sat in his chair, spinning to face the desk. He would have to behave while he was over there. She'd already made it clear she wouldn't date him, even if he knew she wanted him. She was in denial if she didn't recognize the heat that coursed between them.

However, he wasn't going to harass her. He'd just slowly charm her.

In the meantime, he'd take advantage of the quiet office to get some work done.

∼

THERESA STOOD in front of Liam's bed folding and stacking shirts for his trip. She put the stack into his suitcase, a cute little blue and green thing. He'd picked it because it had a shark on the front of it. She closed it and called, "Liam!"

"What, Mom?" he said in an irritated voice right behind her, which made her jump.

She turned around and found him sitting at his desk, drawing. "Oh, honey! I thought you were downstairs. What are you drawing?"

"Dad's house." He turned around to face her, still holding onto his pencil.

"Oh, you remember what it looks like?" She hadn't seen the house, but knew it was in Bellevue, a city on the other side of Lake Washington from Seattle.

"Uh-huh."

She walked the two steps to his desk to take a look, and he wasn't exaggerating about remembering it because it was detailed already. It was big, too. This was enough to satisfy her curiosity—she didn't want to see the house in real life. She'd only met Michael's wife a couple times. She was a very sweet Christian woman who wholly bought into Michael's vision for the role his wife should play. She'd already had three kids with him. She treated Liam well and obviously adored her kids. There were moments when Theresa was a little jealous of the time she got to spend with them. These moments were fleeting, however. She was happy with her decision to continue working because she loved her job, too.

Liam had turned around and started on the drawing again.

"That looks great, honey. Your dad's going to be here soon. Are you ready?"

"Yeah!"

She hoped he wasn't going to be disappointed again. Even though he dreaded the biweekly phone calls from his father, anticipation always built up before the visits, like he thought it would be different this time. Then Michael was his normal aloof self and Liam would come back disheartened. But it was always so hard to say anything that would dampen his enthusiasm. Michael was his father after all.

"Can you take your suitcase downstairs?"

"I'm busy."

"I'm aware, but he'll be here soon. The drawing will still be here when you get back."

Liam looked at her until he smiled and said, "Fine." He jumped up and pulled the blue bag off the bed, Mr. Bark in his other hand. The suitcase bounced, and he righted it on its wheels and started down the hall. She had another small duffel bag that she put a few of his new books in and followed him downstairs.

He sat on the couch kicking the side of it with his heels, his suitcase by the front door.

Theresa set the duffel next to it and sat beside Liam.

"Honey, remember your father might not have a lot of time to spend with you. I don't want you to expect too much, okay?"

"Okay." He wasn't looking at her.

She guessed he didn't want to reveal how excited he was. She'd become so predictable that he didn't want to hear her downer of a lecture. So she left him alone. She sat there just resting, dreading speaking with Michael. They tried to be mostly civil in front of Liam, but there were always undertones of hatred.

She heard the rumble of a truck in the driveway and waited on the couch rather than get up prematurely. Of course, he'd brought the giant truck. What better way to flaunt the money he made than by burning up that much fuel?

The doorbell rang.

She forced herself off the couch, but Liam raced over.

"Dad!" he said after he opened it.

"Hello, son," Michael said. He was a big man, tall and stocky with dark brown wavy hair. She used to like how his big hands felt on her, until she didn't anymore.

He didn't even reach out to touch Liam, much less lean down and hug him like any normal father would have. This didn't stop Liam from giving him a hug of his own, and then Michael did pat him on the back. Poor, sweet Liam.

She steeled herself. "Michael."

He looked up, his eyes completely cold. "Theresa." He'd never forgiven her for not being what he'd wanted her to be.

"Here are his things." She picked up the duffel and suitcase and reached out to hand them to Michael.

"I can take it!" Liam said his face one big smile.

She set it back on the floor and extended the handle for him. Michael took the duffel while she continued looking at Liam's head to avoid Michael's glare.

Michael turned to head off the porch and Liam ran to catch up, the suitcase dragging behind him. Theresa followed them out to the giant black Dodge Ram. Michael pushed the front seat forward to cram the bags behind it and then set the seat back into place. The back seat was full of winter gear.

"Can't you move that stuff to the truck bed so he can sit in the back?" she asked.

"He's fine in the front."

"Come on, Michael, you know it's safer." How could he be so horrible? How was he able to make her feel like such a bad mother?

"No, my snowboards were just waxed, and they're in the bed."

She gritted her teeth as tension rushed to her head. "Did you at least bring his booster seat?"

"Yes," Michael snapped. He pulled the seat forward again and extracted the booster seat.

He wouldn't have used it if she hadn't reminded him. It was bad enough that Liam would have to ride in the front seat, but he wouldn't have even been properly restrained. It was unconscionable and made her face heat up with anger.

"Don't forget it on the way back," she said as Liam climbed inside.

He ignored her, shut Liam's door, and simply said, "I'll see you Sunday at one at the Safeway in Centralia." This time they were meeting about halfway between Portland and Seattle.

"Yep."

"Enjoy your break from motherhood," he said flatly.

The comment still hurt, as angry as she was. She wished he didn't still have the power to affect her so much.

She watched him walk around the front of the truck and get in without another glance in her direction. She stood in the driveway waving at Liam until they were out of sight and went back in to pour herself some wine. She filled a glass, but then she took a big swig from the bottle, shocking herself. She felt surprisingly better afterward.

She set the glass down on the coffee table and fell onto the couch, groaning in frustration. Whenever Liam was outside her realm, her lack of control terrified her. Anything could happen. Please let them arrive safely.

And please let this time be different for Liam.

She took a sip of the wine and thought of nothing for several minutes. It was quiet. Too quiet. Imagining Liam in a truck flying away from her at seventy miles per hour was too much. Time to call Conall.

15

"So what you want to do is measure the amount of space you want to cover on either side of the fireplace," Conall said. He stood next to said fireplace holding a tape measure stretched against the wall.

Theresa stood a few feet back and nodded, unable to avoid noticing the way his jeans hung low on his trim hips.

"And then measure the depth of the hearth and decide if you want your shelves to be that deep." He looked down. "I think in this case since you have a shallow buildout, but your hearth sticks out about eighteen inches. you'll have to just pick a depth less than that and go with it."

"You think it will look good? What's a typical shelf depth?"

"It'll work fine. And ten to twelve inches is common."

Theresa nodded. "Okay. So where would eleven inches meet the hearth?"

Conall turned around and leaned over to hold the tape measure against it.

She glanced at his butt for a second but then he turned around and said, "Come here and I'll show you."

She wondered if he'd caught her looking. Sending the man mixed signals wasn't right. She shook her head and went over to stand just behind him.

Her heart sped up from being this close to him, and she wasn't even that close. She looked down at the tape measure on the brick. "That looks reasonable to me." She watched him as he stood back up to his full height and smiled at her. Their eyes locked for a moment.

"Do you want to put a backing wall on the shelf or just use the wall as the back?" He was so close.

Theresa frowned at her lack of control and leaned back. "Which do you recommend?"

He looked at the wall. "Actually, I'd go with the wood backing. Because the shelves aren't going to stretch all the way to either side wall, are they?"

She tapped her chin. "No, I don't think so. Do you think that'll look okay?"

"It's all in the trim. Did you look at the pictures I sent you?"

Conall had sent her links to several pictures on Pinterest and a handful of blogs, which was pretty thoughtful of him since she was supposed to be looking for them herself.

"I had a quick peek but didn't have a chance to study them," she admitted.

He smiled, which lit his eyes up again. "Too busy for your own good. Have another glance so you can pick the kind of look you want."

She pulled out her phone and brought up the email he'd sent.

He walked to the other side of the fireplace and wrote down some more measurements while she scanned the pictures. They were all over the place in terms of style, and some were quite ornate.

"Can you do any of these?" she asked.

He smiled at her from across the hearth. "Sure."

It was nice to have someone with real DIY know-how helping her, and she even found his expertise attractive. But his smile was at a whole other level. Every single thing about him sucked her in. "Wow, I'm impressed."

"No big."

She scanned through more of the pictures until she found one she liked. "This one looks nice to me. It's simple but classy. Shaker style."

The shelves were relatively short and all of the same height, and they were trimmed with straight boards.

He walked over to stand right next to her and looked at the picture on her phone. Their shoulders touched and her heart jumpstarted.

"Yeah, I liked that one too. It also happens to be one of the easiest to build."

"That's good." For a second she worried he'd be able to hear her racing heart.

"Did you want exactly what's shown here? We could make some of the shelves taller, for instance."

"Can we make the shelves adjustable?"

"Sure. It'll take more time—we have to drill peg holes along the inner sides of the shelves and route each shelf to rest on the pegs. It takes more time than fixed height shelves for sure, but people like them better." He looked over at her. "Not everyone wants book-height shelves."

"That's true." Being this close to him was too distracting and she pocketed her phone and leaned her shoulders against the wall.

Conall turned, and it looked like he might reach out to touch her, but he didn't. "I'm excited to see how it turns out. The room will look great with them once you get them painted like the rest of the trim."

She plastered on a smile and swallowed to calm herself. "Yeah, I'm excited for it, too."

His gaze flicked to her mouth, and the thought that she did want him to kiss her crossed her mind in a flash, but then he looked away and said, "So let me show you how to find the studs."

"Right." It came out barely louder than a whisper, and she had to clear her throat.

He stepped to the side and handed her a yellow box that had been sitting on the hearth. "Stud finder."

Their fingers brushed, and she felt it all the way up her arm. It felt nice. Too nice. "Okay."

"Hold it against the wall vertically."

She did.

"And press the side buttons and move it slowly to the right."

After a couple inches, it beeped and red arrows lit up.

"That's a stud. They're generally sixteen or twenty-four inches apart, so you should find another one over here."

She moved it back in the opposite direction until it beeped again. She smirked at him. "I feel like a real DIYer now."

He laughed. "You even said it right. We'll mark them off when we get back. I just wanted to show you. So should we head over to the hardware store?"

She nodded. "Yeah, let's do it." It would be good to be in a public place, where she'd have an easier time controlling herself.

THERESA FOLLOWED Conall off her porch, admiring his easy gait.

"I can drive," he said, unlocking his car.

Was this one of those things where he wanted to be in control? Like Michael always was? "That's okay. I've got the SUV."

He smiled at her. "Oh, alright. No prob. Your car's better for carrying stuff, it's true."

Okay, so he probably wasn't trying to control the situation. She was likely being oversensitive.

She started up her car and handed him the sheet with all the measurements when he got in.

As she backed out, he asked, "So how was seeing your ex? Always loads of fun, huh? I haven't seen mine in over two years."

Even thinking about it was stressing her out again. She put her hand on her forehead. "You're right, it was no fun at all. He's awful. He was just going to buckle Liam in without his booster seat. And he brought his stupid pickup full of snowboarding crap so there was no room for Liam in the back. He doesn't even care about his own son."

"I'm sorry. Where does he live?"

"Up in Seattle. He has a fancy Amazon job to go along with his pretty little dutiful wife and their own brood of babies." She couldn't keep the disgust out of her voice.

"How long have you been divorced?" Conall asked.

"Five years." She glanced at him.

"And they've managed a brood in that time?"

"Liam is only seven and he has three younger siblings with another on the way." It wasn't that she was opposed to having a lot of kids in theory, but she believed in giving the kids you had adequate attention.

"Oh, wow. That's some serious breeding."

"It is." She laughed. "How long were you married?"

"Seven years."

"Seriously? Wow. But no kids."

"No."

It sounded like there was more to it than that simple word.

She hit the blinker to signal a left turn into the store's parking lot. "I'm sorry?"

He glanced over at her and said, "No, you're fine."

She pulled into a spot in the middle of a row in front of the exit of the store.

Conall said, "I'm excited about building these shelves."

"Yeah? Why?"

"It's fun and they'll look great." They headed toward the entrance and he added, "Plus it'll make you happy."

That made her heart pinch for a second. He glanced over at her but she couldn't read his expression.

He probably hadn't meant anything by it. "I'm looking to you to tell me what to buy, of course. I've just got the credit card."

"Of course. I'm going to pick up a few things for myself, though we'll use them on your shelves."

"Like what?"

They reached the front of the store, where Conall extracted a lumber cart from a cluster of them. "Go ahead and grab a cart, too. We'll be picking up quite a bit. I'm going to get a drill, a circular saw, and a worktable, for me, for starters."

The front doors swished open for them and she pulled a cart from just inside the door, trailing behind him as he turned left to head toward power tools. The cart was jerky. "What is with these things? They're never right, which is ridiculous given the kind of store this is."

He laughed.

Her own drill would be handy, she abruptly decided. "I can get the drill."

"I still need one, but I can help you if you want one, too. They're useful things to have."

"Okay, great."

They walked in silence except for the wheel on the lumber cart that kept bouncing off the floor.

As they passed the plumbing section, Theresa said, "So now that you know all the dirty secrets about my ex-husband, tell me about your ex-wife."

"Oh, there's not a lot to tell. We were quite young when we got married and it just didn't work out." He looked straight ahead when he said it.

"How old were you?"

"Twenty."

Somehow that surprised her. She couldn't picture him at that age. "Was she your high school sweetheart?"

"Yeah."

"That's adorable."

He laughed. "It was at the time. Not so much when we broke up."

"Seven years isn't a terrible run nowadays."

She wanted to ask him what broke them up, but she refrained. He was clearly reticent.

They reached the power tools area and Conall stopped the lumber cart on the outside. "Go ahead and bring the cart with you. We'll be loading it up."

She leaned over on the cart.

He grabbed a saw and drill and put them in the cart like he knew what he wanted. "So for your drill, you just want one for general household use, right?" His face wore an overly innocent expression when he looked at her.

Oh. Unintentional cleavage. She stood up. "Yep."

He put his hand on one of the yellow DeWalts in the display. "Well, a decent 18 or 20V should be good enough."

"Okay. I'd like one with a battery pack rather than a cord."

"Smart. I personally like DeWalt and Milwaukee the best for brands. You'll want to get one with a decent chuck size."

She leaned forward and pointed to the drill Conall was still touching. "So is this one good, then?"

They were so close. If she were in a different place, she might lean into him.

He pulled his hand back and said, "Yeah, it's good. But if you don't mind spending a little extra, I'd go for this one. Good chuck size." He pointed to a Milwaukee, which was $179. "It also comes with a starter set of drill bits."

She cocked her head to the side, still not looking at him. She picked it up to feel how heavy it was. Not too bad.

"How's it feel?"

"Like an expensive drill. I could probably get one for fifty bucks on Amazon."

"You could. It's up to you." He shrugged. "I'm partial to quality tools."

"I was just teasing. I like quality, too."

"Yeah?"

She sensed some overtones in the way he said it, but let it go. "Yeah. Okay, I'll do it. Thanks." She forced herself to smile up at him.

"Let me go grab some drill bits for me," he said.

She rested her elbows on the cart again and leaned forward as Conall went to another aisle.

A man barely her height strolled into her aisle. "Hi there," he said, obviously trying to impress her with his friendliness.

"Hi." She returned his smile.

"What brings a pretty lady like you out to the hardware store?"

Smooth. "Oh—"

"Theresa, I got everything." Conall came up from behind her and stood a little closer than strictly necessary. He dropped a box into the cart.

"Morning," the guy said, stepping back.

She smiled at him again as they left the aisle. Conall grabbed the lumber cart, and they stopped off for the worktable, which they ended up loading in the bottom of the cart. Then they made their way back to the lumber section. Theresa pulled out the sheet of paper with the measurements and they started loading the cart.

"This is a lot of wood," she said.

"Yeah. We'll use most of it but there will still be some scrap left over."

Once they'd gotten the boards ripped into narrower pieces that would be easier to work with, they picked up some screws and checked out before heading over to customer service to find out about renting a truck to get it all to her house.

Once they'd unloaded everything from the truck into her garage, they headed back to the store to return the truck. The conversation was pretty vanilla, as they discussed the plan for the day.

But Theresa couldn't contain herself as they pulled onto her driveway. "I'm so excited!"

"Yeah? Me too. They're going to look so good."

16

When Theresa and Conall returned to the garage, Conall unloaded his tools. He set up the workbench and rested the circular saw and toolbox on top of it. Theresa stood back, looking curious, her blonde hair resting on her shoulders.

She'd tied her hair back and taken her earrings out of her delicate ears.

What he wouldn't give for a chance at a nibble.

He started putting the wood into organized stacks so they could more easily mark the boards up and start cutting. He smiled at her, glad she couldn't read his thoughts, even if they were tame at the moment.

"Do we need to open the garage door?" she asked.

"No, I don't think so. It's not like paint fumes."

"So, how do we start?" she asked, stepping forward before looking down at one of the stacks he'd made.

"We're going to mark off the boards first for each type of cut. First we'll do the sides, then the shelves, then the side support pieces that'll hold up the shelves. Once we get everything marked up, we'll start making the cuts."

"Great." She smiled. "Measure twice, cut once."

He laughed. "Exactly. I'll show you how to operate the saw and everything." He hadn't given it much thought earlier, but now the idea of watching her use the saw struck him as hot.

To get her measuring, he gave her his tape measure and stood at the other end of the first board.

"Eight, two, right?" she asked.

"Yeah." He watched her mark the edge of the board and realized he still wasn't thinking straight. She had him distracted. "Hold on. Let me get the speed square so you can make a straight line across the board." He jumped up and got it from the workbench before handing it over. From his vantage point, he got another view of her cleavage which seemed like a nice bonus for his effort. He returned to the end of the board, ready for the next one.

She finished marking it, and they did the second board, then the third and fourth. Each time, he moved from one end of the board to the other and caught the scent of her hair, overpowering the smell of the wood.

On the last one, Conall stood right next to her, almost shoulder to shoulder, as she held the speed square. He looked at her when she finished drawing the line. Her beautiful face was inches from his, and he longed for her to turn toward him.

Instead, she leaned back and put her hands on her thighs. She gave him a smile that looked a little awkward. "Now we do the shelves?"

He leaned forward to grab the next board. "Okay, now we can do the smaller pieces. These should all be exactly three feet, five inches long. Mark from each end instead of one after the other."

She nodded. "Got it."

They worked off the next stack of boards, just a few feet from each other, a nearness he felt deep down. They were quiet, but at one point, Conall glanced up to see her watching him. She looked down as if guilty. Whatever this thing was between them, it wasn't all him.

Soon they had all the boards marked up and moved on to the back pieces.

Even though they weren't talking very much, it was sort of nice to be working side by side with someone. Some camaraderie. Working with her reminded him of his dad, except for the fact that he'd never sported a semi when he worked with his dad, thank Christ.

She was killing him.

"Done," Theresa said and sat back on her feet.

"Great. Let me finish these, and then I'll show you how to use the saw." The idea of her using it was still a turn-on.

She gracefully pushed off the ground.

"Come here," he said as he picked up one board and stepped over to the workbench, laying the board down across the top of it next to the saw.

She stood a couple of feet away and watched him slide the board so that the mark was over the right edge of the bench.

"Okay, so I'm right handed so we'll cut off the right side."

"Me too."

"I'll do the first few cuts, and then we'll switch to you." He would have to keep her focused on his instructions to keep her from spotting his crotch.

She nodded.

"Okay, first off, this saw has a laser light so you can see exactly where it's going to cut." He held the saw on the board so she could see the light. "I've got the safety on right now." She stepped closer and leaned forward, and he caught her fruity scent. His groin tightened.

He closed his eyes for a second to regain control. When he opened them, she'd turned to face him, and their eyes locked. They were so close that if he just leaned forward a little bit, he could kiss her. She was so tempting. Her eyes were a delicious velvet brown, and they were focused on his. He touched her face with the back of his fingers, and she parted her lips ever-so-slightly and glanced down at his.

He leaned forward and gently grasped her upper arm before brushing his lips against hers. They were softer than he could have imagined.

She inhaled and then her hands were on his chest.

Okay, then.

He set the saw on the board and leaned into her lips. She pressed back and opened her mouth more. He took it for an invitation, and his tongue brushed against hers tentatively until she returned the favor with more force. His hand caressed her lower back.

God, she felt good. And she tasted like peppermint. She moved her arms across his shoulders until her breasts pressed against him, which seemed so natural and right he couldn't believe they hadn't done this earlier. He moved his other hand to the back of her neck as he pulled his mouth away from her lips and kissed his way up her jaw to her earlobe, which he licked and nibbled. Finally.

She whimpered a little, which made him grin. He worked his way down her neck and across her throat with kisses, then up to her other ear.

"Conall," she whispered, sending her hot breath into his ear.

The only thought he had was that she must want his mouth on hers again, so he gave her that, and it felt like she would swallow his tongue.

He'd known how she felt, even if she'd been unwilling to admit it. And even if he hadn't meant to act on it. He palmed her breast and brushed the raised nipple through her thin bra. She moaned into his mouth and pulled him in tighter.

He too needed to be closer, so he wrapped his hands around her and squeezed until her nipples drilled into his chest. She surprised him by grinding against him.

If he wasn't careful, he'd come in his jeans. It had been a long time. He pushed against her. She backed up, and he went with her, their tongues tangling the whole time, until they crashed into the shelf, which shook from the force. He registered a scraping sound and then a dull thud and crack. His head instinctively jerked to the side to see what had fallen, but she palmed his cheek to bring his mouth back to hers.

He gave her mouth the attention it deserved, sucking and licking. Her shoulders were against a shelf but there was room behind her to slip his hands under her shirt in the back so he could finally feel her sweet, soft bare skin.

She moaned again, and it would be impossible for him to say how much he loved it. He rubbed her back, and she dropped her arms, dragging her hands along his chest. When she reached the bottom of his shirt, she lifted it and began toying with his waistband and rubbing her fingers across his stomach.

He couldn't wait any longer. He pulled her shirt up and unhooked her bra, pushing it up so he could take her breasts in his hands. He broke the kiss and glanced at her watching him, before looking back down at where his hands were. Her breasts were beyond perfect, plump and round with big red nipples. He took one in his mouth and sucked until she moaned yet again. That sound would be his undoing.

Her head was back as he moved to the other breast, tweaking the free nipples with his thumb.

"Come here," she said.

He obeyed and started by dragging her bottom lip through his teeth. Then they were kissing again, but his hands remained on her breasts, kneading.

She cupped the front of his jeans, and he groaned into her mouth. When he opened his eyes, all he could see was her hungry eyes.

He grinned. "You want to?"

She nodded. Then she rubbed his erection, hard.

"Mmm." He reached for the hem of her shirt to pull it off, and she stopped him.

"Not here. Upstairs." Her voice was husky

"Wherever you say."

She pulled her shirt down, gripped his hand, and dragged him toward the door into the house.

THERESA FELT the air on her stomach as she led Conall through the kitchen so she yanked her shirt all the way down. On the stairs, she glanced back and saw Conall—a man with need burning in his eyes.

"Don't stop now," he growled.

She scrambled up and lost her balance, letting go of his hand to catch herself with both of hers.

"Whoa, there." Conall grabbed her hips and helped her right herself, but then he turned her around and kissed her, his tongue sliding against hers.

The burn between her legs was unbelievable. She was officially out of control. "Conall. I need more."

His breath hitched. "Yeah?" He squeezed her butt and ground against her so she could feel the hard length of him press into her.

Theresa was so desperate—and here he was teasing her. She shoved his hands off her and turned around. They scrambled up the stairs together. She grabbed onto the banister at the top and raced around it toward the bedroom.

As soon as they were through the doorway into her room, Conall grabbed her hand and spun her around to kiss her again. His fingers gripped the hem of her shirt and pushed it up. When he got to her breasts he squeezed them once and stopped kissing her. She lifted her arms so he could pull her shirt over her head.

He backed her up until her thighs hit the bed, kissing her on the neck the whole time, and undid the button on her jeans before pulling the zipper down. His hand was inside her panties and down to her core.

"Christ, Theresa. You're so wet."

His strong, solid fingers were making her crazy. She kissed his jaw until he turned his mouth back to hers. Then their tongues were sliding against each other while he caressed her until her breath hitched, and she knew—unbelievably—that she was already close.

How could he have had this much of an effect on her, this fast?

He must have known how close she was, too, because he pressed harder and rubbed faster until her legs buckled, and she moaned and trembled through her release. She would have collapsed with it had he not held her up. She stared at his smiling face as he gently laid her down on the bed, her heavy breathing reverberating.

He grasped the waistband of her jeans and tugged until she lifted her hips. Everything came off, and she was fully naked in front of a man for the first time in over five years. And it felt amazing.

He crawled over her as if to kiss her again, but she pushed on his chest.

"What?"

"You have far too many clothes on." She reached for his shirt and pulled on it until he laughed and put his hands on hers.

"I got it." He lifted it over his head as she worked on his jeans before getting distracted by the solid expanse of his chest. She spread her fingers on his abs and moved her hands up. Those shirts he wore at work didn't do him justice.

He reached around her hands to get his jeans unbuttoned and unzipped. She reached into his black boxer briefs and felt the hot and silky skin of his erection.

He closed his eyes and groaned. She pulled the front of his boxer briefs down to release him, watching him flinch as the head of his cock slapped against his lower belly.

"Ooh, sorry," she said with a grimace. She was too out of practice.

He just laughed.

She started to push his jeans down.

"Hold up."

He slipped off the bed and reached into his back pocket for his wallet and the condom it hid.

Seeing the condom made her whimper.

He looked at her and gave her a sly grin. He slipped out of his jeans and boxer briefs and then he tore the packet open and slowly rolled it on, smiling and watching her face the whole time.

Desire flared and she whimpered again. Should she be embarrassed at the noises she was making? No. She was just turned on and nothing else mattered at this point.

He was back on the bed and pushing on her inner thighs to spread her legs, which she did more than willingly. Her breathing was still heavy, but her entire body tingled with anticipation.

He leaned forward and ran his tongue from just above her inner thigh until he reached her belly button, where he dipped his tongue and she squirmed in agony.

"Conall, please."

"You ready?" he asked with a chuckle while he moved up to take her breast into his mouth. He gave her nipple a strong suck, causing her to arch her back, and released it with a pop.

He was torturing her. Now he swirled his tongue around her other nipple.

She reached out to touch his erection but he held her down so she couldn't reach it.

He laughed again, and his whole body shook. Then he bumped her legs even further apart with his knees and positioned himself just outside her sex. She heard herself whimper yet again and instinctively bent her legs to scoot closer to him.

He smiled and notched inside.

She sighed. Even this half inch felt good. The rest of him would feel even better.

He pushed inside slowly, watching her the whole time and holding his jaw tight while he filled her up.

Once he was all the way in, he stopped and leaned down to kiss her. She sucked on his upper lip while he withdrew and pushed back in.

He kissed her through a few thrusts. The tension was already building inside her core again. She released his tongue and said, "Harder."

He didn't hesitate to pull back and anchor his arms. Then he started pounding into her with enough force that it pushed her back on the bed, and she had to hold on to the headboard. The bed creaked with the motion and soon she came like she never had before, moaning his name loudly before sighing in exhaustion.

He pumped rapidly a couple more times, and then sighed and collapsed onto his elbows. When his eyes looked normal again, he fell on the bed next to her, arm over his head. Then he got up and headed into the bathroom before coming back and lying down next to her.

Neither said anything. They simply lay there. She listened to his breathing as it went back to normal and quiet. She hadn't felt this close to anyone in so long, and she didn't want to ruin the moment.

He broke the silence. "It occurred to me that it's good we stopped working on the shelves because we forgot to put on the safety glasses. You distract me so much."

She laughed, but knowing she had such an impact on him swelled her heart with happiness.

"Theresa."

"Yeah?"

"Also, I think if I don't get to do that again, I will die."

She blinked, savoring the sense of power it gave her to know he wanted her that bad, again. "Well, Liam's gone the whole weekend." Where had that come from?

"So you're saying we can do this again?"

"I think so." Maybe she could get him out of her system this way. A few days of great sex, and then she'd be set for a few more years. Maybe for life.

"Thank God." He propped himself up on his side and caressed her belly. "You have the flattest stomach. I'd never guess you'd had a kid."

She laughed and rubbed his chest. "I've worked hard for it." If she wasn't with Liam, working, or cleaning, she was working out. "Do you lift?"

"Yeah. What is it you do to stay so fit?"

"Elliptical and yoga." She pinched his nipples and he inhaled.

"Well, it pays off. You are even more gorgeous without your clothes. I'd suspected, but I'm glad I got to confirm my theory."

Theresa laughed. "You aren't so bad yourself."

His hand moved up to cup her breast and he kissed her shoulder.

She turned toward him, seeing the sheen of sweat on his forehead and relishing the fact that it was all because of her.

He closed his eyes, and she watched him for a moment. She knew he wasn't asleep because he was repeatedly thumbing her nipple, which was driving her a little crazy. She reached for his penis. His eyes popped open the second she grasped it, and she was surprised to feel it already thickening.

"Wow, Conall."

"It's all you."

Hot desire flared up in her again. "Conall?"

"Mmm?"

"This really can't continue after Liam's back. It's just temporary." She felt a twinge of regret just saying the words, but they needed to be said. Her focus had to be on Liam. She couldn't be distracted by Conall with Liam around.

"Okay. We'll get it out of our systems, and when we're back at work Monday, it's back to normal."

She stroked his tight, satiny skin.

He gritted his teeth and then said, "Do you have another condom? That was my only one."

Her heart dropped but she continued to stroke him. "No. And I'm not on the pill either."

"Damn." He grimaced.

"There are other things we can do." She squeezed him firmly, and he groaned.

17

—————

Theresa lay in bed, still naked. Conall had been gone about a quarter of an hour to take care of Maddy, and she needed to get up so she could go down to let him in when he got back. He'd awakened something in her she hadn't known was there.

It must be that it had been so long since she'd had sex.

That must be it.

She headed into the bathroom and opened the blue shower curtain. She'd already shaved her legs and pits that morning—she must have subconsciously known having Conall alone in her house was dangerous. She turned the water on and waited for it to warm up before stepping in. As she soaped herself up, she reflected on the fact that she'd never been this perpetually turned on by a guy. Sex had never been anything like this with Michael.

She rinsed herself and turned the water off. The faucet knob was a little loose—she needed to see about fixing that.

While toweling off she pictured Conall over her, his sexy chest with its spattering of hair—just enough to make him look like a real man without being so much it was gross.

And his penis. Lord, she hadn't ever been enamored of a body part before, but his was glorious.

Ack, she was getting worked up again.

She finished toweling off and put on a pair of black sleep shorts and a camisole.

Once she was in the kitchen, she poured herself a glass of wine and headed into the living room to relax.

She sat on the couch and propped her bare feet up on the coffee table. When her gaze wandered to the fireplace, she thought of the bookshelves they were building, and Conall was hot on her mind again.

He wasn't a bodybuilder, but he was firm and strong everywhere. His long arms had defined muscles, and they'd felt so good wrapped around her.

She took a sip. His mouth had been everywhere. Almost literally. When he'd gone down on her, she'd thought she was having a religious experience. He'd had his fingers inside her while expertly using his tongue.

Her hand slipped under the waistband of her shorts. She stroked herself until she heard a knock on the door.

She jumped up so fast that she sloshed wine out of the glass she'd forgotten she was holding. "Crap!"

She made her way to the door and wiped her guilty hand on her stomach under her shirt before turning the doorknob.

Wow, there he was again. Tall, slightly tousled hair, sexy jeans. And a big grin. "Hey."

"Hi." She moved so he could come in with his two plastic bags. She shut the door. "I got Chinese."

Wine dripped off her elbow. "Man."

"What?" He set one of the bags on the stairs and put the other on the kitchen table.

She followed him into the kitchen. "I spilled wine all over myself." It was on her shorts as well as her arm and hand.

"Yeah? Where?"

She took the glass in her other hand and held the wet one up. "Mostly here."

He came over and took her hand, lifting it to his mouth and licking it. "Mmm. Chardonnay."

She laughed as he sucked on her fingers one at a time, heating up on the inside again. She was getting even wetter.

Then he took her other hand. "What does this one taste like?"

She was a little self-conscious about what he'd notice, but not as much as she figured she ought to be.

He lifted it up to his mouth. "Hey. What's this?"

She arched her eyebrows.

His voice low, he asked, "Were you touching yourself while I was gone?"

"Maybe."

He sucked one of her sticky fingers in his mouth and looked down at her. "Were you thinking of me? When you were touching yourself?"

She recognized the hungry look in his eyes. "Maybe."

He sucked on each of her fingers while pressing his erection against her belly. She reached for it, stroking him through his jeans. He dropped her hand and kissed her neck before moving up to her mouth and taking her lower lip gently between his teeth. Soon his tongue was in her mouth, and she sucked hard on it while stroking him.

"We have to go upstairs," he murmured. "Now."

She led him toward the stairs again, and he snagged the plastic bag on the way up.

He had his shirt off before they were even in her room, and when they reached the bed, he lifted hers off.

"You have the most beautiful breasts. You know that, right?"

"Really?" She reached to undo his jeans, and he pushed her shorts down over her hips while kissing her again.

Once she had his jeans unzipped, he stepped out of them and his boxer briefs while she fell on the bed and scooted up toward the headboard.

He plopped the box of condoms on the bed while she smiled at him and then snuck another peek at his penis, noting the glint of light off the pre-come.

"How many condoms did you get?"

He shook his head. "I'm starting to think not enough."

~

CONALL WOKE SLOWLY with the soft morning light on Thanksgiving. He lay on his side, and his arm was draped over Theresa. He was way too comfortable. He was reminded of mornings with Clarissa, the lying around thinking they had forever.

Conall and Theresa had three more days. That was it.

He brushed her hair behind her ear and kissed the side of her head. She stirred.

"Morning," he whispered. "Happy Thanksgiving."

"Mmm," she said as she stretched her legs.

He ran his hand along her shoulder and down her arm.

Finishing her stretch, she brought her legs back up and pushed her butt back into his crotch, so he was poking her again. She wiggled.

"Theresa," he warned playfully.

"Yes?" She said it with feigned innocence.

He traced his fingers along her arm again and then circled her navel before pushing further south. His fingers slid further down between her wet folds, and she inhaled sharply. He applied a bit of pressure and rubbed.

She turned around to face him and kissed him hungrily. It surprised him but he wasn't going to let the opportunity pass.

A condom later, they lay next to each other while their breathing calmed.

"I'm starving," Theresa announced.

"Me too, now that you mention it. I feel like we've both burned through quite a few calories."

"Chinese for breakfast?"

"Breakfast sounds great, but I don't want Chinese. Do you have eggs?"

"Of course."

"Let's go, then." He slapped her on the butt.

She sat up on the edge of the bed and looked around, standing to put on a yellow cotton robe.

He got up and found his boxer briefs at the foot of the bed, which he slid on before following her downstairs.

She had a nice kitchen setup, though it could be bigger. The only small appliance she had out was a single-brew coffee machine and treated the rest of countertop as work area. He opened the oven door and saw nothing inside, so he fiddled with the settings until he got it preheating to 350.

"Onions?" he asked.

She pointed to a hanging basket he'd somehow missed over the end of the counter.

"Can I raid your fridge?"

"Sure. What are you going to make?"

He opened the fridge door and started looking at what she had. "You'll see."

She sat down in the chair at the table, crossed her legs, and watched him.

He found half a red bell pepper, an opened bag of fresh spinach, and some mozzarella. She had plenty of eggs.

He set everything on the counter and dug around for a knife and cutting board. Theresa watched him the whole time, an amused look on her face.

"Don't you have to go take care of Maddy?" she asked.

"She can wait a little bit longer. An hour or so will be fine." He'd gone home last night to take her out.

He started sautéing the onions and peppers in a skillet he found under the oven. "Mixing bowl for the eggs?"

"In the lower cabinet next to the fridge. Frittata?"

"You guessed it." He waggled his eyebrows. "I'll give you a reward later for your astute guessing skills."

She smiled and uncrossed her legs, which made him glance at them. And he was ready again.

Once he had the pan in the oven and set the timer next to the oven, he went over to stand in front of her. He brushed the hair behind both of her ears. "Quickie?"

"We shouldn't leave the kitchen," Theresa said in Mom voice. "I don't want to burn anything."

"Okay, we won't leave the kitchen. Quickie?"

She looked up at him with desire in her eyes, and he knew he had her. He stepped around her to close the curtains on the window that faced out back and then shut the ones over the sink, too. He glanced around and saw that she must have closed the rest of them when she came down to put the food in the fridge last night.

Her mouth was slightly open as she watched him.

He put his hands on her hips and gently backed her up until she was against the table. "I'll be right back."

She grabbed his arm and reached into a pocket on her robe to pull out a condom.

He grinned. This woman. He slowly turned her, pressing on her back to encourage her to lean over.

He lifted the robe and fingered her slick heat.

"Mmm," she said.

He rolled the condom on and soon everything on the table shook while he slid in and out, the robe bunched up on her back so he could see her beautiful ass.

As he lay stretched out on her back afterward, he whispered, "See, gorgeous? The timer hasn't even gone off."

"You're very efficient," she said as he disengaged.

He tossed the condom in the trash and pulled his shorts back up just as the timer started wailing.

After they took turns washing their hands, he opened the oven door, which belched out a wave of heat and onion aroma that pushed both of them back. Then Theresa reached in to grab the skillet and placed it on the stove, stowing the oven mitts back in a drawer.

The cheese bubbled a little and the frittata looked great, just slightly browned around the edges. As they sat down to eat, she said, "Should we do something for Thanksgiving?"

"The only thing I want to do today is sitting right in front of me."

Still, she blushed a little, suddenly looking a little shy.

Her phone started ringing on the kitchen counter. She jumped up. "Probably my mom." She retrieved the phone and nodded. "I've got to take this. You're not here."

"Hi, Mom. Happy Thanksgiving to you, too." She sat on the couch and propped her feet up.

Conall took another bite.

"Just taking it easy. I'm not cooking anything today."

Theresa looked at him guiltily. "No, of course he's not over here.

133

We barely know each other." She fiddled with the tie on her robe as her mom said something that took a while.

"How's Dad?"

There was another long silence. "That's good."

Conall cut another few pieces off the frittata. He didn't want her to come back and find him all done.

"Okay, I'll do that."

"Mom, I've told you. I'm not seeing anyone and Liam is fine." A pause.

"It's not like that. He helped out a little. Like a neighbor." She glanced at him again.

Conall raised his eyebrows, unable to contain a smile.

"Come on," she said. "Yeah, I'll find one soon."

He took another bite. This thing was pretty good.

"Okay. I should go." A pause. "No, I just have work to do."

She pursed her lips as her mom must have said something unpleasant.

"Okay. I love you."

She ended the call and threw her head back onto the couch. "Argh."

"Rough call?" Conall asked, chuckling. "She doesn't like me, huh? Or is some other man not here?"

She came back to the kitchen and sat. "I have to lie to her. She wants us to go to church, but by Sunday, I'm too beat to go."

"Well, do *you* want to go?"

"I would, actually."

Conall nodded. "But it's a long week, plus you've got Liam. Seems reasonable to me. Who's she to tell you how to live your life? You should stand up to her."

She put her head on her forehead. "You don't know her."

"I don't need to; I know you. You're a good person." He arched his eyebrows. "And a great lay."

"Conall, shush. She might hear." She laughed before cutting into her piece of the frittata with her fork. Then she asked, "So how do you celebrate Thanksgiving in Hawaii?"

"Oh, my family celebrates pretty much like the mainland. They carried on the tradition. My dad always made fun of my mom for it, though."

"Yeah? Why?"

He swallowed. "He's Irish and thought it's a stupid holiday. Celebrating a great evil."

She cocked her head to the side. "The European invasion?" After he nodded, she asked, "How did your parents end up together?"

"They met when my mom studied in Dublin. My dad was a bartender at the time, but once they got married, and she managed to land a job at the university, they moved to Hawaii."

She smiled. "That's a nice story. Were they happy?"

Conall nodded and finished chewing. "How about your parents? Anything cute there?"

"Nope. They met in church." She shrugged. "And I don't think they're particularly happy. Just dutiful."

"That's too bad. Hey, where are you from? I just realized I have no idea."

She set her fork down and said, "Kerrville, Texas," in an unexpected drawl.

He cracked up. Normally, she didn't have even a drop of an accent. "I'd never have guessed it. Southern Baptist?"

She nodded and arched her eyebrows. "Liam mentioned you to my mom, and she freaked out at the idea of him having contact with…"

"A stranger?"

"No. A Catholic." Her smile made it clear she thought this was stupid.

He laughed. "I promise not to try to convert him."

"I wasn't worried." She took a bite.

"I'm not religious, anyway. We only went to church on holidays."

She nodded.

He stabbed the last piece on his plate and popped it in his mouth. She worked on finishing hers and as soon as she did, he stood and took their plates to the sink.

They rinsed the plates off together, and he put the skillet in the fridge.

"What do you want to do now?" he asked, taking her in his arms and giving her a soft kiss that felt sweeter than it should have.

After he pulled back, she asked, "Do you have to take care of Maddy?"

He grimaced. "Yeah, I do. I'll have to feed her and take her out for a few minutes."

"Too bad. Why don't I let you borrow the spare key so you can let yourself back in and come straight upstairs, where I'll be waiting." She reached into a small drawer near the sink.

He arched an eyebrow as she laid the key in his palm. "Sounds good to me."

This was crazy. And he loved it.

18

Friday morning, Theresa had some sausage sautéing and the oven preheating.

The last two days had been a whirlwind. She still couldn't believe what they'd done—and how many times.

She sliced two red peppers in half and cleaned them out.

How was Liam doing? She said a little silent prayer that he was having a good time and was getting along with his siblings. And that his father was paying attention to him.

Theresa beat some eggs and mixed in scallions and a little bit of cheese and then the sausage. Then she stuffed the peppers, topped them with cheese, and put them in the oven.

She went back upstairs and got back on the bed. The movement woke Conall up, and he looked at her sleepily, a lazy smile spreading across his face. She ran her hand along his arm as he gazed into her eyes.

"I've got breakfast in the oven. I need to get back down there."

"I'm awake now. You can." He rested his hand on her hip.

"For some reason, I don't want to."

He leaned in and kissed her. It was sweet and intimate, and she felt something dangerous in her heart. Too much affection. She couldn't go there, so she pulled back and said, "Going downstairs now."

He smiled. "Be down in a minute."

She slid off the bed and got to the kitchen with a few minutes to spare so she set the table. He came down in just jeans, and she couldn't help but again admire his solid chest with its dusting of dark hair.

He raised his eyebrows and came to stand next to her, putting his arm around her waist. The scent of toothpaste emanated off him, so she kissed him.

They were pressed up against each other when the timer went off.

"Aw," he said.

She broke away and pulled the peppers out of the oven.

They ate in relative silence, just enjoying each other's company— or that's how she felt, at least. When they finished, she rinsed the dishes while he ran down to take care of Maddy.

Once he was back, they headed into the garage after changing into better clothes.

The comforting wood smell was still out there and the board lay where they had left it on the worktable.

Conall said, "So I'll start over where we were on Wednesday." He held the saw to the board and showed her the laser light.

"Don't we need the safety glasses?"

"Oh, yeah. You want to grab them?"

She turned around after getting them out of the back and saw him watching her lustily. He shook his head a little and smiled before reaching out for the pair she handed him. He put them on and smiled at her while she donned hers. Who knew clear plastic safety glasses could be sexy?

He reached for the speed square that sat on the workbench and started explaining again how the cutting worked. "Let me cut a few and you just watch."

From a safe distance, she could see the laser light and hear the loud whine of the saw as he pushed it slowly across the first board. The excess fell onto the ground, bouncing with a pop. He did three more boards before turning the safety back on. The absence of the sound left a slight ringing in her ears.

"Do you want to try?" he asked.

"Sure." It didn't look hard.

He scooted over, and she got into position. Then he surprised her by moving behind her and putting his hand on top of hers where she held the saw. "Just to help guide you the first time," he explained.

But having him close to her like this made it really hard to concentrate. His left hand was next to hers holding the board in place, he pressed into her, and she could feel his breath on her neck.

"Ready?" he asked.

"Mm-hmm."

"Make sure the light is on the line."

She looked down and scooted the saw over a tad to get it in place. She could still smell his toothpaste.

"Now hit the safety and squeeze the trigger."

The familiar whine started up, and he guided her hand on the saw.

The right side of the board fell.

"See, not hard, right?" he asked.

If she wasn't wrong, his voice was sexier than it had been a few moments ago. She got the safety back on, and he backed off. She picked up the next board and managed to cut it, but by the time she got to the third one, she set the saw down and turned around to kiss him. He was as into it as she was, and they had to scramble back to the bedroom and shed their clothes. They never made it back out to the garage for the rest of the day.

CONALL WOKE up first Saturday morning, finding himself spooning Theresa again, his arm draped across her front. He knew today would be rough because they had the bookshelves to finish. But for now, her elbows were tucked against her stomach, and his hand rested on hers. He pushed his nose into her hair and breathed in the fruity scent he'd gotten so used to.

After having three days of virtually nothing but sex, they'd showered—together—last night before going to bed. Her citrus shampoo and mint body wash were what made her smell so good. Afterward, they'd fallen asleep before anything else happened, but now it had been about ten hours since he'd been inside her, and he was aching for it again.

He'd never had better sex with anyone. He'd never really thought much about sexual compatibility, but it clearly was a thing, and they had it.

Letting this end would be the hardest thing he'd ever had to do. Going back to work with her and seeing her five days a week. He'd be fighting a semi all day long, all week long. But he knew she'd meant it when she said it was temporary. He understood. She had her son to think about. It was probably best for him, too.

Theresa made a little waking up groan and stretched her arms and legs. She must have felt him poking her because she rolled over to face him and grasped his cock like it was the only thing she wanted to do.

"Mornin'," she said while squeezing him and pulling up slowly.

"Hi, you." He let his hand land on her hip after throwing the covers down so he could watch her.

The next thing he knew, his cock was in her mouth and she was taking him on the best ride possible.

After he came, hard, she slid her mouth off, and he watched her swallow, smiling at him the whole time.

"Christ, woman," he said between ragged breaths. "Come here."

She obeyed, laying her head across his chest. He pulled her further up so their mouths met, and her leg was between his. He kissed her, their tongues tangling sweetly.

He pulled back. "Your turn."

"I'm hungry. Let's go make breakfast."

"Are you sure?"

She put her hand on his cheek, and said, "Mm-hmm."

He got off the bed to find his boxer briefs. "I've got to go take care of Maddy. I'll be back soon. We've still got to get the shelves built today." He located the rest of his clothes and slipped into his jeans.

"Okay. I'll go make some breakfast."

He headed down. Maddy was suitably excited to see him, jumping up and giving a high-pitched yelp. He took her out on a quick walk up and down the street. She was still worked up when they got back to the house, but he needed to get back. Getting everything done in one day would be a challenge. But if they focused, they could do it.

He walked back and let himself in the front door. He could smell some kind of spice in the air as he opened the door.

Theresa was standing at the stove, and he went up behind her and put his arms around her.

"Hey," she said.

He rested his cheek against the side of her wet head. "You took a shower." He could see she had some sausage in the pan and an omelet going in another.

"Yeah, I felt like I needed one." She laughed.

He chuckled. "We're just going to get grungier today in the garage."

She shrugged and he had to step back so she could flip the omelet, which she did expertly. "Grab two plates?"

He returned with two, and she finished the first omelet and folded it onto the top plate. She sprayed the pan with no-stick spray and used a hand blender to rewhip the next omelet mix before pouring it in.

He carried the plate to the table and got two mugs. "Coffee?"

"Sure."

He got two pods out of the cabinet and started the first one brewing.

Once they sat down, he was starving.

"Conall," she said.

"Yeah?" He took a bite of the omelet.

"You know today's the last night of this thing between us. It has to be over when you leave."

He nodded. It was a shame, but for the best. He couldn't give her what she truly needed.

As much as he'd love to. He'd do anything to be able to do that. Live his life with her.

They looked at each other for a moment. She didn't look happy about the choice, either.

"So what's the plan for today?" she abruptly asked.

He went over what they would have to do while they ate. Afterward, they rinsed the dishes off before heading out to the garage.

Then they got to work, in comfortable silence except when they needed to coordinate. Conall felt subdued, sad even since this thing—this glorious thing they'd had—was coming to an end. They finished cutting the boards they hadn't managed to get to yesterday, and he showed her how to drill the peg holes. They shared a few looks, but the looks weren't full of heat. She seemed to feel it ending too. Once they had everything ready, they assembled the shelves and dragged the first one into the living room.

When they set it down, Conall said, "So, Theresa?"

She looked up at him. "Yeah?"

"Am I staying tonight?" He didn't know where things stood.

"I hope so."

He thought for a moment about how things were ending. Although he understood, he was frustrated that she wouldn't consider anything beyond this weird sex fest. "You know, it might be best if I went home."

"Oh." She looked at him sharply. "Okay, if you think so."

"Yeah." He smiled to cover his inner gloom. "Let's get this one on the wall, and then we'll bring the other one in."

19

Theresa was halfway to Centralia already and was still unable to avoid pondering Conall. She kept trying to distract herself by thinking of how great the shelves looked and then focusing on Liam, which would work for a while, but she was already pretty sure how his visit with his father had gone. Not well, and Liam would be all downtrodden again. It was depressing to think about her little boy like that, and thoughts of Conall's hands all over her were much more pleasant.

Maybe Liam's trip had gone better this time. She could hope, couldn't she?

What had she ever seen in Michael?

Maybe Liam. Maybe she'd simply known they'd make the greatest child together. She'd get him reading, and they'd get past this dark time and everything would be good again.

As the miles passed, her dread at seeing Michael, and seeing Liam unhappy, grew and grew. Poor Liam.

She realized abruptly that he was too much like her right now. He felt like Michael didn't love him because he believed there was something wrong with him.

There. She'd thought about something other than Conall for a good amount of time. What was he up to today? Had he spent his entire day thinking about her, too?

If they got together, Liam would be so happy because Conall would be around more. All that attention from Conall, and he'd get to see Maddy a lot more, too.

But she couldn't do it. Because what would happen when they broke up? She couldn't see it lasting. Great sex doesn't make a relationship. Even stellar, world-turning sex.

She tried thinking about work, but that just kept leading back to the Athena project and Conall.

And how well they'd worked together on the shelves. She couldn't deny that. But still, it wasn't enough for a relationship.

Then she thought of the other thing she dreaded today—the phone call to her mom, since Liam hadn't gotten to talk to her on Thanksgiving. She did love her mom, but she never could do anything right with her.

Her phone rang through the car system. An 830 number—her sister, not her mom. She relaxed.

"Hi, Sarah. How are you?"

There was a scuffling sound and Theresa heard something incomprehensible said in the background. Then she barely heard, "Petey, who did you call?" over the sound of the road.

The call ended after more scuffling, which cracked her up. Petey was her three-year-old nephew and he and his twin were constantly butt-dialing her. She was near the top of the list of names—with her family's last name, Alberts—and one of them was always managing to get Sarah's phone unlocked.

The phone rang again. This time it would be her sister intentionally calling.

"Sorry about that, Theresa. My other two were never so much work, honestly."

Theresa laughed. "They're boys, Sarah."

"Too true. So how are you?"

"On my way to pick Liam up."

"Oh, honey. I hope it's not like last time. Paulie! Put that down!"

The madness of Sarah's house always made Theresa feel better about her own household, even if their mom refused to see it.

They chatted about Sarah's kids, and Theresa told her about Liam's reading difficulties. Sarah was afraid her oldest daughter was having sex with her boyfriend and Sarah was stressing over it.

Theresa hoped that wasn't the case, because if she was, she probably wasn't using protection. In small-town Texas, they didn't teach kids about safe sex, believing abstinence-only sex ed was the best route. As though you could wish something into reality.

Petey got into something, and Sarah had to go. The rest of the drive was quiet and left her more time to think about Conall again. Or more, remember him and the incredible things he did to her.

But just to her body. Not to her heart.

Finally, she pulled off I-5 and headed to the Safeway in Centralia where they'd agreed to meet.

When Liam got out of Michael's truck, Theresa could instantly see it was as she'd feared. The poor boy's face said it all. He would be back to his morose self. Her gut twisted. She hated Michael.

Her ex got out and walked around the front of the black truck with Liam's suitcase and duffel and said, "Here's his stuff." He handed it to Theresa and she hated him more. Liam hugged her waist, and she fiercely held on to him. She'd wait until they were in the car to say anything to Liam, in case he cried, which he had done last year after spending Christmas with Michael.

"Thanks," she forced herself to say in a civil voice.

"We need to have a conversation," he said, squinting at her in the sun as he turned back toward the truck. "You look different. Happy." He narrowed his eyes, and she worked to keep a straight face.

Shrugging, he reached in, and handed her a black Nike bag, which she knew contained Liam's Christmas presents.

"Not now." What had that meant? Was she glowing or something?

"No, not now. I'll call in a couple weeks." Michael turned back around and opened his car door. "Bye, Liam," he called.

"Bye." Liam held on to her more tightly.

"Where's Mr. Bark, little man?"

He looked around, panic in his eyes.

"Michael!" she called. "Do you have his dog?"

Michael turned and squinted at them a second before retrieving the stuffed toy from the passenger seat. He'd been glaring. Like neither of them was good enough for him.

Liam went over to take it from him. He stood there next to the truck, watching his father get in.

Once Michael's door was shut, she said, "Let's get you in the car, honey. Did you have lunch yet?"

He shook his head and came back to take her hand.

"You ready?"

"Okay." He let go and got in the back of the car and into his carseat.

She was so angry at Michael that her stomach ached.

She got in and started up the car. "How about McDonald's?" There was one around the corner.

"Okay."

He wasn't even excited about McDonald's. "We'll get you a happy meal with fries this time. And you can play for as long as you want."

"Okay."

Michael. She could kill him.

"How was seeing your dad?" she asked him.

"Okay."

"What did you do?" She pulled out onto the main street.

"Nothing."

Of course, he wouldn't even draw when his dad was around because Liam knew what he thought of art.

"How are your brother and sisters?" She looked at him in the rearview mirror while he looked out the window.

"Fine."

"Honey, if you don't want to talk, we don't have to right now. But I want to hear about your visit."

He was quiet and continued to look out the window until they pulled into the McDonald's parking lot.

"Mom, why don't you want me to read?"

"What?" What was he talking about? How could he ask that? She pulled into a parking spot.

"Dad said that's why I am not good at it."

"Honey, that's not true." She turned around in her seat and tried to catch his eye, but he wouldn't let her. "Learning to read is hard. You're just struggling with it a little, that's all. We're going to find out why and then you'll be able to learn."

"Why do you have to go to work?"

"A lot of moms work, Liam." Defending her choices to her son was not how she thought today would go.

"Lily doesn't." His eyes were angry.

Lily was Michael's wife. Of course, she didn't work—he'd been much more careful the second time, even though it had taken him all of five months to find her.

She wasn't going to explain herself to him, because he wouldn't understand.

"It's your fault I don't like sports," he spat, finally looking at her again.

"Liam." This ticked her off. Michael was such a jerk.

He crossed his arms.

"Every time you try a new sport, you tell me you hate it. You told me you don't like PE. You have other interests."

She could see tears forming in his eyes, and he looked away, probably even angrier now that he was crying.

"Can I take karate?" he asked with a stuffed-up nose.

But he didn't like fighting. "If you want to, we can check it out."

His frowned deepened. "Dad said it will make me stronger, and then I can play football."

"Do you want to play football?" She had to convince him not to. No way was she risking her son's brain on anything so ridiculous.

"Yeah."

Michael. She could wring his neck. "Honey, if you want to take karate, we'll look into it, okay?"

"Okay." He didn't sound enthused.

Time to change the subject. "Let's go inside and see what toy they have now."

"Okay." Still not enthused, but he unbuckled himself.

After they ate in relative quiet, they got back in the car. Once they were back on the road, Theresa asked, "Are you ready to put the tree up when we get back? We can put the ornaments on, too."

He sighed. "I guess."

They continued in silence for a few miles, when Theresa's phone rang. Her mom.

Possibly for the first time ever, she decided not to answer.

The phone rang again and then one more time later, and she still didn't answer. She'd call back when they got home.

Her little rebellion.

FORTITUDE. That's what Theresa needed to get through today, barely forty-eight hours after getting out of bed with Conall for the last time. Ever.

She couldn't think about him all day, or act weird around him. She couldn't even talk about him to her friends—at least not today.

She'd felt so strange about the whole thing—it was so out of character for her, the way she'd acted—that she hadn't called either Casey or Sujata to tell them about it last night. She'd decided to wait until Friday night to tell them, after they each had a glass of wine in them.

So far, she'd avoided him, and it was just after lunch. She'd brought her own lunch today to have a reason to say no to Bernard and Martin, since Conall would probably go with them wherever they went.

She was tired because of the lack of coffee, since she'd been afraid to go to the kitchen. She'd seen him walk by a few times but had avoided eye contact.

"Hey, you."

She'd been so focused on avoiding Conall that she hadn't heard Sujata approach.

"Oh, hi."

"I have your answer, and it's affirmative. Hunky dory. A-OK." She gave a thumbs-up and turned to continue on.

Theresa laughed. "Great." And of course, her mind went straight to Conall, since that's what Sujata was talking about. She was good friends with the office manager, Gwen, who was in charge of the company's tutoring program. Gwen also managed the background checks, and a couple Fridays ago, Theresa had asked Sujata to confirm with her that Conall had had his background check.

Apparently he had. Which meant she was comfortable with him working with Liam.

Which meant she'd see him more, assuming he'd still do it now that she'd rejected him.

Though to be fair, he'd seemed on board with the temporary thing.

For the next half hour, she worked on wrapping up her first programming task of the day since the Athena meeting was coming up. But thoughts of Conall—usually involving his gorgeous naked body—kept interfering, and she didn't get everything done by the time the meeting rolled around.

She instinctively glanced toward his desk when she got up, but he wasn't there. He must have snuck by her. All the way to the conference room, she wondered if he was going through the same torture.

He was the first thing she saw as she walked in. Of course, it was his face that drew her attention, with his magical mouth. Her stomach dropped.

No, she could not get turned on at work. That was just... that was too weird.

He looked at her and winked.

Oh, no.

How could he? Nobody could have seen him wink, but still.

Iryna started the meeting, which is when Theresa realized she'd have to look at Conall anyway, since he was right next to Iryna.

"...Deliverable three," Iryna was saying. "Guru, are you on track for it?"

Conall wore another plaid shirt, this one mostly red. He had his elbows on the table and his fingers interlaced. Those magical fingers. She had to fight a shudder, remembering what he'd done with them Friday night.

Guru talked about what he was doing, but Theresa was barely listening.

Was that a smirk on Conall's face?

The rest of the meeting was torturous enough that she couldn't get out of there fast enough. But Conall stopped on his way back to his desk.

"Hi, Theresa. How was your break?"

Oh, man, he was going to tease her.

She gave him her best platonic smile. "Oh, you know. It was fine. It was nice to get some downtime."

"Downtime, huh? Sounds relaxing."

She looked at her screen and shook her mouse to wake the computer up. "How about you? What did you do?"

"Just something surprising and fun." He paused before adding, "And beautiful."

She blushed and mouthed, "Stop," at him. But she couldn't help feeling a little twist in her heart.

He just arched his eyebrows and grinned at her.

"So, Conall?" she asked.

"Mm-hmm." The corners of his mouth were still turned up.

"Were you serious about being willing to work with Liam?"

"Definitely."

She nodded. "I would love you to. Liam would, too."

"When were you thinking?"

"Well, there's evenings and weekends... it's up to you. You're the one doing us a favor." She had an IM from Sujata asking if she was okay. She closed it.

"Twice a week would probably be good. What about Wednesdays and Saturdays?"

This guy. "That would be wonderful. You're too generous, Conall."

He shrugged. "It's no trouble. He's a great kid."

"Could we start Saturday? Wednesday I have to meet with the psychologist for his test results."

They decided he'd come over at three, and he headed back to his desk. She stared at him the whole time, until his head disappeared behind a pod wall.

This week would be rough.

20

The next evening, Conall met Isaac at the gym for the volleyball team practice. He'd be meeting everyone for the first time.

"You'll get along with the guys on the team," Isaac said. "They're all cool. It's mostly couples, except for a couple girls."

"Cool."

While they walked inside, Isaac chatted with Jenny and Conall thought back to Theresa, who he couldn't get out of his head. Yesterday had been pretty hilarious when she got all flustered during the meeting. Today she hadn't had so much trouble when he'd gone by to talk to her. He took heart in the fact that he'd be working with Liam. At least he'd be in her life—her personal life, not just her work life.

Conall heard the starting and stopping squeaks of shoes on the court before they pushed the doors open. A net stood across the court. They walked over to the corner where several guys in shorts and tanks were standing.

After Conall was introduced around, a guy named Chuck directed them to start warming up.

Isaac walked over to his bag and returned with a volleyball under his arm. "Shall we?" They started bumping it back and forth.

Then the gym door opened and Isaac caught the ball and held onto it. Conall looked at the newcomers and saw Jenny, Isaac's girlfriend, followed by two other women, one of whom was wearing pink sweats and a pink t-shirt with a pink jacket over it all.

No way.

It couldn't be.

"Conall!"

It *was* Iryna.

She waved excitedly as the three women approached. Iryna's floral scent preceded them.

"Hi," Conall said.

Jenny kissed Isaac hello.

"How'd you end up here?" Iryna asked.

"You two know each other?" Isaac asked.

"We work together," she said.

This was… unexpected.

Jenny introduced him to the other woman, Hannah, who was busty and tall.

"Come on, guys, get going," Chuck called.

Jenny and Isaac were passing a ball back and forth, which now left Conall with the two ladies.

They started passing another ball between the three of them.

"Did you just move to town?" Hannah asked Conall.

"Yep, just last month."

"He's a developer," Iryna said. "He's even on one of my projects. He likes my cookies, too."

As Hannah bumped the ball to Conall, Iryna said, "I didn't know you played volleyball."

Of course, she didn't know that. They'd hardly spoken. "Just about everybody in Hawaii plays."

"Oh, that's interesting," Iryna said, passing the ball back to Hannah.

Conall forced a smile, and they continued on, Hannah asking him questions and Iryna finding everything he said fascinating.

"Okay, guys, let's do some serving drills," Chuck called. "Ladies on that side and men on the other and do one at a time."

Conall followed the men over to their half of the court, and they lined up. Each guy served the ball and chased it down, then served it back to the group. The women did the same.

"Scrimmage," Chuck called after they'd gone through the line several times. He mixed the men and women up, and Conall ended up on the same side as Iryna.

After the game, they all headed over to their duffels. Iryna came up to him and touched his wrist. "I've been wanting to offer, since you're new to town. I'd love to show you around, if you're interested."

"Now's not a good time. Getting settled in at work and so on."

Iryna's smile wavered a tiny bit, but she recovered quickly. "Okay, sure. I'll see you at the office tomorrow."

Was she interested?

WEDNESDAY AFTERNOON, Theresa left work early to get to the psychologist's and hear Liam's test results. She wanted to know what was wrong, but she was also afraid. What if he really had a learning disability? How would she deal with that? Would she tell him?

But what if he *didn't*? What would she do then?

The whole drive over there, the tension in her core expanded with each mile.

Once she was sitting across from Dr. Schwartz, who was perched behind an old wooden desk piled with papers, she felt like she would pop if someone stuck a pin in her.

She had the report in her hands, and he went over page one.

"Can you just give me the summarized version first?" She hadn't been this impatient since she'd been eight and a half months pregnant.

He looked up and smiled.

She realized with a start that he looked a little like Conall. He'd shaved the beard. Dark black hair, light eyes. Her heart sped up a tiny bit, remembering what she and Conall had gotten up to last week, and had to concentrate to focus back on real life.

"Sure," he said. "I understand." His voice was nothing like

Conall's. "My basic conclusion is that he doesn't appear to have anything that would qualify as a learning disability. However, he definitely is behind where he should be. I just can't pinpoint why at this point."

"Oh." She deflated. This was worse. What *was* it then? And was it her fault?

"I'd still like to go through the report, because it details some of his strengths and weaknesses."

"Sure."

In the end, she learned that his basic phonemic awareness was good—he understood that words were composed of distinct sounds and understood rhymes and other interchangeable parts of words. He knew all the basic letter sounds. He also knew most simple single-syllable words on sight. But he struggled with longer and multi-syllabic words.

The good news was that his IQ was over 130, which made her very proud again, even though she wasn't surprised.

"So now, recommendations," he said.

"Great."

"Because I don't think he has any specific learning disability, it is likely a problem with self-confidence."

That made her heart hurt. This man probably thought it was her fault, too.

"Can you think of any reason he'd be struggling there?" he continued.

Theresa nodded, nearly gritting her teeth in frustration. "His father. Liam is a talented artist, and his father thinks that is a worthless skill. The only things he values are sports and anything computer-related. Liam's not interested in either. Then, the other thing is I know he knows other kids read better than he does, so it makes it worse."

Dr. Schwartz leaned back in his chair tented his fingers. "You might do well with an outside tutor."

"Actually, there is a..." She wasn't sure what to call Conall. "A friend of mine who has experience with tutoring kids in reading, and I've arranged for him to work with Liam."

"That could be excellent. I would recommend pursuing that, especially because he's male. Boys often respond more positively to male mentors, especially if they don't have regular contact with a male role model."

He knew she was a single mom. "I will." She glanced over the current page of the report, which finished off with his thoughts on tutoring. "Do you have any other specific recommendations for tutoring?" She could always have him in a formal program, too.

"Yes. Next page."

She turned to it and saw several local organizations that offered tutoring in various locations in the area. "Thank you." She flipped back to the front page. "Is that all you have for me?"

"Yes, Ms. Alberts. Do you have any further questions?"

"I don't think so. Can I contact you if I have any?"

He smiled again, still looking like Conall. "Of course. My contact information is on the report." He stood up and stepped to the side of his desk to open the door. "Best of luck with Liam. He's a bright boy, and I think with the right tutor can get back on track."

She stood up. "Thank you again." Then she was out in the hall and heading out to her car.

For the entire drive over to pick Liam up, she pondered the idea that Conall could fix him. Was it right to ask a sort of random guy to tutor him, as opposed to someone at an official tutoring center? Maybe she'd see what happened. Give it a couple weeks just to see if Liam relaxed and would read with her more.

She found him drawing at his unofficial table at the after-school program. She watched him from across the room, his left arm thrown across the top of the paper while he leaned forward and focused on the bottom.

A couple of younger kids—a girl and a boy—were busy making a large, unidentifiable construction out of wooden blocks, which looked about ready to tip over at any moment. That didn't stop them from chattering and busily adding to the mess.

A girl in a pink dress and black shoes sat on the floor reading one of the books from the center's mini-library, a large shelf that was perched against the wall across from Liam.

She looked back at Liam just as he turned the paper sideways and began working on another part of the drawing.

Just then, there was a crash as the block tower toppled in the corner, and the boy shrieked in dismay.

"I told you!" the girl said, but then she laughed. "We can make it again."

Liam hadn't even looked up, his concentration was so deep. Theresa went over to his table and said, "Hi, honey."

He looked up in surprise and blinked a couple times. "Mom! Time to go!"

"What have you drawn today, little man?" She looked down while rubbing his back.

"A caterpillar."

It was indeed a caterpillar, about 12 inches long.

The boy in the corner started sobbing, and Theresa looked over to see the little girl consoling him.

"Where'd you see this caterpillar?" she asked Liam.

"In a book."

One of the staff members, a young college girl, came in to comfort the boy in the corner.

"Well, it's wonderful," Theresa said. "I love it. Is it done?"

"No." He pushed his chair back and stood up.

"Go on and get your backpack."

He trotted over there and came back with it, then pulled out the tube that he'd started keeping in there and rolled up the picture carefully to slide it in.

Theresa glanced over again at the group in the corner around the pile of blocks and saw the boy was done crying, and the three of them were cleaning up.

"Let's go, sweetie."

"Bye, Liam," the college girl called as they headed out.

Liam didn't say anything in return, so Theresa smiled and waved at her.

21

Saturday morning, Theresa's nervous energy had her picking up downstairs while Liam played his vet video game. Conall was due to arrive any minute to work with Liam, and her stomach was doing flips while excitement threatened to go lower.

Conall would be in her house again.

She had to stop thinking about him that way. He was a work friend now. In pod solidarity, she'd ordered a Hawaiian shirt that morning, since the guys had all worn theirs yesterday. She figured, why not? That was the kind of thing she and Conall could talk about. Plus Liam.

But for now, there was something else to focus on. She got the spray cleaner out of the cabinet over the sink. Liam was here, and she couldn't be distracted from him. This was important.

The smell of bleach invaded her nose as she sprayed. She began wiping down the kitchen counter. Last night, she'd gone out with Casey and Sujata, as usual. But although they had teased her about Conall some more, she didn't tell them what had happened. Just that he'd come over, and they'd built the bookshelves.

Of course they'd wanted to know what they looked like and what she was going to do with them. She'd shown them the pictures and said she was painting them white like the rest of the trim.

She finished the counter just as a knock sounded from the door, a knock that reverberated through her heart.

"Got it!" Liam called.

She set the bottle down and slipped her rubber gloves off.

"Hey, buddy," she heard. "Ready to read?"

"Hi," Liam answered. "Where's Maddy?"

By the time she got around the kitchen counter, Conall had stepped in.

"She's at home. I didn't bring her because we're going to spend the time reading, not playing with her."

"But I want to play with her," Liam said. "I don't want to read."

Theresa came up behind him. "Little man, you have to learn to read. And Conall's going to help you."

Liam stood in front of the couch with his arms crossed, looking determined.

"It'll be fun, Liam," Conall said.

Liam didn't budge.

Theresa crossed her arms herself. "I know you don't want to, but you're going to." She said it firmly and continued, "Go upstairs and get four or five books."

The boy didn't move.

"Liam, now."

This time she sounded mad enough that he went.

She looked over at Conall, who chuckled.

"Trying to impress me, is he?"

"Something like that." She sighed. "Thanks for coming. I'll just have you two work down here."

"In the kitchen?" Then he gave her a grin that took her right back to their episode on the kitchen table.

She'd been so uncharacteristically out of control with him. She blinked. "No, I'm going to mop while you work. How about the couch?"

"Sure."

She looked past him at the door.

They were still standing just a few feet apart.

"It's hard to be here and not touch you," Conall said.

She looked at his shoulder. "Should we meet somewhere else? The library?"

"No, I can control myself." He paused and winked. "Can you?"

Theresa turned toward the kitchen. "Yes." She willed it to become true.

"I can't believe it was less than a week ago that I was here making love to you." He took a step closer to her.

That struck her core. How could he say that? She looked at his gorgeous eyes. "Conall, we didn't make love. We just had sex. Really great sex, yes, but just sex." It was the truth.

His jaw clenched. "No, you're right. Just sex." He reached out and touched her face quickly before dropping his hand. "Just fucking amazing sex, that's all." It came out almost a growl.

They stared at each other, Theresa's heart beating faster than it needed to.

"I got four," Liam said as he stepped off the stairs.

Theresa said, "Don't forget your dad's calling in an hour and a half."

Liam nodded and Conall stepped to the side and said, "That's great. Pick which one to read first."

Theresa headed back into the kitchen and put the spray bottle away. She glanced into the living room and saw Liam settled next to Conall on the couch, who was holding the book across their laps. The Christmas tree stood in the corner next to the couch.

"You want to start?" Conall asked.

"No, you."

She went into the garage to get the mop bucket. When she leaned down to pull it off the shelf, she spotted a couple of nails just showing under the bottom shelf. Her face flushed, and her body warmed, because they had missed these as they cleaned up everything that had fallen off the shelf when Conall pushed her into it. A box of nails had popped open and sprayed them everywhere.

She gripped one of the higher shelves to brace herself and catch her breath.

The nails slipped out of her fingers as she tried to grab them, but eventually she got them back in the box and on the top shelf. She snagged the bucket and rushed back into the kitchen, still flustered.

"...butter and jelly," Conall was reading.

"Why does her hair look like that?" Liam asked.

"I think because she likes it."

Theresa put the blue bucket in the sink and turned the hot water on.

Soon steam was rolling up, and she couldn't hear anything over the rush of the water. She reached under the sink for the floor cleaner and poured it in once the bucket was full. Water sloshed out as she hefted it out of the sink and set it on the floor.

"She got the pan out of the cabinet and handed it to Mom," Conall read.

Theresa stole a glance in there as she got the mop out of the closet and saw Liam leaning forward like he did whenever he was entranced with a book. She knew the one they were reading—it was about treating everyone, even a bully, with kindness. A good message for kids, and the story was funny, too.

She dunked the mop in and squeezed it dry with the rollers, the lemony scent wafting by, before starting from the door to the garage and working her way across the room, all the while listening to Conall's sexy timbre as he read to her son.

He did different voices as he read, making Liam laugh and her smile.

The laughter tugged at her heart as she pushed the mop. Conall was already behaving more like a real father than Michael ever had.

Maybe dating him wouldn't be a bad thing...

No. As great as he seemed, Conall was a man. Right now, he was behaving well because he wanted to sleep with her again. How would he act once he understood it wasn't going to happen? Or, if they dated, he assumed it was a given?

Things were risky with Liam. What if Conall realized she wasn't going to invite him into her bed again and bailed on the whole reading-with-Liam thing?

She scrubbed at a dark spot on the kitchen floor.

She didn't think he would. Despite her reservations, she only got a good vibe off Conall. But if he did disappear, they'd be back at square one, and she'd have to find a professional tutor for Liam.

Not to mention that Liam would be devastated. Another man who'd left him behind. She knew he'd blame himself.

Theresa moved a chair out of the way and started mopping under the table, right in the spot where he'd drilled into her while her hands were spread on the top of it.

She should never have let him do that here, because now she could never get it out of her mind. And right here, where she spent so much time.

She knew she was blushing as she finished under the table and made her way toward the dining room.

Once she made it to the carpet, she rested the mop against the wall and turned toward Liam and Conall.

Conall looked up and smiled at her, his eyes glowing.

Her blush deepened.

"Why'd you stop?" Liam asked.

Conall looked back down. "Sorry, kiddo. Where were we?"

"Right here."

MONDAY EVENING CONALL decided to tackle his boxes of books and fill his new shelves. He cut open the top box and began filling the small bookshelf. As he put a couple of books onto the shelf, a piece of paper fluttered out from between them onto the floor. He knelt down to get it, instantly recognizing one of Clarissa's notes. Back when things had been good, she was always leaving little notes. "I love you bunches!!!" this one said.

"Not fucking enough," he muttered, anger filling his chest. She'd decided adoption wasn't a viable option. He wasn't worth it. They'd already been working with an agency when she dumped him. After nine years. Nine years together. And that was it. The last thing he'd heard, she'd married a mailman.

Fuck. Stop thinking about it. It made him feel like such shit. He shoved a few of his books on the shelf in random order.

They really had been good together. She'd just gone baby crazy and they'd tried for so long. When they'd found out he had the same condition his father had—Conall was a miracle baby— she couldn't handle it. He still didn't understand what had turned her against his idea of adopting.

A book with a distinctive black and red cover slipped from his hand and fell to the floor.

Theresa had worn red and black a couple days earlier. He pulled some more books out of the box.

She had looked especially nice that day. The red skirt hugged her butt a little more closely than some of her others, and he'd had to make a concerted effort to control himself, knowing exactly what was under that skirt. Mmm.

And then earlier today, she'd stood at Sujata's desk in a short-sleeve dress that again showed off her lovely arms.

Theresa. She was something else. And Thanksgiving... Christ.

Once he was done unloading the books, he broke the empty boxes down and took them out to the recycle bin, which Theresa kept on the side of the house. The air was cold, and Conall wrapped his arms around himself on the way back in.

The motion reminded him of Theresa holding onto him.

He needed to shake that. It was never happening again.

He shut the front door and fell onto the couch next to his computer, arms stretched across the back. He sighed and pulled it into his lap, lifting the lid.

As soon as he had logged in, a window popped up on his personal email window. His cousin Mark.

mdesouza999: hey, conall

conodonn: hey, bro, MIT still kicking your ass?

mdesouza999: finals are coming up

conodonn: you ready?

mdesouza999: almost. i'm still glad i decided to retake calculus

conodonn: yeah, gives you a bit of breathing room

mdesouza999: python's still awesome

Python was a programming language notoriously easy to learn, as opposed to a lot of the other languages that used to be taught in computer science degrees. Theresa used it in her role more than Conall did.

conodonn: what are you working on?

Mark went into detail about his various projects, and they chatted a bit more about goings-on at home. Nothing exciting had happened, but there was always cousin news. Conall needed to call his mom for his own update.

After he and Mark finished chatting, he did call her.

"Hi, sweetheart." She was obviously smiling, like she always did when he called. "I'm so glad to hear from you! You never call anymore."

Affection for her washed over him. Why didn't he call her more? She always made him feel better. "I know, I'm sorry. Tell me what's going on back home."

She regaled him with stories about his cousins, and he again felt the pang of not being there.

"Honey," she said in a voice that worried him. "I need to tell you something."

Shit, what now? "Okay," he said slowly.

"I saw Clarissa at the store."

Oh, no. What was it?

"She's pregnant."

He closed his eyes against the sense of being nothing. Absolutely nothing.

"Now, I don't want you to let it bother you. She's as big as a house with boats for feet."

"Doesn't help, Mom." It really didn't.

Christ, this fucking sucked.

Her voice was low when she said, "I know, honey. Please don't let it get you down. You're still the best man I know. You're smart and handsome, and some day you'll find someone else who notices."

He thought of Theresa and how perfect she was, and how he'd never have something like that.

"You are getting to a good age, honey. You just need to find yourself a nice widow or divorcee who's already got a gaggle of kids. I know you're going to be the best father."

"Stepfather," he grumbled.

"I don't believe it's that simple. Being a father is something you do, not just a biological condition."

"Okay, Mom. I hear you. I'll work on it." He couldn't keep mild bitterness out of his voice.

"Sweetheart, don't be like that. I know you'll find her someday."

Problem was, he already had, and she would never want him back.

22

Theresa puttered around the kitchen making dinner Wednesday evening while Conall sat on the couch with Liam and a book between them. She glanced in there at them. Liam's grungy stuffed dog was parked next to his hip. He read the first page of the book, one about a farting dog.

"A bath!" Liam laughed. "Do you give Maddy a bath?"

"I take her to a groomer. She gets dirty. But in the summer we can do it in the backyard."

"Cool! Read the next page!"

Conall laughed and began reading. When he got to the part about the bubbles in the water, Liam giggled. And when he got to the end of the page and read that the dog just farted a lot, Liam laughed and jerked back against the couch. His joy was infectious all the way into the kitchen.

She had the chicken baking in the oven and was slicing the carrots and cucumber for a nice salad.

Conall and Liam had gone quiet so she took another peek. It seemed like they were looking at the pictures, which she already knew were wild and fun, with a lot going on.

After a bit longer, she heard Conall say, "For the next one, I want to make a deal with you."

"Okay."

"I'll read one page, and you read the next."

She imagined Liam crossing his arms as he said, "I don't want to."

"Come on, buddy. You need to learn better. I know it's hard, but everyone has to learn." He sounded so patient and encouraging.

"Why?"

"Life is just hard if you can't read well. Your mom and I both had to learn when we were little, too."

"Was it hard?"

"Yeah, I remember it being hard." He paused. "You know something funny?"

"What?"

Theresa dumped the carrots and cucumber into a bowl and started chopping a red onion up.

"English is especially hard to learn because the spelling is so weird. It's not just you. Sometimes the same letters are pronounced differently, depending on the word. You aren't alone." That was true.

She couldn't hear Liam's response.

"So we can take turns, right?"

"Okay."

"Which book do you want to read next?"

She peeked around the corner as Liam stood up rifled through the books on the coffee table. He fell onto the couch and opened the book. "You first."

She continued watching while Conall read the first page. "Your turn. Can you read that?" He pointed at the first word on Liam's page, glancing over at his face, which was scrunched in concentration.

"The... boy... ate." He stalled.

Conall pointed at the beginning of the word. "What's this letter?"

"L."

She got back to her onion.

"And this one?" He moved his finger to the right.

"U."

"And here?"

"N."

"So how does that sound?"

166

"Lun... lunch!" He sounded so excited.

"Exactly, good job. When C and H are together, they make a 'ch' sound."

Once she had the salad mixed, she took the chicken out and sliced it up thinly.

Conall and Liam continued on, eventually making it through the book, though it took a while because Liam was still struggling.

When it sounded like they'd finished a book, she stepped into the living room and said, "I think that's probably enough for tonight, guys."

"Yeah, I do need to get home to Maddy," Conall said.

"Liam, why don't you go get your latest drawing to show Conall?"

"Okay!" He raced up stairs.

"Did you want to get me alone?" Conall teased.

"No." She looked at him but kept her expression blank.

He stood up and walked toward her. "Do you think of me when you're lying in bed at night?" he whispered.

"Don't." But she hadn't broken their gaze.

He stepped forward and brushed her face with the back of his fingers, and when she didn't back up, he leaned in. She still didn't back up, and soon their lips met.

Then she jerked back and said, "Conall, don't. I really can't."

But oh, she wanted to.

MONDAY AFTERNOON, Conall and Theresa headed to the conference room for a meeting. He experienced a moment of uncertainty about where to sit at the ten-chair table. But then he decided he was being stupid—he'd walked in with her so there was no reason not to sit next to her. Weird not to.

He glanced over and smiled before turning to tap his pen against his notebook.

"Liam did a pretty good job reading Saturday," he said.

"He sounds more confident when he's with you than he has been with me. I've been so worried about him. Apparently, I just need to find random men to read with him, since he clearly responds to you people better than me."

Conall laughed a little while their coworkers filed in. "Kids are funny. But I don't think I'm some random man."

She arched her eyebrows and cocked her head to the side. "They are. And no, you're not."

One of the database guys came in with a piece of red velvet cake on a small paper plate.

Iryna waltzed in—again wearing more pink than any human ever should. She sat in front of the keyboard as Conall leaned forward to turn the projector on.

"Hi, Conall. Nice game last week." She smiled.

"Yeah, you too." Not true. She was new to the game and still learning.

She continued looking at him intently, and he glanced over at Theresa, who had a flat expression.

Iryna cleared her throat. "Hi, everyone. Let's just go through the teams to see where we're at. Theresa, why don't you start."

Theresa nodded. "As everyone knows, I've been having to make myself an expert in data warehousing in short time, so I've been spending my time on absorbing everything I can." She finished with, "I should have a basic design complete in about two weeks."

Iryna went around to a couple more people before getting to Conall.

"I am in a holding pattern until we have the design." He turned to Theresa. "But I should mention I have a lot of experience with data warehouses. I can help you with the design."

Theresa eyes narrowed ever-so-slightly. She probably wondered if he was trying to come up with an excuse to be near her. He wasn't. He really could help.

"Great," Iryna said tartly. "You two get together and see what you can come up with by the end of next week."

The meeting ended soon afterward.

Theresa looked at Conall while everyone else left. "The room's booked for another half hour. Do you want to start now?"

"Sure."

Theresa got up and picked up the blue marker. She wrote "DW" on the top left of the board. Her light green dress gave Conall a satisfying glimpse of her toned calves.

"So, why don't you tell me what you're currently thinking in terms of a design?" he said.

His eyes wandered up to her butt. He remembered the feel of it in his hands and wished they could go there again.

Theresa turned around and nodded. "Okay. I feel like I have a decent handle on things, actually, but I'm worried I've made it easier than it should be."

"I doubt it." Conall shrugged, also trying to shrug off his work-inappropriate thoughts. "It's really not that hard. But just realize the warehouse I built before was for an inventory system so it's a little different from what we're doing here."

"Right, that's what I've been reading. Usually a warehouse is focused on a particular type of transaction. But ours will fit under several different categories." She recapped the pen.

Conall's mind wouldn't leave him alone with its thoughts of her. Naked beneath him. He didn't know why it was happening right now, of all times. Mercifully, Theresa didn't seem to notice.

He cleared his throat. "And allow for growth."

She gave him that gorgeous smile. "We might explode with customers, after all."

Conall nodded, still fighting his thoughts.

"Okay, so first—Inmon or Kimball?" Theresa asked, referring to the two gurus of data warehousing who advocated different approaches, which led to different designs.

"Not Inmon," he scoffed.

She smiled again. "That's what I figured."

They continued discussing her thoughts on the design, which were absolutely on track. Maybe the fact that she was so smart was part of what turned him on. He needed to get out of there. "You've got this, Theresa. I'm happy to help. Let me know if you have additional questions."

"Thanks. I'm sure I'll have some more."

He forced an uncomfortable smile and shifted in his chair. "Sure, no problem."

"Let's start with the HR aspect of the warehouse," Theresa said. She began sketching out a plan for the core tables that would make up the warehouse.

When her back was turned, Conall's gaze strayed off the board again so he could admire the shape of her body under the thin dress. He had to adjust himself under the table.

Then she asked, "What do they call it? The one that tracks job changes and so on?"

"Employee Transactions?"

"Yeah, that one. Duh." She added it to the top of one of her tables and kept drawing her model.

They continued on to work on the finance part of the database and then on sales.

After she'd finished, they'd looked it over and made a few small adjustments, but Conall knew they'd nailed it.

Just like he wanted to nail her again.

WEDNESDAY EVENING, Theresa worked on making the crust for a pizza while Conall worked with Liam. She could hear them in there, and it was so sweet listening to someone work with Liam so patiently. She would ask him to stay for dinner, hoping it didn't come across as flirting.

She got out the cutting board and washed off three Roma tomatoes.

She heard Liam laugh. He was so much more engaged with Conall than he was with her whenever she'd try to get him to read. It wasn't like he wasn't engaged with her ever. He loved to talk about his draw-ings after all, and sometimes she played a video game with him. He loved that.

She set the tomatoes on the cutting board and got the knife out of the block. These excellent knives were the second best thing to come out of her marriage. She loved them, but it was hard not to think of Michael when she used them. When he'd first bought them for her, very early in the marriage, he'd made a joke about how now she could cook him real meals. At least she'd taken it as a joke at the time. It had probably been a dig.

"Why don't you read this page?" Conall said.

She was glad making this meal she was quiet so she could hear them.

"He got the... du... dog..." He stopped.

"Not quite, that's a b, not a d."

"Boo... Book."

She began slicing the second tomato, thinking back to how much she'd loved to cook for Michael in the beginning.

"Good, but go ahead and start from the beginning of the sentence." Conall's voice was almost gentle, and it made Theresa's heart pinch. He would be a wonderful father whenever he decided to settle down. She was almost jealous of the woman that he would be with.

"He got the... book... oat."

"Out. Can you try the whole sentence again?"

"He got the doo... book... out." He said the last word with finality, obviously proud he'd remembered it.

"Good job. I'll read the rest of the page, and then you can read the next one." He proceeded to finish it, and they turned the page.

Liam struggled through the next page. He'd make it about three words and falter, but Conall eased him through the page while she added a thin layer of the sauce over the crust. It smelled wonderful— with a kick of basil and oregano. She'd also added small bits of onion to it to give it a little different flavor.

Liam read an entire sentence without stumbling and then was quiet.

"Good job, kiddo. You read that all by yourself."

Theresa sauced the crust and cut the mozzarella into thin slices. She preferred fresh over the pre-grated stuff. Of course, Michael had, too.

She listened to Liam try the rest of the page. He struggled a little more, but still made it through with only a couple redirections from Conall.

He was an amazing man. Seeing him with Liam melted her heart.

Maybe she *could* risk being with him.

No, her thoughts of Michael reminded her why. Theresa finished the pizza and got it in the oven.

Still a bad idea. She couldn't manage it all—a demanding job, being a mother, and a boyfriend. A husband would be a different thing because they'd already be partners. But you couldn't go straight there.

She went into the next room and leaned against the wall next to the stairs to watch them, her arms crossed. Conall as a boyfriend? No. There'd be expectations, and she couldn't live up to them.

While Liam read, Conall glanced up at her and smiled. Her heart warmed more than it should have.

But then Liam finished his page and saw her. "Mom!" he said, stretching out the vowel. "I'm busy!"

"You don't want me to watch, little man?"

"No."

She shrugged while Conall laughed to himself, raising his eyebrows at her. "Okay," she said.

She set the table and started sweeping the floor even though it didn't need it. Conall had sat with Theresa to work on the data warehouse design again today. He'd been very helpful, though she'd of course struggled to keep her thoughts on work.

But she'd managed. They made some progress on the design.

She started clearing the fridge. The expiration date on everything was fine, except for an old yogurt that had escaped her notice, hiding in the back. November 24. That went into the trash.

That was Thanksgiving day. Right in the midst of their shenanigans. She couldn't keep remembering, so she leaned against the counter to listen some more. After the timer went off, she poured a milk for Liam.

Liam and Conall stood just outside the kitchen.

"Is dinner ready?" Liam asked.

"Yes, honey. Did you finish reading? How many books did you read?"

"Three."

"That's great." She looked at Conall. "You're welcome to stay for dinner. There's plenty."

172

"Smells Italian."

"Tomato basil pizza."

"Mmm, sounds good." His eyes held the gaze. "I can stay, thank you."

"Great." She noticed Liam was looking back and forth between them, so she smiled at him instead. "Go on and sit down, honey."

She handed Conall the water she'd just poured, and their fingers touched, which was bad because it got her thinking about the last time she and Conall had been at the table together. She flushed.

Stop it.

He must have noticed because he turned away, possibly to avoid saying something flirtatious. She'd been pretty clear last time.

THURSDAY NIGHT, the squeak of Conall's shoes on the court rang in his ears as he stopped and passed the ball to Isaac. Isaac hit it for a kill. They were losing by two points now.

The other team aced on their serve, leaving Conall's team three points behind. But Hannah's next attack went unanswered and after a bunch of scrambling, they pulled forward for a win at the final buzzer.

So far their record was quite good—they were 3-0. It didn't matter, but it was more fun to be winning.

Conall stood near the wall wiping the sweat off his forehead, his back to the court, when he heard his name.

He turned around and to find Iryna and Hannah. "Great game, ladies. You're both quite the little firecrackers, aren't you?"

Actually, Hannah was, but Iryna was still bad.

"That was some spike at the end," he said to Hannah. "I feel like you've done this before."

Hannah laughed while Iryna looked on with what looked like a fake smile. She probably thought he was flirting with Hannah. He wasn't.

Everyone congregated at the end of the court, congratulating and high-fiving each other.

"You all want to go out for a beer?" Chuck asked.

Conall felt like he should go.

By the time they'd all changed and made it to the large bar, they'd lost one couple. They managed to snag a table, but it only had enough room for the women, who took over it in seconds. So the guys ended up at the bar along with Hannah and Iryna and a smattering of other people trying to get the two bartenders' attention.

"Why aren't you with all the other ladies?" Conall asked them.

"Because we don't have a man to buy them for us." Iryna angled her chin down but looked up and batted her eyelids. "Unless you want to be kind...."

Conall barked a laugh. "You can't pull off bashful, Iryna."

Hannah cracked up. Iryna smiled and said, "Well, I tried."

"Since you made me laugh, I'll buy you both drinks. What would you like?"

Once he managed to get the attention of the nearest bartender—a hipster with large spacers in his earlobes—he bought them both pumpkin ales and Iryna squeezed his arm in thanks.

Conall handed the ladies their ales. When Iryna took hers, their fingers brushed. The touch stirred nothing in him except thoughts of Theresa and her beautiful smile. And how he couldn't have her.

He found the guys hovering around the table. The ladies had saved seats for Hannah and Iryna.

Then Chuck was next to them and slapping Conall on the back. "Man of the night," he said. "Eight points."

Before Conall could say anything, Karen snorted and said, "After Hannah. Try ten."

Chuck laughed. "Okay, good point." He made as if to slap Hannah on the back but instead just put his hand on her shoulder, lifted his beer, and said, "Woman of the night."

Or player of the night.

Everyone raised their bottles in agreement while Hannah laughed.

They chatted for a while about nothing, though he kept noticing Iryna watching him with a smile on her face.

After a hour or so, Hannah said, "Okay, guys, I think that's it for me. I've got an early client tomorrow." She and Iryna headed out. Iryna gave everyone a finger wave—but he expected it was really for him.

23

Saturday morning, Theresa was downstairs vacuuming. She wanted to get all the cleaning done before Conall got there at two because she planned to sit at the dining room table and work so she could listen in better.

"Mom," Liam called from upstairs.

"What?"

"The toilet won't flush."

Crap. She didn't want to have to call a plumber on the weekend. She headed upstairs.

Liam stood outside the bathroom. "It spilled."

She stepped in and saw there was water around the pink toilet and the bowl was full. No more was coming out, but there was enough on the floor it would spread if she didn't get it cleaned up. "Go grab a bunch of towels, honey."

She pulled the one off the towel rack and spread it behind the toilet. Liam returned with an armful of towels and she placed them around the toilet. He stood just outside the pool of water and watched.

Man, she didn't want to call a plumber on a weekend.

There was always YouTube. Nothing was happening at this exact moment so she had time to figure out what to do. So, she headed over to the internet to attempt to solve her problem.

The videos mentioned many things to try, starting with a coat hanger, which didn't work, and a plunger, which also didn't work and spilled even more out of the bowl.

In the end, she thought of Pat. Maybe she had a toilet auger they recommended. Pat was generally on top of things. She was a super-independent woman—she'd been big in the women's movement of the 1970s and knew how to take care of herself and her house.

Theresa called her.

"Yes, I've got one, honey. Come on over." There was something mischievous in her voice.

Theresa called to Liam to stay where he was and sloshed her way across the wet grass.

Pat answered wearing a Berkeley sweatshirt and holding the long, bendable pole. She smiled and said, "Before I give you this, you have to tell me about the man I've seen over there lately. I've been wanting to ask, but not in front of Liam. Who is he? He's yummy."

Hearing that from a woman in her seventies made Theresa crack up.

Once she recovered, she said, "He's just a friend."

"He sure spent a lot of time over there while Liam was away."

Theresa blushed. "We built the new bookshelves you've seen." Pat had babysat a couple times since Thanksgiving when Theresa went out with Casey and Sujata.

Pat arched an eyebrow. "If you say so, honey. Though I wouldn't mind seeing you with someone. You deserve a partner in life."

That made Theresa smile. It sure sounded nice when she put it like that. A partner.

"Anyway, since I'm obviously not going to get the truth out of you, here you go." She reached out to hand Theresa the auger.

"Thanks, Pat. I'll get it back to you soon."

"Bye, honey." Pat waved as she headed back across the yards.

Theresa grabbed a large trash bag and waded into the bathroom, soaked towels slopping as she stepped on them. She gagged.

Once she got over that, she unlatched the auger end, took a deep breath and held it, and stuck the thing in the toilet. She could feel it bending with the S-curve, and finally it hit some resistance.

She gagged again but pushed a few times until the resistance went away. She pulled the thing out, and a little soggy toilet paper was stuck to the end. She grabbed for the dry part of the driest towel and wiped it off, gagging one more time.

She wrung the towels out in the bathtub and crammed them in the trash bag, which she set in the hall.

Now she was faced with a disgusting bathroom that needed significant cleaning. She hoped none of the dirty water had made it onto the subfloor.

"Liam?" she called.

"Yeah?"

"What time is it?" Conall was coming at two.

"1:53."

Crap, crap. She stepped out of her shoes to leave them in the bathroom. She would throw her shoes and clothes in the washing machine as soon as she'd had a shower in her own bathroom.

She poked her head in Liam's room and found him at his desk. "Honey?"

"Yeah?"

"I've got the mess cleaned up. But try not to use so much toilet paper next time."

"I didn't use any. I just went pee."

Well, that was something. She'd been elbows and knees deep in pissy water, not poopy water.

"Okay. Still, try not use too much in general. Also, your dad's calling today."

"Oh." He turned back to his drawing.

"But Conall will be here any minute. I need you to let him in. Why don't you go ahead and pick some books to take downstairs?"

Liam smiled and started flipping through books on his bookshelf.

She didn't want to track anything downstairs.

Then another problem occurred to her.

"Liam, did you walk in the water that came out of the toilet?"

"No, it came out after."

"Okay, good. Go on downstairs with your books so you can hear him knock. Let me know when he's here, okay?"

~

CONALL LISTENED to Liam read from a book. Theresa had asked them to sit at the kitchen table since she had to be upstairs cleaning up the unfortunate results of a toilet mishap. He smiled to himself thinking of her solving the problem on her own—with the help of YouTube, as she'd explained.

Liam was concentrating on his page.

"Bobby rang the... bell. He... hear... it... huh?"

"Heard," Conall clarified.

"Oh. He heard it ring."

Conall felt himself nodding along as Liam read. He corrected him a few times but Liam seemed relaxed and wasn't doing bad. Conall figured he'd just let Liam go and not correct everything because he wanted him to feel less self-conscious.

"Finished!" Liam said as he closed the first book.

"You did a great job, kiddo. Now which one do you want to read?"

There were three library books laid out on the table. One had a picture of a school bus with happy kids hanging out the windows, while another was about seeing-eye and other assistance dogs. Liam surprised him by picking the third one, which had a picture of a kid playing in a creek on it. He figured he'd go for the dog one.

"Max..." Liam faltered on the second page and Conall said, "Asked."

"Max asked to play." He paused for a breath. "But Jonny said no."

Conall glanced at the picture on the page, which showed a boy frowning off to the side of several boys playing basketball. One of the players stood with his hands on his hips, facing Max.

Liam kept reading. When the boy tried to play anyway, the others chased him off the court and pushed him to the ground. Liam got quiet after that before saying, "Conall?"

"Yeah, buddy?"

He looked over at Conall. "Why do they do that?"

"Why are they mean to Max?"

"Yeah."

Conall shook his head. "I don't know why. Some kids are just like that. I had a problem with a boy like that when I was young."

"Really? What happened?"

Conall had been skinny and small until high school, when he'd finally started growing. He put his hand on the back of Liam's chair. "My dad told me to stand up to him, so one time when he hit me, I hit him back in the face."

Liam's eyes went wide. "Whoa."

"He left me alone after that."

Liam looked up at him. "Really?"

"Really. Alright, kiddo, let's keep reading."

"Okay." Liam looked back at the page. "Your turn."

Conall read the next page, and they made it through the story. The kid in the book didn't fight back, but they resolved it by going to a teacher, who made them include Max, and they were all friends by the end.

That might be fine for a kid's book, but that wasn't how the playground really worked.

They started the book about dogs next. A few pages in, Theresa came down with a bulging black trash bag.

"Hi guys, how's it going?" She stopped and looked at Liam.

"I read four books," he said.

"All by yourself?"

Conall smiled at Theresa as she glanced over at him.

Liam said, "Conall helped."

She laughed and looked at Conall again. "Did he?"

Conall said, "We're almost done with this book, actually."

"Perfect timing. I just finished cleaning up the bathroom." She headed into the garage with the bag.

They had made it through several more pages by the time Theresa came back in. She washed her hands in the sink. She wore jean cutoffs and a white t-shirt. He could see the outline of her bra under the shirt, and it made him want her again.

"Your turn," Liam said.

Conall guiltily looked back down at the book and started reading the next page.

"I already read that," Liam scoffed.

"Oops." He turned the page and read the first sentence. He shouldn't get distracted like that. The whole point was to help the kid improve.

Soon they'd finished the book while Theresa puttered around the kitchen in her bare feet—Christ, her legs were gorgeous. How he'd like to feel them wrapped around him again.

"Finished!" Liam announced once they were.

Theresa rinsed her hands and dried them off with a white towel hanging on the oven door handle. She smiled at Liam and said, "Why don't you go upstairs and get your donkey drawing?"

"Okay!" He leapt out of the chair and headed upstairs.

"How's he doing?" she asked Conall.

He nodded. "Not bad. I think he is getting more comfortable. He's still mixing up letters sometimes—b and d—and he doesn't always recognize the same words more than once, but he'll get there." He pushed his chair back and stood to come around the side of the table, a few feet from where she stood.

"Good. I'm still so worried about him. Seven-year-olds shouldn't have confidence crises."

"No, they shouldn't. But he can come out of it."

She nodded. "I hope so."

24

"Mom."

Theresa opened her eyes as she felt a small hand shake her shoulder. There was Liam's face, inches from hers. She registered Mr. Bark, too.

"You're awake! Come on!"

Right. Christmas morning. She smiled at him and then covered her mouth for a yawn. She loved this time with him, when he'd forget all his troubles and just be a happy kid.

Liam pulled the bedspread off her. "Come on!"

Their rule was that he couldn't go down by himself, because what if Santa was running late and was still here?

Theresa grabbed her robe off the other side of the bed and wrapped it around herself because the morning chill had a distinct bite.

Liam grabbed her hand and practically dragged her out of the room. He had on his official Christmas pajamas—a green top with red and white striped bottoms. They did not fit at all, as the cuffs were halfway up his calves. The top was so tight that it couldn't be comfortable. She'd bought them for last Christmas at his dad's, and he'd insisted on wearing them again.

She stumbled after him until they reached the stairs, where he stopped and dropped her hand.

"Go," he said.

Theresa laughed and worked her way down the stairs. "You stay up there, okay?"

"I know, Mom."

When she got to the bottom step, she made a big show of looking left and right around the room and stepped off. "Coast is clear."

Liam pounded down the steps and past her to the Christmas tree, which had about ten gifts under it, all for Liam. She didn't believe in extravagant Christmases. Half the presents were wrapped in her shiny green paper. Liam was on his knees in front of the biggest one near the front, with a green and red Mickey Mouse print, which was from his dad. Or his stepmom, really.

She trotted into the kitchen to preheat the oven and headed over to sit on the couch.

He picked it up and whipped around, his eyes wide with expectation. "Can I open this one?"

Who knew what was in there. Michael didn't have the courtesy to tell her.

"Sure, little man. Let me just get a notepad." She always recorded who gave him what so he could write meaningful thank you notes. She grabbed that, scissors, and a trash bag from the kitchen.

He ripped into the paper, throwing it right and left. Inside was an Amazon box taped shut. He held the box up to her, and she slit the tape so he could yank the tabs open. He fisted the blue fabric inside and dropped the box, which was way bigger than necessary.

She recognized it instantly, and experienced a moment of internal rage.

"A shirt?" he asked.

"It's a Seahawks jersey, sweetie."

"What's that?" He held the shirt in front of him and looked at the front.

"The Seahawks are the Seattle football team." She fumed. But then she realized neither karate or football had come up since the ride home after Thanksgiving. Which was wonderful, but this might bring it back.

"Oh." He studied the shirt in his hands. "Can I put it on?"

"Sure, it looks big enough to fit over your pajamas." She leaned forward to pick up the torn paper and bagged it while he wiggled into the shirt. She snapped a picture of him as he smiled at the phone.

"What do you want to open next?" She grabbed the box and used the scissors to slice open the seams. She lay the flattened box next to her on the couch.

Liam's face was scrunched in concentration while he scanned his options. He picked up the next biggest.

After a handful more, her phone rang. "It's Grammy, Liam."

"Oh!" Liam said, turning with a smile that turned into a grimace. "But I'm busy."

Theresa laughed and answered.

"Merry Christmas, Theresa."

"You too, Mom."

"Are you still doing presents?"

"Yeah, almost done." She watched Liam discover a pair of cute pajamas in a dog print, which didn't get him worked up so he grabbed another box. She laughed and said, "He said he can't talk to you right now since he's busy."

Her mom laughed, too. "Did he like the sweater?"

"Of course." The sweater with a dog on it hadn't excited him, but he'd like it once things calmed down. "You know how he is about dogs right now. He's opening the other one right now. What is it?" She leaned over to pick up the trash as he opened a box.

"Some art paper pads. You know, the higher quality kind."

"Oh, that's wonderful. Thanks, Mom."

"Paper?" Liam looked at Theresa.

"Yeah, honey. It's the kind of paper professional artists use."

He smiled at that.

"Theresa, are you still spending time with that Catholic?"

She flushed at the sudden image of Conall over her in her bed and had to shake off the shiver that went up her spine. She wanted him again more than she should. Not that it was possible.

"Mom, we're not dating. But yes, he comes over to help around the house sometimes." She felt temporarily bold, maybe because of what

Conall had said. She was an adult and should do what she felt was right for herself and her son. "And he reads with Liam."

"What?"

"He's been involved in tutoring kids in reading, so it was perfect." She watched Liam open a stack of books she'd wrapped up as one present. He didn't make a bad face, so that was a good sign. "Liam's doing really well with him. Gaining confidence and everything."

She got up and headed into the kitchen to get the breakfast pizza in the oven.

"Theresa, you need to be careful." Her voice was low. "You'd better make sure you watch that man with him."

"I do. Plus, I know he had a background check to work on the program we have at work. Don't worry. And I added spinach to the breakfast pizza this year."

"Really? That sounds interesting." She sounded genuinely intrigued, and Theresa thought maybe she'd successfully diverted the conversation. "Let me know how it turns out. But I don't trust him."

She sighed. "I know you don't. But I do."

"Theresa," her mom said in a warning tone. "You know you don't always make the best decisions."

She didn't need to listen to this. Liam picked up the last one, the other from Michael. The gift was small and flat, obviously an envelope.

"And those choices are going to hurt that sweet little boy."

That tore at her heart just as Liam ripped open the present and looked inside.

"Hold on a second, Mom. What is it, Liam?"

"I don't know." He handed it to her, and she read it.

Her blood boiled. "You'll get to go to a summer football camp, if you want to go." Michael had paid the tuition for a spot in a Seattle camp.

"Oh." He looked down and scanned his Christmas haul.

"You don't have to go if you don't want to." She needed to convince him he didn't want to go. Karate was one thing, but football was in a different class. She valued his brain too much to allow him to damage it in some stupid, barbaric sport.

To her mom, she said, "Do you want to talk to Liam?"

"Of course."

Liam smiled when she handed the phone to him. He talked with her mom for a few minutes while Theresa picked up the rest of the trash and boxes, chattering about everything he'd gotten.

Theresa tapped him on the shoulder. "Liam, thank her for the paper and the sweater."

He did and then finished the conversation and handed the phone back to her.

"Did you hang up?"

He nodded and stood up to pick up the easel off the couch.

A certain amount of relief washed over her—maybe she wouldn't have to hear the rest of the rant—which was immediately replaced by guilt. The phone rang again.

"Hi, Mom."

"I didn't get to finish. You need to be careful about who you expose Liam to."

"I know—oh, I'm getting another call. Michael. Gotta go. I'll call you. I love you." Before she could lose her nerve, she hung up.

"Liam?"

He was messing with an easel she'd given him, turning it all sorts of different directions.

"It goes like this, honey." She set it upright and pointed to the tray. "See, you put the canvas or paper here."

"Oh." He looked up at her and smiled and her heart swelled with pride for a moment.

"Let's have breakfast."

CONALL REACHED for the doorbell before remembering that he hadn't fixed it for Theresa yet, so he knocked instead. She'd invited him for dinner, knowing he didn't have anyone else local since Isaac had gone to Jenny's parents'.

Liam opened the door wearing a football jersey, which surprised him. But he also wore a good Christmas-day smile, and the smell of turkey wafted out.

"Hey, buddy."

"Merry Christmas!" he grinned.

"You too."

Liam's gaze fell to the box Conall was holding. "What's that?"

"I brought you a little something."

"Really? What is it?"

Theresa appeared behind Liam. "You didn't have to do that, Conall." She put her hands on Liam's shoulders. "Come on, honey, let's get out of the way so he can come inside. It's cold."

She smiled at Conall, and he remembered her laid out on her bed, gorgeous.

Get a grip. She'd said no already.

"Can I have my present now?" Liam asked.

Conall laughed and handed it over.

Liam ran to the couch and started unwrapping it.

Theresa shut the door. "You didn't have to bring him anything."

"I know, but it's fun. Hopefully he likes it."

She stood next to him and crossed her arms while she watched Liam tearing the paper away. "What is it, honey?"

Liam looked at the box like he wasn't quite sure.

"It's a box of art supplies in a nice little case," Conall explained. "It's got pencils, pastels, even charcoal."

Liam worked on opening the box the set came in and slid it out onto the cushion. He smiled, understanding covering his face.

"That's awesome, Liam! Don't forget to thank him."

He smiled at Conall. "Thank you."

She turned to Conall and touched his arm for a second. "Thank you. That was thoughtful of you." She was close enough that she had to look up at him, and he loved it more than he should have.

"It was no big deal."

She smiled. They looked at Liam, who had the case open and was inspecting the pastels.

"Come on in the kitchen. Let me get you something to drink. I bought a winter beer."

"Yeah? That sounds perfect." He followed her in there, and she handed him a bottle from the fridge. He opened the drawer with the can opener, and she quirked an eyebrow at that. Maybe he shouldn't act so familiar with the house.

Not that Liam would notice.

Theresa motioned with her hand. "Let's go sit in the living room while the rolls bake."

Conall sat on the end of the couch opposite Liam, who was still looking through the case. Theresa sat between them and leaned against the back of the sofa.

"So, Liam, what did you get today?" Conall asked.

The boy leaned forward to look at him and listed everything he'd gotten, eyes glowing with happiness while he talked with his hands.

"Did you call your family today?" Theresa asked.

Conall nodded. "Yeah. Talked to everyone."

"Your many cousins?"

He smiled and took a sip of his beer. "All of them except the two that live on the mainland. Everyone goes to one of my aunts' houses, so I just call. She puts me on speaker and everyone yells Merry Christmas and so on. What did you two do?"

Liam held some colored pencils out in front of him and studied the tips.

"We talked to my mom for a bit. Liam's dad hasn't called yet." She swirled her wine. "He'll probably call as soon as we sit down to dinner."

Conall rested his palms on his knees, wanting to turn to face her, but it seemed too intimate with Liam sitting right there. As much as he liked the kid, he half wished Liam was at his dad's so he and Theresa could get up to no good again. Right here, on the couch, maybe.

Theresa took a sip of her wine and put her arm across Liam's shoulders. She looked at Conall and smiled before looking into her glass. He felt guilty for his thoughts. He was in the middle of a comfortable domestic scene. He could really imagine being here on a weekend, watching TV. Or playing that Xbox with Liam. Or even Theresa. Maybe he could convince her to take up gaming again.

No, that sort of thing would never happen, broken as he was.

The timer buzzed, and Theresa scooted off the couch. He had to move his legs for her to squeeze between them and the coffee table.

"Why don't you two sit down at the table?" she said. "I just need to get the rolls."

As soon as she'd dished out mashed potatoes for Liam to go with the slice of turkey already on his plate, her phone started ringing from the living room. "Ah. That'll be Liam's father."

Liam jumped out of his seat and ran to the coffee table to snag the phone. "Hello?"

Theresa added a small amount of green bean casserole to Liam's plate while she cocked her head toward the conversation.

"Merry Christmas," Liam said. He sat back on the couch. Then there was a series of "Yeahs" followed by, "Dad, what's a seahawk?"

Conall smiled. Liam was wearing a Seattle jersey. "I didn't think he was a sports kid."

She poured a little gravy onto Liam's potatoes and looked at Conall with a flat expression. "He's not."

"Ah."

Liam said, "Oh. Okay." Then, "Okay. Bye." He brought the phone back to Theresa, disappointment leaking off him.

Conall smiled at him. "So, Liam, what's a seahawk?"

"I don't know."

"Didn't you ask?" Theresa said as he slid onto his chair.

"He told me it was the football team."

"But you already knew that," she said. "Why didn't you clarify so he'd tell you?"

"He'd get mad." He picked up his spoon and dipped into the potatoes.

She frowned in apparent agreement.

"Well," Conall said, "I think a seahawk is just a type of hawk that hangs out by the sea. An osprey."

"Oh. What do they look like?"

Conall forked a few slices of turkey onto his plate. "I'm not sure, but you could probably find a picture and draw one, don't you think?"

Theresa passed him the potatoes and smiled at him. "We'll look it up after dinner, okay?"

He nodded. Conall thought he didn't seem that excited. He wondered what that was about.

But it wasn't his business, and he might never know. He wasn't truly a part of their lives, which bummed him out more than it should have.

25

_____

Theresa was just grabbing her bag to head out with Sujata and Casey for lunch the Friday after New Year's when her phone rang.

"Oh, I've got to get this," she said. "Hello?"

They headed toward the elevators.

"Ms. Alberts?"

"Yes?"

"This is Principal Turpen from Thomas Jefferson Elementary. Liam is fine, but there has been an incident, and we need you to come to the school."

She stopped walking. "What happened?"

"It's a matter of discipline," the woman explained. "Liam was involved in a fight."

"What? That doesn't sound like him!" How was that possible? She'd taught him to be nonviolent. And did he get hit? "But he's not hurt?"

"No. How—"

"And the other boy?" Theresa was still trying to process the fact that Liam had hit another person.

"He'll be fine. How soon can you get here?"

"About half an hour. I'll leave now." She shook her head as she stood there with wide eyes.

"Okay. We will see you shortly. Thank you."

Casey touched Theresa's arm. "What happened? Is he okay?"

"He apparently got in a fight!" She still couldn't believe it.

"Oh, my God!" Sujata said. "Did a small alien take over your child's body?"

"I know!" Theresa shook her head. "But I've got to go."

Casey reached out and pressed the elevator call button. The whole way to her car, Theresa was going over what could have happened. Who could he have been fighting? And why? He just wasn't like that. He wasn't overly physical, like a lot of boys were. He had his moments, but they were more exceptions than the norm.

She fretted the whole drive there. What if he really was hurt, despite what they'd said? And what did the principal mean when she said the other boy would "be fine?" What had happened to him?

Maybe there was just a mistake. She pulled into a spot in the gravel parking lot across from the loading lanes and headed inside, ducking under a sign that read, "Bully-Free Zone."

Before she even pulled open the office's glass door, she saw Liam sitting with his head down, next to another, bigger boy in a baggy wrestling sweatshirt. His hair was longer than she would have let Liam's get, and she didn't recognize him.

Liam didn't look up until she said his name. His guilty face said it all. She couldn't believe it.

"Ms. Alberts?"

She turned to see the principal.

"Why don't you both come back with me?"

Theresa reached out to take Liam's hand, and they followed Principal Turpen back into her office.

"What's this about?" Theresa asked as the principal walked around her desk. They all sat.

The principal tented her hands and looked at Liam. "Why don't you tell us why you hit Ethan, Liam?"

Liam looked at the floor and shifted in his seat. "I don't know."

"You hit someone?" Theresa asked, still stunned even though she'd believed it before. It was one thing to know it and another to see him admit it.

He nodded without looking at her.

"Please answer me."

Silence.

"Liam," Theresa said sternly.

"Yeah."

She shook her head to clear it. This was crazy. She looked back to the principal. "I'm sorry about this. I don't know what happened. We'll be having a serious conversation when we get home."

"I'm glad to hear it. But you know we have a strict no-fighting policy. We have no choice but to suspend Liam for three days."

Wow. Never did she think her son would be getting in trouble. "Okay, I understand."

Liam didn't say anything on the way to the car. He silently buckled himself into his seat.

Theresa didn't know where to start, so she spent the whole quiet drive home formulating a plan.

Once they parked, she said, "Go on up to your room, and I'll be up there in a bit."

"Okay." He opened the car door and moped his way to the front door.

A glass of wine in hand, she sat on the couch. She leaned back and relaxed a bit. She would have to go upstairs and deal with Liam, but she needed a little break. She finished the glass, sighed, and headed upstairs.

Liam was drawing when she went into his room. She sat on his bed and said, "Come here."

He put his pencil down and sat next to her, looking at his socked feet.

"Tell me what happened."

"I don't know."

She put her arm around his shoulders. "Come on, Liam. I know that's not true."

He didn't say anything so she gently turned his face toward hers. "Come on, honey. I need to know."

He frowned and then said, "Ethan pushed me."

"And then what happened?"

He averted his eyes. "I hit him in the face."

"You punched him?" She couldn't keep the shock out of her voice. This was unbelievable. She dropped his chin.

He nodded, looking both angry and on the verge of tears.

How could he punch somebody? How did he even know how? "Did your dad teach you how to do that?"

"No." He sniffed.

"What have I told you about hitting people?" She rubbed his back.

"Not to."

"That's right. Violence is always wrong, sweetie. It never solves anything. Promise me you won't do it again."

"But, Mom—he pushed me first!"

"You need to get a teacher if he's pushing you."

His frown deepened, and he glanced over at her as if he might say something else, but stayed quiet.

"You promise?"

"Yeah."

"Okay. Now, you know you're in big trouble. I'm going to take away your drawing supplies. I want you to think about what you did."

His mouth formed an O of surprise and horror. He looked like he'd been struck speechless.

Theresa got up and went over to his drawing table to pick up everything. "I'm going to go make dinner. I'll call you when it's ready."

THAT NIGHT, Liam sat at the table with a big frown, pushing his potatoes and chicken around. He'd obviously been crying a little.

Theresa could understand. She felt a little like crying herself. Her little boy had done a terrible thing. Was this the start of something? Would she have to figure out how to deal with it on a regular basis? She was struggling enough this time.

He hadn't even eaten any of his spinach yet. One bite of chicken.

"Liam, eat some of your spinach. And your chicken."

"I don't want to!"

Theresa set her fork down and took a deep breath. She leaned over to be closer to Liam and said, "You will eat three more bites of chicken and all of your spinach."

His frown deepened as he clenched his jaw and gripped his fork tighter.

"I'm serious. You will eat and then go back upstairs to think some more about what you did."

"You don't care that he pushed me!"

She put her hand on his shoulder. "Of course I care, honey. He should not have done that. He's in trouble, too. I'm sure his parents are having the same conversation with him."

Liam muttered something.

"What?" she asked. This attitude of his was something new, and she didn't like it.

"Nothing." He pushed his potatoes around more.

Theresa gripped his shoulder. Not too tight, but enough so he knew she meant business. "Tell me what you said."

He stared at his plate.

"Liam," she said firmly.

"He's mean."

"I'm sorry, honey. We can't control what other people are. But we can control how we act toward them. Have you ever heard the phrase 'turn the other cheek?'"

He shook his head.

"It comes from the Bible. It means if someone does something mean to you, you shouldn't try to get revenge on them. Be the better person and rise above the conflict."

Liam looked up at her and blinked. She thought he might be about to say something else, but he didn't.

"Eat some chicken," Theresa said.

His shoulders slumped, but then he ate a piece of chicken.

They made it through the rest of the meal, and Liam stared at the napkins in the center of the table, swinging his legs.

Theresa got up to take her plate to the sink. "Rinse your plate off, little man. I'm going to go get the mail." In the hubbub of earlier, she'd forgotten.

It was freezing outside so she threw her coat over her shoulders and walked out to the mailbox. She found a plastic bag that must hold her new Hawaiian shirt and grabbed the rest of the mail—junk—before glancing down the street.

A man was walking his dog and heading toward them. Conall.

She needed to tell him not to come for the tutoring the next day. She could just wave and head inside and then text him, but it would be more courteous to wait. She hugged her coat tighter and watched him approach.

Admired him was more like it. He'd spotted her and waved, and now she watched him, even his gait appealed to her. Confident and comfortable.

Maddy stopped but he urged her on.

"Hey, what's up?" he said as he got close enough for talking. Conall smiled at her, and an unexpected wave of desire washed over her.

But it would never work. She couldn't handle a relationship on top of motherhood.

"Hi. Actually, I needed to let you know, the tutoring is off for tomorrow."

Maddy bumped her leg so she reached down to tentatively pet her.

"Maddy," Conall said while tugging on her leash. "Come on now, give Theresa some space."

"She's okay." She leaned forward to pet her, rubbing behind her ears. She held up the package in her hands. "My Hawaiian shirt."

"That's good. I'm excited to see you in it." He grinned before looking thoughtful. "What's up with the tutoring?"

"Oh, geez. It's just for this week. It would be great if you came back next Saturday." Theresa looked up from Maddy to Conall. "The worst thing. He fought another boy at school and got suspended!"

His eyes widened. "Oh. What happened?"

"I'm not quite sure, but it doesn't matter. He knows it's wrong to hit someone for any reason."

"Yeah?" He sounded surprised.

"What, you don't agree?"

"Well, there's always self-defense."

"These are little boys."

"That's true." He opened his mouth like he might say something else, but didn't.

"Maddy!" Liam called as he came running from the front door.

"Hey, buddy," Conall said as Liam started petting her.

"I love her." Liam reached over to hug the dog.

Theresa moved to stand behind her son. "He's still angling for a dog."

Conall smiled at her. "Dogs are nice. I'm a fan."

Liam looked up shyly at Conall and said, "I did it, Conall."

Conall's eyes narrowed with the curiosity that Theresa also felt. "Did what?"

"Ethan."

Now Theresa's curiosity redoubled. Ethan was the name of the kid Liam had fought.

Conall's brow was furrowed until it relaxed and understanding bloomed on Conall's face, and he looked at Theresa sheepishly.

"What's he talking about?" she asked. When Conall said nothing, she looked at Liam again, who was now looking at the ground. Now she got it. "You told him to hit Ethan?"

Conall grimaced. "No, that's not what happened."

"How could you?!"

Liam said, "Mom, he was—"

"I don't care what the reason is! Go to your room, Liam!"

Liam's eyes filled with tears, and he turned and ran inside. Maddy's leash went taut as she chased after him.

"Theresa, I'm sorry. I—"

"I can't believe you." She hadn't been this angry since Michael's Thanksgiving. "You can't be around him. That's just not okay."

"The kid must have been bullying him and I—"

"He was being bullied?" That's what Liam had been trying to tell her at the table. She felt sick. How could she have missed that?

"Look, something similar happened to me when I was his age."

"So you told him to hit this kid?"

"It didn't happen that way, Theresa. I told him what happened with a bully I had when we were reading that book. I didn't realize he was being bullied."

"I can't trust you around him anymore. I'm sorry." She looked at his guilty face. "I appreciate the time you've put into working with him so far, but that's over."

"Theresa... I'm sorry." He was clearly upset, but it didn't move her.

She stood glaring at him, her hands on her hips, until he turned and left. She had a lot to think about, and to talk to Liam about.

26

That evening Conall worked on making his own version of spam musubi, which would keep for Monday's lunch.

He took the pot of rice off the burner and added some rice vinegar to it and stirred, picturing the pot he and Clarissa had had. He shook his head to clear the pain that memory brought and set the pot to the side before pouring a healthy amount of vegetable oil in a skillet. The spam had been marinating in a mixture of oyster sauce and soy sauce for several minutes.

The image of Theresa's face—red with anger this time, not arousal —came back to him, as it had been with him all day. Of course, she was right, at least partially. He should have realized Liam was being bullied based on how he reacted when Conall had told him about his own experiences. If he had, he would have told Theresa.

The oil popped when he placed the slices of spam in the pan, one drop hitting his arm, which stung for a second. The universe was paying him back for missing the obvious.

He'd always been the cool older cousin, so he'd done a lot of pseudo-parenting and should have known.

He was surprised at Theresa, though. She seemed to be one of those "violence never solves anything" people, when that was patently untrue. It solved some things, unfortunately.

Self-defense might have solved Liam's problem, even if he had gotten him in trouble for it. That was how it went, sometimes. You fight back, and the issue disappears. Conall had been shy as a kid, too. And small and scrawny. He hadn't really grown until his last year of college, when he'd hit his six feet. So it wasn't surprising that he'd had to face down his own bully in elementary school.

After wrapping each musubi in nori—seaweed paper—he made up a plate and sat down on the couch, propping his bare feet up on the coffee table. Was Theresa going to forgive him, or was work going to be awkward, too? He chewed away, the slight crispness of the spam against the soft rice distracting him from his thoughts.

Afterward, he went into the kitchen to wrap up the musubi for Monday.

He was worried to see how Theresa would be at work.

THERESA STOOD in the doorway of Liam's room Saturday morning, finally calmed down enough to attempt another conversation with him about what had happened. She needed to understand why he'd done something so out of character, and what Conall had said to encourage it.

She wondered if she should have let Conall explain his side of the story better. Probably. But what could he say that would excuse it?

Liam lay on his bed on his stomach in his jeans and sweatshirt with his face toward the wall. Since he still wasn't allowed to draw, play video games, or watch TV, he was moping like a champ.

"Liam."

"Hmm?" He didn't turn around.

She stepped in and sat down on his bed. His socks were a little big, and the toes of them were stretched out past his feet. When he didn't move, she squeezed his hand. "Sit up, honey."

He shifted until he was sitting and even leaned against her, so she wrapped her arm around him.

She brushed the hair off his forehead and saw his cheeks were red.

"Why were you crying, honey?"

"I wasn't."

"Okay." That wasn't true. "Are you bored out of your mind?"

"Yeah." He sniffed.

"Do you understand why you're in so much trouble?"

"Because of Ethan."

"Because you *hit* Ethan." She put her hand on his chin so he would look at her. "You know how I feel about violence. Did Conall tell you to hit him?"

He averted his eyes. "I don't like Ethan."

"Not liking somebody is not a reason to hit them."

Liam frowned.

Conall had said Liam was being bullied. "Did Ethan tease you?"

He shrugged. "I guess."

"Is that it?" She would have to have a talk with the school. She pulled him tightly into her side and kissed the top of his head.

"He punches me sometimes."

"He *punches* you? Where?" Who was this Ethan? How could anybody punch Liam?

He looked up at her. "On the playground."

"No, I mean where on your body?" She grew queasy just thinking about it.

He put his hand on his stomach.

"On your tummy?"

"I can't breathe."

"He hits you so hard you can't breathe?" This was unbelievable. She pulled him closer against her. She felt him nod but he said nothing.

She wasn't sure what to do with her anger so they sat there for a moment in silence.

"Mom?"

Theresa's phone rang, and she saw it was her mom, but she didn't answer. "Yeah, little man?"

"When can I see Conall again?"

She hadn't told him yet. "He's not going to read with you anymore."

Liam's head jerked up. "Why not?"

"Because I can't trust him."

"But I like him!" His eyes were wide.

"I know, but he's not good for you."

Liam frowned and looked back down. "What about Maddy?"

"I'm sorry, Liam, but you probably won't see Maddy very often, either."

"It's not fair."

"Honey, I need you to promise me you will never hit anyone else."

"Even if they hit me first?"

"You come to me if that happens." She was going to have to work to undo the damage Conall had done.

For now, she went downstairs and poured herself a fortifying glass of wine and sat on the couch to call her mom.

"Hi, honey. Why didn't you answer?"

"Hi, Mom. I was talking with Liam."

"Is everything okay?" She sounded worried.

"It's fine. He just got into trouble at school." She traced her finger along the seam of the seat cushion next to her. "He got in a fight."

"What?!" her mom exclaimed. "See, this is what I told you would happen. It must be that Catholic's fault."

"Mom, it's not Conall's fault." Oh, but it was. This was so much worse because her mom was right.

"Well, you say that. But you don't really know. They can be insidious."

Theresa sighed. Was she right? It wasn't because he was Catholic; that was stupid. But it made her doubt her judgment. Again. She'd truly thought Conall was good for him, but she'd been wrong. Again.

After telling Theresa about her dad, her mom asked, "Have you found a church yet?"

Maybe she did need to start going. Maybe that would get Liam back on the path of nonviolence. But the mere thought wearied her. There wasn't enough time in the week.

"Hmm?" her mom prompted.

Even if he was sort of the devil, Conall might have been right about it being her life and choices. But she just didn't have the nerve to push back. "Not yet. I'll see when I can."

"Theresa, you need to."

"I know, Mom." She took a breath. "Look, I need to go. I have work to do."

"That blasted job of yours, Theresa. You know what I think of it."

"Yes, I know."

27

On Monday a week and a half later, the McDonald's playground was surprisingly empty after she'd picked Liam up. He'd been back at school for three days now. Theresa sent him out there while she ordered. When she sat down with their tray at one of the white tables, Liam was in a red tube that looped above her.

"Hey, honey." She waved at him, and he grinned at her through the plastic window. "Come on down and eat your burger."

He crawled through the tunnel and emerged from the ball pit. "I'm hungry."

"Good. I got you a Happy Meal. With fries this time."

"Oh!" Usually she opted for the healthier choice of apples, but she felt like letting him splurge this time.

He ran over, sat, and picked up the Happy Meal box and dumped it upside down on the tray. The fries fell out of the bag and flew all over the place.

"Whoa there, Liam. Careful."

He unwrapped the burger and took a bite while Theresa scooted some fries to the side and squeezed ketchup out onto the wrapper. She watched him eat while she worked on her salad. He was in a better mood since the car.

"Can I play more?" There were a handful of fries left but the burger was gone.

"Okay. We have to leave in fifteen minutes." He stood up so fast that the chair nearly toppled backward and ran back into the ball pit. She hoped he wouldn't hide in there. It wasn't his style, but you never knew. She'd never be able to get him out.

Soon Liam was buried in the innards of the colorful PlayPlace at McDonald's, climbing around in silence except for the occasional "oof." It was otherwise empty, and he was focused on his own play.

They were going to be there for a bit and then head over to the library to get some new books and do some reading.

"Mom, look at me!"

She looked up at her son, waving to her from a plastic bubble encased in yellow.

"Hi, honey!" She smiled and waved back.

Liam leaped into the ball pit with a small yell, which made Theresa laugh to herself. She was glad to see him happy. He'd been morose since Conall wasn't coming by anymore.

Conall. She couldn't get him out of her head. He'd seemed like a genuinely good guy. All the help he'd given her on the house. Even if it had been just to get her into bed, it was still very nice. She really did get something tangible out of it, after all, in addition to a handful of earth-moving orgasms. A nice set of bookshelves.

She'd never be able to look at those again without picturing the kisses they'd shared in front of them.

The last Friday night she'd spent with Casey and Sujata flitted into her mind, because of their opinions on the matter of whether Conall was entirely in the wrong or not. First off, she'd accidentally revealed that she'd slept with Conall, and they were both fascinated by that. But Sujata hadn't heard the full story of Liam's fight.

"So why are you mad at him?" Sujata had asked.

"He told Liam to fight the kid at school."

"What?" Sujata's eyes were wide.

"In his defense, the kid was bullying Liam," Casey said.

Theresa jerked her head toward Casey. "That doesn't matter. Liam knows how I feel about violence. He should have gone to a teacher."

"Wait, what?" Sujata said. "That would just make things worse."

"That's what I said," Casey added.

"No, it wouldn't. I don't want Liam going around hitting people."

"But if he hits back in defense, how is that wrong?" Sujata asked.

Theresa frowned. If both of them thought it wasn't bad, maybe she should reconsider.

Casey took a sip of her wine before saying, "Things are different for boys, as much as we'd like to pretend they aren't. I think the politics of boyhood sometimes demand self-defense."

"How do you know?" Theresa asked.

"Marcus went through it." Marcus was Casey's younger brother. "It was sort of magical. The kid wouldn't leave him alone and finally Marcus just lost it and started whaling on him. The kid cried and ran off, and then never bothered Marcus again."

Sujata nodded.

"Really?" This gave Theresa something to think about.

"And going to a teacher just leads to retribution," Sujata added.

Theresa rested her forehead in her hands. "I just don't know. I've always been so adamantly opposed to it, and Liam is so nonviolent."

"Maybe this was the same as Marcus's moment," Sujata said.

"Has anything happened this week?" Casey asked.

Theresa had shaken her head. "Not that Liam has mentioned. And I've asked him point blank every day."

Sujata had squeezed Theresa's arm. "Maybe it worked."

"Mom!" Liam called from the ball pit, bringing her abruptly back to the present.

"Yeah?"

"Watch me!"

He climbed up and fell backwards into the pit.

Her heart twinged with the fear she always had. What if he hit his head, or landed weird? But she had to trust the world a bit more. "That's great, honey!"

So, maybe giving Liam advice wasn't the worst thing Conall could have done. Liam had said the kid had left him alone since then.

But still, Conall should have told her about the bullying. Whatever experiences he'd had growing up, it was her right to parent

Liam as she saw fit. She shook her head to clear it of thoughts of Conall.

Theresa watched Liam for a while longer until he disappeared from view. She checked the time and called in the general direction of the slide, "Liam, it's time to go."

He scrambled around a little more and then emerged, rosy-cheeked, at the bottom of the blue slide before coming over to stand in front of her.

"Are we going home?" he asked.

"No, we're going to the library. We need to read a little."

He frowned. "I don't want to."

"I know you don't, but this is what we need to do. You have to practice more." She picked up her bag, and Liam followed her out to the car, head down.

He crossed his arms after he got buckled in and didn't say anything all the way to the library.

He trailed behind her up the steps and through the library's front door. By the time they got to the children's room downstairs, he was way behind her.

"Come on, little man. It's not the end of the world."

He crossed his arms and sat on the bottom step. "Mom, I don't want to read with you."

"Why not?" That sort of hurt. "I know you like stories."

"I want to read with Conall."

"Honey, we've talked about this." She walked back to stand in front of him. "Conall is a nice man and I know you like him, but he isn't going to be around anymore."

"Why not?" He looked up at her with wide eyes.

She sighed. She hadn't told him the real reason, because she didn't need to justify her decisions. But that meant he didn't understand why and it seemed arbitrary.

So she'd give him the modified version. She sat next to him. "Liam, you know how I feel about violence. Conall told you it was okay for you to hit someone else. He should have talked to me about Ethan first. *You* should have talked to me about him first, then Conall wouldn't have had to be the one."

Liam's frown deepened.

"Excuse us." A woman with two young kids stood in front of Theresa.

"Oh, sorry." Theresa stood up so they could get by. The little girl, who looked about four, stared at Liam as they passed.

"Come on, sweetie. Let's go in."

"No, I don't want to."

"You can sit out here if you want, but it means you won't get to choose which books we'll check out."

He crossed his arms again and looked very determined to stay put.

"Liam," she said firmly.

He avoided looking at her.

She thought back to the days when she could solve the problem simply by picking him up. Those days were long gone. This sort of thing made her feel so powerless.

"Liam," she said again, even more forcefully than before. She might have even raised her voice.

He jerked his head up and looked at her. There were tears in his eyes, which stunned her. It also broke her heart a little. This was all about Conall. They both liked him more than they should.

Liam got up and followed her into the room, where he picked out a handful of books.

Once they were in the car, he said, "Mom, I miss Maddy."

"I know you do, honey." And she missed Maddy's owner. There wasn't anything else to say.

CONALL STOOD behind the table in the small conference room to take a picture of the diagrams on the whiteboard. He and Vivek were working through the design for another program they'd be working on together.

"You will send it to me, as well?" Vivek asked.

"Sure." He checked to make sure everything was readable and emailed the picture to Vivek and himself.

There was a knock on the door, and Sujata poked her head inside.

"We're almost done," Conall said.

She nodded and shut the door again.

Vivek's brown cheeks had a distinct pinkish tinge. "You are lucky to sit near her," he said.

Conall laughed as he walked over to erase the whiteboard. "You think so?" So he wasn't the only guy here who admired a coworker.

"Yes."

"Talk to her. She's nice."

"I try, but it is difficult." Vivek looked earnestly at Conall.

"I know what you mean. It can be. But keep trying." He wiped off the last black line on the board and set the eraser down in the tray.

Vivek stood and Conall followed him out, nodding at Sujata as they passed her.

He made his way back to his desk, throwing Theresa a quick glance. What he'd said to Vivek resonated with him. He should keep trying with Theresa—he should apologize. He at least owed her that.

As he neared Theresa's desk, she popped out of her pod into his path, and he had to stop.

"Oh, sorry," she said, flushing. "I wasn't paying attention."

"No problem. How are you?" He really wanted to know how she'd been. He'd missed her.

"I'm good. How about you?"

"Oh, you know. Good. How was your weekend?" This was uninspiring. He thought of apologizing now, but it might not be appropriate at work. It could make her uncomfortable.

"Busy." She wasn't avoiding his gaze, but she wasn't really looking at him, either.

"Yeah." Okay, this was painful. He felt a certain sense of desperation over the fact that things were so messed up. "Alright, I'll let you get to wherever you were going."

She smiled and then looked at him and something flashed across her face, though he couldn't read it.

He moved around her and headed back to his desk.

Fuck, he'd screwed up. He wanted so badly to explain. He would have to go over to her house and convince her to listen.

Not being in Theresa's and Liam's lives felt wrong.

He sat and typed his password into his computer in order to start working on some code, but he couldn't stop thinking about both Theresa.

He not only missed Theresa, but he missed spending time with Liam. How was the kid doing? He hoped Liam didn't backslide in his reading, because he had been improving. They'd worked beyond self-confidence, which was half the battle.

"Conall."

He turned to face Iryna. "Hi."

"You're going to tonight's game?" she asked.

"Of course."

"Great, I'll see you there. I've got to leave early for an appointment, but I'll be there by the start."

That was more information than he needed. They didn't need to coordinate. "That's good. I'm looking forward to it."

She smiled and turned to leave, effectively leaving behind a contrail of flowery pink dust. He glanced over at Sujata and realized she'd probably watched the whole exchange.

He wondered what Theresa thought of him spending time with Iryna. Was she jealous? At least a little?

He sighed and turned back to his desk.

Even though it was pretty clear that any chance with Theresa was over, he'd call her this weekend and hope she'd listen to his apology.

28

Theresa was waiting in the meeting room when Conall appeared in the doorway on Wednesday. He smiled as he came in. The two of them were meeting about the data warehouse again.

Oh, he was such a sight. Her heart twisted at the thought that she could never have a relationship with him. It wasn't fair.

But she'd temporarily forgotten how mad she was at him. He'd undermined her parenting, which was still not okay with her.

"Hey," he said as he pulled out a chair to sit.

"Hi." She forced a smile but looked away, unable to reconcile the two disparate feelings she was experiencing.

"So," he started.

"I was just hoping you could help me out with these aggregations tables."

"Sure." He leaned back in the chair and rested one ankle on his knee. When she looked at his face again, he had an expression she couldn't read. Something like guilt, but she wasn't sure what else was mixed in there.

Theresa stood up and began sketching out the table design she'd been considering. She narrated as she went, and Conall nodded his agreement along the way.

They'd made it through four of the six tables when Theresa's phone rang. She checked the number and saw it was Liam's school.

"Oh, I've got to take this," she said to Conall, capping the marker and setting it on the table.

He nodded and rested his hands on the table.

"Hello?" She tried to keep the sudden nerves out of her voice.

"Ms. Alberts? This is Mrs. Winters." Liam's teacher.

"Yes? Is everything okay?"

"Yes, Liam's fine. I just wanted to talk to you about something if you have a moment."

Conall stood up and mouthed, "I'll go."

She nodded and said, "Sure," into the phone.

"He's behaving differently during reading time. I had noticed he'd become more confident, but starting last week he's been disruptive when we read. Today he refused to read when it was his turn, which is so unlike him."

Theresa's mouth fell open. She'd noticed some improvement? Was that from Conall? And it had been so fast, and noticeable?

The teacher continued. "Is anything going on that it would help me to know about?"

Theresa looked at the door Conall had just shut as he'd left. "I had someone working with him on his reading."

"Oh, that's wonderful."

"But we stopped it a couple weeks ago." Theresa sat and closed her eyes. This might change everything.

"Oh, I see. Is there someone else? I can recommend some professional tutors I know are wonderful."

Maybe that would be the answer. She still had the list from the specialist. Especially if she could find a male tutor to work with him. Maybe he'd respond as well to another man as he did to Conall. "Yes, please send me those contacts. I will look into that. Of course, I'll talk to him about his behavior, too."

"Wonderful. I know we just need to get him past this. He's such a sweet boy. And his drawings are just stunning. I've never seen anything like it."

Theresa smiled, proud again. Though the idea of him being disruptive and refusing to do what his teacher said was disturbing. She hoped it wasn't the start of a pattern.

"Thank you for speaking with me," Mrs. Winters said.

"Thank you." She hit the end call button and sighed. She checked her email on her phone and already had one from the teacher with the recommended tutors, which was remarkable. She must have already had the email ready to go. From their names, there wasn't a man among them, which was very disappointing. But there were some tutoring centers listed, and she could call them. Maybe they'd have someone who could help.

She checked the time and realized they had this room for another twenty-five minutes. She could get Conall back in here, or go ahead and call. She could follow up with him later.

So she called the first center on the list, and then the second. Neither had any male tutors with after-school openings at the moment, which was both surprising and very frustrating.

She finished off the rest of her work for the day and left to pick Liam up.

When she got to the after-school center, he was drawing at his table. But he spotted her when she came in this time.

"Hi, Mom." He smiled at her and set his pencil down.

"Hi, little man. Ready?" He didn't seem to feel guilty about anything, so he probably had no idea Mrs. Winters had called.

He nodded, and soon they were in the car.

She pulled out onto the street. "Liam?"

"Hmm?"

"Do you need to tell me about anything that happened today?"

He didn't say anything. She could see his face in the rearview mirror, and it was clear he was trying to figure out what to say. He knew what she was referring to.

"Mrs. Winters called me," Theresa said.

He was still quiet.

"You have to do what the teacher says. You can't just choose what to do at school."

"But I *hate* reading!" The words exploded out of him.

"You haven't always hated it. And you like it when I read to you. Why is it different now?"

"Why can't I see Conall anymore?"

Ah, so it was still about him.

"Liam, we've talked about this." But maybe letting Conall work with him again wasn't such a bad idea, after all. If she could have a conversation about boundaries and then make sure not to leave them alone. She would have overheard the offending conversation if it wasn't because of the stupid overflowing toilet, because that had to be when it occurred.

Or maybe… Her heart lurched. Maybe she would have never found out about the bullying at all because Liam wouldn't have told anyone.

But still, Liam's behavior was unacceptable.

"Honey, I'm going to have to take away your drawing supplies tonight. You cannot act out that way at school."

"Mom, no!" The utter desperation in his voice was heart-breaking, but he had to learn.

CONALL WAS PACKING up after the game Thursday night when Chuck suggested they go out to the bar to celebrate yet another win. He didn't feel like going because he needed to get some more work done tonight, but he felt obligated.

"Are you coming, Conall?" Iryna asked, approaching from behind Chuck.

"I suppose for a few minutes."

"Great," she said, smiling at him as if she was the reason he'd said yes. She walked back over to where Hannah stood, and the two of them headed out. Iryna slipped the strap of her pink duffel bag over her shoulder.

At least she hadn't offered him a ride.

Should he go for it with her? He deserved to get laid every now and again, right?

The thought just didn't appeal to him at all. She wasn't his type—

anyone who was so committed to a single color couldn't be that interesting. She wouldn't be open to new things.

Also, he had a sense that she wouldn't be good at keeping things quiet at work.

Plus, most importantly, she wasn't Theresa, whose smiling face was what he was picturing right now. Even though it was her pissed off face he should be imagining, since that was how she felt at the moment.

"Ready to go?" Isaac said, clapping Conall on the back.

They headed out with Jenny so Conall took the back seat.

"What's going on between you and Iryna, Conall?" Isaac asked.

"Absolutely nothing."

"She seems pretty fascinated by you," Jenny said.

Conall shrugged and looked out the window. "What can I say?"

His thoughts went back to Theresa except for their meeting. He really hadn't seen much of her this week. She was avoiding him, as much as that was possible at work. Occasionally, they'd pass between pods or see each other in the kitchen, but they didn't chat. And she hadn't visited Sujata much.

He wanted to ask after Liam, but it felt off-limits.

He was going to call her on Saturday.

SATURDAY AFTERNOON, Conall sat on the couch with his laptop on his thighs. He picked up his phone for the tenth time. He'd been meaning to text Theresa all day, but he was worried she wouldn't respond.

Which was ridiculous. He was behaving like a lovestruck teenager. This was about an adult apology.

He composed and sent a text.

—*I wanted to talk to you. Can I call you this evening?*—

There.

And if she didn't reply, he'd just call her anyway. He'd try at nine, when he guessed Liam would be in bed. And if that didn't—

Ding.

Ah. He read her text.

—I'll call you once Liam's in bed—

Good. He could say what he needed to say, and he hoped she'd understand.

He set his laptop on the cushion next to him. After picking up and doing some laundry, he made dinner and then sat back down to continue working. And to wait for Theresa's call.

He dealt with some emails—it had ceased to amaze him how normal it was for everyone to work on weekends—and worked on code.

At 8:53, his phone rang.

"Hello?"

"Hi."

"How are you?" How could talking to her feel so awkward?

"Yeah, good. I'm glad you texted. I wanted to talk to you, too."

That surprised him. "What about?"

"Well, why don't you go first."

Oh, shit. Was she still pissed off at him?

There were few couple heartbeats where neither said anything. He should stop stalling and just go.

"I want to apologize for what happened with Liam. I truly didn't know he was being bullied, but I should have figured it out from how he reacted."

"You didn't know?" she asked.

"No. He didn't say anything, just asked a question or two about what I'd told him, and we continued on with the book."

She sighed. "So, can you tell me what exactly happened?"

"We were reading a book with a bully in it, and Liam asked me why some kids were like that. I ended up telling him about when I was being bullied at school, and how my dad had told me to stand up for myself. When I did, it stopped. He was impressed by that. That was it."

She was quiet.

"I'm sorry for not figuring it out."

"The reason I was angry," Theresa started. She paused before continuing, "Was that I thought you were undermining my parenting by giving him advice against my own."

"Theresa, come on. I think you're a wonderful mother and are doing a fine job, despite what your mom and ex-husband might think."

She was quiet for a moment. "That's sweet of you to say."

He hadn't said it to be sweet. He'd meant it. He kept quiet.

"But do you really think hitting the other kid was the best solution?"

"That's kind of how it is with boys, Theresa. Being physical is pretty normal."

She was quiet again, before saying, "But Liam's never been like that."

"Sure, but that doesn't mean the other kid isn't, which has a direct impact on Liam."

She didn't say anything.

"Listen, I was little as a kid and an easy target. Standing up for myself solved the problem."

"I guess I'm starting to believe it. My friends talked to me about it. Boys just deal with things differently. I think the boy has left Liam alone since it happened." She took a breath. "Conall?"

"Yeah?" He felt hopeful again.

"He misses you so much. And he's started acting up during reading at school. Would you be willing to work with him again, once I get his behavior under control?"

She'd trust him again? "Sure, I'd be happy to."

"But can you promise me you will just read? No secret advice. And anything he says, you have to tell me."

"Of course. I get it. If he tells me anything at all, I will talk to you about it." He would, but then Liam wouldn't trust him with much, but he understood her view. She was Liam's parent; he wasn't.

"Even if it doesn't seem important?"

"Even then."

"Okay." She cleared her throat. "Can you... do you want to start again soon?"

"Sure. We can go back to the old schedule."

"Wednesday?"

Why not? He wasn't too busy. "Yeah."

"Okay, thanks Conall. I... I'll see you at work tomorrow, then?"

"Yep."

Thank God. Things would get back to normal. The new tension between them was intolerable.

29

Wednesday evening after dinner, Theresa finished wiping down the counter and listened to Conall reading to Liam. This time Conall seemed to be doing all the reading. She'd talk to him afterward about why that was. There might be a good reason. She trusted Conall, even if he'd betrayed her once.

What he'd said about her being a good mother had touched her, because she felt like he'd meant it.

She pulled off several paper towels and sprayed down the big window behind the kitchen table, again remembering what she and Conall had done on that table. Conall's deep voice filled her head as she wiped the glass clean, her ears ringing with the memory.

She wiped down the small window over the sink and then moved into the dining room to get the one in there.

Liam looked up at her and seemed surprised to see her there.

"Come on, kiddo, don't get distracted," Conall said. He glanced at her and smiled when he said it.

Liam turned back to the book and Conall started reading again.

Before finishing the dining room window, she stared at the two of them sitting next to each other on the couch, finding the image comforting, almost like Conall belonged there.

She'd done all the quiet chores she could, so she grabbed her laptop and sat down next to Liam, who got distracted by her again, this time making an unhappy face.

"Mo-o-om," he whined.

She raised her eyebrows at him.

"We can still read," Conall said. Liam's frown didn't fade but he turned back to the book and Conall continued.

They read three more books while Theresa worked through her email and a specification she was finishing up. She checked the status of a couple long programming jobs that would run for another day and a half or so. Everything was fine.

"Well, that's all the books we have," Conall said.

Liam leaned forward to pull one of the books off the coffee table. "Can we read this one again?"

Theresa rubbed his back. "Conall's got to get home, sweetie."

"I'll be back on Saturday, buddy." Conall stood up, and Theresa glanced over, realizing her eyes were about crotch-level, which was not a good thing because she still wanted him.

Thinking about him that way was such a bad idea. Even if he was still interested in a relationship, she couldn't.

She averted her eyes, and he stepped around the coffee table toward the front door. She met him there and smiled at him.

"What do you say to Conall, Liam?"

"Thank you."

"No problem, buddy." Conall prompted Liam to fist-bump him, which made Theresa laugh.

"Okay, honey, why don't you go on upstairs and get ready for bed."

Liam asked, "Are you going to talk about me?"

"No, we have to talk about work," she said.

"Then why can't I listen?"

Conall raised his eyebrows and smiled.

"It's adult stuff. You'd be bored. Go on up."

Liam sighed and headed up the stairs.

"Adult stuff?" Conall asked with a smirk. "I know what I think of when someone says 'adult.'"

She rolled her eyes. "Whatever. Now let's talk about him."

He laughed and stepped closer so he was just a comfortable friend distance away. She found herself straining to catch a whiff of his scent, but couldn't.

"What do you want to know?" he asked.

"I'm just curious why you didn't have him read today."

He nodded. "I sensed that he needs his confidence built up again. I want him to be comfortable with me. He might still be, but if he's been acting out, maybe we needed to reset. Saturday I'll have him read."

"Okay, that makes sense to me." He was putting thought into this. Putting her sweet little boy first. "Thanks."

"You're welcome." His gaze flicked down to her mouth for a second.

Desire rushed through her and she mentally cursed herself. She should not be letting him affect her this way.

"Guess I should get going," he said, a tinge of regret in his voice.

As much as she wanted to come up with a reason for him to stay, she opened the door and said, "Yeah. But thanks again for all your help. I appreciate it."

"Sure. I'll see you tomorrow."

Yes, he would. She hoped by then she'd have herself back under control.

On Saturday afternoon, Conall brought Maddy with him to Theresa's. After they finished the tutoring session, Liam went outside to play with her, leaving Conall and Theresa alone again.

"Can I get you a drink?" Theresa asked him from the kitchen.

He headed in there and leaned against the counter, watching her stand with her hand on the fridge door, looking at him. "I'll take a water. All the reading dries me out."

"Sure thing." She stepped over to the cabinet and reached inside to the top shelf for two glasses. In the process, her t-shirt raised up enough that he could see her flat stomach, and wave of unexpected desire tightened his groin.

He really wasn't past this woman. The image of her stretched out on the kitchen table blew into his mind.

She turned around, mouth open like she was going to say something. Instead she stared at him, before swallowing and saying, "Ice?"

She must have seen the look on his face, which reflected his thoughts. He cleared his expression and smiled. "Sure."

She filled both glasses from the fridge dispenser and then pulled a pitcher of water out. She glanced up at him once while filling the first one, looking a little nervous. She still wanted him, of that he was sure.

When she handed it to him, their fingers brushed, and it made him smile again.

She filled the second one, and he followed her to the couch.

She sat sideways to face him, so he did the same.

"Conall," she started, pausing. "I so appreciate what you're doing with Liam. You are a wonderful man, and I'm sure you'll make a great father one day."

That got him through the heart, and he looked away. "That's nice of you to say, but I can't."

"Can't what?"

"Have kids."

When she looked confused, he looked away and added. "Physically. I'm broken."

She stared at him, her face neutral. She was probably concentrating on not looking surprised. Or horrified.

Then she spoke. "I don't think that makes you broken."

He looked out the window and spotted Liam running by with Maddy.

"You'll find someone who already has a child. God works that way." She said it with a certain amount of earnestness but without pity.

Okay, why *not* her?

"Go out with me, Theresa." Where had that come from?

"What?" Her eyes widened.

"We have great chemistry. You know we do." They did. Her understanding and lack of judgment made him bold.

She turned away, and he took the opportunity to scoot closer, close enough that he could reach forward and cup her chin. With gentle pressure, he turned her back so she looked at him again.

Her face was tense, but she was staring at his mouth. So, he leaned forward and kissed her. It was almost tentative at first, but then she opened for him. Yet as soon as he slid his tongue in, she pulled back.

"I can't date you," she said hastily.

He smiled, confidence brewing because although her words were negative, her face showed she was wavering. "Yes, you can."

"Conall, I…"

"Why not? I like you, you like me, even your kid likes me."

"What about work?"

"I can keep it professional. I'm sure you can, too. We have so far, despite the distinctly unprofessional activities we engaged in over Thanksgiving."

She looked off to the side and blinked, then chewed on her lip, something he hadn't seen her do before.

He smiled at her in a way that he hoped was both encouraging and a little bit seductive.

"Okay," she said after a silence. She looked back at him, her face tense. "But, Conall, if this goes south, I'm blaming it all on you."

"It won't go south." He grasped her by the shoulders and pulled her in for another kiss.

She turned her head so he got her cheek. "Not with Liam here."

"Okay." He dropped his arms. "Just know that the next time I get you alone, you're all mine." It took all he had not to growl it.

30

F riday night, Theresa looked up at Conall while they stood just inside her front door. They were starting over, pretending like Thanksgiving hadn't happened. This was a first date.

Conall told Liam all about the new tricks Maddy was learning at obedience training class. Liam was sitting next to Pat on the couch.

"The best is when she rolls over, because she never makes it all the way around without stopping for a belly rub."

Liam laughed. "She loves that!"

"Yeah, she does. Some day, she'll get it right, though." Conall stepped closer to the door.

Theresa smiled at Liam. "Okay, honey, we're going to go now."

Liam jumped up and rushed the door to give Theresa a hug. She hugged him back but wondered what was making him so clingy.

"Okay, honey," she said.

She stood back up and looked over to Pat. "I'll be home by eleven."

Pat gave her a knowing smile and patted the couch. "Come on, Liam. Let your mom go."

Theresa leaned down to kiss him on the forehead and touched his cheek just as he said, "Bye, Mom."

Conall opened the door and they headed out.

"Bye, Conall," Liam said.

"Bye, buddy."

Once they were outside, Theresa said, "Sorry, he's being oddly clingy tonight."

Conall laughed. "No worries. He's probably worried I'm going to take you away."

"I don't think he knows we're on a date."

"I guarantee he does." He opened the door for her, and she slipped inside.

After he'd gotten in the driver's seat, he continued, "Kids always know more about what's going on than people think."

"You think?" She hoped he wasn't right. She didn't like the idea of Liam knowing. What if it went wrong?

"Yep." He started the car. "Does sushi sound good?"

"Oh, perfect." Best not to think about what Liam knew. She didn't want to stress about it all night.

"So did you get all that stuff done for Casey today?" Conall asked.

"Yes." Theresa had had a bunch of work in the afternoon that had taken her away from the Athena project work this week, which was holding Conall up a bit because she hadn't gotten the design changes to him so he could code them. "Just before I left. Monday I'll be able to get back to Athena."

"That's good."

"Just in time to make Iryna happy," she said with a smirk.

"Oh, God, don't mention her. She brought sugar cookies *again* this week."

Theresa laughed. "That's what you get for telling her they're your favorite."

"It just slipped out." Conall accelerated when the light they were at turned green. "If I'd understood the consequences, I'd have been more careful."

Her smile remained as she glanced out the window at a couple walking down the sidewalk holding hands. A twinge of jealousy twisted her heart, but then she realized that could be her some time soon. If things went well. Did she want that? She looked back at Conall. Even his profile was attractive.

"What?" he asked.

"Nothing."

"If you say so." He drove a few more blocks before pulling into a strip mall. "I know it doesn't look that great, but they have good sushi."

"I know this place. And you're right."

"Cool."

They sat down at a wobbly table on black metal chairs with green vinyl padding. A small woman from behind the counter came over to them and handed them menus without saying anything.

"Now that we're here, I'm glad you already know and like this restaurant, because it probably isn't the most impressive place to take a woman on a first date."

She'd almost forgotten this was a date. The realization made her a little nervous.

He must have mistaken her silence for judgement, because he said, "Should we have gone somewhere else?"

She looked at him. "No, it's fine. I'm more concerned with the who's at the table with me than the setting."

He smiled and arched his eyebrows.

"You ready?" the woman asked from next to the table, pad and pen in hand.

They ordered, and the woman hung the ticket in the kitchen.

Conall asked, "Are you excited for the movie?"

"Of course. I'm a big Wonder Woman fan, and I'm dying to see her." Wonder Woman didn't have a major role in the movie—this one belonged to Batman and Superman—but she was going to make an appearance and then eventually getting her own film.

"I've heard Gal Gadot does a great job."

"Yeah. It's going to be great."

He nodded. "So, are you a Batman or Superman kind of girl?"

"Batman. I grew up reading him."

"Comics?" He sounded surprised. Men were always surprised.

"Yep."

"How'd you get into them?"

"My older sister, actually. I have a couple of older brothers but they weren't casual readers."

He laughed. "How'd she get into them?"

"I don't even know. Probably a boyfriend. She's ten years older."

"Ah. So you have a big family?"

The waitress returned with two glasses of water, which she put on the table.

"Yeah, there are six of us. Kids. Parents are still married."

"So you have lots of nieces and nephews?" Conall picked up his glass and took a sip.

"Only four. My older sister's kids. My older brothers haven't settled down yet. One is a singer on a cruise ship and the other is a lawyer in New York."

"I bet your mom is bummed about that. Six kids, and only five grandkids."

"She is. I think she might have sided with my ex in some ways. They weren't big fans of the divorce." That was somewhat of an understatement. Her mom had been pissed at her but at least her dad was mad at Michael for leaving her.

"Oh, really?" His brow furrowed. "That sucks."

"You said you don't have any siblings, right?"

"Yeah. Just a gaggle of cousins."

Theresa laughed. "A gaggle."

The woman returned with plates of sushi and Conall gave her a smile and said thanks. She turned away with a flat expression still on her face.

"I don't think she's glad we're here," he said to Theresa once she'd gone.

"She's always like this. It's not personal."

He cocked his head to the side. "True."

Conall worked on a piece of sashimi with a little bit of wasabi, and Theresa dipped her tuna sushi in soy sauce and took a bite.

He smiled over at her. Once she finished chewing, she said, "So tell me about your cousins."

"Oh, well, the oldest is Henry. He's a lawyer, too. In LA. Doing pretty well for himself. Then there's Mark, who's at in his first year at M.I.T."

"Oh, nice."

"Yeah, he's very smart." Conall smiled, as if to himself. "We're all very proud of him."

Conall went down the list, eleven in total, with the youngest being just four. "I don't know her very well, obviously." He pulled out his phone and swiped through several pictures before holding it out to her. "But here she is."

The photo showed a smiling black-haired girl in a pink princess costume. "She's beautiful. And pink. Is she another Iryna in the making?" She regretted bringing up the woman again.

Conall groaned. "I hope not. What's with that, anyway?"

"Casey has a theory."

"Which is?" He took another bite of sushi.

"She thinks that because she works in a male-dominated field, she's worried people might think she's unfeminine. So, she wants to make sure there's no room for doubt."

"Well, mission accomplished. She's a woman. Good for her."

Theresa laughed and finished chewing.

They talked a little about the Athena project while they finished their food.

"You ready?" Conall asked. We have about half an hour before the movie starts."

"Sure. Let's go."

He walked up to the register to pay, and they headed out to the car.

"So, tell me a little more about your smart cousin. What's his name again?"

"Mark." He started the car and backed out of the parking space. "He's a National Merit Scholar and a Presidential Scholar. He competed on the United States Physics Olympiad Team and on the computer one, too."

Theresa laughed. "Okay, I get the picture."

He arched his eyebrows and pulled out onto the street. "It's kind of a big deal to me because his mom never cared about his academic achievements. Henry and I pushed him and made sure he didn't go astray."

"What's he studying at M.I.T.?"

"Physics."

Theresa said, "Wow, that's impressive."

Conall was quiet, and Theresa was reminded of her nervousness. What was it they were supposed to talk about now? Conall drove through several intersections, and still neither said anything.

He pulled into the theater parking lot.

She had something. "What time do you plan to come over tomorrow?"

He glanced over.

"You know, for Liam."

"Oh, how about ten?" He pulled down a row, looking for a parking space, but there was nothing close. "And he can play with Maddy afterward."

"Great idea. She wears him out."

"He wears her out, too. Plus, it will guarantee a little more semi-alone time with you. Finally, here we go." He pulled into a parking space. "I hope you don't mind walking."

"Not at all."

They headed toward the theater. "I hope they'll still have tickets," Theresa said.

"I bought them already.

"Mr. Prepared."

"I like to think so." He winked at her, which sent a shiver through her because she knew what he meant.

He held the door for her, and they were inside.

"Can't do a movie without popcorn and drinks. What's your poison?" he asked as they got in yet another line.

She glanced at the menu. "Diet Pepsi."

The line moved pretty quickly, and soon they had their drinks and a small bucket of popcorn—light on the butter as she'd insisted.

They found a couple seats in the back row. She took her jacket off, and they settled in. Theresa was a little excited at the thought of being in the dark with Conall. It had been a long time, but the memories of high school dates were still pretty vivid. Her parents were so conservative that she'd had to be careful not to get spotted by their friends, and the dark was good for hiding.

Conall held the popcorn out for her, and she took a handful. The lights went dark just as he took some for himself. They munched away through the previews. Then the movie started, and she was sucked in. She did enjoy a good movie, even though she rarely saw them.

After a while, she started to get cold, so she leaned forward to take her jacket off the back of the seat and laid it across her front.

"Cold?" Conall asked. He obligingly draped his arm across her back, and she warmed all over. She leaned into him a little and felt very happy. She'd been so distracted by the good conversation earlier than she'd forgotten the physical effect he had on her. She remembered now.

They cuddled through the rest of the movie—Wonder Woman didn't disappoint—and filed out with the rest of the crowd.

"You want to hit a bar or head back?" Conall asked and touched her arm as they trekked to the car.

She weighed the options. She felt like she should get back, but what she wanted was to spend more time with Conall. "Let's go to a bar. You have one in mind?"

He smiled at her. "There's one not far from home. Harrigan's. You know it?"

"I've seen it but never been. The only bar I go to is in Portland."

He took her hand, and a surge of lust went through her. She didn't want to go to a bar with him—she wanted to go home with him.

That was not going to happen. It was way, way too soon. Plus, she had to get home. So, a bar would have to do.

They reached the car, and he let go of her hand. They got in, and he headed over to the bar. The drive was short, and they filled it with talk of work, of all things. Theresa started it because she wanted to wind her libido back down.

It didn't work.

31

onall found the two of them a table in the bar.

"Be right back—Chardonnay for you, right?"

Theresa gave him her beautiful smile and nodded.

When he returned with a couple drinks, he said, "No work talk," and put his hand on top of hers, which rested on the table.

She smiled at him and took a sip of her wine.

He moved his hand but scooted his stool over so he was right next to her. He'd been sporting a semi ever since he put his arm across her shoulders in the theater, and his balls tightened when she leaned into him from her stool. He put his arm around her, and they sat like that for a little while, not talking.

Eventually, he said, "So tell me about your younger siblings."

She looked over at him, their faces mere inches apart. Her eyes fell to his mouth, and his dick throbbed.

"Oh, yeah," she said. "I never finished telling you. June is seventeen. She's a senior and will go to a small college in Texas. Kevin is twenty-one and he works for a moving company. He's not very ambitious but he's a nice kid."

"What's your older sister do?" he asked, pulling her closer.

"She's a stay-at-home mom." She took a sip of her wine, nearly finishing it off.

"And your nieces? Nephews?" He loved hearing about her family, though he couldn't say why. Probably because he missed his own.

"Two girls and two boys. They're eighteen, fifteen, and three-year-old twin boys."

Conall drained his glass. "Wow, your little sister is younger than your niece. That's funny. You want another?"

"Actually, let me." She slipped off the stool before he could say anything.

"No, I'll get it."

"No, you won't." She glared at him playfully. "Stay put."

He put his hands up. "If you insist. I won't complain."

When she got back with the drinks, they talked about the movie and finished up their drinks.

"Another?" he asked. "Maybe a coffee?" He wanted to keep her here as long as possible, because otherwise she'd have to go home.

Theresa looked at her phone. She shook her head. "I'd better get home."

The disappointment rested in his gut. "Okay, no problem."

She slid off the stool, wavered a bit, and clasped his arm. "Crap."

"What's wrong?" He stood next to her and held her other arm.

"The wine just hit me a little harder than I realized. I can't go home like this."

"Oh. We could go to my place for a bit. I can make some coffee."

"That sounds like a good idea, actually. Liam will be in bed, but I'd feel ridiculous if Pat saw me this way. Park down the street, though, so we can sneak in from the side."

"No problem." Conall put his hand on the small of Theresa's back, and they left. It wasn't that she needed him to hold on to her—she wasn't so drunk—it was just that now that he'd started touching her, he couldn't keep his hands off. And she seemed to like it, the way she kept leaning into him. She wasn't *that* drunk.

On the drive back to the house, he rested his palm on her thigh, and she put her hand on top of his. He didn't think she was trying to keep his hand from wandering further up. Still, he wasn't going to try. They were quiet for the first part of the drive.

"You tired?" he asked after a time.

"A little. Long day." She turned toward him. "But I had a nice time tonight, Conall."

"Yeah, me too."

She leaned back against the headrest and didn't say anything else. They were quiet again until he parked.

She stood behind him as he unlocked the door, which seemed exciting even though he knew nothing would happen. She had to get home.

Maddy frantically pushed up against him. "I need to take her out for a couple minutes. Make yourself at home, and I'll be right back." He grabbed the leash off the hook by the door and got Maddy outside.

Theresa went inside, and he shut the door.

Maddy was so excited to see him that she kept hovering around him. "Come on girl, do your business." He shivered in the cold and rain.

Once she'd finished, he went back inside his apartment before heading toward Theresa's.

Some day, Theresa would have to get used to Maddy, but he wasn't going to force the issue now.

He sat next to her on the couch so he faced her.

She watched him, soft brown eyes unblinking.

"There's something I've been wanting to do all night," he said and looked at her luscious lips slightly parted.

"What's that?" her lips said.

"This." He moved in for a gentle kiss, but she wrapped her arms around him and pulled him half on top of her. She held on so tight that he deepened the kiss and found even that wasn't enough. He turned his head for better access and explored with his tongue, only to have her suck on it. He took it back and gave her upper lip some serious attention before moving to her jaw. Her head was back, and she moaned a little as he worked his way up to her delicious ear, bumping the hoop earring she was wearing to the side with his tongue.

Conall could feel her heart thumping behind her breasts. She could surely feel the erection against her stomach.

He worked his way back to her mouth, and their tongues battled

232

until she turned and started kissing him on the side of the neck. His hand went to her breast and she moaned again but continued gently sucking on his neck. He moved his other hand to her head and turned it so her mouth was against his, and she kissed him with need.

She pushed against his cock and he sucked her tongue into his mouth, and he was lost.

She brought him back only when she pulled away. "Conall."

"Mmm," he said.

"I think I need to get back home. I don't think this is a good idea."

"What, kissing?"

"This is more than kissing, and we both know where it will lead."

They were still wrapped in each other's arms, so he leaned back and said, "I thought you needed to sober up."

"I feel quite sober now." She smiled with half-lidded eyes. "Thank you very much."

He laughed lightly. "Happy to help." He rubbed her back and ran his other hand through her silky hair.

She rested her head in the crook of his neck. "Really, I should go."

"Okay, no problem. Let's go." He ached with need, but she was setting the pace here.

Theresa didn't let go and neither did he. She kissed his chin. He'd shaved before going out tonight, so she wasn't dealing with stubble. He turned his head so he could find her mouth again, and they kissed hungrily.

She pulled away, breathing hard, and dropped her arms from his back. "Okay, for real this time."

He laughed and dropped his own hands and reluctantly leaned back against the couch arm. But he couldn't help but to reach up and tuck some of her loose hair behind her ear. Then he ran his hand down the outside of her ear and down her jawline before cupping her chin. "Let's get you home."

She smiled up at him and put her hand on his chest. "I really did have a great time tonight."

"Let's go." He took her hand to help her up and headed toward the door.

When he pulled onto her driveway, he asked, "Where's your babysitter's car?"

"She walks. She just lives next door."

"I'll watch her get home." Might as well be the gentleman.

"That would be nice. I just watch her from the porch."

He watched Pat head home from the driveway. Once she was inside —she'd waved at him and winked just before shutting the door—he turned back to Theresa.

He wanted to go up to the porch and touch her again, but unless she specifically asked, he wasn't going to.

She stood with her arms crossed, still watching him.

He couldn't read her right now. So, he nodded at her and stood next to the driver's side of the car. "See you tomorrow around ten?" he called.

He could read her smile, which was all happiness. "See you then," she said as she waved and stepped back in the house.

32

After work Monday, Theresa picked Liam up. She was taking him to the library but was planning to bribe him first, in hopes of a better result than the last time they picked up books.

"Ready for laser tag, Liam?" she said as she took his hand, his backpack in the other.

"Laser tag?" he said with a grin.

"Remember, we're going to the library, but I promised we'd play a little first." She opened the back door.

"Okay." His voice fell at the news of the library.

They were lucky—there was a place for laser tag in Milwaukie, so it was easy for them to get to, and they went occasionally.

"But Mom."

"Yeah?"

"We're not wearing black."

"Oh, you're right." The game was played inside in a dark room, so wearing black made it harder for opponents to see you. "Well, we'll just have to play smarter."

When they got there, Theresa paid, and they got their vests and group assignment. They were teamed up with a group of three teenagers, which wasn't ideal, but they seemed okay.

She handed Liam his vest and helped him put it on, latching it at the side. The lights on the front and shoulders of their vests were flashing bright blue like the rest of their team. The other players—some more teenagers and a couple families—were flashing yellow and red.

They went into the very dimly lit room, and there were fake rocks to hide behind. When they reached the blue base, the staff member explained how the game worked. Of course, Theresa and Liam didn't need the instruction, and he entertained himself by pretending to shoot her, whispering pew-pew noises.

Once the game started, they walked briskly into the neutral zone—no running allowed, as difficult as it was to avoid—and immediately headed upstairs, music pounding in their ears while yellow overhead lights flashed.

Theresa saw Liam's laser beam as it hit another player, and he dodged their return fire, but it hit her. They moved out of the way fast enough to get to the stairs, and the other shooter disappeared.

"Look out, Mom!"

She dodged, and he shot their opponent several times with his killer aim, until the player was dead and had to skulk off to her base to recharge.

They circled the top floor and each got a kill, but when a man jumped out from behind a wall, Theresa was toast.

"Let's go back to base, Mom! I'll cover you." Not that that was necessary, since she was unable to be any more dead, but the sentiment was sweet. She had to get back to the base before rejoining the game.

They made it back, and Theresa recharged her gun, which made a whooshing sound as it refueled. Then they were off again. This time they stayed downstairs and went through the maze, but before they were out, they were both dead and had to go to the other base to recharge again.

They played two more fifteen-minute games before heading out.

"Did you see when I got that one kid?" Liam asked in a high-pitched voice once they were in the parking lot.

"I did—I was right there!" she said, ruffling his hair.

Liam was quiet the whole way to the library, and she knew his good mood needed a recharge it wasn't going to get. Once she'd parked, he got out of the car slowly. She was really worried they'd have a repeat of the last time. She couldn't read his demeanor on the way in—he didn't look particularly defiant.

He followed her to the drop box, then down the stairs and into the kids' room where they headed to the picture books.

So far so good.

He sat down in front of the books and began scanning the titles, cocking his head to the side so he could read the spines better.

This was a surprisingly good sign. "See anything you like, honey?"

He pulled one out. The front had a picture of a couple of young-looking kids dumping a pail at the beach.

"I think we need to find one for older kids," she said.

He nodded and pushed the book back between two others. She sat down next to him and leaned against his shoulder. "What are you looking for?"

"I don't know. Something funny."

"Okay, we'll find something."

He methodically pulled off one book after the other, gave it a cursory glance and slid it back in. He seemed almost laser-focused on getting the right books. They looked through several shelves before they had a stack of five. Theresa decided to push her luck. "Why don't you pick one for us to read right now?"

He looked up at her, his brown eyes uncertain. She smiled at him, hoping it would work.

"Okay," he said after a pause. Then he turned back and continued his search.

She couldn't help being surprised, but she went with it. "How about this one?" She showed him one about volcanoes she'd spotted.

"Okay."

As they were getting up to go to a bench to read, Liam said, "Mom?"

"Yeah, honey?" She sat on a nearby bench and set the stack of books down on the floor.

"Is Conall your boyfriend?" He sat next to her

She jerked her head in his direction. "What?" Crap, Conall must have been right. Liam was paying more attention than she'd realized.

"Is he?"

"No, sweetie. We're just friends." She had to correct him since she did not want Liam mentioning any relationship to her mom or to his father. She knew what her mom would say, but Michael was another matter. He'd probably raise a ruckus.

Liam looked at her with narrowed eyes and a small frown.

"Seriously. We work together and we're friends." She was using the term 'friend' loosely here, but she didn't think Conall was her official boyfriend yet, so it wasn't a lie.

He didn't say anything else and instead took the volcano book from her and opened it.

She wondered if he was going to read it himself, but instead he put it in her lap and looked up expectantly. "You read first. Then me."

"Sure." She read the first page.

Liam dragged his finger under the words as he read the second page. It was bumpy, but he was reading. Actually, voluntarily reading.

She knew she had Conall to thank for this. She texted him, which started off a little back and forth session that kept her up way too late. She couldn't wait to see him again.

WEDNESDAY EVENING, Conall sat on the couch with Liam as he struggled through another book about a dog. This one was pretty funny, but because he was having trouble with it, Liam wasn't enjoying it as much as he should.

"The dog w... want?" Liam read.

"Went," Conall corrected.

"Over the—"

"To."

"Oh."

Conall smiled at him. "Why don't you start from the beginning, buddy?"

"The dog... went... over to the doll."

"Ball," Conall corrected. Still, Liam was doing so much better.

"He hit it with his... nose?"

"That's right." Conall glanced over at Theresa, who sat on the other side of Liam. He couldn't hold back a smile just for her. She glanced sideways at him and half-smiled, but didn't turn her head from her book.

Liam turned the page and put his finger under the first word. "To..."

Conall opened his mouth to say something, but then Liam self-corrected. "The da—ball... um, what is that?" His finger was under the next word.

"Bounced."

"Down the hill. The dog went after it. He ran fast." He paused to look at the pictures on the pages and then turned to the next one. He began reading and stumbled a little, but kept going.

They went through the rest of the book like that, with Conall alternating between correcting Liam's occasional mistakes and glancing at Theresa.

She set her book down on the coffee table and got up. "Be back in a second."

As soon as she was in the bathroom, Liam whispered, "Are you Mom's boyfriend?"

He jerked back in surprise, but then recovered. "You'll have to ask your mom that."

"I already did. She said you're not."

Ouch. "Well, you should listen to your mom. She knows what she's talking about." That sort of sucked.

The bathroom door opened, and Theresa came out. Before he'd arrived, she'd changed into jeans and a white t-shirt that showed her shape. He could also barely make out the outline of her bra. Even in mundane clothes she was sexy.

She smiled in their general direction and sat back on the couch.

Liam picked another book, and they worked their way through it. His confidence was clearly growing, because even though he made mistakes, it wasn't deterring him. He didn't keep begging Conall to read.

Liam finished the last one and closed the book. "All done!"

"Yeah, buddy." Conall rubbed his back. "You read five books. You did a great job, too."

Theresa marked her page and set her book on the coffee table. "Did you like the books, honey?"

"Yeah."

"Why don't you go on up and get ready for bed?" she said.

Conall had come over after dinner this time.

Liam got up and headed to the stairs.

"What do you say to Conall, Liam?"

He turned around and said, "Thank you."

Then he turned around and went upstairs.

Theresa brought her leg up on the couch and turned sideways to face Conall. "I wanted to thank you again—he's doing so much better, isn't he?"

Conall mirrored her and scooted forward. "He is. His confidence is way up. That's the first step."

Their knees were touching, and just from that simple contact his groin tightened. He couldn't help but reach out and stroke her arm.

She looked like she might protest, but instead said, "I'm just so glad. I think he's going to catch up."

"He will. I'm sure of it." He leaned forward, hoping she'd meet him halfway.

"Not with Liam here."

He leaned back. "Alright. He told me you said I wasn't your boyfriend."

"Oh. He said that?" Her eyes were wide.

"Yep. What do I have to do to be your boyfriend?"

She glanced away. "It's a big deal, putting a label on it."

"I want to put a label on it."

She looked into his eyes but he couldn't read her expression. "Let me... let me think about it."

He nodded, still disappointed. "I should probably go."

She stood up, and he followed her to the door. He stepped into her space when she opened the door and turned toward him. He couldn't resist—he grasped her by the hips and kissed her. She kissed him back before breaking it.

"Conall, don't." But she giggled.

He chuckled and stepped into the doorway. That's when he noticed Liam standing at the bottom of the stairs. His mouth hung open a little, and he looked uncertain.

Theresa followed his gaze. "Liam, hi, honey."

"What are you doing?" the boy asked.

"Hugging," Theresa said quickly.

She turned toward Conall and said, "Okay, I'll see you tomorrow."

"Bye." He waved at Liam. "Bye, buddy."

He hoped this didn't make her want to back off.

33

Friday night, Conall added ice to the saucepan of the brine he was using for the huli huli chicken he was making for Theresa. Last night after volleyball he'd made haupia, a coconut milk-based custard-like dessert common in Hawaii, which sat in the fridge.

He was looking forward to seeing Theresa tonight. He'd be able to touch her again. Just thinking about it woke his body up. This had been one of the hardest weeks of his life, being that close to her and keeping his hands off her beautiful body.

He started the huli huli sauce by pouring pineapple juice, ketchup, soy sauce, and sherry vinegar into a pot. It smelled like Hawaii and everything he'd lost. His father and Clarissa.

Once the sauce was simmering, he whisked it until it started to thicken and set it aside. The smell was still getting to him, also reminding him of everything he'd given up by leaving. Seeing his mom. Watching his cousins grow up.

But it was stupid to think of that. Theresa was coming over. *Theresa.* If things went right, he'd be making new cooking memories with her.

The table already looked nice. He'd bought red candles for the occasion. He'd also bought a nice serving dish for the chicken.

As soon as Theresa was inside his house, he planned to kiss her good and long. His hands would be everywhere, and his desire for her would be temporarily quenched. Before it started recharging.

He couldn't get her off his mind the whole time he was out watching the chicken on the grill. He felt so lucky that she seemed to be as into him as he was her. He hadn't felt this kind of connection since the beginning of his relationship with Clarissa. Things with her had been good for a long time, until she kept failing to conceive. Then it all went to hell once they found out it was his fault.

Fuck, stop thinking about it.

He turned the chicken over and went inside to grab the huli huli sauce for glazing.

Theresa knew about his problem and didn't care. He smiled and thought of her luscious mouth, all ready for him.

Once the chicken was done, he took it back inside, placed it on a cookie sheet and proceeded to carve it. Once he had distinct pieces, he placed it neatly in the serving dish and put it in the oven to stay warm.

Ten minutes. He couldn't wait.

He poured the huli huli sauce into a bowl and set it on the table with a ladle next to it. The King's Hawaiian sweet rolls were ready to go into the oven. He went over to the table and straightened the place settings, debating lighting the candles but deciding to hold off in case she was running late. Leaving a kid with a babysitter for the evening could be a complicated and time-consuming task.

He got two wine glasses—which he'd also purchased for this occasion—out of the cabinet and set them on the counter next to a bottle of Sauvignon Blanc.

He paced in anticipation, his hands already craving something delicious to touch. He fell into the couch, bouncing his leg.

The doorbell rang, and his heart leapt as he got up.

Theresa had on a sweater dress that hit just below the knee, which sent a surge through him. Her wavy hair was down. She smiled at him and nothing had been more beautiful. He reached out and took her hand to lead her in.

He kicked the door shut and caressed her face. She looked up at him with half-lidded eyes, and he couldn't wait any longer. Her lips were soft and yielding, and they parted right away. He slid inside and explored her mouth desperately, even though they hadn't said anything to each other yet. Her hands were around his waist, pressing into his back, and her breasts were crushed against him. He was already hard. Christ, he wanted her. But there was dinner to be eaten first.

He pushed his hand through her silky hair, feeling it brush the sensitive space between his fingers.

She pulled away and started kissing his neck, sucking before licking his jawline and coming back to his mouth. He sucked on her upper lip until she moaned with need, and then his tongue started exploring again. When they were together like this, it felt like there was a larger connection between them that the entire universe knew about.

When he needed to breathe, he pulled back and leaned against her forehead. "Hi."

"Hi," she said, her hot breath against his chin.

"How are you?"

"Wonderful."

He let go and took a step back. "Ready for dinner?"

She looked toward the kitchen and sniffed the air. "This smells wonderful."

He needed to touch her again, so he took her hand. "I just need to get the rolls warming, and then we can eat."

They went into the kitchen, and he put the rolls in the oven one-handed.

He stopped and admired her again. "Here, give me your jacket."

She took off her pea coat, and he hung it in the closet next to the kitchen. His balls clenched when he saw that although it wasn't sleeveless, it fit her lovely arms. He knew exactly what they felt like.

She stood in his kitchen, next to the table, looking beautiful with her flushed cheeks. He watched her glance at the table so he pulled the matches out of the drawer and lit the candles.

"You went all out," she said.

He smiled at her. "Of course. I've been wanting to do this since I met you."

"Oh, yeah?"

"Yeah." He put the oven mitts on and got the chicken out of the oven and onto the table.

She was irresistible right now. He walked over and slid his arms around her waist and kissed her gently on the mouth. "I've been dying all week not being able to touch you."

"You kissed me Wednesday."

"Oh, yeah, but I forgot about that. It wasn't enough." But good. She didn't sound stressed about it.

He kissed her again, keeping his tongue in his mouth because the rolls were almost ready. She gripped his shirt but kissed him back as softly as he was. It was like he couldn't get enough of her sweetness.

"I think the rolls are ready," he said, dropping his arms.

"Okay," she whispered.

He put them on the table, and she sat down. Then he went back to pour two glasses of wine and set one in front of her.

"This looks amazing, Conall."

"Thank you. Breast or thigh?"

"Breast."

He dished it out and then gave her one of the baked sweet potatoes. "I put a little butter on them, but let me know if you want more. Here's the sauce for the chicken." He indicated the bowl, and she poured some over her plate.

She smiled and said, "This looks perfect."

He motioned to the sweet rolls. "Have a roll if you want." She didn't but he took two himself.

He filled his own plate and sat down. She was watching him. The flickering candles danced in front of her gorgeous face. He smiled, his heart so filled with happiness at that moment. "Let's eat."

"So, tell me about this chicken," she said.

"This is my mom's recipe for huli huli chicken, and it's one of the many favorite dishes of Hawaii. It's my personal favorite."

She took a bite, and her eyes widened. She nodded in appreciation. "It's very good."

He told her what was in the sauce.

"Liam would like it, I think. It's kind of like barbecue chicken."

"Oh, I meant to ask. Have you found an art program for him?" She'd talked about wanting to find one that catered to especially gifted kids, because the ones he'd done so far had bored him. He was so beyond macaroni art.

"Not yet. But there's a nonprofit that offers children's art programs, so I thought I'd get in touch with them to see if they know any for very advanced kids." She paused. "I still don't know where he gets his talent from."

Conall cocked his head to the side. "Talents like that seem to spontaneously generate in DNA, I think."

Theresa laughed. "Are you saying my child is a mutant?"

"Only the kind that drives evolution."

They continued chatting about Liam and then moved on to a bit about work. Soon, they'd finished dinner.

"Ready for dessert?" he asked.

"Oh, wow. You're seriously treating me."

"Of course." He got up and took their plates to the sink. He got the haupia out of the fridge and cut a couple pieces, delivering hers along with a small spoon and telling her about it.

She tried a bite. "Mmm, it's good. You are quite the cook."

Conall shrugged. "My mom trained me good."

"My mom taught all the girls in my family, too. The boys entered the adult world not knowing how to boil water."

"I think my mom wanted a daughter. So, I had to fill both roles." The candles had burned down about a third of the way.

Theresa raised her eyebrows. "You don't strike me as a mama's boy."

"No, it's not that. She just taught me to cook and clean, that's all. And it took."

"That's good." She smiled.

"She just knew they wouldn't have any more kids. I got my problem from my dad. I was the miracle baby who never should have existed."

She wore a pained expression. "This really hurts you, doesn't it? Personally, I'm glad you exist."

He shrugged. He shouldn't have brought this up. Not now. "It's fine."

"Conall, it *is* fine. It doesn't bother me at all, and I don't think of you as less of a man."

He nodded. "I appreciate that. What movie do you want to watch?"

She looked a little frustrated, but they discussed what he had on hand and after picking one, Theresa said, "But don't you want to wash the dishes first?"

"I could." He went back over to blow the candles out.

"I meant both of us. I'll help."

"That's not very romantic."

"I don't like the idea of dirty dishes in the sink."

He laughed. "Okay, then."

THERESA WAS SO happy that she couldn't imagine having survived without feeling this way for so long. She was lying on Conall's couch resting against him, and he had his arm around her., which felt so natural. They'd picked a comedy, which was good because she felt so charged and emotional that she would have cried like a baby at anything sad.

Conall squeezed her arm after the credits started. "Theresa?"

"Hmm?"

"I'm going to kiss you now."

She looked up at him and laughed a little. Then she saw his eyes were burning with desire. She sat up and leaned forward. The second his lips touched hers, she was awash with emotion laced with a fair dose of raw lust.

His tongue was in her mouth, and she sucked, hard, so he groaned. He made her feel so powerful and sexy. He turned so that he had her pinned against the back of the couch, and she loved it. His hand was in her hair. The other one cupped her breast, and she arched her back into it.

Somehow, she ended up on her back, and he was nipping her ear and massaging her breast and licking her neck and kissing her mouth seemingly all at once. She could feel the length of him against her thigh, and she wanted him so much that she moaned in anticipation. She slid down a little so she could feel his erection in her center and lifted her pelvis to feel it even more.

"Mmm," he said into her mouth as he ground his hips into hers. "You feel so good."

She felt so good, too, but the thought that she had to be somewhere percolated up into her mind. She went limp. "Conall, what time is it?"

"Hmm?"

"I think I need to get home." She wanted to stay so badly that it hurt to say the words.

He stopped moving and opened his eyes. "Really? Now?"

"I think so." She was breathless.

He pushed off her and leaned toward the coffee table to check his phone. "10:43."

"Yeah. I told her 11:00 tonight."

"Oh." He sat back against the couch and ran his hand through his hair, with the smallest frown. "No problem. I understand."

She stood up and straightened her dress.

"Let's go." He headed toward the door.

"I need my jacket."

"Oh, yeah." He laughed. "You have me all flustered."

"I know the feeling." And did she. She hadn't been this turned on since Thanksgiving.

They walked around to the front door hand in hand. She and Conall watched Pat go home.

They were kissing as soon as the door was shut, and it was like they picked up where they were on the couch.

His hands cupped both her breasts. "I want to feel you under this thick fabric."

She moaned, wanting the very same thing. Without thinking about it, she reached down and cupped the front of his jeans.

He grunted and slid his hands around her back to start kissing her again.

She rubbed.

"Theresa, you will be the death of me."

"Conall, let's go upstairs," she whispered.

"Yes, let's," he said desperately.

She reached over and locked the door. Then she broke away from him and took his hand to lead him upstairs. "Be quiet. And you can't stay. Liam can't know," she whispered. They were both breathing heavily, and her heart was about to explode.

As soon as they were past the bedroom door, his mouth was on her again, all over her neck and jaw. She moaned again. He felt the back of her dress for the zipper. He found it and began pulling it down.

"Hold on," she managed. "The door."

He raced over to the door and shut and locked it and then found the light switch. He wanted to see her. "Okay, where were we?"

Conall moved around her and finished the zipper. Then he turned her around and pushed the dress off her shoulders, which fell to her hips.

Her nipples were puckered tight and pushed against her thin black bra. He stared at them and licked his lips. She reached around to unhook the bra, and he stopped her. "Let me."

It fell to the floor, and she felt amazing for causing the hungry look on his face. He leaned forward and down and put his mouth to her left nipple, licking it and then sucking, softly at first and then harder. Her head went back, and she moaned. No one had ever been this good to her. She felt like they were a single, perfect unit. She gripped his shoulders. He switched to her other breast and gave it even more attention.

Then he pushed the dress down over her hips, and it fell to the floor. He cupped her sex and said, "You're so wet, all the way through your panties."

She blinked. "You do this to me."

"I'm glad, because you know what you do to me." He took her hand and put it on his erection and dragged her hand up and down.

She couldn't wait anymore and reached for the button of his jeans to undo it. Before she could go for the zipper, he cupped her ass and pulled her in tight so he was pushing against her stomach.

"You feel so good, sweetheart."

Then he went to his knees and gripped her thighs and kissed the front of her panties. He pushed them to the side and explored her with his fingers, and she threw her head back in both pleasure and anticipation.

34

Conall's hands grasped Theresa's thighs as he gave her one last lick and came up for air. She was still catching her breath. His chin was drenched with her sweetness, and it just turned him on more.

"How are you, gorgeous?" he murmured.

"Unh," she whispered. "Conall…"

"Come here and help me get out of these."

"I can't move."

He laughed, a feeling of satisfaction in his chest. "Come on, Theresa. Give a guy a hand."

She pushed up on her elbows, and he could see the pink patches across her cheeks.

He grinned at her as she sat up and stared at his crotch. The greedy look on her face as she reached to unzip his jeans made him feel like a sex god. He was wearing boxer briefs, which were stretched tight over his erection. His pre-come had leaked through and dampened the fabric. She touched the spot, and he inhaled through his teeth.

She grasped the waistband of his jeans and pushed them down past his hips, all the while staring at the front of his shorts. She fingered his happy trail at his belly button and traced it down to the briefs before reaching up with her other hand to pull them down.

He closed his eyes as the cool air hit him. He leaned forward to push his jeans and shorts down and stepped out of them.

Theresa was still staring at his cock, an unbelievably hot thing. "Wow," she said. "You really are not small. I've been thinking about you so much since November, and I thought I must have inflated you in my head."

"Yeah?" he said with a chuckle.

She cupped his balls and licked the rest of the pre-come off the end.

"Ahh," he said.

She took him in her hot little mouth—not deep, just enough to make him need her more.

"That's not what I want right now, Theresa. Condom?"

She leaned back, releasing him, and nodded. "In the nightstand. Top drawer."

"Scoot back." He rolled the condom on and crawled onto the bed by her feet, working his way closer to her until he was over her. He kissed her deeply, and she arched into him, like she was desperate for more. He moved down to suck on each of her breasts in turn, and she arched again. "Ready, sweetheart?"

"Yes," she rasped.

He leaned back and reached out to spread her legs and then grasped her left leg and rested it on his hip. He inched forward and notched himself inside her wet heat. He closed his eyes, savoring the moment of just before. Then he pushed inside slowly. Christ, she felt good, and when she gave a little moan, he thought he would die.

"You are so tight around me. You feel like heaven." She truly did. Nothing could be better than this—the two of them together.

Her lips were parted, and she was breathing heavily. She needed him as much as he needed her.

He withdrew and pushed back inside, deeper this time. Then again, to the hilt. She grimaced but it was in pleasure.

He thrusted slowly, savoring every inch of friction like it was the last thing he'd ever feel. If it were, he'd die a happy man.

But then he needed to speed up, so he did. Theresa gasped over and over, so he kept up until he felt her shudder and spasm around him as she moaned again. His own orgasm washed over him like a tsunami. He rode it out and dropped her leg and fell onto his side on the bed next to her, his arm across her, just below her beautiful breasts.

"I can't believe you make me come that way," Theresa said. "No one else has ever been able to do it. It usually takes... manual work."

"I like to think I know what I'm doing," he said with a proud chuckle as his hand wandered to one of her breasts and rested there.

"I guess you do."

He peeled himself off her and scooted off the bed. "Let me get rid of this."

After he dumped the condom, he felt happier than he'd been in a long time. Everything felt so right. The realization put a grin on his face that he wore all the way back to bed.

"What are you smiling about?" she asked, catching it from him.

"You. You make me smile." He crawled back in the bed and nestled up against her.

"Let's get under the covers," she said.

They had to get off the bed and pull everything down and get back in, but under the sheets it was even more comfortable to be lying there with her. They were on their sides facing each other, and he played with her hair while her hands wandered over his chest.

Conall scooted closer so they were chest to chest and wrapped his arm around her. "I love being close to you."

"I love it, too." She yawned, covering her mouth with her hand. "Sleepy. Fridays are long days."

He could feel her heartbeat against him, gradually slowing back to normal. He caressed her back and watched her fall asleep. Being with her was so sweet.

Her breathing evened out, but he stayed there, watching her. He knew he should get up and go, but he'd have to wake her to have her lock the door behind him, and he didn't want to do that just yet.

THERESA WOKE SLOWLY, wondering why she felt a weight on her chest. She opened her eyes to find Conall spooning her, his arm possessively across her chest. At first, she just enjoyed it and how it felt so right.

Then she realized it was morning, and Conall was still here. She checked the clock on the nightstand, noting the drawer was still open, and the box of condoms was visible. 7:40. Liam could very well be up by now.

She slid out from under Conall's arm and off the bed to go stand at the door and listen for sounds of life. Was that the TV downstairs? Liam always turned it on too loud when he was playing a video game if she wasn't there to get on his case about it.

Crap.

She turned back toward the bed to see Conall stretched out with his arms propped behind his head on the pillow.

"Morning, sweetheart," he said. He wasn't looking her in the eye at the moment as his gaze was a little lower. She was buck naked, and it hadn't even occurred to her to be self-conscious about it.

The sheet was pulled up to his waist. "Nice tent," she said, motioning to his middle.

He laughed. "Why don't you come here and check it out? We can make fine use of it."

As tempting as it was—and it was indeed very tempting—she was more worried about getting him out of there without Liam seeing. "You weren't supposed to stay the night."

"I know. I didn't mean to fall asleep. Is he up yet?"

"I think so. I think he's downstairs playing a video game."

"Oh." He rubbed his chin. "How can I leave, then?"

"I don't know." The way the house was configured, the stairs led right to the middle, so Liam would see him come down if he was in the living room. Or in the kitchen.

"Will he come up here if he's busy downstairs?"

"Not unless he's hungry." She stared at the door.

Conall laughed. "Will he get hungry?"

"Not if he's in the middle of a video game."

"Come here, then. We're trapped. Might as well make the most of it." He grinned at her.

Theresa tapped her nails on her chin. Maybe if she could get Liam into his room, Conall could sneak out.

"Come here."

She walked back to the bed and sat down. He leaned forward and moved her hair to the side so he could kiss the back of her neck.

"Mmm," she said, closing her eyes and almost forgetting about her problem. His hand reached around and cupped her breast before massaging it. Her nipples instantly puckered and she wanted him again.

Focus. "Normally on Saturday mornings, he gets up and plays a game for a while and then I make him pancakes."

Conall's hand moved lower and lower as he continued sucking on her neck.

Against her better judgment, she spread her legs a little, and he pushed two fingers inside her.

"So wet," he murmured in her ear before sliding them out and rubbing circles around her clit.

Her breath hitched. "Conall," she whispered.

"Come on, you want this as bad as I do."

His hot breath on her neck got her heart pounding even faster. She reached back and wrapped her hand around his cock, and he inhaled through his teeth. She leaned forward to pull another condom out of the box and set it next to her hip.

"You choose wisely," he whispered into her ear. Then he pulled her back and over so she was lying on top of him, and he kissed her like he'd never done before. "How do you want it?"

Desire was coursing through her like wildfire, and she wanted something different. She rolled off him onto her knees. "Like this."

"Christ," he growled before reaching for the condom and getting behind her.

She heard the crinkling of the packet and then without warning he gripped her hips and pushed inside her. She gasped because he stretched her so tight. But it was delicious.

He leaned forward and moved her hair to the side before running his hand down her back and stopping just above her hips. He left it there while grasping her hip with his other hand. He withdrew slowly and pushed inside again.

"Harder," she said, gripping the comforter they were on in her fists.

He moved the hand on her back to her other hip and withdrew almost all the way before slamming into her.

"Ah," she moaned through gritted teeth.

Soon all she could feel was Conall, and all she could hear was their bodies crashing together, over and over.

She knew from his frenzied pace he was close. "Not yet," she managed between moans.

This position was magical. Two more thrusts, and her orgasm ripped through her. Her arms gave way, and she collapsed just as she felt him tense and hold on to her hips tightly.

She panted onto the sheet. He folded over her, and she slid her legs back so she was resting on the bed with Conall lying on top of her and breathing hard.

"You are like nothing else," he said, kissing her ear.

"Likewise." But as her heart rate began to slow, she remembered the original problem. "Oh, no." This was a disaster. "You have to go."

"Thanks, Theresa," he said with a chuckle. He rolled off her and went into the bathroom.

Theresa went to her closet and pulled on a pair of flannel pajama bottoms. After donning the shirt, she turned to find him watching her in the doorway. He stepped and kissed her once. "You are so beautiful."

He was being sweet and distracting, but she was fretting about Liam again. "As much as I'd like to look at you indefinitely, you have to get dressed."

"Okay," he said throwing her a smile before rounding up his boxer briefs and jeans. She watched him dress and could feel herself getting turned on yet again. Her libido was constantly charged when he was around.

She looked away. "Okay, here's the plan. You stay in here, out of sight of the door. I'm going to go down and talk him into working on a drawing while I make breakfast. As soon as you hear me say, 'I'll call you when it's ready,' or something like that, quietly sneak down the stairs."

After some finagling, she got Liam up in his room and promised him she'd make goat-shaped pancakes. Once she was standing inside Liam's room to make sure he'd stay at his desk, Conall sneaked down the hall and made it down the stairs without getting caught. As he crossed in front of the doorway, he brought his legs way up and pointed his toes toward the floor in an exaggerated sneak walk, all while grinning at her like a madman. She couldn't help but laugh out loud. Liam looked at her like she was crazy. Maybe she was.

35

Theresa had Liam settled with Pat on a Friday night several weeks later—not for her regular date with Conall because they were switching to Saturdays, but instead for her night out with Sujata and Casey. She'd ditched them for too long, so she pushed Conall off to Saturday night. She took the MAX into town and waited for Sujata.

"Hey, you," Sujata said as she stepped off the train.

"You look nice," Theresa said. Sujata had on a little black dress. "Is that new?"

"Thanks. No, I just haven't worn it in a while."

They left to head over to Clement's.

"What's the occasion?" Theresa asked.

Sujata shrugged. "I don't know. Just felt like getting a little attention tonight."

That was a little unusual, but Sujata did dress well. "I'm sure you will." She put her arm around Sujata's shoulders and side-hugged her, which made Sujata laugh.

They waited at a crosswalk, and a couple men whistled at them. It had been a while since she'd been at—or near, in this case—the center of street harassment. Fortunately, she didn't get a sense of danger from them, especially with so many people around.

Just as Theresa and Sujata arrived at the bar, a car pulled up, and Casey got out. She always took a Lyft car in so she wouldn't have to deal with the train. A benefit of being rich.

Casey snagged their table while Theresa and Sujata headed to the bar.

By the time they got the table, Theresa was ready to relax. "Long week," she said.

"It's good to have you back, Theresa," Casey said. "I've missed you."

Sujata laughed. "Yeah, it's so nice of Conall to loan you out for the night."

Theresa raised her eyebrows. "Come on, it's not that bad. Besides, you both see me all the time."

"Not the same. It's been what, six weeks?" Sujata bumped her shoulder.

"I think so." Casey nodded and took a sip of the wine Sujata had brought her.

"So, how's Conall?" Sujata asked.

They knew what was going on. Theresa talked to both of them on the phone regularly, and Casey still came over most Sunday nights. They both knew she was sleeping with him.

"You've seen more of him this week than I have."

"True," Sujata said with a smile.

"But I'll see him tomorrow during the day, and then we're going out in the evening, too."

"Nice," Casey said. "Every week. How's Liam doing with Conall anyway?" Casey asked.

"Oh, it's great. Liam's reading on his own. He still makes lots of mistakes, but his confidence is way up, and we think it's just a matter of time before his skills catch up. His teacher says he was even willing to read in front of the class."

"That's awesome," Sujata said.

Casey nodded. "Good for him."

"Yeah."

Sujata bumped Theresa's shoulder again. "I've been meaning to ask. What's with the matching shirts Fridays, anyway?"

"Aloha Friday," Theresa said. "Apparently it's a thing in Hawaii. People—I guess men, mostly—wear Hawaiian shirts and khakis. They convinced me to buy one for pod solidarity."

Casey and Sujata laughed, and they all took a sip from their drinks.

Sujata said, "Guess who I ran into at Srider." Srider was the best Indian grocery store in town.

"Who?" Casey said. "Oh, wait, I can guess."

"Vivek," Theresa said, and Casey nodded with a smirk.

"Yes." She put her head in her hands for a moment. Theresa and Casey left her to her wallowing. She lifted her head and said, "You should have heard him. He was there with his roommates, including Girish from the database admin team. And he was all, 'Allow me to introduce my roommates....'"

Theresa and Casey laughed. Theresa imitated his deep voice, "Allow me to introduce the woman I fancy."

"Exactly." Sujata sighed. "They were all very nice, though. Then they—all of them, like the group—invited me to see a Bollywood film next Thursday. Somehow I said yes."

"What?!" Theresa said as Casey's eyes widened in shock.

"I know, I know." Sujata put her head on her arms again and groaned. "What have I done?" Her voice was muffled but Theresa could hear it.

"This is hilarious," Casey said.

But really, she was a little impressed. She'd thought Vivek lacked all self-confidence and that a relationship with Sujata would be impossible. But if he did have a spine, maybe one was possible. A relationship would be good for Sujata.

"It's supposed to be a good film," Sujata said after lifting her head and taking a sip of her wine.

"Sure it is," Theresa teased.

Casey was still laughing, and Theresa said, "Maybe you'll end up together."

"Fat chance," Sujata said. "That's about as likely as you and Conall *not* ending up together."

That seemed a fair assessment, the way things were going.

THERESA DRAGGED the vacuum into Liam's room. They were working to get it cleaned up, because she'd not gotten to it in over a week. Liam squirted some cleaner onto his table and began wiping it down.

"Don't forget to get your nightstand. And pick up the light so you can clean under there."

"I know, Mom."

"Okay, good." She needed to talk to him, but wasn't sure how to approach the topic. "Honey?"

He looked up from his table, mid swipe. "Yeah?"

"You like Conall, don't you?"

"Yeah." He grinned.

"He might be around more." She'd been considering inviting him to start staying over. Once a week with him was not enough.

"Really? Why?"

"Well, you know he's a good friend to both of us. I just wanted you to know so it wouldn't be a surprise."

His brow was furrowed. "Do I have to read more?"

She laughed and reached down to plug the vacuum in. "I thought you liked reading with him."

"Only sometimes. Not *all* the time."

"Okay, well, we won't make you read all the time."

"Okay." He turned back around and finished wiping down the table.

She started the vacuum up and ran it around the room while he wiped off the nightstand.

"Mom!" he yelled.

She turned the vacuum off. "What?"

"Can we change my sheets?"

Ah, he took after her. Loved his clean sheets. "Sure. Go ahead and grab them and we'll do it."

She finished vacuuming, and she had just spread the fitted sheet over the mattress when her phone rang. Her mom.

She wasn't in the book for another reaming. She'd have her talk to Liam first.

"Hi, Mom. How are you?"

"I'm okay. How are you? How's my little man?"

"We're good. I'm going to let you talk to him while I finish making his bed." She handed the phone to Liam, who was grinning.

"Hi Grammy!"

Theresa finished the bed while they chattered. Liam wandered out into the hall and downstairs so she couldn't hear what was being said.

After she was done and had his comforter in place and smoothed down, she headed downstairs to find Liam on the couch, still chattering away. He was telling her mom about his most recent drawings.

"Mom will send you the best one!" he said. "Okay. Love you." He handed the phone to Theresa. "She wants to talk to you."

"Hi, Mom."

"That Catholic is still coming to your house?"

She didn't know where the resolve came from, but she was done with this attitude. "Liam, why don't you go on up and work on one of your drawings?"

"I want to play my game."

"Go upstairs." She said it more sternly than she'd intended.

His eyes widened, and he left.

"Theresa?"

"Mom, you have to stop." She took a deep breath.

"But—"

"It's my life and Conall's in it and he's going to be in my life indefinitely. He's a great man, and he's wonderful with Liam, and I don't care that his father was Catholic. We don't have time to go to church and I don't plan to start any time soon. But Liam's still going to be okay because despite what you think, I am a good mother." She was out of breath by the time she finished.

"Well," her mom huffed. "I don't know what made you fly off the handle—I just asked a simple question."

Theresa laughed, unable to keep the bitterness out of it. "It's the way you ask it. The way you say everything. I know you aren't happy with the choices I've made, but I am. I'm not going to let you treat me like some failure or substandard person anymore."

"Theresa, I never meant any harm." She sounded alarmed. "You know I love you, and I adore Liam. I know he's a good boy."

Theresa sighed. "Then stop questioning everything I do. You cannot talk to me like that."

"Okay," her mom whispered in a quavering voice.

"Okay, then." Theresa paused. "I am going to go because I have a lot to do today. I love you."

"Love you." Her mom's voice was small.

Theresa hung up and fell onto the couch, closing her eyes and putting her hand on her forehead. Her mom was too much sometimes.

36

When Conall arrived for his Wednesday tutoring session, Theresa opened the door and welcomed him in with a kiss.

He laughed through it and said, "What's the occasion?" Normally she was so careful with Liam around that she was very hands-off, at least until she was sure Liam had gone back upstairs afterward.

"No occasion. I've just been wanting to do that all day." She rested her arms on his shoulders.

"I'm not complaining." He kissed her again until she backed up.

She called up for Liam. "Bring your books down, honey."

Something was definitely up. They'd been seeing each other for close to two months now. He looked at her profile while she stood there at the stairs in her jeans and socked feet. Her t-shirt hugged her breasts, and he still wanted to touch them as much as he had when they'd first met. Now he was lucky enough to know what they looked —and tasted—like. Perfection.

She turned her head and smiled at him. "What's up?"

"Nothing." He stepped over to the couch and fell onto it. He would let her choose to tell him what was going on rather than push the issue himself.

Theresa went into the kitchen to clean up. She'd given up being a helicopter mom and now let them work alone. He didn't want to admit to himself how much he appreciated that she trusted him again.

"Hi, Conall," Liam said.

"Hey, buddy."

He sat down next to Conall.

"What'd you bring?"

"This." He held up a book about dinosaurs and then spread out the others on the table. A couple about artists Conall had never heard of and a couple of fiction ones.

"That one first?" Conall asked, indicating the dinosaur book. "Are you interested in dinosaurs?"

"Yeah."

What boy didn't go through a dinosaur phase?

Liam read through the book pretty well. He still made mistakes, but it didn't faze him so much anymore, which was the most important thing. On top of that, they would discuss the books after finishing them, and he seemed to remember what he'd read, which meant he was concentrating on the meaning now instead of just slogging through the words. This was quite an improvement.

"What next?" Conall asked.

Liam picked up one with a painting of a bunch of kids getting on a school bus and opened it on his lap before starting to read.

He had improved so much that Conall guessed he was a stronger reader than some of the other kids in his class. And Conall was also pretty sure that the bully hadn't started back up again. Theresa told him there hadn't been any other incidents.

All in all, things were pretty good. He was a positive influence in a kid's life, and they weren't even related. He wondered what Liam would be like when he got older. He was starting to imagine himself in Liam's life for good, and he liked it.

By the time they made it through the three books, it was seven thirty, and Theresa sent Liam upstairs to get ready for bed. Conall headed for the door.

Once Liam was out of sight, she stopped Conall, slipped her arms around his neck again and kissed him deeply.

Yeah, something was up. They always kissed before he left, but there was something in it this time that was different.

"Would you stay tonight?"

"What?" He pulled back and grasped her shoulders so he could look at her. She couldn't be really asking him to stay over, could she? Ever since that first, accidental time, he'd always left right after they'd had sex after their dates.

"I want you to stay with me all night tonight."

"Yes." There wasn't anything else to answer with. "I need to go down and get Maddy set up first. But I'd love to come back tonight."

She smiled. "Good, because I have big plans."

His dick twitched in anticipation. Whatever she had, it had to be good.

THERESA SAT on the edge of Liam's bed, finishing up his bedtime story.

She glanced at his face. His eyes were droopy, and she knew he was close to falling asleep.

"Liam?"

"Hmm?"

"Conall is going to stay here tonight. So, you'll see him in the morning." She reached over to push his bangs back. She was so excited and apprehensive that it was hard to keep her voice neutral. How was this going to impact him? This was a big deal.

"Like a slumber party? Are we going to play games?"

She laughed. How did he even know what a slumber party was? "No, not like that. You will stay here and sleep."

"I want to see Conall again."

"You'll see him in the morning, sweetie." She palmed his cheek.

"Is he here now?"

"No, he's at home taking care of Maddy." She couldn't wait for him to return.

That perked him up. "Will he bring her?"

"No, she has to stay at home. Tell you what, when he gets here, I'll have him come in and say goodnight to you."

Liam smiled, looking groggy again. "Can you finish the book?"

"Sure, honey."

She finished it, and he was still holding on, though she didn't think he'd last much longer.

She closed the book and put it on top of his bookshelf before going back to give him a goodnight kiss on the forehead.

"Will Conall..." he started.

"He'll come by." She knew he'd be willing to do it. She was so lucky to have found a man who also loved her son.

She headed downstairs, poured herself a small glass of wine, and sat on the couch waiting for Conall.

She'd finished it by the time he knocked on the door. As soon as she opened it, he stepped in and took her in his arms. His kiss was sweet and slow.

She turned away after a moment. "Can you do me a favor?"

He cupped her chin and gently turned her head back so he could see her eyes. "Anything you want, sweetheart."

She loved it when he called her that. It hit her right in the heart. "Could you say goodnight to Liam, if he's not asleep?"

"You told him I'd be here?" he asked with a surprised smile.

"I didn't want him to be confused if he saw you in the morning."

"Makes sense. Let's go."

She led Conall upstairs and stood at the door as he tiptoed in.

"Liam?" he whispered.

Seeing him in there with her sleeping son seemed so right. He looked like he belonged, and she realized she wished Conall was here all the time.

Nothing from Liam. He was out. Conall turned around, shrugged, and smiled at her.

Theresa stuck her hand out, and he took it and followed her into the bedroom, locking the door behind him.

She sat on the bed, and he stood in front of her. The bulge in his jeans was right there, and a wave of lust washed over her. She unbuttoned his jeans and reached into his boxer briefs, squeezing him and savoring his girth.

"Mmm," he said.

When she took the head in her mouth, he said, "As good as that feels, tonight's not about me."

He lifted her head by the chin and leaned over to kiss her. He reached for the hem of her shirt and soon it was on the floor. He gently squeezed her breasts.

She was glad she'd decided to wear one of her lace bras. For some reason she wanted to impress him tonight. But why had he said tonight was not about him? As far as she was concerned it was.

He showed her what he'd meant, taking her to new heights of pleasure. Once he was finished making her feel better than he ever had before he asked, "How are you doing?"

"Melted butter."

He smiled but he was looking at her with such affection. She hadn't felt so wanted in a long time. Ever. Michael had never wanted her like this.

"Roll over and scoot forward, sweetheart."

She was happy to oblige. He knew she loved it like this. He rolled a condom on, and then she felt him get on the bed and lift her hips so he could position himself. He notched inside. She felt the anticipation build up as he just sat there like that. She needed him to fill her up, now.

"Conall."

He squeezed her hips and then abruptly pushed in as far as he'd go, making her moan in appreciation.

Usually when they did it this way, he went fast and hard, but today he moved deliberately, massaging her hips. Then he lifted her so he could palm both breasts and continued moving.

He surprised her by pulling out, and she turned her head to see him. He rolled her over and said, "It wasn't good enough. I want to see you." He leaned forward and kissed her deeply before notching inside again.

The look on his face as he pushed inside was one she hadn't seen before. His eyes were so intense as he stared into hers, thrusting slowly. She felt like she knew him better than anyone else except Liam, and it had only been a few months, really. Then it struck her—she loved him.

Her mouth fell open in surprise, and he propped himself on his elbows so he could kiss her again. She pushed her tongue in and felt like she couldn't get enough of him. They were joined in two places, and it wasn't enough for how much she wanted him to be just hers.

THE FIRST THING Theresa noticed when she woke was a weight across her stomach. Conall's arm. She looked over at him and smiled at his sleeping face. Dark stubble had grown in overnight, giving him a more rugged look than he normally had.

Then she heard a knock at the door. "Mom!"

She slipped out from under Conall's arm and ran to the bathroom door where her robe hung.

"Mom!" The doorknob jiggled.

"What, Liam? Are you okay?"

"Is Conall here?"

She glanced over at him. His eyes were open now, and he was looking at her sleepily, but a smile crept across his face.

She opened the door to see Liam in his Batman pajamas. He looked up at her expectantly and before she could stop him, rushed past her. She turned around just in time to see him leap onto the bed next to Conall.

"Whoa, buddy," Conall said. Thank goodness the bedspread covered him.

Theresa walked over and leaned down to kiss Liam's head. "Honey, why don't you go on downstairs and I'll be there in a minute to make breakfast."

He looked at Conall again and then Theresa, and slid off the bed.

She quietly shut the door behind him and went back to the bed to lie next to Conall, who rolled onto his side to be closer.

"Morning," he said.

She leaned over to kiss him, then said, "I love waking up with you."

He caressed her face. "I love waking up with you, too."

"Let's make this a regular thing."

He smiled and kissed her again. "Okay. I'm convinced."

"I have to go make breakfast."

"I know. It's too bad. What time is it?"

She smiled and ran her fingers along his firm arm. "A little after six. I've got to go."

"Mm-hmm."

"Okay." She kissed him again, a lingering one that she missed as soon as she slipped away from him and off the bed.

Once downstairs, she found Liam playing a video game. "I'm hungry, Mom."

"I'm starting breakfast now. Do scrambled eggs sound good?"

He nodded while repeatedly pressing one of the game's controller buttons.

Theresa turned a burner on and sprayed a pan with Pam. She broke several eggs into a bowl, then poured some milk in and began whipping it.

When the pan was ready, she threw some turkey sausage patties in.

She heard some movement on the stairs.

"Conall!" Liam said. "Did you have fun spending the night?"

Conall laughed. "Oh, yeah, I had a lot of fun, buddy."

"Do you want to play my game with me?"

"Sure."

He went into the living room.

She flinched when she heard Liam's first question: "What did you do last night?"

She wanted to run out there to make sure Conall didn't say something bad, but relaxed when she heard him say, "We just went to bed, kiddo. We were both tired."

She finished breakfast, getting the table set while it was cooking. When she glanced into the living room, Conall caught her eye and smiled, which pinched her heart. She liked him way too much.

Once she had the eggs dished out, she called Liam and Conall.

Theresa sat and started spreading the almond butter on a piece of toast for Liam.

Liam picked his fork up, and then asked Conall, "Did you read when you went to bed? Mom does."

"Not last night, buddy. I was beat."

Theresa put the toast on Liam's plate and couldn't help lock eyes with Conall for a moment, when they both smiled. When she looked back at Liam, he was looking back and forth between them.

"Do you like your eggs, Liam?" Theresa asked.

"Yeah."

Liam definitely knew something had changed.

37

"Can you get the salad mix out of the fridge?" Conall asked Liam. They were making dinner Friday night a month later, with Theresa laid up in her room, in the throes of the flu.

Liam cheerily pulled it out. "Here you go!"

"Go ahead and put it in a bowl. You want carrots and celery in there?" Conall stirred the pasta he was boiling.

"Sure."

"Grab those, then, and I'll cut them up."

Liam retrieved them and set them on the counter. He got the wooden salad bowl out and tore the bag open, spilling about half of it on the floor.

"Oh."

"Don't worry about it, buddy. Throw it in the sink." Conall chopped up a few carrots and a piece of celery and tossed it in the bowl while Liam picked up the lettuce off the floor.

Conall put the vegetables back in the fridge. "You want to set the table?"

"Okay."

Conall grabbed a couple plates and put them on the counter so Liam could reach them.

"Is Mom not eating?"

"I don't think so. She still feels really bad."

Liam's brow furrowed. "Is she going to be okay?"

"Yeah, buddy. She just has the flu. It's pretty bad, but she'll be fine. I need to go check on her, to make sure she doesn't want to eat something, okay?"

"Okay."

"Why don't you hang out with Maddy, and I'll be back down in a minute."

Liam nodded and went into the living room, where Maddy was curled up in front of the couch. Conall was working on getting Theresa to let Maddy on the couch. He wasn't there yet, but he knew she would fall for her. Just slowly.

When Conall went into see Theresa, he immediately knew she was much worse off than she'd been that afternoon. She was sprawled out in her flannel pajamas with the covers pushed to the foot of the bed. She looked passed out and was covered in sweat.

He rushed to the bed. "Sweetheart, are you okay?"

She opened her eyes and shakily said, "Hi." She gave him a very weak smile.

His heart ached for her because he didn't know what he could do to make her feel better. "Do you want to sit up?"

"No, I don't think so. I'm really dizzy."

He sat down on the bed to feel her forehead. She was burning up, and his hand came away wet from her sweat.

"Can I have some water?" She motioned at the empty glass on the nightstand.

"Definitely. Be right back." He jumped up, glad to have something specific to do, because he didn't know what you were supposed to do for this.

He returned with a cup from the bathroom that he set on the nightstand. "Can you sit up? For the water?"

She attempted to push herself back a little, but when she couldn't do it, he reached under her knees and arms and just moved her into a sitting position himself, grabbing to pillows to put behind her back.

She smiled weakly at him again, which sort of hurt his heart.

He brushed some of her damp hair out of her eyes, and she stared up at him.

"I'm sorry I look so terrible."

"Don't be ridiculous. You look like a sick woman, that's all. Here's the water, sweetheart."

"Oh, thanks." She took it and drank some small sips before setting it back on the nightstand.

He went to the bathroom to grab a towel and came back to wipe down her face and neck. She coughed feebly.

"Do you want to lie down again?" He loved her. This was a truth.

"I think so."

He wanted to punch the flu in the face. Seeing her like this was unbearable. He got her lying down flat again.

"I'm cold again."

He brought the covers back up to her chin and brushed her hair back with his fingers.

"Mom?" Liam said from the doorway.

"Hey, buddy."

"Hi, sweetie. Don't come close—I don't want you to get this. It's terrible. But I love you from over here."

Liam looked at Conall, wide-eyed, probably from how she sounded. Like she was on the verge of passing out.

"Your mom's feeling really bad. Why don't you finish setting the table and get the salad on there?"

He nodded and left.

"You're so good with him," she said. Her eyelids drooped.

"I'm going to let you sleep, okay, sweetheart?" He touched her cheek again.

"Mmm."

He didn't want to leave her, but he needed to get back down to Liam.

Right before he reached the bottom step, Conall heard a clang, a gasp, and a thunk.

He ran into the kitchen to see Liam standing there, blood dripping down his hand and off his elbow onto the floor. A knife was on the floor next to the step stool he stood on in his bare feet.

"Oh, my God, Liam! What happened?"

Liam's mouth was in an O, and tears started rolling down his face.

Conall raced over to look at his fingers. He'd apparently cut himself on the inside of multiple fingers, and the cuts looked deep.

"I dropped the knife!" Liam said between sobs.

Conall picked up the knife and dropped it in the sink before grabbing a towel out of a drawer and wrapping it around Liam's fingers. The only cuts were on his fingers. But he was going to have to take him to the emergency room. Liam would need stitches.

He maneuvered Liam over to the kitchen table and onto a chair. The boy was sobbing and moaning a little from the pain.

"Hold the towel tight on your fingers, okay?" He had to take Liam's other hand and wrap his fingers around the towel. "Tight, okay?"

Liam's face was white, and now Conall worried that Liam would pass out. So, he picked him up and carried him to the couch.

Then he raced upstairs, grabbed a pair of shoes from Liam's room, and ran into Theresa's room.

"Theresa?" he called.

She didn't stir. As much as he hated to, he had to shake her awake. She stared at him groggily.

"Liam's cut himself. I have to take him to the emergency room."

"Oh." Her eyes went wide, and she jerked forward like she was going to try to get up, but Conall held her down.

"You're in no condition, Theresa. I'll take care of it."

"Is he okay?"

"He'll be fine. He'll need stitches, though."

"Please take care of him, Conall," she said, apparently losing the fight against closing her eyes.

Conall touched her face again but then raced back downstairs. Liam was still awake, thank God, and crying. He threw shoes on Liam's feet and picked him up to get him standing.

They made it to the car, and Conall got Liam situated in the back. "Remember, hold on tight."

"It hurts," Liam said through his tears.

"I know, kiddo. Hang tight."

He ran around to the driver's side, and they were off.

How could he have let this happen? And he'd thought he was made for parenting. Obviously, it wasn't that simple.

LIAM CRIED EVEN MORE FERVENTLY when the doctor gave him the first of the numbing shots in his index finger. Conall's heart broke a little. Liam's wounded left hand was strapped down with velcro straps to a soft board to keep him from moving it.

"Hey, buddy, you can do this." He wasn't going to tell him to be tough. "This is the worst part of it, okay?"

Liam wiped tears off his face with his good hand and nodded.

"You're doing great, Liam," the doctor said. He was a young man, probably not long out of his residency. But he clearly knew what he was doing.

Conall rubbed Liam's back while the doctor gave him another shot. Should he take his good hand? It seemed like a fatherly thing to do.

This was all his fault. He should have put the knife away. Some father figure he was.

But this was about Liam so he took his hand, and the kid squeezed hard at the next shot, whimpering a little.

The doctor patted Liam's shoulder. "I'll be back in a few minutes, to let the numbing take effect."

Liam nodded and leaned against Conall's arm. The doctor slipped past the curtain.

"Liam?"

"Yeah?"

"What were you doing with the knife?" He reached over to push Liam's bangs from his eyes.

"I wanted to be like you. I thought I would cut up a red pepper. Mom puts it in salads, and I like it."

Liam wanted to be like him. So, it really was his fault. He should have put the knife away. "What happened?"

"I dropped it."

"And you tried to catch it?"

"Yeah." He sniffed. The crying had subsided.

"I'm sorry that happened to you, buddy."

They were quiet except for Liam's stuffed-up breathing.

"How does your hand feel, kiddo?" Conall asked.

"Okay. It doesn't hurt now."

"Good." He rubbed Liam's back. "You know, when you get the stitches, it will feel weird, okay? Because you can't feel what they're doing, but your hand will move. It's kind of creepy."

"You had stitches?"

"Right here." He showed Liam a scar on his forehead. "I fell off my first bike and landed head-first on the curb."

"Whoa. Did it hurt?"

"A lot. I got a terrible headache after, too."

"Ready for your stitches, Liam?" the doctor called from outside the curtain before coming in. A nurse was with him.

Liam nodded.

"You're being really brave, Liam," Conall said.

The nurse handed the doctor the needle and thread. "This will tug a little, okay?"

Liam nodded as the doctor started.

He jerked his head to look at Conall.

"Told you—feels weird, huh?"

"Yeah!"

The doctor chuckled as he continued stitching. He finished Liam's pinky and ring fingers and continued on to the middle finger.

Liam watched, fascinated.

The doctor finished and bandaged the fingers. "Good job, Liam." He patted Liam on the shoulder and left.

The nurse smiled at Liam. "You were very brave." She handed Conall a sheet of paper detailing care for the wounds and went over it.

On the way to the car, Liam took Conall's hand again and climbed silently into the back.

God, what would Theresa think of him once she was awake again?

THERESA WAS SPRAWLED out on the bed with her arms over her head. She stank, but couldn't really care right at the moment since she still felt so awful. The worst of it did seem to have passed, and she didn't feel borderline delirious anymore, which was good.

It was still dark outside, and she had to pee. She shifted so her feet were on the floor and sat there a moment to make sure she wasn't going to get dizzy again.

"Theresa?"

"Hi," she turned around and said, a feeling of such strong affection overtaking her that she thought her heart might burst. He hadn't minded sharing the bed with her. Michael never would have done that. He would have grumpily taken the couch, for fear of getting sick himself.

"How are you? Are you feeling better?" Conall jumped up and raced around the bed to stand in front of her, despite looking quite sleepy himself.

She smiled, still happy he was here and cared so much about her. "I'm much better. How's Liam?"

"He's good. I've changed the bandage again. He says his fingers itch, but he's handling it pretty well."

She took his hand. "Thank you so much for taking care of him."

He smiled, but it didn't quite reach his eyes, which was odd. "Are you going somewhere?"

"I just need to go to the bathroom."

He stuck his hand out, and she took it so he could help her stand, but she didn't need it.

"I think I can make it, Conall." Then she remembered she still stank. "I need a shower."

"Why don't I run you a bath instead?"

Ooh. "That would be really nice. Thanks." She squeezed his hand, and he leaned down and kissed her forehead.

Theresa pushed him away. "I smell. Stay away."

"I didn't even notice. And I'm glad you're feeling better." He pushed hair back from her forehead. "I'll go run that bath."

She smiled stupidly at him until he went into the bathroom and then fell back on the bed. Even the way she felt right now, she wanted him. She couldn't get away from that fact.

She heard the water start up, which just made the situation with her bladder more of a concern. She pushed herself back up onto her elbows and then sat up.

Once the water stopped, she stood up, leaning back against the bed, but she wasn't dizzy, so she headed to the closet for some clean pajamas. Conall came out of the bathroom, and she looked up at his face, feeling lucky he was hers.

He smiled at her and said, "It's ready. Are you sure you're okay?"

She put her hand on his forearm. "I am. I'm going to get back in bed after, but I'm desperate for a bath."

Once she was in the pink tub and scrubbing herself clean, the hot water felt amazing, like it was melting away the flu itself.

She was so glad she had Conall. How could she have ever thought of pushing him away? He was pretty much perfect. She closed her eyes and pictured his smiling face with that jaw and those eyes, and then she imagined him coming in for a kiss. And just like that, she knew she couldn't wait to feel up for making love again.

She squeezed some shampoo into her palm and scrubbed her hair clean, dunking her head to rinse it off. Now the tub was full of dirty water, and she wondered what the point of a bath really was—it didn't seem like you could get truly clean. So, she pulled the plug and then carefully stood up to turn the shower itself on and rinsed off. Now, that was washing away the flu, for sure.

When she got back to her bed, she found that Conall had changed her sheets. Perfect man.

She settled in just as her phone vibrated on the nightstand. She picked it up. "Hi, Mom."

"What's wrong?"

Theresa pulled the comforter up to her neck. "I've had the flu this week."

"Oh, I'm sorry. Has it been bad?"

"Yeah. I would have been in trouble if it hadn't been for Conall. He's been taking care of both Liam and me."

"Well, that's nice. I'm glad you've found someone who's there for you."

She seemed to mean it, a clear improvement. Her mom appeared to have adjusted as much as possible to the idea of Conall in Liam's life. Perhaps she appreciated a good male role model for Liam.

"How's everybody there?" Theresa asked.

Her mom started on the goings on in Kerrville. Her younger sister's boyfriend had broken his arm in an ATV accident. Sarah's twins were playing t-ball and were adorable to watch. Sarah's daughters were both doing well in school, and the older one still loved cheerleading. Her older brother was on a different cruise liner now. And so on.

Theresa was glad to hear about everybody, but she was getting tired.

Her mom wrapped up the family talk. "So, can I talk to Liam now?"

"Yeah, but I'll have him call you in a couple minutes." She couldn't get up again, so she'd just call Conall and have him send Liam up. "Love you."

"Love you, too, honey."

Maybe her mom really would stay off her case.

38

Almost two months later, Theresa and Conall were in the garage working on bookshelves for Liam's room. They were going to build some just like the ones downstairs. Theresa watched Conall operate the circular saw and listened to the whine of it. She was competent with it, but they wanted to finish today, and he was a little faster. They had the garage door open because it was a nice, not-too-hot summer day, and she looked out and saw her neighbor across the street. She waved.

Then she turned around and saw Liam standing in the doorway. She put a hand on Conall's shoulder, appreciating how solid he was. He stopped and looked over at her so she nodded in the doorway.

"Conall, I made you something," Liam said, stepping into the garage.

"Stay back, honey," Theresa said.

Conall stepped over to him, and Liam handed over the card he'd made. It had a picture of Maddy he'd drawn.

"Look at that!" Conall said. "It looks just like her!"

Liam beamed.

"Open it up," Theresa said.

He did. When he saw what was written inside—I Like you! Thank you for helping me read better—he said, "Aw, buddy. Thanks." Then he reached down to hug Liam, who still looked happy.

"Honey, can you take Maddy outside and play with her?" Theresa said. "It's too dangerous for you out here while we're working."

"But I want to watch."

"Maddy needs a little exercise, Liam. You're good at running her tired."

Liam looked annoyed but said, "Fine."

Once he was gone, Conall turned around and said, "He's such a good kid. I can't believe he made me something."

"He had to make one for his father, and he wanted to make one for you, too," Theresa said.

Conall looked at her in confusion.

"It's Father's Day."

Understanding spread across his face. "Ohh," he said. "I didn't realize. Ever since my dad died, I've kind of ignored it." But he was smiling so much he looked almost goofy.

He set the card down on a shelf, and Theresa went over to hug him.

"You're already like a father to him," she said, breathing him in, his soap scent mixed with the wood they were cutting.

"I'm not sure about that."

Maybe she shouldn't have said that. She might be scaring him off with what might sound like commitment talk.

He smiled at her again and kissed her nice and slow. "Let's get back to it."

They worked on sawing more boards, but between a couple when the saw was off, they heard another noise coming from inside.

"What is that?" Conall asked.

But Theresa realized with a racing heart what it was. "The smoke alarm!"

Conall's eyes widened.

They raced inside and the acrid scent of smoke was everywhere. Theresa went straight for the backyard. "Liam!" He didn't come. "Liam!" When she ran out into the yard, he wasn't there. She shot back inside, her heart going crazy, and found Conall stepping off the bottom step, carrying Liam, who was crying and holding on tight to Conall's neck. She touched Liam's back, and without another word, they ran outside the front door.

Theresa ran into the garage for her phone while Conall put Liam down, and then she dialed 9-1-1. When she got back to them, Liam fell against her, still crying. She gave the operator her address.

"I'm going to go get Maddy," Conall said. He ran around the side of the house to the gate.

Theresa could hear him calling for Maddy until he came back looking panicked. "She's not there!"

"Where's Maddy, Liam?" Theresa asked.

"In my room," he said in the smallest voice.

"Shit!" Conall ran toward the house.

Theresa couldn't believe it. Her panic rose, and she cried, "Conall, no!" But he was already inside.

After a few seconds, he came back out. "The smoke's too thick!"

Theresa was still holding the phone, and she said, "There's a dog inside the house! When will they get here?"

Conall raced into the garage and came out carrying her extendable ladder and ran around the side of the house. She trailed him and saw him extending the ladder and resting it just under Liam's window.

"Conall, you can't go in there!"

"I have to! I have to get Maddy!"

"But they're on their way!" She held on to Liam, whose arms were wrapped around her again.

He rooted around on the ground and picked up a palm-sized rock. "You didn't see the smoke." He started climbing the ladder and broke the window, picking the glass shards out on the bottom and dropping them while smoke snaked out the top of the window.

Then he was inside.

"Conall!" Theresa yelled, still not believing this was happening. She could hear Liam sobbing, then she heard fire trucks in the distance.

She was torn between calling for Conall to come back out and keeping Liam a safe distance from the house. They ended up standing on the curb where she could see the bedroom window. She couldn't leave Liam on his own.

No Conall. She leaned over and rested her palms on her thighs. Was she going to throw up.

Liam put a hand on her back but didn't say anything. He was still crying.

Sirens wailed in the distance.

A police car pulled up, and she cried, "My boyfriend is in there! He's trying to get his dog!"

"Where?" asked the tiny woman officer.

"This way!"

Theresa led her back toward the window, dragging Liam behind her.

Just then, Conall's head emerged from the window, holding Maddy's head out. They were both coughing violently.

"Conall, please come down!" she begged, so relieved to see him alive that she knew she couldn't bear to lose sight of him again. She was holding on to Liam's hand so tight she knew it must be hurting him.

He hefted Maddy onto the window's edge and then started trying to get himself out, but it was clear it was going to be impossible.

The officer made them move back toward the curb, which is when Theresa saw two firetrucks pull up, and firefighters started unrolling the fire hose. Then Pat was next to her, giving Liam a hug.

"Where's Conall?" Pat asked.

Theresa pointed at the house. Smoke was flowing out the window.

"Oh, my God!" Pat said, not masking her alarm at all. She let go of Liam and ran toward the window, but was bumped out of the way by two firefighters.

The one carrying a ladder moved Conall's before racing up his own.

Theresa watched in terror as the man climbed into the room and made Conall leave Maddy and climb down.

By now, more neighbors had emerged and some were talking to Pat. Then Conall was on the ground, and Theresa ran to him, so glad he seemed okay that she burst into tears of relief. He reached out to hug her, but looked back up to see them start bringing Maddy down.

Oh, no. She looked bad, all limp.

Then a paramedic took Conall away from her and left her watching the firefighter with Maddy.

She ran after Conall, who they were taking to an ambulance she hadn't known had arrived. Liam ran up to her, and she put her hand on his back.

"Thank God he's okay!" Pat said.

The paramedic had to force Conall onto the back of the ambulance despite his coughing.

Theresa looked back and saw the firefighters giving Maddy oxygen in the grass next to the first firetruck. She didn't know what to do. She held onto Liam, watched Conall, and felt Pat holding her hand.

How could this have happened?

THE PARAMEDICS HAD to forcibly sit Conall at the back of the open ambulance and put a mask over his face. His heart was pounding while he breathed in the oxygen. He'd been trying to find out how Maddy was. He knew the firefighters were giving her oxygen, too, but that was all he knew. She'd been inside longer than he had, and his lungs and throat burned from just his own exposure.

Theresa and Liam came rushing over. Liam was still crying deep, wracking sobs.

Theresa took Conall's hand and said, "Are you okay?"

Conall nodded as he held up the mask.

"I didn't mean to!" Liam wailed.

"Didn't mean to what?" Theresa asked, holding onto his hand with her other.

He took two sobbing breaths.

"I just wanted to see what would happen!"

"What are you talking about?" Theresa asked.

"It exploded!"

What on earth was the kid talking about? Did he start the fire?

"What did you do?" Theresa crouched down to look Liam in the eye.

Liam hiccuped. "I found your lighter in the kitchen."

"What did you light?" she asked.

"The toilet paper." He cried, "And then it went up the shower curtain!"

Liam had started the fire? On purpose?

Theresa gripped him by the shoulders. "Liam, how could you do that? What were you thinking?"

"I don't know!" He was sobbing again. "And Mr. Bark is still in there!"

Conall stared at them, listening to the sound of his breathing through the respirator. Confused anger was rising like flames licking at his insides.

"Conall," Liam started shakily.

Conall put his hand out to stop him and said, "If Maddy dies, it's going to be your fault."

Liam's crying escalated quickly, and he clung to Theresa.

"Conall!" Theresa cried. "How could you say that?"

He couldn't look at her. Her son had nearly killed Maddy. Or maybe had.

THERESA HAD herself propped up on the bed, leaning against two pillows, and watched Liam drawing at the hotel's table. It was Monday evening after the fire. One of the first things she'd bought, after some more clothes, was drawing supplies for Liam. As angry as she was at him—and she was very angry—he was clearly sorry and traumatized by what had happened.

What he'd done.

She couldn't believe he'd set a toilet roll on fire. It was unbelievable and so out of character. They'd talked about it some more, and he had explained he was just curious. She didn't think she needed to worry about having a pyromaniac on her hands, as he was so freaked out by his role in the fire that she had no

286

doubt he'd never do it again. But he was going to therapy to make sure.

She knew art was considered good for therapy, so she figured encouraging him to draw was the right thing to do. She didn't feel like punishment was in order yet.

She had her work laptop open but couldn't focus. She was worried because Conall hadn't been at work today. She'd gone in—and Liam had gone to school—because she figured it was best to keep up with the normal routine. For both of them.

Where was he? Because she needed to talk to him. She needed to tell him she was sorry about yelling at him, and she understood why he'd snapped at Liam. She got it. She imagined he felt bad by now, anyway. He was such a good man.

She couldn't believe it when he'd gone back in for Maddy. That had been one of the most terrifying moments of her life.

She tried calling him—again—but it went straight to voice mail. Like his phone was off, not like he just didn't answer.

What if he was in the hospital?

"Mom?"

"Yes, honey?"

He'd turned around in his chair and looked at her. "Is Conall going to be mad at me forever?"

"I don't think so." But what if he was?

But no, he was a reasonable man.

"I want to say sorry."

He must be in the hospital.

No, he was probably with that friend of his, recuperating on his own. If they went over there, she could find out how he was, herself.

"That's a good idea. Let's go."

When they got to Isaac's house, it was the same—no cars and dark inside. Liam held her hand while they went up to the door to knock, but no one answered. He could be in there, but she couldn't picture him just not answering.

Now she was really worried. She parked in front of her own house, and his car was indeed still there. She and Liam both looked at the house, which had black streaks out over the tops of the broken

287

windows. Otherwise, you couldn't really tell how damaged it was. They'd gotten the garage door closed the old school way. The inside was soaked, and the upstairs bathroom was destroyed. Every porous surface was smoke damaged. Fixing it would be so awful. And after all the work they'd put into it. The whole thing was gut-wrenching.

This was awful, just awful. She felt tears forming, the first time. She'd just been too shocked up until now, but somehow it really struck home, now that she was looking at her house.

And where was Conall?

"Mom?"

"Mm-hmm?" She wiped her eyes.

"Are you crying?"

"Just a little."

"Oh. I'm crying, too."

"Why, honey?"

"I miss Mr. Bark." He sniffed. "Will I get him back?"

"No. He'll smell too bad." She hoped he'd take this okay. "We're going to have to get you a new one."

He cried openly now. "I don't want another one! I want Mr. Bark!"

"Liam, you did a bad thing, and this is one of the consequences."

"But I didn't mean to."

She turned around to face him. "You knew you weren't supposed to play with the lighter. This is why. You're going to have to let Mr. Bark go."

His face was tear-stained but he nodded weakly.

She called the hospital from the car to see if Conall was there, but they wouldn't tell her if he was. And since she wasn't a relative, even if she went in, they wouldn't tell her—unless he'd mentioned her by name. The only way to find out if he had would be to go by, so they did, but either he wasn't there or he hadn't named her as someone who could visit.

She drove back to the hotel and she and Liam went back inside, dejected.

39

Wednesday morning, Theresa dropped Liam off at school and headed in to work. She dumped her bag under her desk and looked over at Conall's empty desk. She hadn't heard from him, and he hadn't been into work yesterday, either. She'd gone by the hospital last night, too, but no luck.

Then she looked toward the kitchen and saw him heading her way. Her heart pinched as she watched him approach. He looked at her but she couldn't read his expression.

"Hi," he said in a raspy voice when he reached her and stood right next to her desk.

"Where've you been? I've been so worried. I left you so many messages." She focused on keeping her voice at work appropriate levels but she wanted to hug him and cry and tell him she loved him.

"I was in the hospital until yesterday afternoon. My phone battery died."

"Oh! I'm so sorry—are you okay now? I called them, and they wouldn't tell me if you were there."

He nodded. "Hurts a little to talk, but I'll be okay."

She couldn't help but reach out and touch his arm, but then she didn't know what to say.

"Theresa, I'll be fine. How are you holding up? And Liam?" He didn't seem angry when he said Liam's name, so she thought that was a good sign.

"We're fine. How's Maddy?" That poor dog.

"She's still at the vet, but he says she'll be fine, too."

"Oh, Conall. I'm so glad she's going to be okay. And I'm so sorry about everything." She was about to cry.

"Don't worry, sweetheart," he said quietly. "It'll all be fine."

"Okay," she whispered.

"Hey, man, where've you been?" one of the other developers said as he approached.

"Talk to you later, Theresa," Conall said as he walked off with the guy, explaining what had happened.

The rest of the day was a frustrating blur, and she didn't have another chance to talk to Conall. She felt like maybe he was ignoring her, but it was more of a feeling than anything concrete.

She picked Liam up from his after-school program, and once they were in the car, she said, "I saw Conall at work today, honey."

"Did you tell him sorry?"

"You need to do that yourself. But he and Maddy are both going to be okay."

"Can I see them?" He sounded very excited by the idea. Theresa guessed he needed to get his apology off his chest.

"Let me call him first. But we need to have another conversation, Liam."

"About what?"

"The fire." They still hadn't really talked about it. She'd been dreading it, and didn't know how to start the conversation, because it was so important.

"Oh." He didn't say anything else, but she could hear the dread in his voice, as well.

"We're going to have dinner first, though."

They ate their dinner in silence until he started talking about a painting he'd done in art class that day.

"When will I get to see it?" she asked.

"I don't know."

The server returned with her credit card, and she signed the receipt.

"Are you ready?"

"Yeah."

Once they got back to the room, she said, "Sweetie, I need you to tell me everything that happened on Sunday."

He sat down on the bed, and she sat next to him.

"I don't know."

"Be honest with me. After you came to the garage and gave Conall his card, what did you do?" She squeezed his shoulder.

"I went to play with Maddy."

"Outside?"

"Yeah." He was looking away from her.

"Then what?"

"I wanted to draw but I didn't want to be alone."

"So you brought her up to your room?" She reached over to brush the hair off his forehead. He needed another cut.

"Yeah."

"Why did you get a lighter?"

"I already had it."

"Who gave it to you?" she asked.

"It was in the kitchen."

Ah. The one lighter she kept buried in the back of the junk drawer. So stupid of her.

"Okay, so why did you light the toilet paper?"

"I don't knooow." He sounded miserable.

"Liam."

"I didn't know it would do that!"

"What really happened?" she asked.

"I lit it, and then I dropped it because it went whoosh, all fire. Then it caught the shower curtain on fire, too."

"You have to promise me you will never, ever play with fire again."

"I won't!" He looked up at her with an earnest face, and she believed he meant it.

"Okay." Still, she would have to watch him closely.

"When can we see Maddy and Conall?"

She dialed Conall's number, but he didn't answer, which was a little odd. She left him a message: "Conall, it's me. We need to talk to you. Can we come by? Or you could come here." She gave him their hotel and room number and hoped he'd call back, at least.

$\sim$

CONALL SAT on the couch at Isaac's on Friday evening and thought about what he was about to do.

It was the right thing, however wrong it felt and however wrong Theresa would think it was.

He clearly couldn't handle being a father. His condition was a message from the universe. He wasn't meant to have kids, even if he thought he wanted them.

How could he have talked to Liam that way? He was just a kid. And his fingers had these little white scars stretching across them, a forever mark of Conall's failure.

He dialed Theresa.

"Conall, I'm so glad you called. Can we come over? Liam wants to talk to you."

"I'd rather come by your hotel room."

"Okay." She sounded happy, which twisted his gut. What he was about to do to her...

She'd live through it. She was tough.

"Do you want to come to dinner with us?" she continued.

"No, I have some stuff I have to do around the house. Can I catch you before you go out?" He assumed she was still meeting Casey and Sujata in town.

"Why don't you come by about 6:30."

"Okay, see you then."

"I can't wait to see you."

She would if she knew. "Bye, Theresa."

He leaned back with his arms stretched out and closed his eyes. Christ, he'd miss her. And seeing her every day at work would be so hard for both of them. He never should have started dating her. He should have listened to those internal reservations that told him dating a coworker was a bad idea.

He was so exhausted because he hadn't been sleeping well. Without Theresa next to him, everything felt wrong, for one, but also his lungs still hurt.

Maddy was in the same kind of shape. He could feel the weight of her head on his foot, as she was all drugged up on pain meds. He'd only picked her up yesterday after work. She'd gotten a lot more of the smoke than he had.

But she would be okay, thank God.

He drifted off. When he woke up, it was already 6:30.

"Shit," he muttered, jumping up to throw his shoes on and head out.

All the way to the hotel, the pit in his stomach grew. This was likely going to be the hardest thing he'd ever had to do.

He parked and headed in the front door. The desk clerk, in her white blouse, smiled at him and said, "Good evening."

He nodded in response and continued on down the right hall.

125, 127, 129. Here he was. He took a deep breath and knocked.

Theresa opened the door wearing a big smile. "Hi," she said.

"Hi."

"Come on in." She opened the door wide.

He hadn't even thought about the fact that she'd want him to come in. He couldn't do this in front of Liam. "Can you come out here?"

Her smile faded, and her eyes conveyed concerned. But she stepped out after turning the latch to block the door from completely closing.

"Why aren't you out with your friends tonight?" Conall asked.

"Liam's really traumatized. I'm staying with him."

He nodded.

"Conall. I love you."

His heart twisted, and he looked down the hall at the green and blue patterned carpet. How could she love him? Him, of all people.

"Theresa, I'm not the man you think I am. I can't be what you need. What you deserve."

"No." Her voice cracked. "Don't say that. It's not true. You are exactly what I need."

"I think we need to end things."

She inhaled sharply. "Conall, no. No." She reached for his hands and held on to both.

He didn't squeeze back but he looked at her beautiful face, which was already tearing up. "It's the best way. It's best for both of us. For all of us."

"No. No, no, no. You can't do this."

He disengaged his hands and touched her shoulder once. "It's best, Theresa."

Then he turned and started down the hall.

"Conall!" she called.

He almost stopped and went back and took it all back. But no, he was right. This was the best thing for both of them.

He made his way through the hall and into the lobby.

"Have a great night," the clerk called.

There was nothing to say to that.

Everything sounded weird, and he got into his car and stopped. But he was afraid she might come after him, so he backed up and headed to Isaac's. Back home.

40

Two Mondays after the breakup, Theresa was at work setting up the database software on another couple of new servers. Conall had just passed by and headed into the bathroom, so she knew he'd be by again shortly. She didn't want to be there and feel even more of her feelings. Because they were awful. Physically painful. She was so raw that it still took a concerted effort to not tear up at work when she saw or even thought about him.

How could he just throw everything they had away? She did not understand why, and he refused to explain himself even after she'd called him.

So, she popped into an empty conference room to do something else she hadn't wanted to do—call Michael. Liam would be going for his month-long summer visit on Saturday and they hadn't planned the exchange yet. Because they were living in a hotel room, she didn't want to call Michael where Liam could hear. Things could get nasty.

The football camp was during the visit, and she was still hoping to get Liam out of that. He didn't want to go. She'd talked to him about it again. She had an idea for a compromise Liam was on board with that she hoped Michael would go for.

She dialed, half hoping Michael wouldn't pick up. But he did.

"Theresa." His voice was flat.

"Hi. I just wanted to plan for Liam's visit." She'd get to the other thing in a moment.

"Centralia at eleven."

"Okay, sure." Now it was time. "Michael, we also need to discuss the football camp."

"What's there to discuss? It's already paid for, Theresa."

She pressed on her forehead with fingers and closed her eyes. "Michael, Liam doesn't want to go. And you know how I feel about violent sports."

"What boy doesn't want to go to football camp at the Seahawks training center?" It was the kind of thing that would be a dream for a lot of kids—with a lot of the players making cameo appearances.

"You know Liam has no idea who these people are."

"He will. I'll make sure of that."

Theresa opened her eyes and wondered how. Would he sit Liam down and make him watch recorded videos of games and point the players out? Her son would be bored out of his mind.

"Would you consider a compromise?" she asked.

"What?"

"He's open to taking karate or tae kwon do. There are a couple of studios—whatever they're called—nearby, and I'm willing encourage him since you're so keen on him doing a sport."

Michael was silent for a moment, and she waited, hoping.

"What's the compromise?" he asked.

"Don't make him go to the camp. And I'll get him started in martial arts as soon as he's back."

"He's not going to get hurt at this camp, Theresa. It's for little kids. They don't tackle."

Okay, at least there was that. "Still. He doesn't want to go."

"How about this for a compromise." She could hear air quotes when he said "compromise." "He goes to the camp. If he doesn't like football even after that, I'll be happy with a martial art."

She closed her eyes again and rubbed her forehead. Even though it felt like a loss, this was a win if Michael followed through. The camp wouldn't turn Liam onto football. She just knew it. He wouldn't be starstruck like the other kids. So, the football pressure would go away after this summer.

She also knew wasn't going to win this argument. Even if Michael said he'd agree, he'd just send Liam anyway, once he was there. She'd even talked to her lawyer about legally blocking him from the camp. He'd said it was feasible but would be difficult to win, and the timing was problematic.

"Okay. But I also need you to read with him while he's there. He struggled this past year and has only recently gotten back on track." She'd talked to Michael about it before, but it never hurt to remind him.

But of course, thinking about Liam's reading had her thinking about Conall, and that hollow, sick feeling came on strong.

"I'll have Lily read with him."

Great. He couldn't even do this small thing for his own son.

But she shouldn't complain. Lily would read with Liam and eventually Michael would be off his case about football. Maybe Liam would end up really liking martial arts. And he wouldn't get hurt at the camp —she had to trust that.

"Theresa, I need to go."

"Okay. Saturday at eleven in Centralia."

He was gone without another word.

She left the room, nearly running into Conall, who was carrying a cup of coffee.

"Oh, sorry," he said, veering out of the way. He gave her a sideways glance but that was it.

She felt it all the way to the center of her heart. What was he thinking? What was the real reason he'd broken up with her? And he didn't even seem to care.

She let him walk ahead of her and waited for him to get past her pod before she went back to her cube.

After a few silent heavy breaths, she got back to the servers.

She could do this. She had no choice.

~

Conall left work a little earlier than he should have Monday afternoon, but he was fed up. He was fighting a bug in his code he couldn't find. And ever since breaking up with Theresa, his concentration was shot. Especially after nearly mowing her down that afternoon.

He was going to build a desk with shelves in an alcove in the bedroom he was staying in at Isaac's. He *needed* to build a desk with shelves in an alcove in the bedroom he was staying in at Isaac's. He was going crazy.

So, he got home, took care of Maddy, measured, and headed over to the hardware store. He barely had enough time to get everything and get the rented truck returned after unloading into Isaac's garage before they closed. But he had everything he needed in time for the next day, which was Independence Day, so they were off work.

Isaac wasn't at home, so he got to work measuring in the garage.

Every time he used the speed square, he pictured Theresa with it. He could smell her in his mind. How could that be over?

He'd made his choice, and it was the right thing. Liam needed the best man to be his stepfather, and Conall wasn't it. The fact that he was sterile was a clear message from the universe that he wasn't a fit father.

He dragged the pencil across the last board. Then he set up his worktable and the saw, but as he made the first cut, he could practically feel Theresa in front of him as he showed her how to use the saw.

They were almost perfect together. If it hadn't been for Conall's deficiency with Liam, everything would be great. Conall hadn't been able to keep his cool when he should have.

He tried to focus and made another cut. Eventually, all the boards were done, and he drilled the peg holes. He dragged everything inside and moved the little bookshelf he'd picked up at IKEA out of the alcove, tossing his books on the bed first.

He attached the inside boards to the wall, including the more-or-less triangular pieces that jutted out from the alcove the desktop would sit on. He kept on going, getting the desk with its front and sides in place. Now for the shelves.

He looked at the pile of boards that would become the shelf, and an image of Theresa on the stairs that first day they'd made love, in that frenzied, desperate way. Christ, she was beautiful. The fact that they couldn't be together tore at him, but he knew it was right.

He installed the shelves spaced at nice intervals and then started with the trim. Once that was done, he still had the desk drawer to complete, but he was beat and it was two a.m. He had all day tomorrow—he'd have to paint the shelves, which he would do tomorrow if he felt like it—and crawled into bed, trying not to think about Theresa and failing miserably.

41

The following Wednesday evening, Liam scrambled over the climbing dome at the park, making happy sounds. He was not over Conall, but his mind was off it for a moment. Theresa, on the other hand, felt the same as she did every morning, when she had to fight to get out of bed. Once she was out, things were okay because life kept her busy. Downtime was the enemy. With the exception of the near-miss Monday, she and Conall avoided each other. He had nodded at her in the Athena meeting on Monday, when she'd managed a smile and looked at the screen.

Theresa watched Liam dangle from one of the bars and laugh as he dropped into a pile on the ground.

The fact that he was okay right now must mean he'd be okay long term. She had him starting therapy, both to help with the triple loss of his home, his father figure, and his favorite dog, and in case the fire-starting thing wasn't a fluke. She hoped it was. She'd done some stupid things as a kid, too. One time, when her brother dared her, she'd spit on a hot light bulb, which exploded in her face. Miraculously, she'd ended up with only a cut cheek, but it could have been much worse.

She still was in shock over Conall, though. She cried every night while trying to fall asleep, but felt like an even bigger breakdown was overdue, and she was dreading it. She missed him every second of the day. He was the first thing she thought of when she woke up, when she'd wonder why he wasn't holding her.

She still couldn't believe how quickly she'd gotten used to him. Like they were meant to be, and he was just in denial.

Thinking of him made her a little woozy so she closed her eyes.

She sat like that for a moment until she heard, "Mom, look!"

She watched Liam go around fast on the spinner, until he let go and wobbled around, before ending up on the ground again. "Did you see?"

"I did, honey. It looks like fun. But are you about ready to go?"

"Aw, no." He tried to stand up but was too dizzy, as he fell again.

"You okay?"

He lay down, arms and legs stretched out. "Just need a minute."

That made her smile. "I have some stuff I have to do tonight. We'll go back to the room and you can work on your drawing." He was drawing her car.

He lifted his head. "Mom?"

"Yeah?" She picked up her bag off the ground and stood up.

"When can I say sorry to Maddy?" He pushed into a sitting position and then got up.

She had to clutch her stomach to hold in the pain. But maybe it would be good to get it over with. Conall was free Wednesdays, and she knew that he had Maddy back. "Why don't we go by tonight?"

"Okay." Liam was serious again.

They got in the car and headed over to Isaac's house. The whole drive, Theresa was unable to stop herself from imagining a heartfelt take-back of his breakup speech.

She parked on the street, and they headed up to the door. Conall's car was next to his roommate's in the driveway.

A man answered the door holding a sandwich and chewing. They'd never met, but she assumed it was Isaac.

"Hi, is Conall here?"

Then Maddy was at the door and licking Liam's face, but she was way more subdued than normal. Liam laughed happily. Conall appeared behind her, and Isaac stepped back into the house.

"Theresa," Conall said with a smile she knew was forced. He looked worried. His voice was still a little off, too.

She looked down at Liam and put a hand on his back. "What were you going to say, honey?"

Liam looked serious now. He turned his head up toward Conall, then away. "I'm sorry about the fire. I didn't mean to. I'm sorry Maddy got hurt. And you, too."

Then he hugged Maddy and said, "Maddy, I'm glad you're okay."

Maddy rolled over on the porch and Liam crouched down to scratch her belly.

Conall glanced at Theresa before crouching down himself and saying to Liam, "Thank you, buddy. Sometimes adults say things they shouldn't, just like how sometimes kids do things they shouldn't. So, I'm sorry, too."

Liam stood up. "Oh."

"What do you say, Liam?" Theresa prompted.

"Thank you."

Conall reached for Maddy's collar and took her back inside, standing next to her and holding on. He had to lean over to be able to reach her, and it didn't look comfortable. Liam leaned into Theresa. She couldn't read Conall's expression, but she felt like it was time to go.

There'd be no reconciliation.

"Come on, little man, let's go." She looked into Conall's eyes as she said it and thought maybe there was a flicker of something there, but it passed.

She put her hand on Liam's shoulder and prodded him to move, and they headed to the car.

She was numb. This was really it.

As soon as they were both buckled in, Liam said, "Why didn't he kiss you goodbye?"

"I told you, honey." She started the car. "We're not friends like that anymore."

"Oh." She could see the frown on his face. "So, I won't see Maddy anymore? Or Conall?"

"Probably not."

"Oh." He sniffed a few times on the way home.

"Liam, it's going to be okay. It was just you and me before Conall, and it's just you and me again."

Words, they were just words.

~

CONALL LET GO of Maddy and leaned against the door he'd just shut. Seeing Theresa had been torture. And Liam. His buddy.

Isaac strolled in from the kitchen with his peanut butter and jelly sandwich. "Jesus, man, was that Theresa?"

"Yeah."

"She's hot. Why the hell did you dump her?"

"It just wasn't working out." He stepped away from the door and fell onto the couch.

"You've been a mess since the fire. Are you sure you don't want to get back with her?"

Conall propped his head up on the arm of the sofa and threw his arm across his eyes.

"I can't. The boy…"

"What? The little pyromaniac?"

"He's not," Conall said, pondering it. "I don't think."

He felt the couch shift as Isaac sat on the other arm.

"I mean, I think he just did a dumb thing, and it went bad."

"It's possible," Isaac said. "We all did really stupid shit when we were kids."

This was true. Conall had once poured salt on a slug and watched it dissolve. It hadn't occurred to him that he was killing something. He'd felt horrible about it and never done anything like it again.

Then there was the time the neighbors were getting some work done in their yard, and the workers left a small dozer overnight. With the keys. Conall had taken it for a joyride and ended up in a ditch. He'd broken his arm when he'd been tossed out of the cab.

"So, what's the deal, then?" Isaac asked.

"I yelled at Liam after the fire. I just think I can't do this parenting thing." Conall sat up on the couch and put his feet on the coffee table.

Isaac barked a laugh. "Because you got pissed at him after he nearly killed you?"

Conall clenched his jaw. The situation wasn't that simple.

"Conall, come on, man."

"It wasn't just that. Also, the thing with his hand."

"What do you mean?" Isaac slid onto the cushion.

"He cut the shit out of his hand a while back, practically cut his fingers off. Every time I see the bandages—the scars now—I know it was my fault."

"What happened?"

Conall explained while staring at his feet.

"Man, he's old enough to bear some responsibility. It's not like he's two years old. He knew he shouldn't use the knife, I'm sure."

"I know, but I shouldn't have left it out."

"You can't protect a kid from everything. It's like I said, we all did really dumb shit. It still amazes me we survive our childhoods."

"True, I suppose." Technically, Isaac was right. Liam knew better than to use the knife. And the lighter. But he was young enough that grasping the consequences was hard.

"Fuck," Conall said. He dropped his feet onto the floor. "I'm going to go read."

"Okay, man."

Conall went back to his room and pulled a book off the still-unpainted shelf. Yesterday he'd been a complete bum, playing video games all evening. Now, he tried to read, but it was hopeless. He couldn't focus.

So he took Maddy to the dog park and moped some more there. But also while there, his brain started into overdrive. Maybe Isaac was right. And if he wasn't a bad father, what did that mean? Should he get back with Theresa?

Fuck, of course he should. Assuming she'd have him.

He'd been such an idiot. He was in love with her.

42

From the hotel bed, Theresa watched Liam sit at the table drawing his bedroom, as it had been before the fire. They had no idea what it looked like now because they weren't allowed in.

It was Friday night, two weeks since Conall had first broken up with her, and Theresa was still as raw as she had been when it happened. But now the shock had worn off, and she'd had her big over-the-top cry Wednesday evening after they'd gotten home from Conall's house. She was emotionally wobbly at work all day yesterday and today, and especially when Conall smiled at her in a way that didn't seem forced this afternoon.

The expression was strange, and it had hurt. Was he already over her? Had she meant that little to him? Or had he just done the guy thing and gone out and gotten drunk and hooked up with some random chick? Iryna?

The idea of anyone else with him was impossible to tolerate. She couldn't think about it.

"Liam, how's your drawing coming along?"

"Huh?"

"How's it going?" She needed the interaction with him. She was so lonely without Conall and needed every distraction she could drum up.

"Fine."

Fine. Of course, it was fine. He was keeping himself busy, keeping his mind off Conall. Normally work was a good distractor for her, but it just made her think of Conall.

So, she was stuck with the guy she'd thought was perfect occupying her mind.

Okay, she might as well work then. She extracted her laptop from her bag and opened it up. She checked some running programs that she'd kicked off on the server before she'd left. They were still going strong and wouldn't finish until Sunday or early Monday morning.

She had just started coding some queries Bernard needed when there was a knock on the door.

Liam's head jerked up. "Who's that?"

"I don't know," Theresa said as she got off the bed.

"Is it Conall?"

"No, it's probably someone at the wrong door."

But when she opened the door, it was Conall.

"Conall!" Liam cried and raced to the door. "Is Maddy here?"

Conall laughed a little. "No, not this time."

"Is she okay?"

"She's fine," Conall said.

"Then why are you here?"

Theresa stared at Conall, also wondering why he was here. He looked back, jaw tense. Did he want to get back together?

No, that was stupid. Yet his face conveyed nothing.

He looked down and said, "Liam, can I talk to just your mom for a moment?"

Liam didn't budge.

"Honey, go on back to your drawing. I'm just going to talk with him for a minute."

He sat down, looking defeated.

"One minute," Theresa said. She grabbed her key card off the TV shelf and went out into the hall with Conall.

Her heart raced. She was hoping for good news, but then the idea that maybe he wanted to sue her for Maddy's vet bill came to mind.

"Theresa," he said, taking her hand. "I just wanted to tell you...."

She looked at their joined hands, which relit hope in her heart.

But then he faltered, staring at her in awkward silence.

"Conall, you don't have to explain why you broke up with me. You're free to make your own decisions." Even if she did feel like a teenager with her first ever broken heart.

"Theresa, I'm sorry for what I said. I love you, and this time apart has made me realize what a mistake breaking up with you was. And I miss Liam. I can't imagine you two not being a part of my life."

Happiness flooded her, and she had to tell him how much she forgave him. "Conall, I—"

"I'm not done." He squeezed her hands. "You are the best thing that ever happened to me. You and Liam both. I love you and want to be a part of your family. Theresa, I know you have no reason to, but will you forgive me? Will you take me back?"

He looked at her with an expression that could only be called terrified. She'd never seen him so vulnerable, and it broke her heart all over again to see him imagining her saying no.

"Yes," she said. She took his hands and put them on her hips, grasped his shirt in her own hands and got on her tiptoes to kiss him. It was by far the most tender one they'd shared. So much emotion that she was almost in tears.

No, she was absolutely in tears.

He broke the kiss and leaned back, grinning. "Thank God. I was so afraid I'd ruined everything."

She nodded again. "You almost did, but I can't live without you. I am desperately in love with you." She wrapped her arms around him and pulled him close.

"What are you doing?"

Theresa and Conall both turned toward the room door, where Liam stood watching them. He'd seen them kiss before, but they generally kept it light in front of him.

"Oh, honey," Theresa said, finally finding her voice. Conall followed her back inside, taking her hand.

"What's going on?" Liam asked.

She touched his cheek. "We're friends again."

His face brightened. "When can I see Maddy?"

Theresa and Conall laughed, fingers intertwined.

TWO DAYS LATER, Conall was on I-5 driving Theresa and Liam to Centralia.

Liam was entertaining himself in the back with a graphic novel about dogs that Conall had bought him last night for the trip. He wasn't sure Liam wasn't just looking at the pictures, but even that would be a positive thing. Any appreciation of books was a good thing.

"Theresa?" Conall said quietly.

"Yeah?"

"Does Michael know we broke up temporarily?"

"No. The only person I told was my mom. And my friends."

"Oh, yeah?" He glanced at her, admiring her profile for a second. "How'd that go?"

Liam laughed at the book in the back.

Theresa glanced back and then said, "Amazingly, she was very sorry for me. I think she liked you, after all her resistance."

"It's going to be an uphill battle for me to get her to like me again after that... misstep."

Theresa laughed. "Maybe. But we'll get there."

They'd already talked about what Michael would be like. In all the time he and Theresa had been together, Conall had never met or even spoken to him. So, this would be interesting. If Michael was anything like he expected, it would be a challenge to not punch the man.

"Conall?" Liam asked.

"Yeah, buddy?"

"Did you play football when you were little?"

Theresa glanced back. Conall knew how unhappy she was about the football camp.

"No, just volleyball. And basketball."

"Okay." Apparently, Liam was nervous about it, too.

"The camp will go fine." Conall said. "They won't make you do anything you don't want to do. Just remember, it's supposed to be fun."

"Yeah."

"Did you finish your book, honey?" Theresa asked.

"No. Almost."

"Do you like it?"

"Yeah, it's funny."

So, he was reading it for real. But maybe worry about the camp had him distracted. Conall didn't know what to say to make him feel better.

Liam didn't say anything else. Theresa turned around and then said in a low voice, "He's reading again."

Conall smiled.

After another quiet half hour, Theresa directed him to the Safeway where they were to meet Michael.

"Over there," she said, pointing to a big black truck in the back corner of the lot. She didn't sound happy.

Conall pulled up next to the driver's side of the truck, several feet away. Theresa closed her eyes for a second while Liam unbuckled himself. He was out the door just as Michael opened his.

Then Theresa put on a fake smile and got out.

Conall walked around the side of the Rogue and noted that Liam was talking to Michael, who looked at him and said, "That's nice, son."

"Go on and get your stuff, honey," Theresa said. She leaned against her car door as if to stay as far away from Michael as possible.

Conall stepped forward, stuck his hand out, and said, "Hi, I'm Conall."

Michael's handshake was overly firm, and he looked Conall in the eye in a way that said, "I had her first."

Anger bubbled in Conall's stomach, but he simply squeezed back equally hard.

Michael said, "Good to finally meet you."

"Same here."

They finished the shake and each let go, Michael studying him through narrowed eyes.

Theresa helped Liam get his bags out of the back seat. Once he had the two duffel bags, he ran around to the other side of the truck.

Michael turned away to look at Theresa again.

"I'm going to call every Sunday at four."

Michael nodded. He looked at Conall again and turned to get in the truck.

Conall and Theresa stood there while they backed up, both waving at Liam who was grinning and waving back. They watched the truck leave the lot and Theresa turned to Conall and said, "I hate when he goes."

"I know. But just think about it. I can finally make love to you all throughout the day again."

Theresa laughed. "We just have to get back to Portland."

"Or we could rent a room here." Conall waggled his eyebrows, and she folded over, hands on her thighs.

Then she straightened up, stepped toward him and pulled him down for a slow kiss. "I think we can wait another couple hours. It'll be worth it."

EPILOGUE

Conall set the book down on the nightstand and pulled the bedspread up to Liam's neck. Liam yawned, and Conall laughed and stood up.

"Ready to go to sleep, buddy?"

Liam nodded sleepily. "You promise we'll go to the zoo tomorrow?"

Conall chuckled and leaned over to give Liam a kiss on the forehead and ruffle his hair. "Of course, we're going. I promised, didn't I."

"Good." Liam barely got the word out before his eyes were closed, and his mouth hung open.

Conall turned the light out and headed into the bathroom in the master bedroom. He could hear Theresa's electric toothbrush going. He stepped in and hugged her from behind, resting his head on her shoulder and looking at her in the mirror.

"Hi, sweetheart," he said.

Her mouth stretched into a smile, and she said something around her toothbrush that was probably, "Hi." She cupped his hands with her free one.

"Hurry up and come to bed," he whispered into her ear before brushing her hair out of the way and kissing her neck.

~

Thank you for reading *It's Technically Love*. I hope you enjoyed Theresa's and Conall's story.

All honest reviews are appreciated, and I would love it if you would take the time to leave one on Amazon.com or your country-specific Amazon site.

THANK YOU FOR READING!

Thanks for reading *It's Technically Love*. If you enjoyed it and haven't read *Finally in Tune* (the second in the series Coded for Love, with Casey's story), I'd love for you to check it out. Sujata's story is coming in late 2023.

To find out more about me and my books at my website, katvinson.com.